Praise for **Mr** ☑ **W9-AEH-089**

"Brilliant . . . a novel with an amazingly inventive structure . . . The energy and imagination that Elkin invests in Mrs. Bliss, the most ordinary of women in ordinary circumstances, is extraordinary . . . With his old magic . . . he transfigures her in the course of her final years from a hoot in pink polyester to a heroine of depth and grace."
—Maureen Howard, *Los Angeles Times Book Review*

"In MRS. TED BLISS, Stanley Elkin is such a down-to-earth and funny writer that how smart he is sneaks up on you. Although he's making you laugh a lot, he's brilliantly playing out the inescapable seasons of human life . . . Great pleasure and wisdom, and a hymn of an ending."
—John Casey, American Book Award-winning author of *Spartina*

"One of the best books of the season . . . a dark and subtle satire on the neuroses of a Jewish widow."
—*Vanity Fair*

"A delight . . . quirky, hilarious and poignant, with a complement of black humor . . . Dorothy Bliss seems less a creation than a full-fledged person. Elkin simply inhabits her."
—*Detroit Free Press*

"A smart, generous, melancholy, funny, even elegiac work by a prodigious practitioner."
—*The New York Times Book Review*

"Stanley Elkin's imagination should be declared a national landmark. When the moment comes to write the history of American English in the late twentieth century, his novels will be a fundamental source."
—Paul Auster, author of *Mr. Vertigo*

"One of our most talented and original literary voices . . . Mrs. Ted Bliss may be his most enduring heroine in a long career of obsessive dark humor . . . Jewish mothers tend to be unforgettable, but Mrs. Ted Bliss is truly one for the ages."
—*Chicago Sun-Times*

"Stanley Elkin never lets us down. In MRS. TED BLISS he impressively proves once more that he is a true artist . . . I read his books with pleasure and also with respect."
—Saul Bellow, winner of the Nobel Prize for Literature

"Intense and touching . . . MRS. TED BLISS is more straightforward, less given to verbal pyrotechnics and metaphysical experimentation, than many of his novels. It's also sweeter and more forgiving, a gentle if slightly mocking paean to the kind of Jewish mother now out of favor."
—*New York Newsday*

"Elkin is at his best here, blessed with the gift of one-liner insight and a definite, if reluctantly exercised, ability to tug on a reader's heartstrings . . . Countless retirees in America—Jewish or otherwise—will recognize themselves and people they know in Dorothy Bliss. But finding her in a novel—Who would have thought?"
—*Publishers Weekly*

"One of America's finest writers . . . Elkin is a grand master of rhetoric, his characters tossing off stunning, teeming arias of diction."
—*Philadelphia Inquirer*

"In MRS. TED BLISS, Stanley Elkin is his usual brilliant, hilarious, and wrenching self."
—Hilma Wolitzer, author of *Tunnel of Love*

Other Books by
Stanley Elkin

Van Gogh's Room at Arles
Pieces of Soap: Essays
The MacGuffin
The Magic Kingdom
George Mills
Criers and Kibitzers, Kibitzers and Criers
The Rabbi of Lud
The Six-Year-Old Man
The Living End
Early Elkin
The Franchiser
Searches and Seizures: Three Novellas
Boswell
A Bad Man
The Dick Gibson Show
The Coffee Room

STANLEY ELKIN

Mrs. Ted Bliss

AVON BOOKS ◆ NEW YORK

AVON BOOKS
A division of
The Hearst Corporation
1350 Avenue of the Americas
New York, New York 10019

To Joan and her brother, Marshall

Mrs. Ted Bliss

ONE

S ometimes, two, three times a year, there would be card parties, or at least invitations to them. Notices by the security desk in the lobby, or left by the door at each condominium, or posted in the game or laundry rooms, or maybe nothing more than a poster up on the easel near the lifeguard's station on each of the half-dozen rooftop swimming pools in the condominium complex, announced that scheduled at such-and-so a time on so-and-such a Saturday night there was to be a gala, come one come all, sponsored by the residents of this or that building—"Good Neighbor Policy Night," "International Evening," "Hands Across the Panama Canal." Usually there would be a buffet supper, followed by coffee, followed by entertainment, followed by cards.

It wasn't that Bingo didn't have its partisans. Wasn't Bingo, like music, an international language? But that's just the point, isn't it, Dr. Wolitzer, chairman of the Towers' Entertainment Committee, argued: The idea of these evenings was to get to know one another, and there was no nutritional value in the conversation of Bingo. G forty-seven, O eleven, I twenty-four. What kind of exchange was that? It was empty of content.

"Cards is better?" Irv Brodky from Building Number Four might counter. " 'I see your quarter and raise you a dime?' This is hardly the meaning of life either."

"It could be a bluff," the doctor responded. "A bold bluff an-

1

swered by a bluff more timid. There's character here. There's room to maneuver.''

Wolitzer had been a professional man, had two or three years to go before he'd have to step down as chairman of one of the complex's most influential committees. Brodky was nobody's fool; it would come as no surprise to him that if it came to a vote cards would win out over Bingo. Wolitzer was the glibber of the two and, though it hadn't passed Brodky's notice that the old doc might not himself be bluffing, Irv B. wasn't going to the wall on this one and didn't press the issue. Indeed, he backed down with considerable grace, taking it upon himself to suggest that the Entertainment Committee adopt a cards resolution by acclamation. Also, unless you were actually in it for the tsatske prizes—travel alarms, artificial plants, shadow boxes—practically everyone appreciated a good game of cards.

They did not, could not, know that the bloc of Colombian and Chilean and Venezuelan condominium owners along with the tiny contingent of Cubans couldn't have cared less for these evenings. They had enough friends already, muchas gracias very much, good northern neighbors to last a lifetime and, if truth be told, commanded a sufficiency of English to lord it over this group of retired and fixed-income refugees drifted south from places frequently even farther from Miami Beach—Cleveland, Chicago, New York, St. Louis, Detroit—than the homelands of the South American newcomers.

Actually, these ex-Chicagoans and Clevelanders, former New Yorkers, Detroiters, and erstwhile St. Louisans, were, for all the variety of their geographic, financial, political, and even educational backgrounds, pretty much cut from the same cloth. They were Americans. Really, in existential ways they might not even understand, except for the fine, almost nit-picking distinctions between the Democrat, Socialist, and Republican parties, they *had* no political backgrounds. They were Americans. If not always at ease, then almost always easy to get along with. They were reasonably affable, eager as Building Four's Irving Brodky to meet you halfway. They knew in their gut that life was short, and put up with it graciously.

They were Americans, cocks-of-the-walk, stereotypical down to the ground, and would have expressed astonishment to know that the very people to whom, no questions asked, they would have extended their hands in friendship during all those galas on all those international evenings, generally dismissed them as just so many babes in the wood. And who, though the South Americans lived among them and to whom they sometimes, if, say, a death in the family forced the surviving party, by dint of the sheer weight of loneliness, to list a condo in the *Miami Herald* as For Sale by Owner (this would have been during the flush times, from the late sixties through the mid-to late seventies, when the building boom was still on, when it was still a seller's market), would have paid fabulous fees, handsome key money, vigorish, baksheesh that the Southern Hemispherians accepted as the cost of doing business and the surviving parties looked on as the very act of business itself, something maybe even a little sacred and holy not about profit per se but almost about the idea of appreciation, contemptuous of them not so much because they were giving far above par but because these naive, bereft Americans never suspected that their good neighbors to the south already knew it, expected it, may actually have been surprised or even a little disappointed that they hadn't been asked to buy them out at still dearer, more exorbitant prices. Despising them, too, perhaps, for the failure of their imaginations, blind not only to the source of the money with which they were so free but also to the reasons they were so free with it. (Granted, they were Americans, but weren't they Jews, too?) It never seemed to occur to the Americans that some complicated piece of history was happening here, that certain seeds were being planted, certain stakes claimed—that certain bets were being hedged. (Didn't they ever get past the Wednesday Food Section in the newspapers, didn't they read beyond the Winn-Dixie coupons? The pot was being stirred in El Salvador. Nicaragua was starting to simmer. Not fifteen miles from where they stood the Contras were already setting up. In Peru, the Shining Path was in place. Everywhere, the hemisphere seethed along all its awful fault lines, along politics' ancient tectonic plates, meaningless to them as the Spanish language.) As if safe harbor were an alien concept to them, diaspora, exodus, the notion of plans.

They'd been around the block, Jews had, and, to hear the world tell it, had a reputation for being complicated and devious as Jesuits. Why, then, did they overlook in others what they so blithely practiced among themselves—the luxury of a private agenda? Were they so *very* arrogant that, while completely caught up in their own shrewd plots, they declined to believe in the schemes of others? Unless of course their bark was so much worse than their bite. Unless of course they were all hype and fury and didn't deserve their notoriety as a people who bore a grudge. Even so, the Venezuelans and Chileans, Cubans and Colombians did not much trust (to say nothing of enjoy) such innocent, credulous souls. Why, there were a *dozen* unexplored reasons the South Americans might be interested in buying up modest, middle-class properties like those to be acquired in the Towers. As long ago as 1959, when Fidel Castro first made his revolution a couple of hundred or so miles from Miami, it should have been clear to anyone that the next wave of immigration would be from the south. These Chileans and Colombians, Cubans and Venezuelans were merely advance men, outposts, an expeditionary force. A party (in a tradition that went back five hundred years) of explorers. Testers of the waters who would one day accomplish with drugs what their proud Spanish forebears had accomplished with plunder.

They were only preparing the way.

(And another thing. It did not apparently register with the old-timers that there was, on average, probably a ten- or fifteen-year difference in their ages, advantage South America. Could they fail to project that it wasn't the survivors who sold their condos to the Latin Americans who would ultimately survive? Something was happening in Miami and Miami Beach, up and down the south coast of Florida, that went unmarked on the Jews' social calendars. It was history.)

But it wasn't just the queer, naive provincialism of the natives that kept most of the Latin Americans away from those Good Neighbor Policy, International Evening, and Hands Across the Panama Canal galas. Much of the nasty secret lay in the naïveté itself. They were—the Latinos—not only a proud people but a stylish, almost gaudy one. The high heels of the women, the wide, double-breasted, custom suits of the men, lent them a sexy, perky, tango air; sent unmixed signals of something like risk and danger that sailed right over the Jews' heads.

So not very many South Americans ever actually saw the "Hispanic" motifs set up in the game rooms by the Committee on Decorations on these poorly attended, floating occasions that traveled from Building One to Building Six, completing on a maybe semi-annual or triquarterly basis a circuit of the six buildings every two or three years, depending. The transmuted, phantasmagorical visions, themes, and dreamscapes of a South America that never was mounted on the tarted-up walls of the game rooms in brightly colored crepe- and construction-paper cutouts of bullfights, sombreros, mariachi street bands, and, here and there, rough approximations of piñatas suspended from the ceiling like a kind of straw fruit. All this brought back and made known to the vast majority that had declined to see these wonders for themselves.

"I tell you," Hector Camerando told Jaime Guttierez, "these people get their idea of what anything south of Texas looks like out of bad movies. It's all cantinas and old Mexico to them, sleeping peasants sprawled out under the shade of their hats."

"Ay, ¡caramba!" Jaime said flatly.

"There's no stopping them," Hector reported to Guttierez the following year. "You should have seen it, Jaime. The door prize was a lamp that grew out of the back of a burro. Come with me next time."

"I don' need no stinkin' door prize."

But one time, when the gala was hosted by Building Two, Camerando's building, several of the resident Latinos in the Towers complex—Carlos and Rita Olvero, Enrique Frache, Oliver Gutterman, Ricardo Llossas, Elaine Munez, along with Carmen and Tommy Auveristas, Vittorio Cervantes, and Jaime Guttierez himself—their curiosity having been piqued by Hector Camerando's almost Marco Polo–like accounts of these evenings, joined Hector to see for themselves what these galas were all about.

When Guttierez arrived in the game room a handful of his compatriots were already there. He picked up his paper plate, napkin, plastic utensils, and buffet supper and struck out to find where Hector Camerando was sitting. Hector, a veteran of these affairs, spotted him and rose in place at his table to signal his location, but just as Jaime saw him he was stopped by a woman who put her hand on his arm, jiggling the plates he carried and almost causing him to spill them to the floor. She invited him to join her party.

"I see my friend," Jaime Guttierez said.

"So," she said, "if you see your friend he's your friend and you already know him so you don't have to sit with him. Here. Sit by us."

She was actually taking the plates and setup out of his hands and arranging them on the table.

"You look familiar to me. Are you from Building One? They'll come and pour, you don't have to get coffee. Dorothy, you know this man, don't you? I think he's from Building One."

"Three," Guttierez said.

"A very nice building. Three is a *very* nice building."

"Aren't they all the same?"

"Yes, but Three is as nice as any of them. You get a nice view from Three."

"I'm just looking around," Guttierez said. "The decorations. Who makes them?"

"Oh, thank you," said the woman, "thank you very much. I'll tell my friends on the Decorations Committee. They'll be so pleased. This is just another example of your maintenance dollars at work."

The woman's name was Rose Blitzer. She was originally from Baltimore and had moved south in 1974 with her husband, Max. Rose and Max had a three-bedroom, two-and-a-half bath, full kitchen, living/dining-room area with a screened-in California room. Max had been the manager of Baltimore's largest hardware store and had a guaranteed three-quarters point participation in net profits before his stroke in 1971 from which, thank God, he was now fully recovered except for a wide grin that was permanently fixed into his face like a brand.

"People don't take me seriously," Max said. "Even when I shout and call them names."

Giving brief, lightning summaries of their situations and accomplishments, she introduced Guttierez to the others at the table. It was astonishing to Jaime how much information the woman managed to convey about the people and even the various political factions in the Towers. Within minutes, for example, he learned about the rift between Building One (not, despite its name, the first to go up but only the first where ground had been broken) and Building Five (which enjoyed certain easements in One's parking garage). He was given to understand, though he didn't, that Building Number Two was "a sleeping giant." She sketched an overview of the general health of some of the people at their own and nearby tables.

Jaime clucked his tongue sympathetically. "No, you don't understand," Mrs. Blitzer said. "Those people are survivors. What do they say these days? 'They paid their dues.' They came through their procedures and chemotherapies; they spit in their doctors' eyes who gave them only months to live. They laughed up their sleeves."

And she even filled him in on who had the big money. "The little guy over there? He could buy and sell all of us, can't he, Max?"

"I don't dare go to funerals, they think I'm laughing," Max said.

A woman in an apron came by. She held out two pots of coffee—decaf and regular.

"You forgot sugar," one of the women at the table said.

"Ida, she's got her hands full. Don't bother her, take Sweet 'n Low. Look, there's Equal."

"I can't digest sugar substitutes without a nondairy creamer."

"Really?" another woman said. "I never heard such a thing. Have you, Burt?"

"Nothing surprises me anymore. It's all equally fantastic."

"How about you, Mr. Guttierez? She wants to know if you want some coffee."

"I better get back to my friend," Jaime said. "He expected me to sit with him."

"Oh, he's *very* good looking," Rose Blitzer said.

"He has a nice smile," said Max.

"She thinks you're good looking," Guttierez told Hector Camerando.

"Olé."

They were gentlemen. They were from South America. They lived according to a strict code of honor. It would never have occurred to the one to question the word of the other.

So despite the commanding two- or three-gala advantage Hector Camerando held over Jaime Guttierez, the gentleman from Building Three, armed with the bits of information Rose Blitzer had provided him, ate the gentleman of the host building alive that evening in a fast game of human poker.

Hector drew first. He picked Max Blitzer.

"Stroke," Jaime said.

"Stroke? Really? He seems so animated."

"The Gioconda smile is a residual."

Jaime picked the woman pouring coffee.

"I check," Guttierez said, and picked Ida.

"Something with her stomach," Jaime said. "She can't digest Equal unless she has Coffee-Mate."

Guttierez picked Burt.

Jaime checked and picked the guy who was supposed to have the big money.

"Check," Hector said.

Though he had to check when Camerando picked Dorothy, Jaime took the next few hands easily (a brain tumor, liver transplant, two radicals, and a lumpectomy) and was up five hundred dollars when Hector, laughing, said that Guttierez was murdering him and threw in the towel. Jaime declined to take his friend's money but Hector insisted. Then he offered to return it but Camerando congratulated him on his game and said he hoped he was at least as much a man of honor as Guttierez. There was nothing to do but pocket the five hundred dollars as graciously as he could. "You really had me on that, Dorothy. I thought the tide was about to turn," Jaime Guttierez said.

Though he wouldn't remember it, Jaime Guttierez's initial reaction was to be stumped when Hector Camerando had bid Dorothy and taken the hand in their friendly little game, had been about to say that the woman was either incredibly shy or very, very deaf. Shyness wasn't even listed on the scale of infirmities, abnormalities, and outright deformities that counted for points in scoring human poker, and he had no genuinely corroborative evidence that the woman was deaf. The fact that she hadn't spoken a word all evening, or, for that matter, even seemed to have heard one, was beside the point. Guttierez really was an honorable man. Honorable men did not bluff. Though he might well have taken the hand, Camerando was also an honorable man. He would never have called him on it. Knowing this, it wasn't in Jaime's character to bluff. Had he been a tad more observant, however, he might have seen the woman's deformity, declared it openly to his friend, and humiliated him even more soundly than he already had.

Shorn now not only of decibels—unenhanced, Dorothy could no longer make out the ordinary noises of daily life, such as traffic, machinery, the singing of birds—but, in a way, even of the memory of them. She couldn't recall, for example, the sound of her accent, her rough speech, or, even in her head, how to decline the melody of the most familiar tune.

It made her fearful, almost craven, in the streets, and she never entered them without making certain that her hearing aid was securely in place. (Which, hating its electronic hiss and frightful cackle as though storms were exploding inside her skull, she rarely wore in public and, sloughing it like too-constrictive clothing, never at home, even on the telephone or in front of the television, preferring instead to ask friends and visitors to speak louder or actually shout at her or endlessly repeat themselves as if she were carefully going over a tricky contract with them, something legalistic in her understanding.) And taking into account the time of day, whether it was rush hour, or the Christmas holidays, Spring Break and the kids down visiting on vacation, sometimes wore her spare, too, arranging the awkward, ugly hearing aid on the perfectly smooth flap of skin that covered her right outer ear like a long-healed amputation, the flap shiny and sealing over all the ear's buried working parts—the tympanic membrane, auditory meatus and nerve, eustachian tube, cochlea, semicircular canals, stapes, anvil, malleus, and all the little wee chips of skull bones like a sort of gravel—so that even before her increasing, cumulative nerve deafness she heard everything at a slight remove, the profound bass of all distant, muffled sound. This was the deformity Guttierez had missed, for she made no attempt to hide it, never swept it behind her hair. Quite the opposite in fact. Displaying the ear like a piece of jewelry, or a beauty mark. Which, for a considerable time—almost until she was seven or eight—she truly believed it was, or believed it was since she first observed her older sister Miriam, may she rest, scooping wax from her right ear with a wooden match. This was back in Russia, and Dorothy was much too sensitive ever to draw the girl's attention to the pitiable extra hole in her head, and much too modest ever to invite envy in either Miriam or her other sisters by boasting of the beauty of her own perfectly uninterrupted, perfectly smooth and complete right ear. (Indeed, when Miriam died, Dorothy, even though she knew better by then, even though she realized that most people's ears did not enjoy the advantage of an extra flap of skin to prevent cold and germs and moisture from gaining access to the secret, most privy and concealed parts of her head, couldn't help but at least a little believe that something of her dead sister's illness might have been brought about by the vulnerability *two* open ears must have subjected her to.)

So it was a matter of some irritation to her during those times of the day and those seasons of the year when heavy traffic caused her to affix the bulky backup hearing aid in place, planting it and winding it about her ear like a stethscope laid flat against a chest, but better safe than sorry. She did it, as she did almost everything else, uncomplainingly, her only objection reflexive—a knowledge of her smudged, ruined character; her heavy sense, that is, of her vanity, which Dorothy had at least privately permitted herself and privately enjoyed at twenty and thirty and forty and fifty and even, to some extent, into her sixties while Ted, olov hasholem, was still living, but which she fully understood to be not only extravagant and uncalled for but more than a little foolish, too, now that she was almost eighty.

Extravagant or not, foolish or not, she removed them, the good one and the bad one, too, once she was inside the movie theater, preferring the shadowy, muffled, blunted voices of the actors to the shrill, whistling treble of the hearing aids. Most of the dialogue was lost to her. What difference did it make? What could they be saying to each other that she hadn't heard them say to each other a thousand times before? The handsome boy declared his love for the pretty girl. The pretty girl didn't know whether to trust him or not. He'd fooled her before. She should trust him. She should settle down and have his kids. Life was too short. It went by like a dream. It's what Ted always said. And now look at him. He was dead too many years.

And what troubled Mrs. Ted Bliss, what wounded and astonished when sleep eluded during all those endless nights when thoughts outpaced one another in her insomniac mind, was the fact that now, still alive, she was by so many years her dead husband's senior.

He wouldn't recognize her today. She had been beautiful even into her sixties. A dark, smooth-skinned woman with black hair and fine sweet features on a soft, wide armature of flesh, she had been a very parlor game of a creature, among her neighbors in Building Number One something of a conversation piece, someone, you'd have thought, who must have drunk from the fountain of youth. She had been introduced in the game room for years to guests and visitors from the other buildings that lined Biscayne Bay as an oddity, a sport of nature unscathed by time.

"Go on, guess how old she is," more than one of her friends had challenged newcomers while Dorothy, her deep blush invisible to their pale examination, sat meekly by.

"Dorothy is fifty-nine," people five and six years older than herself would hazard.

"Fifty-nine? You think?"

"I don't know. Fifty-nine, sixty."

Even the year Ted was dying.

"*Sixty-seven!*" they shouted, triumphant as people who knew the answer to vexing riddles.

Even after his cancer had been diagnosed Ted smiled benignly, Dorothy suffering these odd old thrust and parries in an almost luxurious calm, detached from the accomplishment of her graceful, almost invisible aging as if it had been the fruit of someone else's labors. (And hadn't it? Except for her long, daily soaks in her tub two and three times a day, she'd never lifted a finger.) Grinning, a cat with a canary in its belly, a reverie of something delicious on its chops.

"Is she? Is she, Ted? Can it be?"

Ted winked.

"Of course not," Lehmann, whose own wife at sixty-seven was as homely as Dorothy was beautiful, said. "They're in a witness protection program, the both of them."

Several of the men at the table understood Lehmann's bitterness—many shared it—and laughed. Even Dorothy smiled. "I came to play," Lehmann said, "deal the cards already. Did I ask to see her driver's license? I don't *know* what they're up to."

"I'll be sixty-two my next birthday," Dorothy Bliss said, shaving years from her age. (It was the vanity again, a battle of the wicked prides. It was one thing, though finally a lesser thing, to look young for one's age, quite another to be the age one looked young for.)

The truth was no one really knew, not Ted, not her sisters. Not her two younger brothers. Certainly not her surviving children. It was as if the time zones she crossed on her ship to America shed entire blocks of months rather than just hours as it forced its way west. Not even Dorothy was certain of her age. It was a new land, a younger country. The same immigration officials who anglicized the difficult Cyrillic names into their frequently arbitrary, occasionally whimsical record books could be bribed into fudging the age of a new arrival. That's exactly what happened to Dorothy. In order for the daughter to get work under the new child labor laws, Dorothy's mom had paid the man fifteen dollars to list her kid as two or three years older than her actual age. She always knew that her clock had been pushed forward, that Time owed her, as it were, and somewhere in her twenties, Dorothy called in a marker that, by the time it was cashed, had accumulated a certain interest. The mind does itself favors. She really *didn't* know her true age, only that whatever it was was less than the sixteen that had appeared on her documents when she'd first come to this country.

Because she didn't have a driver's license to which Lehmann might have referred. Because she had never learned to drive. As though the same fifteen bucks her mother had offered and the official had taken so she might get her work permit had finessed not just the late childhood and early adolescence that were her due but the obligatory education, too. *Most* grown-up Americans' streetish savvy. Paying by check, applying for charge cards, simply subscribing to the damn paper, for God's sake. As though the eleven or twelve thousand dollars she brought in over the nine or ten years before she hooked up with Ted and that her mother's initial fifteen-dollar cash investment had cost for that green card, had purchased not merely an exemption from ever having to play like a child when she was of an age to enjoy it but had been a down payment, too, on ultimate, long-term pampering privileges, making a housewife of her, a baleboosteh, lending some spoiled, complacent, and self-forgiving pinkish aura to her life and perceptions, a certain fastidious cast of mind toward herself and her duties. She shopped the specials, she snipped coupons out of the papers for detergents, for canned goods and coffee and liters of diet soft drinks, for paper products and bottles of salad dressing. She spent endless hours (three or four a day) in her kitchen, preparing food, doing the dishes till they sparkled, mopping the floor, scouring the sink, wiping down the stove; yet she had never been a very good cook, only a driven taskmistress, seldom varying her menus and never, not even when she entertained guests, a recipe, obsessive finally, so finicky about the world whenever she was alone in it that she was never (this preceded her deafness) entirely comfortable outside the door to her apartment (where she conceived of the slipcovers on her living room furniture, and perhaps even of the fitted terrycloth cover on the lid of the toilet seat in the bathrooms, as a necessary part of the furniture itself; for her the development of clear, heavy-duty plastic a technological breakthrough, a hinge event in science, up there with Kem cards, washable mah-jongg tiles, lifelong shmutsdread, a first impression she must have taken as a child in Russia, a sense of actual biological trayf, fear of the Gentile, some notion of caste deeper than a Hindu's, a notion, finally, of *order*), something stubborn and stolid and profoundly resistant in her Slavic features, her adamant, dumb, and disapproving stance like that of a farm animal or a very picky eater.

So it was possible, perhaps, that those long soaks in her tub, the two baths she took every day, were not a preening or polishing of self so much as part of a continual scour, a bodily function like the need for food. Not beauty (who knew almost nothing about beauty) but just another step in a long campaign, some Hundred Years War she waged against the dirt on fruits and meats and vegetables, the germs on pennies, the invisible bacterium in the transparent air, building up a sterile field around herself like a wall of hygiene.

She tried to replicate in her personal appearance the same effects she strove for in her habits as a housekeeper. In her long pink widowhood she started to dress in bright polyester pants suits, bright because bright colors seemed to suggest to her the same buffed qualities of her kitchen's sparkling dishes, mopped floors, scoured sinks and counters, her wiped-down stoves; and polyester because she could clean the suits in the washer and dryer every night before she went to bed. Dorothy had merely meant to simplify her life by filling it with activities that would keep her within the limited confines of her apartment, to live out what remained of her widowhood a respectable baleboosteh life. But her neighbors in the Towers saw only the brightly colored clothes she wore, and the carefully kempt hair she still bothered to dye, and thought of her as a very brave woman, a merry widow; attributing her steady, almost aggressive smile to her friendly outlook and not to the hardness of her hearing, her constant fear that people were saying pleasant things and making soft and friendly jokes she believed only her constant, agreeable, chipper grin and temperament could protect her from ever having to understand.

And now, since Ted's death and the piecemeal disappearance of her beauty, she had ceased to be their little parlor game and game room conversation piece and had become instead a sort of mascot.

About a week or so after she had buried her husband in the Chicago cemetery where almost all the Blisses had been interred, Dorothy Bliss was approached by a man named Alcibiades Chitral. Señor Chitral was from Venezuela, a newcomer to the United States, a relative newcomer to the Towers complex. He had a proposition for Dorothy. He offered to buy her dead husband's car. When Mrs. Bliss heard what he was saying she was outraged, furious, and, though she smiled, would, had she not been so preoccupied by grief, have slammed the door in his face. Vulture, she thought, inconsiderate, scavenging vulture! Bang on my nerves, why don't you? Indeed, she was so chilled by the prospect of a bargain hunter in these terrible circumstances she almost threw up some of the food (she hadn't had a good bowel movement in a week) with which her friends and relatives had tried to distract her from her loss the whole time she had sat shivah in Chicago. (Even here, in Florida, her neighbors brought platters of delicatessen, bakery, salads, liters of the same diet soft drinks she had purchased with discount coupons. To look at all that food you'd have thought death was a picnic. It was no picnic.) When he divined her state Alcibiades excused himself and offered his card.

"Call me in a few days," he said. "Or no," he said, "I see that you won't. I'll call you."

She had not even wanted to take Ted back to Chicago. She was so stunned the day he died she didn't even call her children to tell them their father was dead, and when she phoned them the next morning she passed on her news so dispassionately it was almost as if it had already been written off (well, he had been so ill all year) or had happened so long ago that she might have been speaking of something so very foreign to all their lives it seemed a mild aberration, a curiosity, like a brief spell of freakish weather.

Dirt was dirt, she told the kids, she could make arrangements to get him buried right here in Miami.

They had to talk her into sending the body home, and then they had to talk her into coming to Chicago.

Her son Frank said he would come for her.

Maxine offered the same deal. "Ma," she said, "I'll come down and help you pack. You shouldn't be by yourself. When we're through sitting shivah you'll come to Cincinnati with me. Stay as long as you like. We'll fly back together."

She resisted, it was crazy, an extravagance. What was she, a decrepit old lady? She couldn't pack a suitcase? Anyway, she said, she really didn't like the idea of shlepping Ted back to Chicago. And she didn't, it would be like having him die twice. In Chicago he would be so far away from her, she thought, he might as well be dead. When she realized what she'd been thinking she started to laugh. When she heard herself laughing she began to weep.

"Ma," said her daughter, "I'll be on the next plane. Really, Mama, I want to."

In the end she said that if she couldn't go by herself she wouldn't attend her husband's funeral. Though the idea of that old boneyard sent chills. Maybe Ted really *should* be buried in Florida. The cemeteries were like eighteen-hole golf courses here. She wept when she went to make a withdrawal from her passbook at the savings and loan to get cash to give to the undertakers, and to pay her plane fare at the United ticket counter in the Fort Lauderdale airport, and could not stop weeping while she sat in the lounge waiting for her flight to board, or even for the entire three-hour-and-five-minute nonstop ride to Chicago.

Weeping, inconsolable, not even looking up into the faces of the various strangers who tried to comfort her, the airline hostess who served her her dinner, the captain, who actually left his cabin to come to her seat and ask what was the matter, if there was anything he could do. Looking out the plane window, seeing the perfect green of those eighteen-hole cemeteries, and thinking, oh, oh Ted, oh Ted, oh oh oh. It occurred to her as they flew over

Georgia that she had never been on a plane without her husband before. Weeping, inconsolable, it occurred to her that maybe they had put his body in the hold, that the undertakers had checked him through like her luggage.

And she really *didn't* want to take Ted there. The place was too strange. It was where her mother was buried, her sister, Ted's twin brothers, cousins from both sides of the family, her uncles and aunts, her oldest son. May *all* of them rest. A plot of ground about the size of a vacant lot where an apartment building had been torn down, a plot of land about the size of the construction site where Building Number Seven was going up.

It had been purchased in 1923 by a rich and distant uncle, a waggish man none of them had ever seen, who had bought up the property and set it aside for whomever of the Bliss family was then living or would come after, and had then made arrangements to have himself cremated and his ashes scattered from a biplane over Wyoming's Grand Teton mountains in aviation's earliest days when it wasn't always a dead-solid certainty that airplanes could even achieve such heights. The waggish uncle's curious legacy to the Blisses was possibly the single mystery the family had ever been faced with. Yet more than anything else it was this cemetery that not only held them together but distinguished them as a family, like having a common homeland, say, their own little Israel.

You lived, you died. Then you were buried there. Dorothy had not been the first of the Blisses to speak out about breaking the chain. Others had pronounced the idea of the place as too strange, or claimed it sent chills. And had found other means to dispose of themselves. One Bliss had actually chosen to follow in the flight path of the founder, as it were, and put it in his will that his cremains float down through the same patch of Wyoming altitude as had the waggish uncle's so many years before. Dorothy—this would have been while Ted was being interred—had long since ceased her long, twelve- or thirteen-hundred-mile crying jag. Ceased the moment her flight touched down at O'Hare. The people who met her plane to take her to her sister Etta's apartment on the North Side and those who came over to Etta's later that night to embrace Dorothy—just touching her set them off, just offering their condolences did—and came up to her the next day at the chapel where she sat with her children in the first row, all observed her odd detachment. In Chicago, she knew that among themselves the family spoke of how well she was taking it, as well as could be expected. "Under the circumstances," they added. She couldn't help herself, she didn't mean to take it well. She couldn't help it that at the very moment her husband's coffin was being lowered into the ground she had looked away for a moment and seen all the other graves where her people—the immediate, extended, nuclear, and almost genealogical family of Blisses—were buried and somehow understood that what had so repelled her about the idea of this place was the holy odor of its solidarity.

Back in Florida, where a sort of extended, informal shivah (perpetuated by her friends and neighbors in the Towers) continued to roll on, people came from far and wide throughout the complex to offer their condolences. Dorothy would have preferred that they all stop talking about it. Didn't they understand how exhausting it was to be both a widow *and* a baleboosteh? To have to deal with all the soups and salads, fruit and delicatessen and *more* salads, cookies and cakes and all the other drek she had to find enough jars and baggies and tinfoil and just plain space in the freezer for . . . How, with her grief, which wouldn't go away and which, like the tears, she could handle only in public among strangers she would never see again, people who'd never known Ted, or else only in the privacy of her bed where she couldn't sleep for the sound of her own sobbing. In two years she would see her doctor, who would prescribe sleeping pills to knock her out and on which she would become dependent, a sixty-nine- or seventy-year-old junkie Jewish lady, making her old, piecemeal beginning to break down her gorgeous looks, a fabulous beauty into her sixties, gone frail and plain before her time, a candidate for death by heartbreak, quite literally draining her (she was constantly thirsty, and would rise two or three times a night to take a glass of water) and making the tasks in which, while her husband lived, she had once taken a certain pleasure (the dishes and floors, the sink, wiping down the stove) now seem almost Herculean, too much for her strength. (And now she had the living room to contend with, too, heavy furniture to move in order to vacuum the rug, using attachments she'd rarely bothered with before just to suck crumbs from the sofa and chairs, even an ottoman, from which she now removed the slipcovers every evening in time for her guests and replaced again in the mornings. Cleaning the bathrooms, too, now, wiping stains from beneath the rims of the toilets with a special brush, rubbing off stuck brown tracks of actual turd, flushing them until they disappeared into a whirlpool of blue water, fifty cents off with the coupon.) She didn't know, maybe she *was* brave.

Gradually the visits became less and less frequent and then, about two months after Ted's death, Dorothy received a notice that her personal property taxes were about to come due. When she saw how high they were (her husband had always taken care of such things), she was stunned. They wanted almost two hundred dollars just for the automobile. She couldn't understand. They didn't owe on the car. Ted had paid cash for it. She looked and looked but there was no telephone number on the bill that she could call. She took a bus down to City Hall. They sent her from this office to that office. What with the long lines, it took at least two hours before she found a person she could talk to who didn't chase her to another department. She told her story for maybe the tenth time. She had received this bill. Here, Miss, you can look. They owned the car outright. If he had it Ted always paid cash, even for big-ticket items—their bedroom suite, the sofa, their dining room table and chairs. Even for their condominium. Though he had a couple—they had sent them to him in the mail—he never used his credit cards. Only for gas, he liked paying for gasoline with his Shell credit card. He wrote down how many gallons he put into the tank, he could keep track of his mileage. Dorothy heard how she spoke to this perfect stranger and realized that it was maybe the first time since he'd died that she'd really talked about Ted, that it wasn't just people telling her how sorry they were and if there was anything they could do and Dorothy sighing back at them, thank you, but there really wasn't. She thought she might start in again with the tears. But she didn't.

She organized her thoughts. She didn't know how to write checks. Even if she did she wouldn't know how to keep her accounts. She'd gone to business almost ten years but not since she was a girl, and anyway, back then they gave you wages in a pay envelope that she turned over to her mother. Her husband did everything; she never had to lift a finger. She knew for a fact it was in Ted's name, did she really owe two hundred dollars on the car?

She couldn't help it, she was a baleboosteh. She wasn't so much house proud as efficient. It gave her great satisfaction to know where everything was. There was so much in even the simplest household. It was really astonishing how much there was. Every day the newspaper came, announcements of upcoming events in the building, in the Towers complex. Every day the mail came. (It still came for Ted, and though it broke her heart to read letters from people who hadn't yet gotten the news, and though she never answered them because to write that he had died to someone who hadn't heard about it would be like making him just a little more dead than he already was, she never threw any of her husband's mail away.) She knew which letters of her own to keep (just as she knew what coupons to cut out or which articles to clip from the paper to send her children and grandchildren) and which to throw away.

So as soon as she needed to find the card Alcibiades Chitral had left with her—it was a business card and, because a man had given it to her, she had been certain it was important—she knew where she had put it.

It was in with a stack of current and already expired warranties, instruction manuals, and lists of potentially useful phone numbers and addresses. She called him that evening.

"Are you having your dinner," she said, "did I take you away from your programs?"

There was a pause at the other end of the connection, and it crossed her mind that though she'd given her name and broadly broached the reason for her call—Ted had died two months ago, it had been maybe seven weeks since Chitral had come to her door—he might not remember her, or she might have hurt his feelings—she'd almost closed the door in his face—and though she'd tried to smile he must have seen how upset she was. Hadn't she been an immigrant herself one time? She'd felt slights, plenty of them, other people's warinesses. "It can wait, it can wait," she said. "Or maybe you changed your mind."

"No, no," Alcibiades said suddenly. "Look," he said, "I have an appointment. I have to go to this meeting. I should be back in two, two and a half hours. If you're up I could drop by then."

Dorothy felt herself flush. In two and a half hours it would be about ten o'clock. All of a sudden, just like that, implications of Ted's death that hadn't even occurred to her, occurred to her. Who goes to sleep at ten o'clock? Old lonely people. Soured ones. If her husband were alive they'd still be watching television. Or playing cards with neighbors. Or listen, even if he'd just died—well, he had just died, and she was still sitting shivah—the gang would still be there, no one would even be putting on coffee yet. What could happen? She needed to get rid of Ted's car before she paid the personal property, didn't she? What could happen? Even only just thinking in these directions was a sin. Blushing over a telephone to a total stranger was an insult to Ted's memory.

"I still don't sleep so good," she told him vaguely. "Two hours don't bother me."

She drew a third bath. She dried and powdered herself. She put on the black dress she had worn for the funeral.

This wasn't funny business. She was too old for funny business. Her funny business days were gone forever. If she was nervous, if she blushed over telephones, if she bathed and powdered and put on fresh makeup, if it suddenly occurred that there were ramifications, if she straightened the chairs and made the lights and plumped the cushions, if she defrosted cake and set out fruit, if she was embarrassed or felt the least bit uncomfortable about her husband, dead two months though it seemed either forever or the day before yesterday (and she couldn't remember how his voice sounded), it didn't have the first thing to do with funny business.

She had no education to speak of and her only experience with the world had to do with her family. She had been a salesgirl in a ladies dress shop for maybe ten years more than forty years ago. (For most of those ten not *even* a salesgirl, more like a lady's maid. She fetched dresses to the changing rooms in the back of the shop, handed them in to the customers, or helped while they tried them on.) She had dealt only with women, seen them in their bodies' infinite circumstances, shy, pressed in the crowded quarters of the curtained-off dressing room for intimate opinions. She took care of the family. Ted took care of her. So if she fidgeted now, if she fussed over the fruit and furniture, it was, all over again, the way she'd been when Mrs. Dubow of whom she was terrified (the first woman in Illinois to pay her husband alimony), had pulled her from her duties in the close quarters and sent her out front to deal with the public. Where she was no longer required to give up her reluctant opinions but had actually to force them on others. Whether she held them or not. Volunteering styles (who knew nothing of style), stumping for fashions (or of fashion either), who was not even a good cook, merely one who could be depended upon to get it on the table on time. A baleboosteh manqué who spent twice the time she should have needed to put her condominium in order. Who was uncomfortable dealing with those women in the dress shop some forty-odd years ago let alone a man she was staying up to receive in her home in order to sell him a car.

Dorothy had given up on him and was already turning off lights when Security buzzed from downstairs.

He was almost an hour late. He apologized for having inconvenienced her but he'd been inconvenienced himself. The start of his meeting had been delayed while they waited for stragglers in a hospitality suite at the Hotel Intercontinental. It was inexcusable for people to behave like that, inexcusable, and he hoped Madam would forgive him. And, startling her, he presented her with a bouquet of flowers, which he produced from behind his back. "Oh," Dorothy said, jumping back, "oh." Then, realizing how this could have given offense, she tried to regain some composure. "They're wrapped," she said.

"Wrapped?" Alcibiades Chitral said.

"In that paper. Like florists use. Like my children send me for Mother's Day."

"Yes?"

Then, embarrassed, Dorothy understood that they were not a centerpiece he'd removed from the table in the hotel. "Jewish people," she explained gently, "Jewish people don't send flowers to a person if a person dies."

"Oh," Alcibiades said, "they don't?"

"Sometimes they give a few dollars to a person's charity in honor of the person," she said.

"I see," Alcibiades said. "What charity in particular?"

"The cancer fund," Dorothy said meekly and wiped her eyes.

"Well, that's a good idea," he said. "I'll write a check. But these are for you," he said. "To make up for my being so late."

She didn't know what to say. Of course she had to accept them. If for nothing else then for going to the trouble. What florist was open this time of night? Maybe it was true what people said about the South Americans, not that they had money to burn but that they put it on their backs—the men's gorgeous bespoke suits, the fantastic glitter of their wives' gowns and dresses, the fabulous shoes with their sky-high heels they bought at a hundred dollars an inch, their jewelry and diamond watches that any person in their right mind would keep in a locked-up safe-deposit box and not wear on their wrist where a strap could break or a clasp come undone, or any bag boy in a supermarket or stranger on the street could knock you down and hit you over the head for.

So it was not with an entirely undiluted gratitude that Dorothy accepted his flowers but with a certain scorn, too. Rousting emergency twenty-four-hour-a-day florists to open the store and paying a premium let alone just ordinary retail, never *mind* wholesale. Though it was sweet of him. Very thoughtful. Unless, of course, he was just buttering her up to get a price on the car.

"I know I called you," Dorothy said, "but to tell the truth I'm not sure I'm ready to sell."

"You've changed your mind, señora," said Alcibiades Chitral and then, startling Mrs. Bliss, abruptly rose and moved toward the door.

"Who said I changed my mind?" she said. "Did I say I changed my mind? I haven't made it up, I meant."

Alcibiades smiled. He was a good-looking man, tall, stout, ruddy complected, with bushy black eyebrows and white wavy hair. He looked like Cesar Romero; Dorothy Bliss felt nothing about this observation. Her heart didn't stumble, no nostalgic sigh escaped her. She did not feel foolish. If anything, saddened. In this place, in all the places in the world really, there was something faintly humorous about a recent widow. They consoled and consoled you, distracted you with their calls and their company from morning till night (until, in fact, at least in those first few days of your grief, all you needed for sleep to come over you was to put your head on a pillow), with their hampers of food to feed an army, and she wasn't saying right away, or next month, she wasn't even saying next year; she wasn't saying *any* particular time, but sooner or later, married friends saw your single condition and pronounced you eligible. Have your hair done, get some new clothes, what are you waiting for, time marches on. Because sooner or later it struck people funny. Like you lived in a joke, something comic in the deprived, resigned life. No matter your age, no matter your children were grown, that *they* had children. Something funny about the life force. Because God put you here to be entertained, to make the most of whatever time, however little it was, you had left. And pushed men on you, old farts with one foot in the grave. To make accommodation, to come to terms and spin your heart on its heels like a girl's. They'd change your life, have you cute, almost like you'd get a makeover in Burdines. They didn't care if you didn't get married. You didn't have to marry, he could move in with you, you could move in with him. Marriage was too much trouble. Who needed the aggravation? There were wills to think about, prenuptial agreements. Like living in the old country, dowry, like America had never happened. Or starting all over again.

So if Dorothy was a little sad it wasn't because she found this stranger attractive so much as that, as a widow, she felt like a figure of fun in his eyes. The gallantry, the expensive flowers, his predatory smile when she balked as he got up to leave.

"So what would you give?" she said, determined not to dicker.

He wanted to be fair, he said. He said he'd placed a few calls, taken the trouble to find out its blue book value. "That's the price a dealer will pay for your used car."

She knew what a blue book was. Ted, olov hasholem, had had one himself.

"Of course," Alcibiades said, "I don't know what extras came with your car, but air-conditioning, electric door locks and windows, if you have those it could be worth a little more. Even a radio, FM, AM. And if it's clean."

The baleboosteh in her looked offended. "Spic and span," she said evenly.

Alcibiades, solemn, considered. "Tell you what," he said seriously. "Let's take it for a spin."

She was as stunned as if the Venezuelan had asked her out on a date. Yet in the end she agreed to go with him. She would need a sweater, he said, a wrap. He would wait, he said, while she got it.

The car keys were in a drawer in the nightstand by their bed. Oddly enough, they were right on top of the blue book, and Mrs. Bliss, out of breath and feeling a pressure in her chest, opened it and looked up the value of the car. They'd had it over two years.

Ted never kept a car more than three years. If he'd lived he'd be looking for a new one soon.

Downstairs, in the underground garage, she didn't even have to tell him where it was parked. It was the first time she'd seen it in months and she began to cry. "I'm sorry," she said.

"No, no, señora," Alcibiades said, "please. I understand very well."

"You'll have to drive," Mrs. Bliss said. "I never learned."

She handed him the keys and he opened the door on the passenger side. He held it while she got in and closed the door after her. But Mrs. Bliss was on guard against his charm now. She knew the blue book value.

Then something happened that made her want to get this all over with. Before Chitral had even had time to come around to the driver's side and unlock the door Dorothy was overcome with a feeling so powerful she gasped in astonishment and turned in her seat and looked in the back to see if her husband were sitting there. She was thrown into confusion. It was Ted's scent, the haunted pheromones of cigarettes and sweat and loss, his over-two-year ownership collected, concentrated in the locked, unused automobile. It was the smell of his clothes and habits; it was the lingering odor of his radiation treatments, of road maps and Shell gasoline. It was the smell of presence and love.

They drove to Coconut Grove; they drove to Miami. She went past places and buildings she had never seen before. She didn't see them now. It was a hot night and the air-conditioning was on. She asked Chitral to turn it off and, hoping to exorcize Ted's incense, pressed the buttons to open all the windows.

She knew the blue book value. She would take whatever he offered. When he drove into the garage and went unerringly to Ted's space he shut off the engine and turned to her.

"It drives like a top," he said, and offered her five thousand dollars more than the car was worth.

"But that's more—" Mrs. Ted Bliss said.

"Oh," said Alcibiades Chitral, "I'm not so much interested in the car as in the parking space."

TWO

Excepting the formalities—the transfer of title when his check cleared, surrendering the keys—that was about the last time Alcibiades Chitral had anything to say to Mrs. Ted Bliss. The whirlwind courtship was over. That was just business, Dorothy explained to more than one of her inquisitive, curious friends in the Towers when they saw the fresh flowers—still fresh after more than a week, as though whatever upscale, emergency florist Alcibiades had had perforce to go to to purchase flowers at that time of night and charge what had to have been those kind of prices, would have had to provide not only the convenience of his after-hours availability but, too, something special in the nature of the blooms themselves, a mystery ingredient that imbued them with some almost Edenic longevity and extended scent—some of which Mrs. Ted had transferred from the cut crystal vase into which she'd originally put them and now redistributed in three equal parts into two other vessels.

She was at pains to inform them that there had been but the single presentation from Mr. Chitral, that she herself had thought to place these remarkable flowers in additional vases so that she might enjoy them from various vantage points throughout the room. They cheered her up, she said.

"Sure they do," Florence Klein said. "Believe me, Dorothy, I only wish I had an admirer."

"He admired me for my parking space."

"I'm only *kid*ding," Florence Klein said. "Don't get so cock-cited."

"I'll say this much for Latins," said Mrs. Ted Bliss, "they always try to sell you a bill of goods. During the war, when Ted had the meat market, it was the same thing. He could have opened a liquor store with all the cases of wine those thieves gave him. They climbed all over each other to get you to take their black-market, Argentine meat. I *wanted* to sell."

Had Chitral heard of any of this he would have been offended. The bitch was good-looking enough for an old bitch, but who did these people think they were?

Seducing her into selling her husband's automobile was a non-starter, the *last* thing on his mind. It was insulting. One gave out of respect for the proprieties, the civilized gesture. Was he some nasty tango of a man? Had he kissed her hand? Had he offered serenades?

But no whiff of imagined scandal reached his ears. No wink of conspiracy, no gentle nudge to his ribs in the elevator. Even on those rare occasions when they ran into each other at this or that Towers do, Mrs. Bliss barely acknowledged him. He thought he understood her reasons. He imagined she still felt shame for having sold her husband's car. Chitral was a gentleman, no more given to grandstanding or bluffing than Hector Camerando or Jaime Guttierez. Taking his cue from Mrs. Ted Bliss, he affected a discretion as palpable (though of course not as nervous) as her own. He was not *just* a gentleman. He was a man of parts. In addition to his decorums, he had his sensibilities as well. In the matter of the automobile she may have been shamed as much by the windfall profit she had made from the sale as by the sale itself. All you had to do was look at her. She was like the woman of valor in Proverbs. Any idea of benefit from the death of a spouse would have gone against her nature. She had known he'd overpaid her. That's why he'd told her about the parking space. It was a matter of record that the people in Building One could sell their garage privileges. He'd meant to make it seem like a package deal—which of course it was. The space would have been worthless to him without the car, the car of no value without the space.

So the last time they saw each other without the mutual buffers of an amiable, pretend nonchalance was two years later, when Mrs. Bliss testified against him, a witness for the prosecution, in court. She never entirely understood how they worked it. Nor, for that matter, really understood why the government subpoenaed her.

But don't think the family didn't fight to have the subpoena quashed. Frank, her son, and Maxine, her daughter, wanted her to have representation and even hired a lawyer for her, although when Mrs. Bliss learned what they were being charged she gathered her outrage, joined it to her courage, and fired her. Manny, from the building, had been a lawyer before retiring and moving to Florida, and Mrs. Bliss told him that the kids thought she needed representation. Just using the word sounded dangerous in her mouth, and important.

He told her up front that he had been strictly a real estate lawyer, that he really knew nothing about the sort of thing Dorothy was involved with. "Besides," he said, "I'm retired. I practiced in Michigan. I don't even know if Michigan and Florida have, whadayacall it, reciprocity."

"What's reciprocity?" Mrs. Bliss asked.

Manny came to see her an hour later and told him he had called a man he knew, a registrar of deeds in the Dade County Courthouse.

"You know what?" he said. "He told me I have it." He seemed very excited. "I'm going to take your case," he told her solemnly.

"Ma," Maxine said when she learned Mrs. Bliss had fired the attorney she and her brother had obtained for her, "do you think that's such a good idea? No offense, Mother, but do you really believe Manny is up to this? These are people from the Justice Department, *federal* people. Can Manny go one on one with these people?"

"Manny's no fool."

"If it's the money—"

"Of course it's the money," Mrs. Bliss said. "You know what she charges? Two hundred fifty dollars an hour!"

"Ma, Ma," Maxine said, "this guy is a big-time Venezuelan cocaine kingpin."

"He's a *farmer*."

"Mother, he's a *drug* lord! They want to put you on the stand so you can identify him as the man who bought Daddy's car from you. You're a very important government witness. I'm not even talking about the emotional strain, what going through all that stress could do to a person half your age and with a much better blood pressure. I don't mean to scare you, Ma, but Frank and I are concerned"—she lowered her voice; Dorothy had to press her left ear tight against the receiver to hear her—"what these people could do to you."

"Sweetheart, sweetheart," Mrs. Bliss said, "your daddy, olov hasholem, is dead two years. Two years I've been without him. A lifetime. Who's left to share Marvin's death with me? Who's around to miss him? What trouble can your kingpin make for me?"

Manny couldn't get her out of it. He gave it his best effort, pulled out all the stops, tried tricks he'd learned in thirty-five years of real estate law in the great state of Michigan when clients required additional time before they could move into their new homes or out of their old ones. He brought a note to the government from Mrs. Bliss's doctors. He had her put a dying battery into her hearing aid when she went to be deposed, but these federal boys knew their onions. They wrote their questions out on yellow, lined, 9×14-inch legal pads and handed them to her.

Dorothy put on her glasses.

"Wait, hold your horses a minute. Those ain't her reading glasses."

"Does he have to be here?" asked one of the lawyers.

"Behave yourself, Pop," said another.

In the end, when she was finally called and sworn, she was very calm. She had no great wish to harm this man, she bore him no grudge. Indeed, she was even tempted to perjure herself on his behalf, but thought better of it when she realized the signals this might send to her neighbors in the Towers. So she drew a deep breath and implicated him. She was very careful, however, to point out what a gentleman he'd been, how he'd brought her roses that were still fresh as a daisy after more than a week, and recalled for the jury the lovely drive he had taken her on through Coconut Grove and Miami.

Chitral was sentenced to one hundred years. Dorothy felt terrible about that, just terrible. And although she was told they would have had more than enough to convict him even without her testimony, she was never quite reconciled to the fact that she had damaged him. She asked her lawyer (on the day of her appearance Manny had accompanied her to court for moral support) to get word to Alcibiades's lawyer that there were no hard feelings, and that if he ever wanted her to visit him she would make every effort to get one of her friends in the building to drive her. He said, "Out of the question."

She read about the case in the paper, she watched televised excerpts of it on the eleven o'clock news (though she herself never appeared on the screen she heard some of her actual testimony as the camera showed Chitral's face in all its friendly indifference; he looked, thought Mrs. Bliss, rather as he had looked when they had run into each other in the elevators or passed one another in the Towers' public rooms), but try as she might, she never commanded the nuts and bolts of just how Ted's Buick LeSabre and parking space fit into the kingpin's schemes. It all seemed as complex to her as the idea of "laundering money," a concept alien to even Dorothy's baleboosteh soul. Building on this vaguely housekeeping analogy, however, she gradually came to think of the car serving Chitral and his accomplices as a sort of dope hamper. It was the closest she came. Manny said she wasn't far off.

Then, under the DEA's new federal forfeiture laws, the government confiscated the car. Two agents came and affixed a bright yellow, heavy iron boot to its rear wheel. Mrs. Bliss came down to the garage when a neighbor alerted her to what was happening and wanted to know what was going on.

One of the government agents said there was no room for a pile a shit back on the lot, and they were putting her husband's car under house arrest.

"How would it look?" said the other agent. "People would laugh. A seventy-eight Buick LeSabre next to all those Jags, Benzes, Rolls-Royces, Corvettes, and Bentleys? Folks would think we weren't doing our job."

"Please," said Mrs. Ted Bliss, "you can't leave it here. You're dishonoring my husband's memory."

"Lady," the agent said, "you should've thought of that before you started doing business with those mugs."

She called Manny and told him what was happening. Manny from the building was there within minutes of her placing the call.

"Aha," Manny told her, rubbing his hands, "this, this is more

like it. This appertains to real estate law. Now they're on *my* turf!"
The agents were fixing a long yellow ribbon from four stanchions,
in effect roping off Ted Bliss's old parking space. The lawyer went
up to the government. "Just what do you gentlemen think you're
doing? It looks like a crime scene down here."

"It *is* a crime scene down here," an agent said.

"That parking space is private property. It belongs to my client,
Mrs. Ted Bliss. It was included in the deed of sale when the condominium was originally purchased."

"Oh yeah?" said the agent who had finished attaching the last
ribbon to the last metal stanchion and was just now adjusting the
posts, pulling them taut so the ribbons formed a rectangle about
the parking space. "How's it look?" he asked his partner.

The other agent touched his forefinger to his right thumb and
held it up eye level with his face. "You're an artist," he said.

"Oh yeah?" the agent, turning to Manny, said again. "We're
not just confiscating the car, we're confiscating the parking space,
too. She wants it back, she can come to the auction and make a bid
just like any other American in good standing. She can make us an
offer on the piece a shit, too."

"Sure," said the agent who'd said it *was* a crime scene down
there, speaking to Manny but looking directly at Mrs. Ted Bliss,
"she can start with a bid five, six thousand bucks over the blue
book value of the parking space."

The two DEA agents got into a sparkling, silver, late-model
Maserati and drove the hell off, leaving Manny and Dorothy looking helplessly down at the rubber tire tracks the car had burned
into the cement floor of the garage.

It was as if she were a greenhorn. She felt besmirched, humiliated,
ridden out of town on a rail. In the old days her mother had bribed
an immigration official fifteen dollars and he had changed the age
on Dorothy's papers. Her alien status had never been a problem
for her. There had never been a time when she felt awkward, or
that she had had to hold her tongue. The years in the dress shop
when she'd been more like a lady's maid than a salesgirl, and had
attempted (and sometimes actually seemed) to hide in changing
rooms narrower and less than half the length and width of her
husband's cordoned-off parking space in the garage hadn't been

nearly so degrading. Even in the presence of the terrifying Mrs. Dubow, who somehow managed not only to speak to Dorothy with her mouth full of pins but even to shout at her and come after her (at least five times in the almost ten years she had worked for the deranged woman), brandishing scissors and cracking her tailor's yellow measuring tape at Dorothy's cowering figure as if it were a whip, she hadn't felt the woman's dislike so much as her pure animal rage. The next week there was likely to be an additional six or seven dollars in her pay envelope.

It may have been nothing more than the glib way in which the two DEA men had addressed her (or addressing Manny but really speaking through him to Dorothy), but she had never felt so uncitizened, so abandoned, so bereft of appeal. Her protests would have meant nothing to them.

Dorothy had never experienced anti-Semitism. During all the years Ted had owned his meat market, or even after he'd sold it, bought a fifty-unit apartment building in a declining neighborhood on Chicago's North Side and become not only its landlord but, with Dorothy's assistance, went around collecting the rent money on the first Monday of every month, she hadn't sensed even its trace. Neither from Polack nor shvartzer. Goyim liked her. Everyone liked her, and although there were people *she* disliked—some of Ted's customers when they had the butcher shop, several of her husband's four-flusher tenants in the North Side apartment building— she herself had always felt personally admired.

Now she wasn't so sure. The agents had spoken in front of her as if she were the subject of gossip. From some superior plane of snobbery like a sort of wiseguy American Yiddish, they added insult to injury.

And now the continued presence of her late husband's car seemed like nothing so much as an assault, a kind of smear campaign. She found herself averting her eyes from the blighted automobile whenever she went down to the garage with neighbors who'd offered to drive her to her hair appointment, or take her shopping, or invited her out to restaurants.

Actually her odd fame—she'd become a human interest story; a reporter from the *Herald* had written her up in a column; the host of a radio talk show wanted her as a guest—had leant her a swift cachet in the building, and people with whom she had barely exchanged a few sentences invited her to their condos for dinner. In the days and weeks following the trial Mrs. Bliss found herself accepting more of these invitations than she declined if for no other reason than that she genuinely enjoyed visiting other people's condos in the Towers. With the exception of the penthouses, there were essentially only three basic floor plans. She got a kick out of seeing what people had done with their places and regretted only that Ted wasn't there to see them with her.

It was peculiar, really, Mrs. Bliss thought, that she should be interested in such matters. She was, of course, house proud. Yet the fixtures and furniture in her apartment were not only pretty much what she had brought down to Florida with her from Chicago but many of her things were pieces they'd had from the time they were first married. Massive bedroom and dining room suites that looked as if they had been carved from the same dark block of mahogany. They had bought, it would seem, for the ages. Even their living room furniture, their sofa and side tables and chairs, seemed somehow to have come from a time that predated fashion, was prior to style. In Florida, their dining room table, too big for the squeezed, sleek, modern measurements of a condominium's efficient, reduced rooms, had had to be cut down so that what in Chicago had accommodated eight people (a dozen when there was poker and the family—the gang—was over) now barely had room for five and overwhelmed the space in which it was put. Like every other piece of their giant furniture—the great boxy chairs in the living room like the enormous chairs of Beijing bureaucrats, their thick drapes and valances—it appeared to absorb light and locate the apartment in a more northerly climate in a season more like winter or autumn than summer or spring. An air of disjointedness and vague anachronism presided even over their appliances—their pressure cooker and metal juice squeezer, their electric percolator and carving knife.

And though Mrs. Bliss was neither jealous nor envious of other people's possessions, or of the way they utilized space under their new dispensations, or translated their old New York, Cleveland, or Toronto surroundings through the enormous sea change of their Florida lives, nor understood how at the last moment—she didn't kid herself, with the possible exception of the Central and South Americans (and a few of the Canadians), this was the last place most of them would ever live—they could trade in the solid, substantial furniture of their past for the lightweight bamboo, brushed aluminum, and canvas goods of what they couldn't live long enough to become their future. And, indeed, there'd been considerable turnover in the Towers in the three or so years since Ted Bliss had died. From Rose Blitzer's table alone three people had passed away—Rose's husband, Max; Ida, the woman who couldn't digest sugar substitutes without a nondairy creamer; and the woman who'd poured their coffee.

Yet it was never from a sense of the morbid or any thought to mockery that Mrs. Bliss accepted invitations to other people's apartments. She went out of deep curiosity and interest, as others might go, say, to anthropological museums.

And now, for the first time since she'd moved south, Mrs. Bliss was visiting one of the Towers' penthouses. She had emerged from the penthouse's private elevator. First she had had to descend to the lobby from her condo on Building One's seventh floor, cross the lobby to the security desk and give her name to the guard, Louise Munez. Louise had once confided that while she didn't herself live in the Towers, she was the daughter of Elaine Munez, one of the residents here. She dressed in the thick, dark serge of a night watchman, wore a revolver that she carried in an open, strapless holster, and held a long, heavy batonlike flashlight that doubled as a nightstick. A pair of doubled handcuffs that clanked when she moved was attached to a reinforced loop at the back of her trousers. Though she didn't appear to be a big woman, in her windbreaker and uniform she seemed bulky. On her desk, spread out before her closed-circuit television monitors, was an assortment of tabloids—the *National Enquirer*, the *National Examiner*, the *Star*—along with current numbers of *Scientific American*, *Playboy*, *Playgirl*, *Town and Country*. An open cigar box with a few bills and about two dollars in change was just to the left of a red telephone. A walkie-talkie chattered in a pants pocket.

"Interest you in some reading matter tonight, Mrs. Ted Bliss?"

"Maybe some other time, Louise. I'm invited to attend Mr. and Mrs. Auveristas's open house."

"I have to check the guest list."

"It's an open house," Mrs. Bliss said.

"I have to check the guest list." She referred to a sheet of names. "Stand over there by the penthouse elevator. You don't have a key, I'll remote it from here."

Dorothy stepped out of the elevator into a sort of marble foyer that led to two tall, carved wooden doors. She had to ring to be let in. A butler opened the doors, which were electric and withdrew into a cavity in the marble walls. Without even asking who she was he handed her a name tag with her name written out in a fine cursive script. "How did you know?" she asked the butler who smiled enigmatically but did not answer.

The place was like nothing she'd ever seen. She knew she hadn't worn the right clothes, that she didn't even own the right clothes. What did *she* know, it was an open house. If she'd known it was supposed to be dress-up she'd have put on the dress she'd worn in court the day she testified. She had a queer sense she should have brought opera glasses.

"Ah, it's Mrs. Bliss! How are you, Mrs. Bliss?" called a youthful-looking but silver-haired man who couldn't have been in more than his early forties or perhaps even his late thirties, immediately withdrawing from an intense conversation in which he seemed to be not merely engaged but completely engrossed. It occurred to Dorothy, who couldn't remember having met him, that she'd never seen anyone so thoroughly immaculate. So clean, she meant (he might have been some baleboss of the personal), not so much well groomed (though he was well groomed) as buffed, preened, shiny as new shoes. He could have been newly made, something just off an assembly line, or still in its box. He seemed almost to shine, bright, fresh as wet paint. The others, following the direction of his glance, stared openly at her and, when he started to move toward her across the great open spaces of the immense room, simply trailed along after him. Instinctively, Dorothy drew back a few steps.

As if gauging her alarm the man quite suddenly halted and held up his hand, cautioning the others as if they were on safari and he some white hunter fearful of spooking his prey. "Madam Bliss!" he said, exactly as if it were she who had surprised him.

Dorothy nodded.

"Welcome to my home," he declared, "welcome indeed." And, reaching forward, took up her hand and bent to kiss it. This had never happened to her before, nor, outside the movies, had she ever seen it happen to anyone else. It even crossed her mind that she was being filmed. (People were beginning to buy those things . . . those camcorders. Even one of her grandsons had one. He took it with him everywhere.)

"Oh, don't," Dorothy said smiling nervously. "I must look terrible."

Bemused, Tommy Auveristas—that's who it was, she could read his name tag now—looked at her. It was one of those moments when neither person understands what the other person means. No matter what happened between them in the years that would follow, this was a point that would never be straightened out. Auveristas thought Mrs. Bliss was referring to the overpowering smell of cheap perfume coming off her hands and which he would taste for the rest of the evening and on through the better part of the next morning. Oh, he thought, these crazy old people. "No, no," he said, "you are delicious," and then, turning not to one of the two servers in the room but to a very beautifully dressed woman in a fine gown, told her to get Mrs. Bliss a drink. "What would you like?" he asked.

"Do you have diet cola?"

"I'm sure we must. If we don't we shall absolutely have to send out for a case."

"Oh, no," said Mrs. Bliss, "I wouldn't put you to the trouble. I'll have 7-Up. Your home is very beautiful."

"Would you like me to show you around? I will show you around."

"I mustn't take you from your guests. I just came, there's time, I'm not in any hurry."

Mrs. Bliss felt overwhelmed. She could have been the guest of honor or something, the way they treated her. It was, like that kiss on her hand, outside her experience. Or if not outside her experience exactly, then at least outside earned experience, the cost-effective honors of accomplishment. She'd been a bride. She was a mother, she and Ted had married a daughter, bar mitzvahed two sons, buried one of them. She was a widow, she had buried a husband, so it wasn't as if she'd never been the center of attention. (She had been a witness for the government in a high-profile drug case.) But who's kidding who? Let's face it, except for the trial, all those other occasions had been affairs of one sort or the other, even the funerals, may Ted and Marvin rest, bought and paid for. So unless they were exaggerating their interest in her—Tommy Auveristas was polite, even, she thought, sincere—she couldn't remember feeling so important. It was exciting. But she was overwhelmed. As she hadn't known what to do with all the attention after Ted's death, she didn't know what to do with the solicitude of these strangers.

Many of them drifted away. New guests were arriving and Tommy Auveristas, excusing himself from Mrs. Bliss as if she were indeed the guest of honor, went off to greet them.

Ermalina Cervantes came back with her soft drink.

"Here you go," she said. "It wasn't cold enough, I put ice in it. Can you drink it with ice?"

"Oh, thank you. Cold is fine. This is good, I'm really enjoying it. But you know," Mrs. Bliss said, "they fill up your glass with too much ice in a restaurant, they're trying to water it down. I don't let them get away with that. I send it back to the kitchen."

"If there's too much ice . . ."

"No, no, it's perfect. Hits the spot. I was just saying."

Ermalina Cervantes smiled at her. She had a beautiful smile, beautiful teeth. Beautiful skin. Mrs. Bliss set great store in pretty skin in a woman. She thought it revealed a lot about a person's character. It wasn't so important for a man to have a nice skin. Men had other ways of showing their hearts, but if a woman didn't have sense enough to take care of her skin (it was the secret behind her own beauty; why people had bragged on her looks almost until she was seventy), then she didn't really care about anything. The house could fall down around her ears and she'd never notice. She'd send her kids off to school all shlumperdik, shmuts on their faces, holes in their pants. But this was some Ermalina, this Ermalina. Teeth *and* skin! Butter wouldn't melt.

Ermalina Cervantes, nervous under the scrutiny of Mrs. Bliss's open stare, asked if anything were wrong.

"Wrong? What could be wrong, sweetheart? It's a wonderful party. The pop is delicious. I never tasted better. You have a beautiful smile and wonderful teeth, and your skin is your crowning glory."

"Oh," Ermalina Cervantes said, "oh, thank you."

"I hope you don't mind my saying."

"No, of course not. Thank you, Mrs. Bliss."

"Please, dear. Dorothy."

"Dorothy."

"That's better," she said, "you make me very happy. I'll tell you, I haven't been this happy since my husband was alive. Older people like it when younger people use their first names. If you think it's the opposite you'd be wrong. It shows respect for the person if the person calls the person by her first name than the other way around. Don't ask me why, it's a miracle. You're blushing, am I talking too much? I'm talking too much. I can't help it. Maybe because everyone's so nice. You know, if I didn't know pop don't make you drunk I'd think I was drunk."

A pretty blond named Susan Gutterman came by and Ermalina introduced her to Mrs. Bliss.

"Susan Gutterman," Mrs. Bliss said speculatively. "You're Jewish?"

"No."

"Gutterman is a Jewish name."

"My husband is Jewish. He's from Argentina."

"You? What are you?"

"Oh," Susan Gutterman said offhandedly, "not much of anything, I guess. I'm a WASP."

"A wasp?"

"A White Anglo-Saxon Protestant," Susan Gutterman explained.

"Oh, you're of mixed blood."

"May I bring you something to eat?" Susan Gutterman said.

"I haven't finished my pop. We haven't met but I know who you are," said Mrs. Bliss, turning to a woman just then passing by. "You're Carmen Auveristas, Tommy Auveristas's wife." Like all the other South Americans at the party she was a knockout, not anything like those stale cutouts and figures with their fancy guitars, big sombreros, spangled suits, and drooping mustaches thicker than paintbrushes that the Decorations Committee was always putting up for the galas on those Good Neighbor nights in the gussied-up game rooms. And not at *all* like the women who went about all overheated in their coarse, black, heavy mourning. Was it any wonder those galas were so poorly attended? They must have been insulted, Mrs. Ted Bliss thought. Portrayed like so many shvartzers. Sure, how would Jews like it?

"And I know who you are," Carmen Auveristas said.

"Your husband's very nice. Such a gentleman. He kissed my hand. Very continental. Very suave."

"Have you met Elaine Munez?" Mrs. Auveristas asked.

"Your daughter, Louise, let me up. She tried to sell me a paper. Oh," she told her fellow guest, the cop-and-paper-boy's mother, "she must have called up my name on her walkie-talkie. That's how the servant knew to give me my name tag. I was wondering about that."

"May I bring you something to eat?" Elaine Munez said flatly.

"No, thank you," she said. "I ate some supper before I came. I didn't know what a spread you put on. Go, dear, it looks delicious. I wish I could eat hot spicy foods, but they give me gas. They burn my kishkas."

The three women smiled dully and left her to stand by herself. Dorothy didn't mind. Though she was having a ball, the strain of having to do all the talking was making her tired. She sat down in a big wing chair covered in a bright floral muslin. She was quite comfortable. Vaguely she was reminded of Sundays in Jackson Park when she and Ted and the three children had had picnics in the Japanese Gardens. In the beautiful room many of her pals from the Towers, there, like herself, in the penthouse for the first time, walked about, examining its expensive contents, trying out its furniture, accepting hors d'oeuvres from the caterers, and giggling, loosened up over highballs. Dorothy amused herself by trying to count the guests, keeping two sets of books, three—the Jews, those South Americans she recognized, and those she'd never seen before—but someone was always moving and, when she started over, she'd get all mixed up. It was a little like trying to count the number of musicians in Lawrence Welk's band on television. The camera never stayed still long enough for her to get in all the trumpet players, trombonists, clarinet players, fiddlers, and whatnot. Sometimes a man with a saxophone would set it down and pick up something else. Then, when you threw in the singers . . . It could make you dizzy. Still, she was content enough.

Closing her eyes for a moment and concentrating as hard as she could—she was wearing her hearing aid; this was in the days when she owned only one—she attempted to distinguish between the English and Spanish conversations buzzing around her like flies.

Tommy Auveristas, kneeling beside her armchair, startled her.

Quite almost as much as she, bolting up, startled him, causing him to spill a little of the food from the plate he was extending toward her onto the cream Berber carpeting.

"Son of a bitch!"

"I'm sorry, I'm sorry! It's my fault," Mrs. Bliss volunteered. "If we rub it with seltzer it should come out! I'll go and get some!"

"No, no, of course not. The maid will see to it. Stay where you are."

Mrs. Bliss pushed herself up out of the armchair.

"Stay where you are!" Auveristas commanded. "I *said* the girl would see to it. Where is the nincompoop?"

Seeing he'd frightened Mrs. Bliss half to death, he abruptly modulated. "I've offended you. Forgive me, señora. You're absolutely right. I think you'd be more comfortable someplace else. Here, take my arm. We'll get out of this woman's way while she works." He said something in Spanish to the maid who, on her hands and knees, was picking a reddish sauce out of a trough of sculpted carpet before wiping the stain away with a wet cloth. He led Dorothy to a sofa—one of three—in a distant corner of the room. Seating her there, he asked again that she forgive him for his outburst and promised he'd be right back.

He returned with food piled high on a plate. "Ah, Mrs. Bliss," he said. "Not knowing your preference in my country's dishes, I have taken the liberty of choosing for you."

She accepted the plate from the man. She respected men. They did hard, important work. Not that laundry was a cinch, preparing and serving meals, cleaning the house, raising kids. She and Ted were partners, but she'd been the silent partner. She knew that. It didn't bother her, it never had. If Ted had been mean to her, or bossed her around . . . but he wasn't, he didn't. As a matter of fact, honest, they'd never had a fight. Her sisters had had terrible fights with their husbands. Rose was divorced and to this day she never saw her without thinking of the awful things that had happened between her sister and Herman. Listen, scoundrel that he was, there were two sides to every story. And everything wasn't all cream and peaches between Etta and Sam. Still, much as she loved Etta, the woman had a tongue on her. She wasn't born yesterday. Husbands and wives fought. Cats and dogs. Not her and Ted. Not one time. Not once. Believe it or not. As far as Dorothy was concerned he was, well, he was her hero. Take it or leave it.

What she told Gutterman and Elaine Munez was true. She *wasn't* hungry; she had prepared a bite of supper before she came to the party. She wasn't hungry. What did an old woman need? Juice, a slice of toast with some jelly in the morning, a cup of coffee. Maybe some leftovers for lunch. And if she went out to Wolfie's or the Rascal House with the gang for the Early Bird Special, perhaps some brisket, maybe some fish. Only this wasn't any of those things. These things were things she'd never seen before in her life.

Bravely, she smiled at Tommy Auveristas and permitted him to lay a beautiful cloth napkin across her lap and hand her the plate of strange food. He gave her queer forks, an oddly shaped spoon. She didn't have to look to know that it was sterling, top of the line.

Nodding at her, he encouraged her to dig in.

Mrs. Ted Bliss picked over this drek with her eyes. From her expression, from the way her glance darted from one mysterious item to the next, you'd have thought she was examining different chocolates in a pound box of expensive candy, divining their centers, like a dowser, deciding which to choose first. Meanwhile, Tommy Auveristas explained the food like a waiter in one of those two-star restaurants where you nod and grin but don't know what the hell the man is talking about.

"Which did you say was the chicken, the green or the blue one?"

"Well, both."

"I can't decide," Dorothy Bliss said.

Auveristas wasn't born yesterday either. He knew the woman was stalling him, knew the fixed ways of the old, their petrified tastes. It was one of the big items that most annoyed the proud hidalgo about old fart señoras like this one. She was his guest, however, and whatever else he may have been he was a gracious and resourceful host.

"No, no, Dorothy," he said, snatching her plate and signaling the maid up off her knees to take the food away, "you mustn't!" he raised his hand against the side of his head in the international language of dummkopf.

The señora didn't know what had hit her and looked at him with an expression at once bewildered, curious, and relieved.

"It isn't kosher," he explained, "can you ever forgive me?"

"Oh, sure," she said. "Of course."

"You are graciousness itself," Tommy Auveristas said. "May I offer you something else instead? We have grapes. I bet you like grapes."

"I do like grapes."

He had a bowl of grapes brought to her, wide and deep as the inside of a silk hat.

He asked if it was difficult to keep kosher, and Dorothy, a little embarrassed, explained that she didn't, not strictly, keep kosher. Now that the children were grown and her husband was dead she didn't keep pork in the house—she'd never tasted it—though there was always bacon in her freezer for when the kids came to visit. She never made shellfish, which she loved, and had always eaten in restaurants when Ted was alive, and it didn't bother her mixing milchik and flayshig. And although she always bought kosher meat for Passover, and kept separate dishes, and was careful to pack away all the bread in the house, even cakes and cookies, even bagels and onion rolls, she was no fanatic, she said, and stowed these away in plastic bags in the freezer until after the holidays. In her opinion, it was probably an even bigger sin in God's eyes to waste food than to follow every last rule. Her sisters didn't agree with her, she said, but all she knew was that she'd had a happier marriage with Ted, may he rest, than her sister Etta with Sam.

He was easy to talk to, Tommy Auveristas, but maybe she was taking too much of his time. He had other guests after all.

He shrugged off the idea.

"You're *sure* my soda pop wasn't spiked?"

"What?"

"Oh," Mrs. Bliss said, "that was someone else, the girl with the skin. Ermalina? We had a discussion about my soft drink."

"I see."

"What was I going to tell you? Oh, yeah," she said, "I remember. Chicken.

"One time, this was when Ted was still alive but we were already living in Miami Beach. And we went to a restaurant, in one of the hotels with the gang to have dinner and see the show. The girls treated the men. (Every week we'd set a percentage of our winnings aside from the card games. In a year we'd have enough to go somewhere nice.) And I remember we all ordered chicken. Everyone in our party. We could have had anything we wanted off the menu but everyone ordered chicken. Twenty people felt like chicken! It was funny. Even the waitress couldn't stop laughing. She must have thought we were crazy.

"Now the thing about chicken is that there must be a million ways to prepare it. Boiled chicken, broiled chicken, baked chicken, fried chicken, roast chicken, stewed chicken. Just tonight I learned you could make green chicken, even blue chicken. And the other thing about chicken is that every different way you make it, that's how different it's going to taste. Chicken salad. Chicken fricassee."

"Chicken pox," Tommy Auveristas said.

Mrs. Bliss laughed. It was disgusting but it was one of the funniest things she'd ever heard.

"Yeah," she said, "chicken *pox!*" She couldn't stop laughing. She was practically choking. Tommy Auveristas offered to get her some water. She waved him off. "It's all right, something just went down the wrong pipe. Anyway, anyway, everyone ordered their chicken different. I'll never forget the look on that waitress's face. She must have thought we were nuts.

"But you know," Dorothy said, "when you really stop and think about it, it's not that much different from eggs." She stopped and thought about it. "There are all kinds of ways of making eggs, too.

"Well," Mrs. Bliss said, "the long and the short is that chicken is a very popular dish. I don't know anyone who doesn't like it. We were saying that, and then one of the girls—she's in this room now—wondered how many chickens she must have made for her family in her life. She thought it had to be about a thousand chickens. But she was way off. Way off. I didn't want to embarrass her so I kept my mouth shut, but later, after we got home, I took a pencil and worked it out. Figure you make chicken twice a week. Say I've been making it for 53 years. It's probably more. I must have helped my mother make it when I was a girl, but *say* 53 years. If there are 52 weeks and 365 days in a year, that's 104 chickens a year. You times 104 by 53 years, you get 5,512 chickens. I didn't do that in my head. I worked it out on a gin rummy score sheet when we got home. I never forgot the number, though. When I told Ted,

MRS. TED BLISS ~ 43

you know what he said? He said 'I knew she was wrong. She had to be. I moved more chicken than anything else in the store.' Ted was a butcher. He had a meat market on Fifty-third Street."

"Which one is she?" Tommy whispered.

"Is who?"

"The dope who thought she made only about a thousand chickens."

"I don't want to embarrass her."

"No," he said, "go on. I won't tell a soul. You have my word of honor."

"Maybe they ate out more than we did," Mrs. Bliss said, "maybe she hasn't been cooking as long."

"Still . . ." Tommy Auveristas said. "You can tell me. Come on."

"Well," Mrs. Ted Bliss, who hadn't laughed so hard in years, said slyly, "if you promise not to tell." Auveristas crossed his heart. Mrs. Bliss took a moment to evaluate this pledge, shrugged, and indicated he lean toward her. "It's that one," she said softly, "Arlene Brodky."

"Arlene Brodky?"

"Shh," Mrs. Bliss warned, a finger to her lips.

The gesture made her feel positively girlish. It was as if forty-odd years had poured out of her life and she was back in Chicago again, in the dress shop, gossiping with the real salesgirls about the customers, their loony employer, passing confidences among themselves like notes between schoolmates. Frivolous, silly, almost young.

She had come to see the penthouse. She couldn't have articulated it for you, but it was simply that interest in artifact, some instinctive baleboosteh tropism in Mrs. Ted Bliss that drew her to all the tamed arrangements of human domesticities. She had never expected to *enjoy* herself.

Maybe it was the end of her mourning. Ted had been dead more than three years. She'd still been in her forties when Marvin died, and she'd never stopped mourning him. Perhaps thirty years of grief was enough. Maybe thirty years stamped its quitclaim on even the obligated life, and permitted you to burn the mortgage papers. Was she being disloyal? He'd be forty-six, Marvin. Had she been a better mother than a wife? She hoped she had loved everyone the same, the living and the dead, her children, her husband, her parents whom God himself had compelled her to honor and, by extension, her sisters and brothers, her relations and friends, the thirty years dredging up from the bottom of her particular sea all the sunken, heavy deadweight of her overwhelmed, overburdened heart.

Still, it was one thing not to keep kosher (or not strictly kosher), and another entirely to have caught herself actually *flirting*. She could have bitten her tongue.

Dorothy was not, of course, a particularly modern woman. She had been alive at the time others of her sex had petitioned the franchise from dubious, reluctant males and, though she'd been too young to rally for this or any other cause, the truth was she'd have been content to leave it to others—to other women as well as to other men—to pick the federal government, or even vote on the local, parochial issues of daily life. She had never, for example, attended a P.T.A. meeting when her children were young or, for that matter, spoken up at any of the frequent Towers Condominium Owners Association meetings. On the other hand, neither did she possess any of the vast scorn reserves some women called upon to heap calumny on those of their sisters they perceived as, well, too openly pushy about their rights.

There was something still essentially pink in Mrs. Bliss's soul, some almost vestigial principle in the seventyish old woman, not of childhood particularly, or even of girlhood, so much as of femininity itself, something so obscurely yet solidly distaff in her nature that she was quite suddenly overcome by the ancient etiquette she thought females owed males, something almost like courtship, or the need to nurture, shlepping, no matter how silly she knew it might sound—to Auveristas as well as to herself—the old proprieties of a forced, wide-eyed attention to a man's interests and hobbies from right out of the old beauty-parlor magazines.

Right there, in his penthouse, within earshot of anyone who cared to overhear, she said, "Your home is very beautiful. May I be so bold as to ask what you gave for it? What line of work are you in?"

"Didn't Señor Chitral mention to you?" Tommy Auveristas said evenly. "I'm an importer."

It wasn't the implied meaning of his words, nor his distance, nor even the flattened cruelty of his delivery that caused the woman to flinch. Mrs. Bliss had never been struck. Despite her fear of Mrs. Dubow from her days in the dress shop, though she knew the old dressmaker was mad and perfectly capable of violence; the alimony she paid her husband had been awarded because of physical harm—she couldn't remember what—she'd inflicted, and her memories of being chased about the shop had always been bordered in Dorothy's mind by a kind of comedy. She'd experienced Mrs. Dubow's rage then, and remembered it now, as having taken place in a sort of silent movie, something slapstick and frantically jumpy and Keystone Kops about all that futile energy. So all it could have been, all that had lunged out at her so unexpectedly to startle her was hearing Alcibiades Chitral's name, and hearing it moreover not from the mouth of any of her retired, Jewish, starstruck friends but straight out of the suddenly cool, grim lips of her South American host. It was the way the two DEA agents had spoken to her in the garage, in that same controlled, despising banter of an enemy. She had sensed from the beginning of the evening that she was somehow the point of the open house, even its guest of honor (as far as she knew it was the first time any Towers Jew had set foot in a penthouse), and in light of all the attention she'd received from the moment she entered she'd felt as she sometimes did when she was feeding her family a meal she'd prepared. Tommy Auveristas had practically exclaimed her name the minute he saw her. He'd introduced her around, excused himself if he had to leave. He had kissed her hand and paid her compliments and brought her food. He was all ears as she prattled on about the degree of kosher she kept, listened as she counted her chickens.

He did not strike her as a shy or reticent man. She was an old woman. He could have easily answered her question, a question she knew to be rude but whose rudeness he'd have written off not so much to her age and proprietary seniority as to the feeling of intimacy that had been struck up between them during all the back-and-forth of their easy exchange. He could have told her the truth. What would it hurt him? He had nothing to lose. If anything the opposite. The higher the price the more she'd have been impressed. Up and down the Towers she'd have gone, spreading the word about the big shot in Building One.

Who did Mrs. Bliss think she was kidding? Offended? No offense intended. No, and none taken. Of that she was positive. It was her second question that had set him off, the one about what line of work he was in, if you please.

She had, she saw, overestimated her celebrity. It may have

given the gang a thrill and she certainly, as she'd once heard her son-in-law say about serving on the jury during the trial of an important rock star, that he'd "dined out on it for months," a remark Mrs. Bliss thought so witty and catchy that she found herself repeating it each time anyone offered her a glass of tea or a slice of coffee cake.

Still, though she knew he must have had a reason for spending all that time with her (almost as if it were Auveristas who'd been doing the flirting), all that sitting beside her on the sofa, never once inviting anyone to join them but instead rather pointedly continuing their conversation every time someone sidled up to the couch, even if they were holding a plate of food, or a hot cup of coffee, she now understood that he wasn't pulling on her celebrity—he was indifferent to the fact that her picture had been in the paper, or that people wanted to interview her, or that her testimony had been heard on TV.

Mrs. Bliss was not a particularly suspicious woman. Well, that wasn't entirely so. She was, she *was* a suspicious woman. She'd never trusted some of her husband's customers when he'd owned the butcher shop, or his tenants in the apartment house he'd bought. On behalf of her family, of her near and dear, there was something in Dorothy that made her throw herself on all the landmines and grenades of all the welshers and four-flushers, lie down before all the ordnance of the deadbeats and shoplifters. "Dorothy," Ted had once said to her, "how can you shoplift meat?" "Meat nothing," Mrs. Bliss had replied, "the little cans of spices and tenderizers, the jars of A.1. Sauce on top of the display cases!"

This was like that. Tommy Auveristas was like Mrs. Ted Bliss. He was watching her carefully.

"Didn't Señor Chitral mention to you? I'm an importer," he'd said, and with that one remark brought back all the dread and alarm she'd felt from the time she learned she had to testify against the man who'd bought not only Ted's car but the few square feet of cement on which it was parked, too. Feeling relief only during the brief interval between Chitral's sentencing and the day the federal agents came to bind up Ted's car in metal as obdurate as any Alcibiades Chitral would be breathing for the next hundred years. The dread and alarm merely softened, its edges blunted by the people who had invited her to tour their condominiums. And only completely lifted for the past hour or so when she had ceased to mourn her husband. (Not to miss him—she would always miss him—but, pink polyester or no pink polyester, lay aside the dark weeds and vestments of her spirit and cease to be conscious of him every minute of her waking life.)

Now it was a different story. Now, with Auveristas's icy menace and sudden, sinister calm like the eye of ferocious weather, it was a ton of bricks.

Mrs. Ted Bliss had always enjoyed stories about detectives, about crime and punishment. On television, for example, the cops and the robbers were her favorite shows. She cheered the parts where the bad guys were caught. It was those shoplifters again, the case of the missing A.1. Sauce, the spice and tenderizer capers, that ignited her indignation and held her attention as if she were the victim of a holdup. (Not violence so much as the ordinary smash-and-grab of just robbers and burglars, looting as outrageous to her as murder. This infuriated her. Once, when thieves had broken into the butcher shop and pried their way into Ted's meat locker, making off with a couple of sides of beef, she had described the theft to the policeman taking down the information as the work of cattle rustlers. It was Dorothy who had encouraged her husband to buy a revolver to keep in the store; it was Dorothy who went out and purchased it herself and presented it to him on Father's Day when he had balked, saying owning a gun only invited trouble. And though Ted hadn't known this, it was Dorothy who took it along with her when they went around together collecting the rent money from their tenants in the building in the declining neighborhood on Chicago's North Side.) So Mrs. Bliss suddenly saw this attentive, handsome hand-kisser in new circumstances, in a new light.

Now he leaned dramatically toward her.

"It must be very hard for you," Tommy Auveristas said tonelessly.

"What?" said Mrs. Ted Bliss.

"For you to have to see it," the importer said. "The LeSabre. Turning away when you have to walk past it in the garage. As if it were some dead carcass on the side of the road you have to see close up. A machine that gave your husband such pleasure to drive. That you yourself got such a kick out of when you rode down from . . . was it Chicago?"

"Yes."

"North Side? South Side?"

"South Side."

"Did he follow baseball, your husband?"

"He rooted for the White Sox. He was a White Sox fan."

"Ah," said Tommy Auveristas, "a White Sox fan. *I'm* a White Sox fan."

"Did you get the White Sox in South America?"

"I picked them up on my satellite dish."

"Oh, yes."

"So much pleasure. Driving down the highway, listening to the Sox games on the radio in the Buick LeSabre. So much pleasure. Such happy memories. And now just a green eyesore for you. You turn your head away not to see it. It makes you sad to pass it in the underground garage. Locked up by the government. When they come down to visit kids stooping under the yellow ribbons that hang from the stanchions. Daring each other closer to it as though it was once the car of some mobster. Al Capone's car. Meyer Lansky's."

Dorothy held her breath.

"Tell me, Mrs. Bliss, do you want it out of there? It has to be terrible for you. Others are ashamed, too. I hear talk. Many have said. I could make an arrangement."

Dorothy, breathless, looked around the room. If she hadn't been afraid it would knock her blood pressure for a loop she'd have stood right up. If she'd been younger, or braver, or one of the knockout, gorgeously got-up women at the party, she'd have spit in his eye. But she was none of those things. What she was was a frightened old woman sitting beside—she didn't know how, she didn't know why or what—a robber.

Frozen in place beside him, not answering him, not even hearing him anymore, she continued to look desperately around.

And then she saw him, and tried to catch his eye. But he wasn't looking in her direction. And then, when he suddenly did, she thrust a bright pink polyester arm up in the air stiffly and made helpless, wounded noises until, with others, he heard her voice and stared at her curiously until Mrs. Ted Bliss had the presence of mind to raise her polyester sleeve, waving him over, her lawyer, Manny from the building.

THREE

Manny was on the phone to Maxine in Cincinnati. He was at pains to explain that he was on the horns of a dilemma. It had nothing to do with tightness. Maxine had to understand that. He wasn't tight, he wasn't not tight. He didn't enjoy being under an obligation; he was just a guy who was innately uncomfortable when it came to accepting a gift or even being treated to a meal. On the other hand, he didn't particularly like being taken advantage of either, or that anyone should see him as something of a showboat, so he was just as uncomfortable wrestling for a check. All he wanted, he told Maxine, was to be perceived as a sober, competent, perfectly fair-minded guy. (He'd have loved, for example, to have been appointed to the bench, but did she have any idea what the chances of *that* happening might be? A snowball's in hell! No, Manny'd said, they didn't pick judges from the ranks of mouthpieces who all they did all day was hang around City Hall looking up deeds, checking out titles, hunting up liens.) It was a nice question, a fine point. A professional judgment call, finally.

"What's this about, Manny?" Maxine asked over the Cincinnati long distance.

"Be patient. I'm putting you in the picture."

"Has this something to do with my mother? Is my mother all right?"

"Hey," Manny said, "*I* placed the call. I go at my own pace. Your mother's all right, and yes, it has something to do with her."

"Manny, *please*," said Maxine.

"Listen," he said, "the long and the short. I didn't call you collect. I would have if I was clear in my mind I was taking the case. This is the story. Mom thinks I'm her lawyer. It's true I represented her, but technically, since you and Frank paid the bills, I'm working for you."

"I'm not following you, Manny."

"What, it's a bad connection? You I hear perfectly. You could be in the next room.

"Listen, *sweet*heart, maybe you should go with someone else. I may be in over my head here. It's one thing to help out a woman, could be my older sister, to see does she absolutely have to testify, or can I get her out of it (I couldn't, she was a material witness), then hold her hand when she goes into court, lend her moral support; another entirely when she asks me to make some cockamamy investigation of this fancy-pants South American mystery man— *she* says—who may or may not be involved in this whacko-nutso dope scheme operating right here from the penthouse of Building Number One."

"A dope scheme? Another dope scheme?"

"*She* says," said Manny from the building.

And then went on to run down for Maxine, and again for Frank not half an hour later when Maxine called her brother in Pittsburgh and asked him to phone the old real estate lawyer to hear straight from the horse's mouth what was what.

"Walk me through this, will you, Manny, please? I didn't entirely understand all Maxine was telling me."

"Yeah," Manny said, "I guess I wasn't absolutely clear. Even in law school I had trouble writing up a brief. I don't see how they do it, the trial lawyers, make their summations and offer their final arguments. I guess that's why I never got into litigation."

He told Mrs. Bliss's son about the Auveristases' open house. He tried to be thorough, for, to be honest, he was just the smallest bit intimidated by this young man, an author and professor who on his occasional trips to Florida to spend some time with his mother sometimes struck him as cool, distant, even impatient with the people in the Towers who were only trying to be helpful, after all. He found the kid a little too haughty for his own good if you asked him, a little too quiet. One time Manny had attempted to reassure him. "Don't be so standoffish," he'd said, "they're just showing off some of their famous Southern hospitality."

So he tried to be thorough, walking the little asshole through the evening in the penthouse, past the buffet table, the open bar where you could ask the two mixologists for any drink you could think of, no matter what, and they would make it for you, describing the abundant assortment of hors d'oeuvres that the caterers or servants or whoever they were passed around all night even after the buffet supper was laid out, until you wouldn't think anyone could take another bite into their mouth, no matter how delicious.

Which was why, he told Frank, he suspected there might actually be something to the old woman's story after all.

"I mean," Manny said, "we don't hear a peep from these so-called South Americans in a month of Sundays, and then, tra-la-la, fa-la-lah, they're all over the old lady with their soft drinks and mystery meats. Do you know how many varieties of *coffee* there had to be there?"

Manny had been walking him through it by induction, but Frank seemed confused.

"Listen to me, Manny . . ." Frank said.

"It ain't proof, it isn't the smoking gun," Manny admitted, "but think about it, that's all I'm asking. The ostentation. That affair. That affair had to cost them twice what we spend on our galas and Saturday night card parties all year. Who throws around that kind of money on an open house? *Drug* dealers! And what did he say to Mother in his very own words? 'I'm an *importer!*' "

"Manny . . ."

"Even *she* picked up on it."

"My mother's under a lot of pressure."

Then, quite suddenly, Manny lowered his voice. The bizarre impression Frank, a thousand miles off, got from his tone was that of a man to whom it had just occurred that his phone was bugged and, to defeat the device, had resorted to whispering. Frank giggled.

Manny from the building was more hurt than shocked. Shocked, why should he be shocked? He considered the source. The little prick was a prick.

"Hey," Manny, still sotto voce, said, "put anybody you want on the case. It ain't exactly as if I was on retainer. Get your high-priced, toney, Palm Beach lawyer back, the one you wanted to get Mother's subpoena quashed. Get her. If you can talk her into even coming to Miami Beach!"

Maybe it was because he'd been through it four times by now. Once when Dorothy had told him about it the night of the famous open house, twice when he tried to organize his thoughts about the information he'd been given, a third time when he'd explained to Maxine what her mother had told him, and now repeating the facts of the matter to Frank. But he'd raised his voice again. He'd journeyed in the four accounts from disbelief to skepticism through a rather rattled, scattered objectivity till he'd finally broken through on the other side to a sort of neutral passion as he'd laid their cards—his and Mrs. Bliss's—on the table during his last go-round for the benefit of the creep.

Could it be he was a better lawyer than he'd thought? Could it be that he'd been bamboozled by all the glamour-pusses of his profession, the big corporation hotshots with their three- and four-hundred-buck-an-hour fees, all those flamboyant, wild-west criminal lawyers with their string ties and ten-gallon hats, the famous ACLU and lost-cause hotdogs who'd have defended Hitler himself if the price was right or the press and TV cameras were watching? Hey, he'd passed the same bar exams they had, and courtroom or no courtroom, had satisfied just as many clients with the careful contracts he'd drawn up for them for their real estate deals, commercial as well as residential. So maybe all there was to being a good lawyer or working up an argument was just to go over it often enough until you began to believe it yourself.

"Well, thanks for filling me in, Manny," Frank said. "I'll talk it over with my sister, see what she has to say. We'll get back to you."

"Sure," he said. "And when you do," Manny suggested slyly, "ask how she explains the car?"

Because the fact was the '78 Buick LeSabre was gone. One minute it had been there in the garage and the next it had vanished, a ton or so of locked-up, bolted-down metal carried off, disappeared, pffft, just like that!

He knew well enough what he must have sounded like to them.

A troublemaker. A busybody. Some self-important Mr. Butt-insky. And in fact, though he resented it, he could hardly blame them. Sometimes, down here, retired not just from the practice of law but from the forty-or-so-year pressure of building not just a professional life, or even a family one, but the constant, minute-to-minute routine of putting together a character, assembling out of little notes and pieces of the past—significant betrayals, deaths, yearnings, successes, meaningful disappointments, and sudden gushers of grace and bounty—some strange, fearful archaeology of the present, the Self to Now, as it were, like a synopsis, some queer, running quiddity of you-ness like a flavor bonded into the bones, skin, and flesh of an animal. Of course the curse of such guys was that they didn't know how to retire. Or when to quit.

Hadn't Manny run into these fellows himself? There seemed to be at least one on every floor of each building in the Towers. Tommy Auveristas himself, if he weren't a dope-smuggling Peru-vian killer, might have been such a one, an arranger of favors who insinuated himself into the life of a widowed neighbor; one of those aging Boy Scout types who offered to drive in all the carpools of the quotidian; shlepping their charges to doctors' offices; dropping them off at supermarkets, beauty parlors, banks, and travel agents; hauling them to airports; picking up their prescriptions for them or organizing their personal affairs. Bloom in Building Three had ac-tually filed an application with the Florida Secretary of State to become a notary public. He paid the fee for the official stamp and seal out of his own pocket and offered his services at no charge—he personally came to their condos—around the Towers complex. "Best investment I ever made," Bloom, patting his windbreaker where the weight of the heavy kit tugged at its pocket, had once confessed to him. Manny, flushing, knew what he meant. (More than a little jealous of the secrets Bloom must know or, if not secrets exactly—these were people too old and brittle for scandal—then at least the sort of interesting detail that must surely be contained in documents so necessary to the deeds, affidavits, transfers, powers of attorney, and protests of negotiable paper, that they had to be sworn to and witnessed by an official designee of the State.) Subtly, over time, making themselves indispensable, breeding a kind of dependency, a sort of *familiar*, a sort of super who changed locks and replaced washers and often as not had their own keys to the lady's apartment. A certain satisfaction in being these amici curiae to the declining or lonely, heroes of the immediate who filled their days with largely unresented, if sometimes intrusive, kindnesses. In it, Manny guessed, harmlessly, to retain at least a little of the juice spilled from the bottom of what had once been a full-enough life in the bygone days before exile, retired not just from the practice of law but of character, too, that forty-or-so-year stint of dependable quiddity, individual as the intimate smell of one's trousers and shirts.

Poor shmuck didn't know what to count as a billable hour. Finally decided as he went around eating his liver waiting on the cold day in hell for Frank or Maxine to get back to him—ha ha, hoo hoo, and next year in Jerusalem—that all he'd say, *if* they asked, which they wouldn't, was that all he ever was was a small-timer, a lousy little Detroit real estate lawyer, and that until their mom he'd never put in a minute of pro bono in his life and that this was his chance, Frank, my pleasure, Maxine, though he might call them collect once in a while to keep them posted. No no, that wasn't necessary, he already *had* a large-screen TV, he already *had* a fine stereo, he already *had* a Mont Blanc pen, but if they insisted, if it made them more comfortable, then sure, they could give him dinner once the dust settled and Mother was easy again in her heart.

As it happened, he didn't have to wait long after all. Frank and Maxine were there not long after he'd placed his first phone call to the DEA people.

He looked them up in the Miami Southern Bell white pages. Quite frankly, he was surprised that they were actually listed. The CIA was listed, too. So was NASA and the Bureau of Alcohol, Tobacco and Firearms. This brought home to Manny from the building that law degree or no law degree, senior citizen or no senior citizen, Golden Ager or no Golden Ager, just exactly what a naive babe-in-the-woods he actually was. He even had second thoughts about his mission. Here he was, proposing to go up pro bono against possible drug lords, dances with assholes, with nothing to be gained except the thrill of the chase. He was a married man, he had grandchildren, responsibilities. He and his wife were hosting the seder this year, ten people. Flying down—his treat—his graduate student daughter-in-law, his thirty-eight-year-old, out-of-work, house-husband son and their two vildeh chei-eh; his sister and brother-in-law—also in Florida, Jacksonville not Miami—and a couple of old people from South Beach one of the Jewish agencies would be sending over—a matched pair of personal Elijahs. (It was his wife's idea; Manny *hated* the idea of having strangers in his home, no matter how old they were.) So it wasn't as if he needed the additional aggravation.

Personally, if you want to know, like a lot of the people down here, the strangers from South Beach, and even Mrs. Ted Bliss herself, Manny was a little terrified of the very idea of Florida. Hey, who's fooling who? Nobody got out of this place alive. It was like that place in Shakespeare from whose bourn no traveler returned.

Was that why he did it? Was *that* why? Him and all the other old farts, the buttinskies and busybodys, that crew of Boy Scouts, shleppers, and superannuated crossing guards—all that gung-ho varsity of amici curiae? For the last-minute letters their good deeds might earn them? Not the thrill of the chase at all, finally, so much as the just pure clean pro bono of it? Was that what all that tasteless, vaudeville clothing they wore was all about—their Bermuda gatkes and Hawaiian Punch shirts? Their benevolent dress code like the bright colors and cute cuddlies calming the walls on the terminal ward of a children's hospital.

So he placed that first phone call to the agency. Getting, of course, exactly what he expected to get, talking, or listening rather, to a machine with its usual, almost infinite menu of options. "Thank you for calling the Drug Enforcement Agency. Our hours, Monday to Friday, are blah blah blah. For such-and-such information please press one; for such-and-so please press two; for so-and-such please press three; for . . ." He listened through about a dozen options until the machine, he thought a bit impatiently, told him that if he was calling from a rotary phone he should stay on the line and an operator would get to him as soon as it was his turn. (Manny was fascinated by the DEA's choice of canned music.) It had already been established that he was naive, a babe-in-the-woods, but he was no dummy. He realized that no one calling the main number of the DEA on that or any other day would have any better idea than Manny had from the various choices, which went by too swiftly anyway, which button to press, that they would *all* be staying on the line. He hung up, called again, and, for no better reason than that it was the number of Mrs. Ted Bliss's building, pressed one.

He explained to some employee in the Anonymous Tips Department that he was interested in finding out why a certain party's car that had been last seen in the parking garage of this particular address he happened to know of had been suddenly been removed from the premises.

"Who is this?" asked the guy in Anonymous Tips.

"A friend of the family."

"Unless you can be more specific . . ." the bureaucrat said.

He was Mrs. Bliss's counsel now and acting under the Midwest real estate bar association's scrupulous injunction to do no harm. He didn't want to get his client in Dutch. And he was terrified, a self-confessed, small-time old-timer from the state of Michigan who'd earned his law degree from a night school that shared not only the same building but often the same classrooms with a local business college, so that it had been not just his but the experience of several of his classmates, too, that they frequently met the girls they would marry there, striking up their first halting conversations with them during that brief milling about in the halls between classes, the seven or eight minutes between the time Beginning Shorthand or Advanced Typing was letting out and Torts or Contracts was about to start up, an ideal symbiosis, the future secretaries meeting their future husbands, the future lawyers, the future lawyers courting their future wives and secretaries, but something the least bit provisional and backstairs about these arrangements, so that, well, so that there was a sort of irremediable rip in the fabric of their confidence and courage. Which explained his hesitancy and pure rube fear, and made Manny appreciate the nice irony of his having been connected to a division of the agency that dealt under a promise of the condition of anonymity. But didn't mitigate a single inch of who he was. In fact, all the *more* fearful when he gazed down at his brown old arms coming out of the colorful, short-sleeved shirt he wore, the deep tan of a younger, healthier, sportier man, tan above his station, as if there were something not quite on the up-and-up about his appearance. How many Jews, Manny wondered idly, could there even *be* in the DEA?

And how could he be more specific when what he needed to hear was something he didn't even want to know?

But he was on the clock, even if it were only a courtesy clock. He came suddenly out of his withering funk, inexplicably energized, inspired. "Put me through to the fella drives that late-model, silver Maserati as a loaner," Manny demanded sharply.

"Yeah," said a man, "this is Enoch Eddes." The voice was hesitant, suspicious, perhaps even a little fearful. Manny guessed it was unaccustomed to taking phone calls from members of the public.

"Enoch Eddes, the repo man?"

"What the fuck!"

"Enoch, Enoch," Manny said as though the man had just broken his heart.

"What the fuck," Enoch said again, a little more relaxed this time, gentled into a sort of compliance, Manny supposed, by the faintly compromised argot of Manny's thrown, ventriloquized character. Vaguely it felt good on him, like those first few moments when one tries on new, perfectly shined shoes in a shoe store, but Manny knew he couldn't maintain it or hope to keep pace with this trained professional. In a few seconds it would begin to pinch and he would revert to his old Manny-from-the-building self.

So he swung for the fences. He had to.

"Enoch," he said, "*please.*"

"Who is this?" the DEA guy said.

"Hey," Manny said very softly, "hey, Enoch, relax. I'm a repo man, too. Tommy Auveristas has turned you over to me."

"Who?" Eddes asked, genuinely puzzled, totally, it seemed to Manny, without guile or affectation, nothing left of his own assumed character and more innocent than Manny could ever have imagined, as innocent, perhaps, as he'd been when he'd eaten his breakfast in his suburb that morning, when he'd hugged his kids and pecked his wife on the cheek, his own shoes pinching first and crying uncle in his surprised stupidity. "Who did you say?"

"I think," said Manny from the building, "I may have reached a wrong number," and hung up.

Later, Manny told Mrs. Ted Bliss's children, they'd all have a good laugh over it. And by the way, he told them, smiling, they were off the hook and didn't owe him dinner after all.

"Dinner?" Frank said.

"Well, I didn't do anything to earn it, did I? What did I do, place a couple of phone calls to the Drug Enforcement Agency? Please. It's nothing. You see, Frank, you see, Maxine, did I lie? Did I? I *am* a friend of the family. Just another good neighbor even if I'm not from South America and all I ever was was a Detroit real estate lawyer. It was my pleasure. It really was. I don't say I wasn't nervous. I was plenty nervous. You don't live in the greater Miami area, you don't know. I don't care how many times you've seen reports on TV, all those Haitian and Cuban boatload exposés, the drug wars and race riots, the spring break orgies and savings and loan firesalers, all the Portuguese man-of-war alerts—unless you live down here and take the paper you have no idea what goes on. There are migrant workers not an hour away who live in conditions South African blacks would not envy. I'm telling you the truth, Maxine and Frank. You think it's all golf and fishing and fun in the sun? You have a picture in your head of beautiful weather, round-the-clock security guards, and moderate-priced, outside cabins on three-day getaway cruises to the islands. What the hell do *you* know?''

Maxine rather enjoyed listening to him. He was a silly, heavily cologned, pretentious fool, but at least he was on the scene down there, a self-proclaimed stand-up sort in her mother's corner. If he knew too much about her business, well, who else did the woman have? She wouldn't hear of selling the condo and coming to live with them in Cincinnati. God knows how many times Maxine had invited her to. It was exasperating. If she didn't want to be a burden, she would have understood. If she treasured her independence. If she'd made friends with whom she was particularly comfortable. But keeping the place up so that when she died Frank and Maxine and their dead brother Marvin's fatherless children should have an *inheritance?* A roof over their heads? This was a reason? Not that Maxine wasn't secretly glad—and not so secretly, she'd discussed it with George—that Dorothy refused to take her up on it, but let's face it, her mother was getting to an age when sooner or later—probably later, her health, knock wood, was pretty good but there were no guarantees—something would have to give. A way would have to be found to deal with her physical needs. Manny from the building was a nice enough guy, but let's face it, fair-weather friend was written all over him. And why shouldn't it be? He had a wife, Rosie, who was decent enough, and

God knows she'd always seemed willing to put herself out, but quite frankly had to be at least a *little* conflicted where Maxine's mother was concerned. And who could blame her, all the time he'd spent with her in the year since Alcibiades Chitral's trial?

What, Frank Bliss wondered, was with this guy? He wasn't nervous? He was *still* nervous, or why would he be talking so much? And what was all that Florida Confidential crap about, the Miami killing fields? What was he up to? Was he selling protection, was this some kind of special condo old-guy scam? Did every retired old-widow hand down here have some corner he worked, spraying some dark territoriality, pacing off places where he might grind his particular ax?

What the hell do *I* know? Well, heck, Manny, he'd felt like telling him, sure, I know all about it. That and stuff you never even mentioned, the it's-never-too-late and lonely hearts bobbe myseh and December/December alliances. The two-can-live-cheaper-than-one arrangements. That's what I know, old boy, so just watch where you grind your particular ax.

He reined himself in. It wasn't that he knew his mother simply wasn't the type. She wasn't of course, and he thought he understood what a Chinese water torture loneliness must have put her through in the years since his father had died, but all of a sudden and out of the blue, God help him, he thought he saw his mother through Manny's eyes, through the eyes, he meant, God help him, of another man. She had to have been six or seven years older than Manny. And despite the pride Ted had taken in his wife's appearance, her reputation for beauty even deep into her sixties, the woman had aged. Manny, on the other hand, still seemed to be in pretty good shape. All you had to do was look at him, his tan the shade of perfectly made toast. If he weren't married he could have had the pick of the litter. What could a guy like Manny possibly see in his mother? A man would have to be pretty desperate to want to sleep with a woman like her.

Then, another bolt from the blue, he felt blind-sided by shame. What was it in the air down here that poisoned your spirit? Why, he wondered, did he despise Manny more now that he understood there could have been nothing between them, than when he worried about the guy's officious, overbearing manner?

It's all this fucking humidity and sea air, he thought, some steady oxidizing of the soul.

Maxine was feeling shame, too. She realized not only how glad she was her mother didn't want to move to Cincinnati but how happy it made her that Dorothy wouldn't sell the condo, how nice it would be to have it after, God forbid, her mother had died. She thought of all the times Dorothy had shown her records of the certificates of deposit she was accumulating, how she rolled them over whenever they came due, reinvesting, building on the booming interest rates they were earning just now, showing where she kept her bankbooks with their stamped, inky entries like marks in a passport, proud of her compounding interest, of living within her means on social security, on Ted's pension from the butcher's union, the monthly benefit of a modest insurance policy he'd taken out, the miracle of money, mysteriously richer now than when Ted was alive, showing off even the rubberbanded discount coupons she cut, the fat wads of paper like a gambler's stake, Maxine all the while superstitiously protesting, "Spend it, Ma, spend it; it's yours. Don't stand in the heat waiting for a bus when you have to go out someplace. Call cabs, take taxis. You don't even have to wait outside. Whoever's on duty at the security desk will buzz you when it comes."

I'm such a shit, Maxine thought, pretending to change the subject, deliberately averting my eyes whenever she tries to show me this stuff, but glad of Mother's miserliness, even, God help me, dependent on it.

"You know," Manny was saying, "when your dad, olov hasholem, passed away I don't think your mother had made out more than three dozen checks in her whole life. Is this true, Dorothy?"

"I never needed," Mrs. Bliss said defensively. "Whatever I needed—for the house, for the kids—he gave me. If I needed . . . needed? If I *wanted*, he gave me. My every whim—mah-jongg, the beauty parlor, kaluki, the show."

"Ma," Maxine said, "Daddy kept you on an allowance?"

"He didn't keep me on an allowance. All I had to do was ask. What? It's so much fun to make out a check? It's such a delight? Ted paid all the bills. Once in a while, if he ran out of checks, he gave me cash and I went downtown to the post office and they made out money orders to the gas and electric. He didn't keep me on an allowance. All I ever had to do was ask. I didn't even have to specify."

"Ma, I'm *teasing*," Maxine said.

"Of course," Mrs. Ted Bliss said, "once Ted died I had to learn. Manny taught me."

"Taught her," Manny said modestly, "I showed her. I merely reminded her."

"I write large," Mrs. Bliss said. "The hardest part was leaving enough room to write the figures out in longhand. And fitting the numbers into the little box."

"All she needed was practice. She caught right on," Manny said.

"Not with the stubs," Mrs. Bliss said. " 'Balancing my check book,' " she said formally, looking at Manny. "It was like doing homework for school. Farmer Brown buys a blue dress on sale at Burdines for eighteen dollars and ninety-five cents. He has five hundred and eleven dollars and seven cents on the stub."

"His previous balance," Manny said.

"Yeah," Dorothy said. "His previous balance."

"Don't worry," Manny reassured, winking at them. "I went over it with her."

"Not now," said Mrs. Ted Bliss.

"No," Manny said, "not for a *long* time."

"Not since he showed me how to work the computer."

"Ma, you have a computer?"

"She means a calculator. I picked one up on Lincoln Road at Eckerd's for under five bucks."

"It works on the sunshine. Isn't that something? You never have to buy batteries for it."

"Solar energy," Manny said.

"Solar energy," Mrs. Bliss said. "It's lucky I live in Florida."

Frank didn't know how much more of this he could take. What was it, a routine they'd worked out? Even Maxine was starting to feel resentful.

"He wrote out the hard numbers for me in spelling on a little card I keep in the checkbook. Two. Ninety. Nineteen. Forty. Forty-four. Other hard numbers. Eighty with a 'g.' "

"Five bucks?" Frank said to Manny.

"Sorry?"

"The calculator. Five bucks?"

"Under five bucks."

"Here," her son said, and pushed a five-dollar bill into Manny's hand. What was wrong with Frank? She had to live with these people. What did they think? Why didn't they think? Did they think that when one was off in Cincinnati and the other in Pittsburgh her life here stopped, that she lived in the freezer like a pot roast waiting for the next time one of them decided to visit or they spoke on the telephone? They were dear children and she loved them. There was nothing either of them did or could do that would stop that, but please, give me a break, my darlings, Mother doesn't stand on the shelf in a jar when you're not around to help me, to take me out on the town, or let me look at my grandsons. I have my errands. I go to my various organizations and play cards, ten percent of the winnings to charity off the top. We gave ORT a check for more than six hundred dollars this year. How do they think I get to these places? Do they think I fly? I don't fly. I depend on Manny from the building. On Manny and on people like him. Even when the game is right here, in a building in the Towers, and the men walk along to escort the women, not just me, *any* widow, at night, in the dark, to the game, to protect us because security can't leave their post, so no one should jump out at us from behind the bushes to steal our pocketbooks or, God forbid, worse comes to worse. I know. What am I stupid? What could Manny or five more just like him do in a *real* emergency? Nothing. Gornisht. It's just the idea. Like when Marvin—olov hasholem, olov hasholem—he couldn't have been much older than Maxine's James is now and wouldn't lay down his head, never mind sleep, unless I left on a light in the room so if the apartment on Fifty-third caught on fire he could find his slippers and wouldn't have to walk barefoot on the floor in a burning building. Kids are afraid of the craziest things. Oh, Marvin, Marvin! At least you had the sense to be afraid. That wasn't so crazy even if there never was a fire. When the time came and you got sick you burned up plenty, anyway. We're not so stupid after all. Older than James and so much younger than your mother is now, I'm also afraid of the dark, of danger and horror from the bushes. Isn't it strange? When Ted was still alive I'd go anywhere by myself. Even after his cancer was diagnosed and he was laying in the hospital I'd wait alone outside for the bus

after visiting hours were over and never thought twice about it.
Who knows, maybe worry cancels out fear, maybe just being anxious about something makes you a little braver.

God, thought Mrs. Ted Bliss, please don't let him make a scene,
just let him put the five dollars into his pocket as if everybody
understood all along it was a legitimate debt. Don't let anyone get
up on his high horse, please God. Good. Good for you, Manny, she
thought, when Manny accepted the money, you're a mensh.

"I'm sorry," said Manny, "I don't have any change."

Maxine looked down at the carpet and prayed her brother
wouldn't tell the man he could keep it or make some other smart
remark, like it was for his trouble or something.

Frank wondered why he could be such a prick sometimes and
was immensely relieved when Manny didn't make a fuss. He'd
seen the awful look on his mother's face when he'd forced the
money into the old man's hand. It was too late to undo what he'd
done. Maybe it would be all right, though. Maybe it was enough
that he should be seen playing Asshole to the other's mere Big Shot.

Manny bit his lower lip and, preparing to rise, leaned forward
in Mrs. Bliss's furniture.

"Well, guess I better be moseying along," said Manny from the
building.

"There's coffee, there's cake," Dorothy said.

"Muchas gracias, but Rosie'll wonder what's happened to me."

"Do what you have to," Dorothy said, not so much resigned
as quite suddenly disappointed and saddened by the heavy load
of face-saving in the room, all that decorous schmear and behavior.
Why couldn't people talk and behave without having to think
about it or count to ten? Why couldn't it be like it used to be, why
wasn't Marvin alive, why wasn't Ted? Why wasn't what was left
of the gang—the real gang, not the bunch down here with which
she had to make do, the real gang, the blood gang, her sister Etta,
her sister Rose, the boys (grandfathers now), her younger brother
Philip, her younger brother Jake; Ted's deceased brothers, her twin
in-laws, Irving and Sam, their wives, Joyce, the impossible Golda,
their children, grown-ups themselves, Nathan and Jerry, Bobby,
Louis and Sheila, Eli and Ceil; all her dead uncles, her dead uncle
Oliver, her dead uncle Ben; Cousin Arthur, Cousin Oscar, Cousin
Charles, Cousin Joan, Cousins Mary and Joe, Cousins Zelda and

Frances and Betty and Gen; Evelyn, Sylvia, David, Lou and Susan, Diane and Lynne, Cousin Bud—all that ancient network of relation, all that closed circle of vital consanguinity, and all the broken connection in the great Chicago boneyard, too, shtupped in the loam of family, a drowned mulch of death and ancestry, an awful farm of felled Blisses and Plotkins and Fishkins, *all* of them, the rest of that resting (may they rest, may they rest, may they rest) lineage and descended descent; the *real* gang, down here? At ease in their tummel and boosted noise. Shouting, openly quarreling, accusing, promoting their voluble challenges, presenting all their up-front, you-can't-get-away-with-thats in their pokered and pinochled, kaluki'd, gin- and Michigan-rummy'd bluster (and on one famous, furious occasion, Sam, her brother-in-law, so distracted by rage he actually stormed out of his own house, vowing that until Golda received an apology from the entire family he would never sit down to play a game of cards with them again) for, on a good day, a *good* day, at most a two- or three-dollar pot.

Because family didn't have to be nice to each other, thought Mrs. Ted Bliss. Because they didn't always have to dance around tiptoe on eggshells. *Because Golda never got her apology, and Sam did too sit down with them again to play cards*. And the very next time, if she remembered correctly!

They didn't even have to love each other if you want to know. Just being related gave them certain rights and privileges. It was like being born in Canada, or France, or Japan. Herman, her sister Rose's ex, she'd written off. When they got their divorce he'd been revoked, like you'd cancel a stamp. Even though she'd rather liked Herman. He'd been a kidder. Mrs. Bliss, in her good humor, was a sucker for kidders.

But nice as Manny was, kind to her as he'd been, dependent on him as she would always be, and even though he was Jewish, *and* a neighbor, and a *good* neighbor, who shlepped for her and treated when she and Rosie and Manny went out together, to the show or for a bite to eat afterward, he just wasn't related. He was only Manny from the building, and if Dorothy had been protective of his feelings where Frank and Maxine were concerned, it was because push shouldn't have to come to shove in a civilized world, in Florida, a thousand miles from her nearest distant relative. Because Mrs. Ted Bliss knew what was what, was practically a mind

reader where her children were concerned, as certain of their attitudes as she'd been of their temperatures when she pressed her lips
to their foreheads or cheeks when they were babies. She knew
Frank's outrage that this stranger had moved in on her troubles,
understood even her daughter's milder concern. Didn't Dorothy
herself feel buried under the weight of all the blind, indifferent
altruism of Manny's professional courtesies? So she knew all right.
Nobody was putting anything over on nobody. Nobody. Which
was probably why all of them had backed down, why Maxine just
watched the carpeting and Manny just stuck the five dollars into
his pocket and Frank held his tongue when Manny told him that
he had no change.

And why Dorothy, who hated decorum and standing on ceremony, welcomed it then.

And why, above all, Dorothy was thankful to God that Manny
was leaving, without his coffee, without his cake. So he wouldn't
have to be in the same room with Frank even just only *thinking* to
himself, Why the little *pisher*, the little *pisher*, the little no goddamn
good *pisher*! And Mrs. Ted Bliss wouldn't have to yell at Manny
and ruin it for herself with him forever, goodbye and good luck.

FOUR

Nothing had been decided. Even during the little visit to Miami Maxine and her brother had undertaken after Manny's all but incoherent telephone calls and the alarms they set off regarding her state of mind. To Frank's assertion that the lawyer was probably not only a troublemaker but a shyster into the bargain, his sister said that even if he were she doubted he'd made up Tommy Auveristas's end of the conversation.

"Meaning?"

"Frank, she's a *housewife*. All she knows is 'Tips from Heloise' and how you get nasty stains out of the toilet bowl. She's my mom and I love her, but she doesn't have the imagination to make up that crap."

"So what are you saying, Maxine, that this Manny guy is actually onto something, and that Mother's in trouble with south Florida's criminal element?"

"No. Poor Manny hasn't a clue, but I think Mother's in trouble all right."

"What are you talking about?"

"The guest of honor at Mr. Big's house party? The guest of *honor*? A helpless old lady in a pink polyester pants suit among all those diamonds, furs, and high-fashion shoes? And that he practically never left her side the whole evening? Or that he hung on her every word? The never-ending saga of Mama's epic recipes? And what about the part where he tore into the help because he spilled food on the rug when he came up beside her sealed-over ear and startled her? Come on Frank, he *fed* her? Or told her he was a Sox fan? This is good evidence? This is the bill of particulars she presented to Manny?"

"Well," Frank said, "he told her he was an importer. You know what *that* could mean down here."

"Sure. That he buys and sells bananas. Frank, listen to me, the strongest card in her suit, the *strongest*, is the car, the LeSabre in the parking lot, and there could be a hundred forty explanations for that. And all that talk about his *tone*, Tommy whatsisname's sinister menace."

"He scared the shit out of her, Maxine."

"She's deaf, Frank. The woman is deaf."

"What are you doing, Max? What are you trying to say?"

"She *never* goes downtown. At night . . . at night she hardly ever leaves the building unless she has an escort even if it's only to cross over to the next condominium."

"Hey, she's nervous. Her husband is dead. She's frail and vulnerable."

"She's a suspicious old lady."

"She doesn't have a right to be?"

"Frank, she bought Daddy a *gun!*"

"Oh, please," said her brother.

"She carried it in her purse when they collected the rents. 'Just in case,' she told me one time, 'just in case.' "

"Just in case what?"

"Just in case anything. *I* don't know. If they called a rent strike, if they demanded new wallpaper."

"You think she still has the gun?"

"Who knows?"

"You want us to confront her?" Frank asked. "Jesus, Maxine, why start up? We're both of us out of here tomorrow. If she feels more comfortable with a gun around the place I don't think that's so terrible. She'd never use it."

"As a matter of fact," said his sister, "I don't believe she even has that gun anymore. I mentioned it to point out her state of mind before Daddy even died."

"So what are you getting at? You want to go one-on-one with Tommy A., take the bullshit by the horns?"

"I think she ought to talk to somebody," Maxine said.

"Talk to somebody."

"See someone."

"You mean like a shrink? Can you really picture our mother going through analysis?"

"No," Maxine said, "of course not. Just to have somebody to talk to. You see how she relies on Manny."

"Mr. District Attorney."

"Manny's not so bad, Frank. He's been very helpful."

"Manny's a jailhouse lawyer. The woods down here are full of them. Self-important experts and know-it-alls. Manny's *base*, Maxine. That junk he fed us about Enoch Eddes? How he jabbed him with a left, and another left, then finished him off with a right hook?"

"Don't be cruel, Frank. He told that story on himself."

"Well, then he ain't very reliable, is he?"

"They both see things in the dark, I think," Maxine said.

They had less than twenty-one hours between them. Maxine's flight was scheduled to leave Fort Lauderdale at nine the next morning, Frank's an hour and a half later. While Mrs. Bliss was still in the kitchen, preparing at two o'clock in the afternoon the dinner she would not put on the table until at least six, her children concluded that Dorothy had not yet come to terms with her grief, that it was devouring her, and that in a kind of way she was reemigrating, first leaving the old country to flesh out the substance of a new life in America, and now quitting America to abandon what was left her of life in a sort of old country of the soul and spirit where she could be one with that bleak race of widowed grief cronies, woeful, keening sisters in perpetual mourning for the deep bygones of their better days.

The trouble was they had no real clout in Florida, no one to whom they could turn in a pinch. Their dad's doctor hadn't given him such a terrific run for his money. Diagnosed, dead, and buried in just over a year from a relatively slow-growing tumor. He was the *last* one they'd turn to. The little details of life were a sort of word-of-mouth thing, a piecemeal networking, but one needed one's own turf before that kicked in, and the truth was that neither Maxine nor her brother had any. *Their* only contact was Mrs. Ted Bliss herself, so where did *that* leave them? High and dry. Nowhere. Between the devil and the deep blue sea.

Meanwhile, during Mrs. Ted Bliss's sudden appearances in the living room, bearing gifts from her labors in the kitchen—bolts of kishka; sips of soup; little offerings of chopped liver in the making; k'naidlech; defrosted, freezer-burned challah; bites of jarred gefilte fish; ragged flags of boiled chicken skin; strings of overdone brisket—Frank and Maxine, shushing each other, making all the smiling, sudden, guilty moves of people doing ixnay and cheese it to one another, all the high signs and rushed semaphore of lookouts feigning innocence, their meter running out on them, less than nineteen hours to go now, eighteen, eleven or twelve if you counted the seven or eight they'd be asleep, nine or ten if you figured in the couple of hours it would take them to shower and dress, call a taxi to take them to the airport, eight or nine if they were caught up in rush-hour traffic. And no closer to solving their problem than when Maxine first suggested they had one.

"You know what I think?" Frank said.

"What?"

"I think we're going to have to turn this one over to Manny."

"Manny's 'base,' Frank. You said so yourself. Nothing but a jailhouse lawyer. Self-important, a know-it-all."

"He's the only game in town, Maxine," Frank said, sighing, resigned.

So that night while Dorothy was going back and forth from the dining room to the kitchen, they put it to Manny and Rosie that they thought Mrs. Bliss ought to be seeing someone with whom she might talk out her problems. Was that possible? Did either of them know of such a person? Someone reliable? He or she didn't have to be a psychiatrist necessarily, they could be a psychologist, or even a counselor, but someone reliable. Was that possible?

"What, are you kidding me?" Manny wanted to know. "Half the people down here are nutty as fruitcakes. Rosie, am I right or am I right?"

"More like three-fifths," said his wife.

So that's how they left it. With Mr. Buttinsky, the eminent shyster, Manny from the building. Charging him not only with the duty of securing a reliable therapist for Mrs. Ted Bliss but with the responsibility of actually getting Dorothy to agree to see one. The children would help out of course, though all four—the Tresslers (Manny and Rosie), Frank and Maxine—agreed it would be unwise to spring their campaign on Mrs. Bliss the very night before her kids were scheduled to go back North. They had time yet. Their window of opportunity wouldn't slam shut for a while. Tonight should be given over to the feast Mrs. Bliss had been preparing since just after her morning shower. Mrs. Bliss passed out hors d'oeuvres—herring with sour cream on Ritz crackers, chopped chicken liver on little rounds of rye, pupiks of fowl, egg-and-olive salad—and, though Dorothy didn't drink, cocktails—Scotch and Diet Coke, bourbon and ginger ale.

Then they sat down to a heavy meal.

And then, dealer's choice, they played cards—gin, poker, Michigan rummy. Dorothy, no matter the game, offering up the same comment over and over: "You call this a hand? This isn't a hand, it's a foot!"

It wasn't until after midnight that the game broke up and Dorothy's guests left.

"Ma," said Maxine, forgetting she'd be gone the next day, "what are you doing? Leave it, we'll do it in the morning."

"Darling," her mother said, "go to bed, you look exhausted. It'll take me two minutes."

"You've been working all day."

"So what else have I got to do?"

Maxine and Frank fell in after their mother, clearing the dining room table of cups and saucers, emptying Manny's ashtrays, picking up the jelly glasses, the liquor in most of them untasted, adulterate in the melted ice and soda pop. Frank sat down with the poker chips, sorting them according to their values and depositing the bright, primary colors into their caddy like coins into slots. Afterward, he scooped up the cards and tamped them into smooth decks.

Mrs. Ted Bliss scraped food from plates, then rinsed the dishes and cutlery and scrubbed down her pots and pans before placing everything in the dishwasher.

Maxine and Frank sat at their mother's kitchen table, watching her through half-shut eyes.

"You know," she was saying, "neither of them are big eaters, but I think Manny loved the soup. It wasn't too salty, was it?"

"Of course not, Ma, it was delicious."

"It wasn't too salty?"

"It was perfect," Frank said.

"Because nowadays, with their hearts, people are very finicky about the salt they take into their systems. You ask me, soup without salt tastes like pishechts."

"Pishechts is salty," Frank said.

"All in all," Mrs. Bliss said, "I think it went very well. I think everyone had a good time. I know speaking for myself, having you here, I don't think I've been so happy since your father was alive."

She looked as if she were about to cry.

They needn't have worried. Not two days later, Manny reported she hadn't needed much convincing after all. It was no big deal. He'd not only arranged an appointment for her, she'd already had her first meeting with the therapist, someone, he said, with whom she was evidently very pleased.

"You know what she told me?" Manny said. "She said, 'Manny, I think I made a very good impression.' "

"Oh," said Maxine, "her therapist's a man."

Mrs. Ted Bliss was not without sympathy for the women's movement. Indeed, if you'd asked, she'd probably have said she was many times more comfortable in the presence of women than in the presence of men. She had an instinctive sympathy with women and, though she'd never have admitted it, she secretly preferred her sisters to her brothers, her aunts to her uncles, her daughter to her son. (Marvin, her dead son, she loved in the abstract above all of them, though that was probably because of the wide swath of grief and loss his death had caused, all the trouble and rough, unfinished business his passing had left in its wake—his fatherless child; Ellen, her hysteric, fierce, New-Age daughter-in-law in whom Marvin's death had loosed queer forces and a hatred of doctors so profound that when her children were young and ill, she so deprived them of medical attention that they might as well have been sick in an age not only before science but prior to the application of *any* remedial intervention—forest herbs and leaves and roots and barks and grasses, sacrifices, prayers and spells, and left them to cope with their diseases and fevers and pains by throwing themselves onto the mercy of their own helpless bodies.) Ted was merely an exception. And if she had loved her husband almost beyond reason it had more to do with reciprocity than with romance. Quite simply, he had saved her, had given the unschooled young woman with her immigrant's fudged age a reason to leave Mrs. Dubow. It was as if his proposal and Dorothy's acceptance had suddenly lifted the shy young salesgirl's mysterious indenture and released her from the terror of her ten-year bondage. Terror not only of her employer but, even after a decade, of the customers' shining, perfumed, and profound nudity, rich, lush, and overwhelming in the small, oppressive dressing closets, fearful of all their lavish, fecund, human ripeness, steamy and vegetal as a tropical rain forest. Dorothy was still more lady's maid and dresser than clerk, and had become a kind of confidante to women who wouldn't even talk to her, beyond their few curt instructions—"Button this, hold that"— let alone solicit opinions from her or offer up secrets; privy to their measurements, to the ways they examined their reflections, studying blemishes or lifting their necks and turning their heads back over their shoulders to catch glimpses of their behinds in the wide glass triptych of mirrors. These confidences struck like deals between the ladies and the bewildered, untutored maid, done and done, and signed and sealed by the unschooled young girl barely literate in English but who could by now read numbers well enough on the nickels, dimes, quarters, and fifty-cent pieces slipped to her by women, the secret of whose fragile disappointments in their female bodies she not only well enough understood but by accepting their coins was positively sworn to protect. Terrified, or, at the least, made terribly aware and uncomfortable by the awful burden of what she perceived to be a sort of collective letdown and discouragement in their even, enhanced appearance in their new gowns and dresses.

Which may actually have been at the core and source of her sympathies with her gender. It was men these women dressed for. ("I hope this blue isn't *too* blue, I'll die if it clashes with my husband's brown suit.") Dorothy had not, beyond the universe of her own family, known all that many men, but even in her family had noticed the tendency of the women to leave the choicest cuts, ripest

fruits, even the favorite, most popular flavors of candy sourballs—
the reds and purples, the greens and the oranges—for the men. The
most comfortable chairs around the dining room table. The coldest
water, the hottest soup, the last piece of cake. Her smallest little
girl cousins cheerfully shared with their smallest little boy cousins,
voluntarily gave up their turns in line. They worked combs through
the boys' hair gently; they scratched their backs.

She was not resentful. Her sympathies were with her sex because that was the way *she* felt, too.

Indeed, if she resented anyone, it was her employer, Mrs. Dubow, she resented. A resentment that was something beyond and
even greater than her fear of the terrifying woman who not only
chased her through the confines of a dressmaker's shop no larger
than an ordinary shoe store, clacking her scissors and flicking a
yellow measuring tape at her, but shouting at her, too, her mouth
full of pins, and calling her names so vile she could only guess at
their meaning and be more embarrassed than hurt. Because now
she remembered just what it was Mrs. Dubow was supposed to
have done to become the first wife in the history of Illinois ever
required to pay alimony to the husband. She'd thrown acid in his
face! Thrown *acid* at him, defiling him forever where the tenderest
meat went, the sweetest fruits and most delicious candies.

Mrs. Ted Bliss shuddered.

Because there was a trade-off. A covenant almost. Women honored the men who put food on the table, who provided the table
on which the food was put, and the men saved them. That was the
trade-off. Men saved them. They took them out of awful places like
Mrs. Dubow's and put food on the table and kept all the books.
Women *owed* it to them to be good-looking, they *owed* it to them
that the shade of their dresses did not clash with the shade of their
suits, to hold their shapes and do their level best to keep up their
reflections in mirrors. It wasn't vanity, it was duty. And it was what
explained her calm when neighbors had marveled at her beauty,
her almost invisible aging, the two or three baths she took each
day. You needn't have looked farther when people had complimented her than at the benign smile on Ted's face (even in that
last, malignant year) to see that she had kept up her end of the
contract, had proved herself worthy of being saved.

So *of course* Mrs. Ted Bliss, having been saved once before by

a man, and who saw no reason to fiddle with what worked, chose
to see a man to save her this time, too, when her children thought
she was going crazy.

Her therapist, Holmer Toibb, was not Jewish, and did not live
in the Towers. He'd been recommended by Manny's physician,
who thought the lawyer had used the story of a depressed "friend"
as a cover for his own bluff despondency. Manny, at sixty-eight,
was at a difficult age. A few years into his retirement and the bloom
off his freedom, the doctor thought Manny a perfect candidate for
the sort of recreational therapeusis in which Toibb specialized, offering options to patients to open up ways that, in the early stages
of their declining years, might lead them toward fresh interests in
life. Himself in his sixties, Toibb had studied with Greener Hertsheim, practically the founder of recreational therapeusis, after
twenty-or-so years still a relatively new branch of psychology
whose practitioners eschewed the use of drugs and had no use for
tie-ins with psychiatrists. Like a page out of the fifties when doctors
of osteopathy faced off with chiropractors and spokesmen for the
AMA on all-night radio talk shows, RT, in southern Florida at least,
had become a sort of eighties substitute for all the old medical
conspiracy theories. Mrs. Bliss, apolitical and passive almost to a
fault, couldn't get enough of controversial call-in shows. She had
no position on the Warren Commission findings, didn't know if
she was for or against detente, supply-side economics, any of the
hot-button issues of the times, including even the battle between
traditional psychiatry and the recreational therapists, yet she ate up
polemics, dissent, her radio turned up practically to full volume—
she was deaf, yet even at full throttle their voices on the radio came
to her as moderate, disciplined, but she was aware of their anger
and edge and imagined them shouting—somehow comforted by
all that fury, the baleboosteh busyness and passion in their speech.
It was how, distracted from thoughts of Ted in the mutual family
earth back in, and just under, Chicago, she managed to drift off to
sleep.

So she was totally prepared when Toibb undertook to explain
the principles of recreational therapeusis to her, and what he proposed (should he accept her as his patient) to do. Indeed, she rather
enjoyed having it all explained to her, rather as if, thought Mrs.
Bliss, Toibb was a salesman going over the good points in his

wares. Faintly, although she was familiar with most of it from the call-in shows, she had the impression, always enjoyable to her, that he was fleshing out the full picture, a fact that (should he accept her as a patient or not) she liked to believe gave her the upper hand.

"I don't want to leave you with a false impression," Holmer Toibb said.

"No," Dorothy said.

"You'd have to undergo an evaluation."

"Of course."

"A medical evaluation."

"You're the doctor," Dorothy said.

"I'm not a doctor," Holmer Toibb said. "I'm not even a Ph.D. You have to see a physician, someone to do a work-up on you before I'd consent to treat you."

"Specimens? Needles?"

"Well," Toibb said, "whatever it takes to give you a clean bill of health."

Mrs. Bliss looked concerned.

"What?" Toibb said.

"Nothing," said Mrs. Ted Bliss, "it's just. You know something, Doctor?"

"I'm not a doctor."

"What do I call you you're not a doctor?"

"Holmer. My first name is Holmer."

"I can't call you your first name. I won't call you anything."

"Suits me," said Holmer Toibb. "So what were you going to tell me?"

"Oh," said Dorothy, "Ted, my husband, may he rest, took care of all of the paperwork. Medicare, supplemental, Blue Cross, Blue Shield—all the forms. The year he lost his life even. You know something, I haven't seen a doctor since. Isn't that crazy? It ain't just the forms. I can't look at them."

"Here," Toibb said, "use these. Please don't cry, Mrs. Bliss."

She was crying because, in a way, it was the last straw. What was she, stupid? Frank and Maxine had shpilkes to get home, out of Florida, away from her. To ease their consciences they dumped her with Manny from the building. Speaking personally, she liked him. Manny was a nice man. Generous, a lovely neighbor. She needed him and he always tried to be there for her as they said nowadays, but you know what? He was a clown, Manny. He was putting on a show. Perhaps for Mrs. Bliss, or other people in the building, maybe even for God. But a show was a show and anyway every time Manny did something nice for her, every single time, Dorothy felt like someone too poor to buy her own being offered a Thanksgiving turkey. So of course, overwhelmed as she was by the prospect of paperwork, official forms for the government, and the supplemental insurance gonifs, of course she was crying.

"Mrs. Bliss," Holmer Toibb said.

"I'm not Mrs. Bliss."

"You're not?"

"You're not a doctor, my husband is dead, I'm not a Mrs."

"Please," he said, "please Mrs. Bliss, all right, I'll see you. If you want me to see you I'll see you."

That was their first appointment.

"Just out of curiosity, Doctor," she said, and this time he didn't correct her, "just out of curiosity, I don't look healthy?"

"I'm sorry?"

"I look frail? My color is bad?"

"That's not what I said, Mrs. Bliss." And this time she didn't correct him either. "I've no expertise in these matters. It's something else entirely. I don't treat people if there's a chemical imbalance. If they're bipolar personalities, or suffer various mental disorders. I thought you understood that."

"I was a little worried."

"Well," Toibb said, "worried. If you were only worried. Worried's a good sign."

"Well, when you said . . ."

"I have to be sure," Toibb said. "Only if they're at loose ends, sixes and sevens. Only if they have the blues or feel genuinely sorry for themselves. Otherwise . . ." He left the rest of his sentence unfinished.

Mrs. Bliss wasn't sure either of them understood a single word of what the other was saying, but she felt oddly buoyed, even a little intoxicated by the sense she had that she was adrift in difficult waters. For all the times she had gone on picnics with Ted and the children to the Point on Lake Michigan, or out to the Dunes, for all the summers they'd been to resorts in Michigan City, Indiana, with their Olympic-size pools, or even, for that matter, to the one on the roof of the Towers building in which she lived, Mrs. Bliss had never learned to swim. She had taken lessons from lifeguards in the shallow ends of a dozen pools but without the aid of a life preserver she couldn't manage even to float. Though water excited her, its mysterious, incongruous clarity and weight, its invisible powers of erosion and incubation—all its wondrous displacements. This was a little like that. The times, for example, Mrs. Bliss, giddy, alarmed, suspended in inner tubes suspended in life jackets, hovered in the deep end weightless in water, her head and body unknown yards and feet above drowning. This conversation was a little like that. She felt at once interested and threatened, its odd cryptic quality vaguely reminiscent of the times her Maxine or her Frank or her Marvin were home on vacation trying to explain to her the deep things they had learned in their colleges.

"... like the collapse of arteries under a heart attack," Holmer Toibb said. "The heart muscle tries to compensate by prying open collateral vessels. That's what we'll work on. It's what this therapy is all about—a collateralization of interests."

"What heart attack?" asked Mrs. Bliss, alarmed.

"Oh, no," Toibb said, "it's an analogy."

"You said heart attack."

"It was only an example."

There was little history of heart attacks in Mrs. Bliss's family. What generally got them was cancer, some of the slower neuropathies. (Despite her sealed ear, Mrs. Bliss's deafness was largely due to a progressive nerve disorder of the inner ear, a sort of auditory glaucoma.) Yet it was heart disease of which she was most frightened. It was her experience that things broke down. Lightbulbs burned out, the most expensive appliances went on the fritz. Washers and dryers, ranges, refrigerators, radios, cars. No matter how carefully one obeyed the directions in the service manuals, everything came fatally flawed. How many times had she sent back improperly prepared fish in restaurants, how many times were her own roasts underdone, the soup too salty? You watered the plants, careful to give them just the right amount, not too much and not too little, moving them from window to window for the best sun, yet leaves yellowed and fell off and the plant died. Because there was poison even in a rose. So how, wondered Mrs. Bliss, could a heart not fail? A muscle, wound and set to ticking even in the womb. How should it endure its first birthday, its tenth, and twentieth? And how, even after you subtracted those two or three years that the man in Immigration tacked on, could it not be winding down after seventy or so had passed? How could a little muscle of tissue and blood, less substantial than the heavy, solid, working metal parts in a courthouse clock, that you couldn't see, and couldn't feel until it was already coming apart in your chest, hold up to the wear and tear of just staying alive for more than seventy years of even a happy life? It was like the veiled mystery of the invisible depths between herself and her death in the water of a swimming pool.

He wanted to see her again later that same week, he told her, and sent her home with an assignment but, so far as Dorothy could tell, without starting her in on her therapy.

"Tell me," Holmer Toibb said the next time she came, "what name is on your mailbox?" It was the first real question he'd ever asked her, and Mrs. Bliss, who thought it was for purposes of billing, which, since this was the third or fourth time they'd seen each other and he still hadn't started to treat her, she rather resented. In fact, she was still stung by his heart attack remark.

"Mr. and Mrs. Ted Bliss," said Mrs. Ted Bliss.

"And Ted's dead . . . how long?"

"My husband passed away three years ago," she said primly.

"Three *years?* He kicked the bucket three years ago?"

"He's gone, may he rest, three years next month."

"And does he get much mail at this address since he cashed in his chips, may he rest?"

Mrs. Ted Bliss glared at him.

He didn't even pretend to acknowledge her anger. "What," Holmer Toibb said, "he *ain't* dead? Come on, Dorothy, it's been three years, it's not natural. Well, it is, actually. Many women keep their husband's name on the box after they've lost them. Even more than three years, the rest of their lives. It's guilt and shame, not respect, and it doesn't make them happy. You have to make an accommodation. You want to show me your list? Where's your list? Show me your list. Did you bring it?"

The list Toibb referred to was her assignment—a list of her interests—and though she had brought it and actually been at some pains to compose it, she'd been hurt by this disrespectful man and was determined now not to let him see it. If she'd been bolder or less constrained in the presence of men, she might have ended their conference right then and, scorcher or no scorcher, gone back out in the sun to wait for her bus. But she was practical as well as vulnerable and saw no point in cutting off her nose to spite her face. Also—she knew the type—he'd probably charge for the appointment even if she broke it off before it had properly begun. Who am I fooling, Dorothy thought, how many times have I put Band-Aids on after cutting myself clipping coupons out of the papers? Climb down off your high horse before you break something.

Mrs. Bliss reddened. "I didn't write one out," she told him, avoiding his eyes.

"Well, what you remember then."

Dorothy was glad he'd insisted. She hadn't been to school since she was a young girl in Russia and, while she still remembered some of those early lessons and even today could picture the primers in which she'd first learned to read and been introduced to the mysteries of the simplest arithmetic and science and historical overviews, or seen on maps a rough version of the world's geography, education had been the province of the males in her family, and she could still recall her guilty resentment of her younger brothers, Philip and Jake, and how they'd been permitted to take books overnight to study at home while she'd merely been allowed to collect the books of the other girls in the class and put them back on the shelves each afternoon and pass them out again the next morning. She'd never been given anything as important as an "assignment." Even when Manny taught her to make out her own checks and fill out deposit slips, list the entries and withdrawals in her passbook, even when he'd taught her how to work her solar calculator and balance her checkbook, he'd been right there at her side to help her. He'd never given her one single assignment. It was a little like being a young girl back in Russia.

So it was quite possible, now she had regained her composure, that even if he hadn't asked to see a list of her interests she might have volunteered anyway.

"Cards," she began.

"For money?" Toibb said.

"Yes, sure for money."

"Big money?"

"Friendly games. But rich enough for *my* blood."

"How friendly?"

"Friendly. If someone loses five dollars that's a big deal."

"Go on," Toibb said.

"Cooking."

"Mexican? Continental? Japanese? What sort of cooking?"

"Supper. Coffee, dessert. Cooking."

"What else?"

"Breakfast. Lunch. Not now, not so much."

"No, I mean do you have any other interests?"

"Oh, sure," Mrs. Bliss said. "I'm very interested in television. We bought color TV back in the sixties and were one of the first to have cable. If you mean what *kind* of television I'd have to say the detectives."

She had known while she wrote the list out that it made her life seem trivial. Even those interests she hadn't yet mentioned— her membership in ORT and other organizations, things connected with events in the Towers, her visits to Chicago and Pittsburgh and Cincinnati—even that which was most important to her, her children and grandchildren, *all* her family. The trips, when Ted was alive, they'd taken to the islands and, one time, to Israel with a stop in London to visit Frank and his family Frank's sabbatical year. (Her childhood, the years she'd spent in Russia, even farther than London, farther than Israel.) All these were real interests, yet she was ordinary, ordinary. Everyone had interests. Everyone had a family, highlights in their lives. She had considered, when she made her list, putting down Alcibiades Chitral's name, the business with the car, the time she'd had to testify in court, but wasn't sure those experiences qualified as interests. Unless Ted's death also qualified, her twelve-hundred-mile crying jag on the plane to Chicago, Marvin's three-year destruction. *All* the unhappy things in her life. Did *they* interest her?

"Other people's condominiums," she blurted. "Tommy Auveristas," she said. "*All* the South Americans."

"You *know* Tommy Overeasy?" Holmer Toibb said.

"Tommy Overeasy?"

"It's what they call him. But wait a minute, you *know* this man?" Toibb said excitedly.

She'd struck pay dirt but was too caught up in her thoughts to notice. Not *even* thoughts. Sudden impressions. Saliencies. Bolts from the blue. And she rode over Toibb's lively interest. Not her loose ends, her sixes and sevens, not her blues or sadness or even her grief. Maybe she wasn't even a candidate for Holmer Toibb's therapies.

I know, she thought, I want to go visit Alcibiades Chitral!

Speak of the devil, thought Mrs. Ted Bliss.

She had just left Holmer Toibb's office on Lincoln Road and was sitting on a bench inside a small wooden shelter waiting for her bus. The devil who'd come into her line of sight just as she was thinking of him was Hector Camerando. Camerando from Building Two and his friend, Jaime Guttierez from Three, were two of the first South American boys she had met in the Towers. Mrs. Bliss, like many unschooled people, had an absolutely phenomenal memory when it came to attaching names to faces and, since in her relatively small world, her limited universe of experience, strangers were almost always an event, she was usually bang on target recalling the circumstances in which she'd met them. She'd met Hector through Jaime on one of the old international evenings that used to be held in the game rooms on Saturday nights. Rose Blitzer had thought him quite handsome, recalled Mrs. Bliss. Even Rose's husband, Max, olov hasholem, had remarked on his smile. Dorothy sighed. It had been less than four years yet so many were gone. Just from Mrs. Bliss's table alone—Max; Ida; the woman on coffee duty, Estelle. Ted. She didn't care to think about all the others in the room that night who were gone now. (Not "cashed in his chips," not "kicked the bucket." "Who had lost his life." That's how Toibb should have put it. As if death came like the account of a disaster at sea in a newspaper. Or what happened to soldiers in wars. He should have honored it for the really big deal it was.) Let alone the people who'd been too sick to make it to the gala and had stayed in their apartments. Plus all those who'd been well enough but hadn't come anyway. In a way even Guttierez hadn't survived. Oh, he was still alive, touch wood, but Louise Munez had told Mrs. Bliss he'd taken a loss on his condo and moved to a newer, even bigger place in the West Palm Beach area that Louise told her was restricted.

And, if you could trust Louise (even without her mishegoss newspapers and magazines the security guard was a little strange), Hector Camerando was thinking to put *his* place on the market.

Mrs. Ted Bliss hated to hear about Towers condominiums being put up for sale. Everyone knew the Miami area was overbuilt, that it was a buyer's market. But interest rates were sky high. It could cost you a fortune to take out a loan, and what you gave to the bank you didn't give to the seller. That's why the prices kept falling. Or that's what Manny from the building told her anyway. Poor Rose Blitzer, thought Dorothy Bliss. As if it wasn't enough that her husband had lost his life. Poor Rose Blitzer with her three bedrooms, two and a half baths, full kitchen, California room, and a living room/dining room area so large all she needed to have two extra, good-sized rooms was put in a wall. She must rattle around in a place like that. She'd never get back what they'd put into it before Max lost his life. (Crazy Louise was floating rumors.) But selling at a loss was better than renting or leaving it stand empty. Not that it made a difference to Mrs. Ted Bliss. She'd never sell *her* place. When she lost her life it would go to the kids and they'd do what they'd do. Till then, forget it. She and Ted had picked their spot and Mrs. Bliss was perfectly willing to lie in it.

But what, Mrs. Bliss wondered, was Hector Camerando doing on Lincoln Road? What could there be for him here?

Dorothy remembered Lincoln Road from when it was still *Lincoln Road*. From back in the old days, from back in the fifties, from when they first started coming down to Miami Beach. From when all the tourists from all the brand-new hotels up and down Collins Avenue would come there to shop—all the latest styles in men's and women's beach-wear, lounging pajamas, even fur coats if you could believe that. Anything you wanted, any expensive, extravagant thing you could think of—cocktail rings, studs for French cuffs, the fanciest watches and men's white-on-white shirts, anything. Hair salons you could smell the toilet water and perfumes blowing out on the sidewalks like flowers exploding. You want it, they got it. Then, afterward, you could drop into Wolfie's when Wolfie's was Wolfie's.

Now, even the bright, little, old-fashioned trolley bus you rode in free up and down Lincoln looked shabby and the advertising on the back of the bench on which Dorothy sat was in Spanish. Half the shops were boarded up or turned into medical buildings where chiropractors and recreational therapeusisists kept their offices; and in Wolfie's almost the only people you ever saw were dried-up old Jewish ladies on sticks with loose dentures hanging down beneath their upper lips or riding up their jaws, and holding on for dear life to their fat doggie bags of rolls and collapsing pats of foiled, melting butter that came with their cups of coffee and single boiled egg, taking them back to the lone rooms in which they lived in old, whitewashed, three-story hotels far down Collins. Either them or the out-and-out homeless. It stank, if you could believe it, of pee.

What could a man like Hector Camerando want here?

He had seen Mrs. Ted Bliss, too, and was coming toward her.

Does he recognize me? They'd bumped into each other maybe a grand total of three or four times since they'd met. He lives in Building Two, I live in Building One. It's two different worlds.

She waved to him while he was still crossing the street.

"Oh," she said, "how are you? How are you feeling? You're looking very well. I'm waiting for my bus, that's why I'm sitting here. I saw you when you were still across the street. We're neighbors. I live in the Towers, too. Dorothy Bliss? Building One."

"Of course. How are you, Mrs. Ted Bliss?" Hector Camerando said.

"I'm fine. Thank you for asking," Dorothy said, at once flattered and a little surprised he should remember her name, a playboy and something of a man, if you could believe Louise, about town. And just at that moment Mrs. Bliss saw her bus approach. She frowned. She distinctly frowned and, exactly as if she had suddenly sneezed without having a Kleenex ready, she hastily clapped a hand over her face. "Oh," she said, gathering herself and rising to go, "look. Here's my bus."

Hector Camerando lightly pressed his fingers on her arm. "No," he said, "I have my car, I'll drive you."

And wasn't being the least bit coy or too much protesting when she told him that wouldn't be necessary, that she enjoyed riding the bus, that she liked looking out its big, tinted windows and studying all the sights on Collins Avenue, that she loved how, on a hot afternoon like this, the drivers, if only for their own comfort, kept their buses overly air-conditioned. She loved that feeling, she said.

"I'll turn my thermostat down to sixty degrees," he said. "And at this time of day the traffic's so slow you'll be able to study everything to your heart's content. Besides," he said, "why should you pay for a fare if you don't have to? Come," he said, taking her arm once more and leading her away gently, "I'm just around the corner."

It was his point about the fare that turned her. Mrs. Bliss was not a venal woman. That she cut discount coupons out of the paper or, because of her premonition that she'd be charged for the visit anyway, hadn't bolted from his office when Holmer Toibb referred so disrespectfully to the manner in which Ted had lost his life, was testimony not to parsimony as much as to her understanding that money, like oil or clean water or great stands of forest, was a resource, too, and must not be abused.

His hand on her arm, Mrs. Bliss felt almost girlish (she wasn't a fool; it never crossed her mind she might be his sweetheart, he her swain), moved by the pleasure of being humanly touched, and virtuous, too, proud of his physical handsomeness and of the scrupulous innocence of her reasons for accepting his ride. Though he was doing her a favor and she knew it, and she might even be taking him out of his way, and she knew *that*, she was not made to feel (as she often did with Manny) that she was being patronized, or that there was anything showy about this guy's good deeds. Rather, Mrs. Bliss felt for a moment he might be doing it out of something like camaraderie.

Only then did the network of coincidence strike her. Not half an hour earlier she'd mentioned Tommy Auveristas to Toibb, her interest in all the South Americans. She'd declared her interest, too, in other people's condominiums. Perhaps that's what put her in mind of what the security guard, Louise, had told her about Jaime Guttierez's determination to sell and, then, auf tzuluchas, there he was, plain as the nose, a man she didn't run into once or twice in two years.

And, gasping, stopped dead in her tracks, catching her breath.

"What?" said Hector Camerando. "What is it, what's wrong? Is it the heat? Do you want to sit down? We'll go into that Eckerd's. I think there's a soda fountain."

"No," said Dorothy Bliss. "I'm all right."

She was. She was breathing regularly again. She felt no tight-

ness in her throat or chest, no sharp shooting pains up her left arm
or in her jaw. What stopped her, what she'd run into like a wall
was the thrill of conviction, a presentiment, almost a vision. Her
ride, the favor Hector Camerando had crossed the street to press
on her, was to lead her to his car, which, plain as the nose, was
sure to turn out to be Ted's Buick LeSabre, washed, waxed, and
green as the wrapper on a stick of Doublemint gum.

"You're sure?"

"Thank you for asking," said Mrs. Ted Bliss.

They turned the corner.

"Where is it?" she said. "I don't see it."

"We're there," he said, and opened the door on the passenger
side of his Fleetwood Cadillac.

Mrs. Bliss was as stunned by its not being their old car as she
had been by her conviction it would. She couldn't catch her breath
but she was still without pain.

"Let me turn this on," Camerando said, and leaned across Mrs.
Bliss and put the key in the ignition. Almost instantly Mrs. Bliss
felt sheets of cold air. It was like standing at the frontier of a sudden
cold front.

"Would you like to see a doctor? Let me take you to your
doctor."

"That's all right," she said.

"No, really. You mustn't let things slide. It's better if you catch
them early. No," said Camerando, "there's nothing to cry about.
What's there to cry about? You mustn't be frightened. It's nothing.
I'm certain it isn't anything. You waited for the bus in all that heat.
That's enough to knock the stuffing out of anyone."

"You shut up," said Mrs. Ted Bliss. "You just shut up."

"Hey," Camerando said.

"Shut up," she said. "Don't talk."

Camerando stared at her, looked for a moment as if he would
say something else, and then shrugged and moved his oversized
automobile into play in the traffic.

Mrs. Bliss giggled. Then, exactly as if giggling were the rudest
of public displays, removed a handkerchief from her white plastic
handbag and covered first one and then the other corner of her
mouth with it, wiping her incipient laughter into her handkerchief
like a sort of phlegm. She returned the handkerchief to her pock-

etbook, clicking it shut as though snapping her composure back into place.

"Do you happen to know," Mrs. Bliss said, "a gentleman from Building One by the name of Manny?"

The bitch is heat struck, Hector Camerando thought. Her brains are sunburned.

"Manny?" he said. "Manny? Building One? No, I don't think so."

"A big man? Probably in his late sixties, though he looks younger?"

"No," Hector Camerando said.

"You remind me," said Mrs. Bliss. "He's not as sharp a dresser."

Camerando, squinting his eyes as though he were examining some rogues' gallery of Manny-like suspects, shook his head.

The trouble, she thought, was that no one, not her Marvin, not anyone, could hold a candle to Ted. All there was, if you were lucky—oh, you had to be lucky—was someone who didn't sit in judgment waiting for you to make a mistake. The trouble with kindness, Mrs. Bliss thought, was that there was a limit to it, that it was timed to burn out, that if you slipped up one time too many, or didn't put a brave enough face on things, or weren't happy often enough, people lost patience. She felt almost lighthearted.

She wasn't good at expressing things in English. She'd forgotten her Russian, didn't, except for a few expressions and maybe a handful of words, even speak Yiddish. Odd as it seemed to her, English was her first language and, though she couldn't hear it, she knew that her accent was thick, that the sound of her words must be like the sounds characters made in jokes, routines, that she must, even as a young woman in her prime, have come across to others as more vulnerable than she really was, more tremendously naive, less interesting, a type, some stage mockery. (Had she been a murderess her lawyer might have used her voice as a defense; its quaintness like a sort of freckles and dimples and braids.) She wished Ted were alive so she could explain her mood.

It was funny; she thought well enough. She knew this. Not much escaped her. The sights were all up and down Collins Avenue, and everywhere else, too. Holmer Toibb was a sight, the big ugly car she rode in, the man who drove it. Mrs. Bliss wished she had words for the words in her head, or that people could read her mind as she had her impressions. But no one could do that, not even Ted. All Ted could do was not judge her. And now, may he rest, he couldn't do even that. Yet she knew he wasn't resting, he wasn't anything. The thing about losing your life was that you lost everyone else's, too. You lost Marvin's, you lost Frank's, you lost Maxine's. You lost your wife's, Dorothy's. By dying, thought Mrs. Ted Bliss, you lost everything. It must be a little like going through bankruptcy. Mrs. Bliss felt as if he'd set her aside. He'd set her aside? Then may she rest, too.

As, in a way, she did. She was. In the presence of a stranger, she was completely calm. If she'd allowed herself to she could have shut out the sights altogether, closed her eyes, and slept. It was only out of politeness that she didn't, and it was as if they'd exchanged places, as if he were her guest instead of the other way around. She could have offered him coffee, the paper, the use of her phone. She could have broken out the cards and dealt him gin rummy. It was nuts, but that's how she felt. The least she owed him was conversation.

"Louise Munez tells me you're thinking of selling," Dorothy said.

"Selling?"

"Your condominium. When I remember, I say 'condominium.' It's one of the biggest investments we make. Why use slang?"

Mrs. Bliss had no such principles. She was paying him in conversation.

"Louise Munez?"

"Louise Munez. The security guard with the magazines. Very friendly woman with a gun and a nightstick. Talks to everyone. I don't know where she learns all the gossip she knows but she's very reliable. Oh, you know her. Elaine Munez's daughter? No? I thought you did. I don't think they get along very well. I think she asked to be assigned to One because her mother lives there. She probably does it just to aggravate her. Kids! I know the woman won't let her live with her. It must be a secret, she never said what. She's quiet enough about her own business. *I* don't know what's going on. People don't foul their own nests. Sure, when it comes to *their* nests mum's the word."

She paused and looked sidelong at Camerando. Maybe he had something to contribute to the conversation. No?

"Anyway," Dorothy continued, "it was Louise Munez who said you're thinking of selling. The same one who told me your friend Jaime Guttierez bought a big place in West Palm Beach. You've been there? I hear it's nice. Is it nice?"

"Es muy bueno," Hector Camerando said.

(But restricted? thought Mrs. Bliss. They'll take a Spaniard or a Mexican over a Jew?)

"Oh," she said, "you speak Spinach."

"Spinach?"

"It's a joke. In the buildings."

"Si."

She wondered if he knew what was going on. Her moods this afternoon were giving her fits. Now she was impatient to be home. She could almost have jumped out of her skin. What did they all want from her? Why had he crossed the street and made such a fuss if he was going to act this way? She wasn't that vulnerable, she wasn't. Or naive or uninteresting either. If she *did* need her Mannys and protectors. She was a woman who'd carried a gun. In Chicago, on the first of the month, covering her husband, a Jew Louise.

It was just that Miami alarmed her. The things you read, the things you *heard*. All the drugs and factions. There was offshore piracy. Yes, and this one had machine guns in the Everglades, and that one slaves in the orange groves, and another sold green cards, phony papers, and everyone practicing the martial arts against the time they could take back their countries.

The Cubans, the Colombians, the Central Americans. The blacks, and the Haitians beneath the blacks. The beach bums and homeless. Thugs, malcontents, and the insane invading from Mariel. And somewhere in there the Jews, throwbacks, who'd once come on vacations and now went there to die. It wasn't a place, it was a pecking order.

Something sinister in even the traffic, some stalled, oppressive sense of refugee, of the bridge down and the last flight out of wherever (Dear *God*, couldn't he go faster? Didn't he know shortcuts?), and Mrs. Bliss, as much out of distraction and a need to make the time pass, tried to get Camerando to pitch in. She started to ask him questions. (Though, truthfully, were she back in Toibb's office now, she would have opened her pocketbook, removed the homework she'd been at such pains to prepare, and torn it into a dozen pieces. This was no country for baleboostehs. Her husband was dead, her family scattered. She *had* no interests!)

"Do you know Susan and Oliver Gutterman?" she said.

Camerando shook his head.

"Enrique Frache? Ricardo Llossas?"

Mrs. Bliss noted the absence of recognition on his face and went on as though she were reading from a prepared list both of them knew was just a formality, so much red tape.

"Vittorio Cervantes? No? What about his wife, Ermalina?"

He shook his head again and again and Mrs. Bliss wondered how much longer he could answer her questions without actually speaking. She would make this the point of the game.

"Carlos and Rita Olvero? They live in your building."

"I know Carlos," Hector Camerando said. "We're not close."

So much for the point of the game, she thought. And then, remembering what they said on TV, she laughed and said, "Wait, I have a follow-up. Carmen and Tommy Auveristas?"

She hit the jackpot with that one, she broke the bank at Monte Carlo, and suddenly didn't know whether to be pleased or terrified that they had made contact. It was tiresome to have to acknowledge that one no longer had any interests, yet there was something reassuring and comfortable about it, too. To live by second nature, the seat of your pants.

"Listen," Camerando exploded, "put up or shut up! What do you know about it anyway? What do you know about *anythin'*? An old Jew lady cooking soup, making fish! You want some advice? These are your golden years. You should shuffleboard the livelong day. You should tan in the sun till the cows come home! Join the discussion groups. What's wrong with you, lady? These are your golden years. You shouldn't leave the game room!"

He'd scared her shitless. And the odd thing, the odd thing was he liked the old woman. When he came out of Rita de Janeiro's and saw her waiting for her bus he'd been happy to see her, first on her account and then on his. It was already the middle of the afternoon and he hadn't found an opportunity to make reparation, do his good deed. Well, he thought as he'd seen her waving at him, it's Mrs. Ted in the nick of time.

Though that part was superstition, the little self-imposed ritual upping the degree of difficulty. Logically, of course, if the time of day made no difference to God it certainly shouldn't make a difference to Camerando. And if it did (and it did), then maybe *none* of it made any difference to God. And maybe, too, he could have saved himself the trouble and stopped the whole thing altogether. On the other hand, he thought (though this had occurred more times than he could remember), perhaps God not only wasn't in it but wasn't even in *on* it! Boy, he thought, wouldn't *that* be a kick in the nuts?

So he took God out of the equation (Hector Camerando, he scolded, Hector Camerando, you are one good-looking, well-dressed fuck; you can't lose, can you, Fuck?) and decided for more times than he could remember that he'd been doing it for himself all along.

And that degree of difficulty was the whole point.

Hey, if it wasn't, shit, if it wasn't he could have tossed ten, twenty, thirty bucks to the first bum he saw on the street, said, "Starlight, Starbright," and made a wish on the damn creep.

But nah, nah. He played by the rules even if they were only his rules. It had to be all done by at least an hour before sunset, Fall back, Spring forward inclusive. And it was having to wait until the last minute that made it exciting. Well, it was in the blood, wasn't it? Flowing free all up and down his proud red hidalgo.

Still, he hoped the royal reaming he'd just given Mrs. Ted's old ass hadn't spooked her to the point where it canceled his reparation. It probably had, though, and now he'd either have to look out for an accident he could stop for, or pull up to some kid selling newspapers at a stoplight, slip him a ten, and then not take the paper.

Sometimes, compulsive superstition could be a pain in the ass. He wondered whether Jaime Guttierez had similar tics. The guy was one of his best pals, but they had never talked about it. Sure, Camerando thought, he must have them. They were compadres— the both of them dashing macho gentlemen spirit sports with a word and code of honor big and wide as a barn door.

He hated his temper, his temperament. It had cost him a wife, a couple of relatives, and not a few friends. Though he personally doubted that was what had gotten him into the loopy tit-for-tat of his life. And, frankly, he didn't think being Catholic had all that much to do with the endless appeasement that made up at least a part of his days. Even when he'd been a strict observer, confession and penance were things he could do with his soul tied behind his back. In spite of—maybe even because of—the fact that he never really understood those mysteries. To him, God had always seemed something of a pushover. Surely, he thought, reciting all the Our Fathers and Hail Marys in the world didn't make a dime's worth of difference to the human heart, and he'd long ago wearied of such pale, puny recompense. What's more, making restitution to the injured party made as little sense. Why go to the bother of injuring a party if all you had to do to wipe the slate clean was give back his money or restore his health? It slipped all the punches and didn't do a thing for your character. It was hypocritical, if you want to know.

Yet he'd stung and frightened her, rammed words down her ears that, at that close a range, she couldn't help but hear even if she was deaf. (And to judge by the size of the hearing aid that hung out of the side of her head like a fucking Walkman, she was plenty deaf!) So what he decided to do, he decided, was make her the beneficiary of a *second* reparation. She'd been poking her nose, sniffing around his business, trying to get him to spill the goods on his life. All right then, he'd pass up the accidents and paperboys, go straight ahead and rat on himself.

"I know Frache," he told the old woman, "I know Llossas. I know them all. I'm in with Aspiration de Lopardoso."

"Aspiration de Lopardoso?"

"You don't know him?"

She shook her head.

"You didn't just ask me about de Lopardoso?"

"I never heard of him," Mrs. Bliss said.

Ay ay ay, Camerando thought. Macho gentleman spirit sport or no macho gentleman spirit sport, he was frankly astonished that he should be sitting beside this particular woman in this particular place. True, she was only one more familiar absolute type of woman. Throw a mantilla around her shoulders or a dark shawl over her head and she could be a stand-in for any widow in the world, any lachrymose madre, ma, or mama who ever was. Any old, enfeebled pietà of a dame crying over the spilled milk of a lost child. Though it was beyond imagining (as it was with so many of that order) how she could have set aside the housework and tatting and nursing of babes ever to have lain still long enough to conceive one, impossible to drum up in her—not love, she was a pillar of love—but the juices of anything like enjoyment or passion. It was for her that the long distance was created, floral remembrances on birthdays and holidays, all the merely token requitals of pure blind will in the service of sacrifice. She was *such* a dope! *So* stupid! Running only on instinct without the intelligence or fury to refuse anything to anybody, so simply and purely biological as to once have tumbled out of her silly-ass womb. Up to her eyes in forgiveness and long-suffering and incapable of cutting, or even of recognizing, a loss. Who knew nothing of odds, and believed that, by God, so long as it were her blood, she didn't care a damn *what* damage it did! Selfishness like hers—mother selfishness—made guys like him and Auveristas and Chitral and Guttierez pikers. So *dumb!* Now there was someone who knew how to work the reparations!

But what astonished him, what he couldn't get past, were their disparate worldviews. By golly, thought Camerando, I *am* a dashing macho gentleman spirit sport. I *am*. Next to her I am! I do, too, have a code of honor. I *do*. Next to her I do!

He knew her type all right. She wasn't human, she was a cliché quivering in the corner. Of course she was a pillar of love. She was a pillar of love capable of any greed, nastiness, bad manners, gossip, or folly. A patriot only to consanguinity, this cowering special pleader of blood who traded on her revenant, immemorial widowship and mommyhood.

Had she been putting on an act, then? What were all those tears? What had that gasping and shortness of breath been all about, the staggering stutter step when she walked toward his car, or struck her heatstroke poses?

And the odd thing, the odd thing was he liked the woman. She reminded him of his mother. That's why he felt free to poke about the holes in her character.

While she, in her turn, had poked about his. All her damn questions.

All right, Camerando thought, I'll turn myself in.

"Do you know, Mrs. Ted, what I do?"

She didn't. Again, she was without interest and could barely manage to muster the energy to look at him.

"I'm with the jai alai interests," he said.

He didn't look at her and couldn't tell whether she was watching him or even, for that matter, if she'd heard him or, if she had, taken his meaning. "Oh, yes," he said, "I'm a major jai alai kingpin. From little Rhode Island to South Florida important Basque athletes sit by their phones waiting for my calls. Ditto the greyhounds, so to speak. Ditto almost the little fucking mechanical rabbit.

"What, you don't believe me? Lady, I could give you tips, make you big winners. Spread your bets around, lay them off wisely, you don't get impatient or too greedy, I could fix it up pretty good with your life. I could put you in a three-bedroom, two-and-a-half bath, full kitchen, living/dining room area with the convertible screened-in/glassed-in California rooms and a view of Biscayne Bay to knock your eyes out. And this is just starters, openers. I see you in penthouses. I see you in the great gorgeous restricted digs of West Palm. I can do this. Truly. No fooling. What do you say?"

"Sure," said Mrs. Ted Bliss, "why not?"

FIVE

She took him at his word. She bet sparingly, did not grow impatient or, at least in a conventional sense, greedy, and two years later was still in the same condo.

She was very proud of this. It became a sort of referent of her character, a means by which she took her moral temperature. Mrs. Bliss knew her stuff. The lessons of those caper crooks in movies was not lost on her, those essentially victimless-crime villains enjoined to hold their horses, to wait out the statute of limitations before they cashed in on their shady bonanzas. Always, in these shows, one or another of the partners couldn't hold out, snapped, failed the rest, and drew down destruction on their mutual enterprise. And, since she had no other partners, Mrs. Bliss felt all the better about her self-control.

If she didn't feel entirely honorable she had only her embarrassment to blame, her modesty; even, in a way, another aspect of what wasn't even personality anymore so much as a matter of some long-standing tidiness of spirit. It would, after all, have required her actually to *call* Hector Camerando to ask him to give her the winner of a particular match, a specific race, and she could no more have abused this privilege than she could have asked her husband for extra money to run the household. Not that either of them would have refused. It was her need not to appear needy, a saving of face, that held her bets down. Indeed, if she hadn't infrequently run into Hector Camerando—he hadn't moved, he still lived in the Towers; Louise Munez's information was either faulty or he'd changed his mind—she might never have placed a bet at all. Yet always on the rare occasions he saw her he chastised her for not asking for his tips. That he hadn't forgotten his offer made him, well, heroic to Dorothy and, on these occasions, she almost always felt obliged to place a bet or, rather, allowed him to place one for her. The first time this happened she hadn't even known she'd won until he came to her door to hand her her winnings. He gave her four hundred dollars.

"So much? Why so much?"

"It was a lock. A dead-solid certainty. The dog went off at twenty to one. I put down twenty dollars for you."

Surprisingly, her first reaction was one of anger, her second of shame, because although she said nothing to indicate her disappointment that if it was such a certainty he could easily have put down more than twenty dollars, she knew he'd seen the momentary blister of rage on her face. "Wait," she said. Then, to cover her confusion, she excused herself and went off to get her purse. When she returned Camerando thought she had been looking for a place to put the money; instead she began to fumble with the bills in her wallet. She wasn't wearing her glasses and had to hold them up close to her face. "Here," Mrs. Bliss said, and handed Camerando a ten, a five, and five singles.

"What's this?" Hector said.

"The twenty dollars you put down for me."

She knew they weren't quits, but it was the best she could think to do at the time.

Afterward, she tried to avoid him. She really did. And, once, just as she was leaving the apartment of a Towers friend she had been visiting and she spotted him step out of an elevator and walk down the corridor toward her, she quickly reversed fields and turned back to reenter the apartment she had left just seconds before. She had moved with such agility—this would have been when she was in her early seventies—that she quite startled her friend who was still in the process of shutting the door. "Oh," Dorothy said, "did I leave my purse here? I think I left my purse here."

"Dorothy," said her friend, "what's wrong, sweetheart? You're carrying your purse. It's right there on your arm."

"Is it? Oh, my," she explained, "it's been like that all day. I'm running around like a chicken with its head cut off."

"Maybe you should say something to Robins."

"Robins?" said Mrs. Bliss. "No, it's nothing. You don't see a doctor because once in a while you're absentminded."

When she thought it was safe, she bade her friend goodbye a second time and stepped out again into the hallway. She could feel the woman watching her and turned back to look. Her friend smiled broadly and made an exaggerated gesture in the direction of the elevator as if to assure Dorothy she was headed in the right direction.

Is that how they thought of her? Like she was an idiot? She'd give them idiot. She bet she could spot most of them the names of ten people who lived in the Towers and come up with more of their buildings, floors, and apartment numbers than anyone. She could have been the damn postman here!

It occurred, of course, that she could have given that oysvorf, her friend so-called, something to think about. All she had to do was explain Camerando and why she was trying to avoid him.

Then they'd *really* have me going to the doctors, Dorothy thought, and giggled. Running away from some tall, dark, and handsome character who was trying to force money on her without, except for lifting her hands to receive it, her lifting her hands.

"You're too proud," they'd say, "introduce *me!*"

But she wasn't. Too proud, that is. It had nothing to do with pride. Nor, like so many of these widowed, tummy-tucked, liposuctioned, double-dentured, face-lifted, hair-dyed, foolish old husband hunters, the Never-Too-Late brigade, was she looking for a man, or a boyfriend, or even a companion with whom she could go to a movie. In Mrs. Ted Bliss's experience, it wasn't true what they told you, the experts, the AARP people, all the high-powered gerontologists and aging-gracefully crowd—that desire burned a hole in your pocket even on your deathbed. Speaking personally, she hadn't felt that way about a man since Ted, olov hasholem, had lost his life. Or even, if you want to know, since the time his cancer was first diagnosed. Well, she'd been afraid of hurting him and, more shamefully, of his hurting her, of her contracting, though she knew better, a piece of his illness.

And, if you had to know *all* the truth, she'd never so much as touched herself, not once, not in her whole life. So, as far as Mrs. Bliss was concerned, it was bunk, and they were full of it if they said that the sex drive in a healthy person didn't die. What, she wasn't healthy? She was healthy. She was plenty healthy. It was those others, the oversexed ones, who couldn't accept that there was a time and a place for everything and went on searching for the fountain of youth long after it ceased to be appropriate.

Like her friend, who'd only have snickered and kidded her about having a fancy man if she so much as said a word about Camerando.

But even that wasn't the reason she not only kept Hector Camerando's name out of the picture but took actual pains to avoid him. She was saving him. He was money in the bank, something she'd set aside for a rainy day, and she was, she liked to think, playing him like some of the men in the Towers played the stock market.

Now Dorothy was no fool. Just as she knew there was a time and a place for everything, she understood, without ever having come across the actual words, the notion that there is a tide in the affairs of men which taken at the flood, et cetera. He might be riding high right now with his Basques and his greyhounds, but she had known plenty of his type back in Chicago, high rollers, heavy winners and losers in a thousand enterprises, men, competitors of Ted's who followed the trends and locations like dowsers, and opened stores and businesses first in this place, then in that, who had buildings, sold them here, bought them there—wiseguys, into the rackets some of them, always with some new deal on the books, mavins one day, bankrupts the next, but make no mistake, people you had to take seriously, men who always seemed to have good reasons for what they did. Ted, who'd lost his life, had never been one of them, knock wood and thank God. He told Dorothy that what it finally came down to was a failure of nerve, and asked her forgiveness as if, in a way, he held her responsible, their three, then two, children, his family responsibilities. Only one time, during the war, when he splurged and bought the farm in Michigan where he raised and slaughtered his own cattle to sell on the black market, had he behaved otherwise. It wasn't Dorothy, though he used her as an excuse to sell it at a loss only eleven months after he bought it. They'd made money hand over fist; he'd had no reason to sell. It was his failure of nerve and not her complaints about having to live on a place that morning to night stank of cow shit and urine and God knows what awful odors of sour milk and fermenting hay. In town, she had turned even the odd stares of the grauber yung and anti-Semites into reluctant grins with her cheery, preemptive greetings and comments and deliberately clownish ways.

What, they'd never seen Jews before? They thought they had horns, tails? They never dreamed Jews could be comely and clean? If, before going into the little village for supplies, she showered in the infrequently hot water of their primitive bathroom and got herself up in her nicest hats and dresses and furs and nylons and shoes, if she put on her makeup as carefully as she might if she'd been going to synagogue on the highest holiday, it wasn't to flaunt her beauty or show off her big-city fashions but to defy the epithet of "dirty Jew." She took the insult not only personally but literally, too, and, drawing on all her old, childish notions of shmutsdread and trayf, meant to get round it literally, by turning herself into a sort of sterile field. (And wasn't that freezing Michigan village with its wood houses and all its big, powerful goyim and blond, rosy-cheeked shiksas enough like its old Russian counterparts that as soon as she saw it it was like forty years had dropped away from her just like that?) So it wasn't just for herself that she went to these ridiculous lengths. (To avoid getting shit on them, she wore galoshes over her high heels and removed them, setting them down on the side of the road only after coming within sight of the tiny town.) On the contrary. As far as she was concerned she would have donned overalls and walked all the way into town without so much as bothering to scrape the muck from her boots. No, it was for Ted that she went to extremes, for Marvin and Frank and Maxine. To honor her mother and her father and the memory of all her Jewish relatives and all her Jewish playmates who had ever suffered some Cossack's insult. To rub her cleanliness in the faces of the gentiles.

Who of course she thought too benighted ever to take her point, but doing it anyway, as much a victim of her own rituals and superstitions as Hector Camerando with his degree-of-difficulty reparations.

Because, for herself, he needn't have bothered. She'd never

have made it an issue between them or thrown it in his face. Sure. She hated the farm, was appalled from the first moment she'd seen it. Which was at night, so how much of its ramshackle and disrepair could she have actually seen? The darkness at the cozy edges of the candlelight was soft, a layered dark of flickering, unfocused textures. Even the chill beyond the thrown heat of their woodstove seemed a sort of complementary, necessary fiction, lending a kind of magic, olly-olly-oxen-free privilege to the room, a port-in-a-storm illusion of harbor. In the morning she could see just how close they'd actually come to shipwreck. What was wooden in the room was splintered, the fragile chairs they sat on just steps up from kindling. The homespun of the curtains that hung above their windows was so dusty it seemed clogged with a kind of powder. Only Marvin, ten or eleven at the time, was excited by their new arrangements. Four-year-old Maxine was frightened by the animal noises. The baby choked on the dust. Ted, as if he'd been born to it, was already out working the barns.

He hadn't told Dorothy a thing. For months he'd been placing and taking mysterious phone calls at all hours. The voices, if she managed to get to the phone before Ted, were mostly unrecognizable to her. Sometimes they were even female, and once or twice she thought they may have been customers from the store. Another time she thought she distinctly recognized Junior's voice. She'd even asked, "Junior, is that you?" but he'd hung up without answering her. Junior was Milton, Herbie Yellin's boy. Nobody knew why he was called Junior. Dorothy had other, less polite names for him. Early on, and for only a very brief time, he'd been the single partner Ted had ever had. Dorothy had never liked him. He was married to a very nice girl and had two beautiful children, but he was a drunk, a heavy gambler, a philanderer, and flirted with every pretty woman who came into the shop. Once, before the holidays, when they'd been very busy and Mrs. Bliss was helping out behind the counter, he even tried to rub up against Dorothy in a disgusting, filthy way.

Now Dorothy wasn't blind. All butchers were flirts. The female customers seemed to expect it and were flattered by it. (It was good for business, even.) Mrs. Bliss had a theory that she'd mentioned to Ted.

"I think butchers flirt because they're always working with meat."

Her husband blushed.

"That's why, isn't it? Ted? No, I'm serious."

"Sure," said Mr. Bliss. "You hit the nail on the head. Some go for the pot roasts, the rest for the chickens."

She would have mentioned the incident with Junior, too, but she was afraid of what might happen. Ted was a gentle man, but it wasn't unknown for partners to use their carving knives in a fit of temper. It wasn't Junior's life she feared for but her husband's. Since he'd touched her she imagined Junior capable of any outrage. If it happened again, though . . .

And that's why she was so bothered by those telephone calls at all hours. Dorothy was frightened Ted might be taking up with Junior again. The gonif had stolen from them once (tricks with the books), and though Herbie Yellin, Junior's father, had made good their losses (or Dorothy might have taken up a carving knife herself and cut him where it would do the most good), she knew he could rob them again. It was in his nature to be a thief, and not just a thief but someone who deliberately went out of his way to betray the people who were closest to him. Look how he treated his wife, or, fallen down drunk, how he must have appeared to his beautiful children. Look what he'd done to Ted, and how he ran to his daddy whenever he got too far behind in his gambling debts. Was it any wonder Mrs. Bliss didn't want him back in their lives?

But whenever she tried to bring up the subject of the calls with Ted her husband just shrugged and denied that there was anything going on and changed the subject. Sometimes he smiled and winked, conveying that if he really was up to something it wasn't anything she needed to worry about.

Then he sprang the farm on her!

Then he told her—it was in the old, ruined farmhouse that first night after the children had fallen asleep—that the thing of it was that it was a black-market operation. He knew he could trust her, he said. It was no big deal, he said. It was 1942, probably already the middle of the war, and time to strike while the iron was still hot. It was the first time they'd really ever had any opportunity to cash in big. Fortunes were to be made in meat. And did Dorothy remember what it was like during the Depression, how no one had the money for the better cuts of meat and the only way they'd managed to get by was by eating up half their inventory? And every independent butcher he knew was into it directly or indirectly. Some were taking under the table for monkey business with the ration books. And some were charging whatever the traffic would bear no matter how hard the OPA tried to hold prices down. And some sons of bitches had given up the butcher profession completely and had become full-time ration-stamp counterfeiters. Now that was *really* a dirty thing to do, and hurt the war effort, and Ted wouldn't touch it with a ten-foot pole. What he was trying to accomplish with his little operation was just to go to the source, *become* the source and set up his own little business. Why let big shots like Swift and Armour and Mr. Hormel Ham soak up all the profits and leave nothing over for the little guy? It was supply and demand, he said. Didn't Dorothy know anything about supply and demand? It was how business did business, he said, and if Dorothy didn't understand that even the war effort worked by that principle, then all he could say was that he was offering her a very valuable lesson. "Well," Ted said, "what do you think?"

"Does Junior Yellin have anything to do with this?"

"Junior's out of it. He found the place. Then all he did was put me in touch with the guy who owned it."

"And took a cut, I suppose."

"He took his commission. He's entitled to his little commission. Even Junior Yellin has a right to live, Dorothy."

This last was not something Dorothy entirely agreed with—the philandering, the gambling, the drunkenness, the lovely wife and beautiful kids, the funny business with Ted's books, the funny business when he tried to try something with her—and although she knew her husband hated anyone speaking ill of his old partner (despite the fact that the no-good had cheated him), she understood that if she found out that Junior still maintained the slightest connection with this new operation, she would say something, she would have to, even if it meant spilling the beans about what had happened to her in back of the case in which the meat was displayed. (Though she understood her husband's loyalty to Junior. She really did. It was the loyalty of family and, in a way, she shared it. The old loyalty of battle stations and circling wagons—all the closed ranks of blood. The world was humiliating enough. You couldn't afford to live in a double-dealing world where you thought you were subject to being humiliated by partners, too. Of *course* old man Yellin had bailed out his boy by making restitution. Of *course* Ted had not broken up their partnership; of *course* it had been Herbie Yellin who had insisted that his son, so ruthlessly charged, so mercilessly done in by a partner who actually took the word of the accountant, an outsider, against the needs of a son who if he futzed the books did so out of necessity—those mounting gambling debts and the high price of his high nature with the floozies and bimbos he kept on the side. You came, you *sprang* to the defense of family. Dorothy understood this and even admired old Yellin for paying them back, then telling them off, and then insisting that it was Junior who had dissolved the partnership. Your dear ones were dear, no matter. Whatever was yours was.

(And if she'd gone to Ted that time and warned him about Junior and that what he pulled on the housewives and customers he had no compunction about pulling on Dorothy, too, then what? Would Ted have had it out with him, or would he have given her his old song and dance about how Junior was an artist, the best man in Chicago with boning knives, paring, carving knives, hacksaws and cleavers, an artist who could trim every last ounce of fat from a steak so that even the T-bones and porterhouses in their display cases, even the stringy briskets, looked like filet mignons, and you couldn't say to an artist what you could say to an ordinary butcher? He loved her, she knew that, but she wasn't so anxious to see push come to shove, never mind what she had told herself about carving knives and the temperaments of outraged butchers.)

It wasn't even the discomfort of their life in the country she objected to, and certainly it wasn't the problematic criminality of Ted's being a black marketeer. She was innocent, and naive, and a woman of valor, but she was a wife, too, after all, and a mother with mouths to feed and babes to protect. What, she should be less than the simplest creatures, a lioness with her cubs, say, or a bear with its? So if she wished for the conclusion to the interval of their life on the farm, it was as much for the benefit of her three children as it was for her husband or for herself. Chicago represented an ideal of progress and comfort. It represented the future. Indeed, life in Michigan seemed so like life in Russia to Dorothy (though she could barely recall her girlhood in Russia) that the idea of Ted's dumping the farm and moving the family back to Illinois seemed as much an ordeal and adventure as contemplating the journey from Russia to the New World must have seemed to her own parents. After only a few months away from the city, Chicago, raised to almost mythic stature, began to take on an atmosphere of enchantment and fable. Mrs. Bliss regaled her children with stories of how water had poured freely from every faucet in their apartment. All you had to do to fill a pitcher for lemonade was turn a tap. A pitcher for lemonade? To run a bath. To run a bath? To flush the toilet! She was a keeper of the flame, Mrs. Ted Bliss. She told them that in Chicago *all* the streets were paved, and the only paths you ever came across were the trails in Jackson Park or the Forest Preserves. Mail, she reported, was delivered by the postman directly to a letter box in the hall. The radio crackled with static only during thunderstorms. You could get all your programs clear as a bell.

It was the public schools, however, that were the city's greatest asset. The different grades weren't all jammed together in a single room, and the children didn't have to share books. Also, she whispered, in Chicago, it was the goyim who were the exception, and there was a synagogue every three or four blocks.

In the end, though, it wasn't Mrs. Ted Bliss's relentless dislike for their farm that sent them back to Chicago. It was that failure of nerve that Ted simultaneously took responsibility for and ventriloquized over to Dorothy that drove them off.

It was the rustlers. He admitted as much to Dorothy.

"Rustlers?"

"What, you think these spindly, broken-down sparrows that pass for cattle around here were hand cared for by Farmer Brown or old McDonald on Michigan Avenue feedlots? They're runts of the litter rustled off the wrong side of a rancher's tracks by gangster gangsters in cahoots with gangster cowboys in cahoots with their gangster rancher bosses who winked their eyes and left instructions to leave the gate open."

She had never heard him so passionate about anything. It was how Ted's high-roller, go-for-broke pals back in Chicago talked, the mavins and machers butting in on the lines outside shows and in fancy restaurants.

It was his failed nerves whistling in the dark.

"I tell you, Dorothy, Junior Yellin himself couldn't trick those beeves out into anything resembling anything respectable as steak or maybe even just ordinary hamburger."

Of the toughs and heavy-lifter moving-men types who came every week or so to drop off their living, stolen, scrawny cattle in exchange for Ted's slaughtered and dressed beef carcasses, the various rounds, rumps, ribs and roasts, shanks, flanks, chucks, and other moving parts of meat, her husband would whisper, shuddering, that they were the *real* black marketeers, an almost anonymous, dark lot of men who seemed only a few steps up the evolutionary scale from the very animals in which they dealt. *They* were the rustlers; dominant males of the herd, *they* were the ones who with something almost like instinct had a nice feel for just which sacrificial cows and steers the ranchers who owned them and collected insurance on them when they disappeared through those now several times cahooted unlocked gates least minded losing.

They were ugly customers and unnerved Mrs. Bliss, too, whenever they appeared on their rounds. To expedite pickups and deliveries they enlisted Mr. Bliss into helping them with the transfers, transforming her handsome husband, once not only president of the Hyde Park Merchants' Association but a prominent member, too, of the Council of the Greater South Side Committee for Retail and Growth—a tribal elder of sorts, if not by nature himself one of the flashy, loudmouth speculators and get-rich-quick bunch, then a solid burgher of a man, at least someone who had the ears of the loudmouths, a man whose approval and interest in them they openly sought and even vied for. And now look at him, Mrs. Bliss secretly thought, down on the farm, a good two-hundred-plus miles from the city of Chicago, bowed almost to the breaking point under the weight of the sides of slaughtered meat he carried, the wet, red blood not only staining his white protective aprons beyond the point where his wife could ever get them clean again but the shirt he wore beneath them, and the undershirt he wore beneath that, too.

"Ted, what goes into one pocket from this black market," Dorothy would tell him, "goes right out the other with what I spend in Clorox and Rinso."

"Dorothy, it's almost 1943. It'll only be a year the war will be over."

But Ted Bliss's formula for a short, three- or four-year war was off the mark, of course.

It was November, and the news from the fronts was bleaker and bleaker. Loss of life in the Pacific and Africa was already too heavy. In Europe, our troops hadn't really engaged the enemy yet. What happened when they finally did was awful to contemplate. What might have been acceptable in a lightninglike war where you got in and got out was one thing, but to continue to be what not even a year ago the papers had already begun to describe as a "war profiteer" was not something Ted Bliss particularly relished, never mind he was making money hand over fist. Also, word was getting out that the quality of his meat (even though everyone knew there was a war on, and that the government was buying up the best cuts for the boys) was going downhill fast. Plus his real fear of the toughs with whom he had to do business. And his fear, too, of the G-men whose pledge it was to shut down operations like his, find the perpetrators, lock them up and throw away the key.

Him? He did these things? The Hyde Park Merchants' Association prez? Some merchant. The merchant of Venice!

Also, there was no denying the fact of how uncomfortable he'd made Dorothy and the children by shlepping them out to the sticks and making them live in East Kishnif the better part of a year.

"I'm going to sell this place," he announced to his family one day in late March.

"You are?" Dorothy said.

"Just as soon as I get a reasonable offer."

"That's swell, Dad," his son Marvin said. "I really miss my friends back in Chicago. I don't fish. You won't *let* me hunt. There's nothing for a boy my age to do up here."

"Well, you'll be home soon enough. I'm sorry. I didn't look before I leaped. I just didn't think. I didn't realize how unhappy I was making you all. I thought you'd adjust, but, well, you didn't. So I'll wait till I find the right buyer who will give me my price, and then just sell the place."

Marvin and Maxine ran up to their father, threw their arms around his neck and kissed him. "Oh, Daddy," Maxine said, "it's just exactly what I wished for." Ted Bliss hugged his two children, then leaned over and pulled Frank up on his lap. The toddler squealed in delight.

"Well, Dorothy," her husband said, "did I give you what you wished for, too?"

"Just what I wished for. You really did, Ted. Hey, thanks a million," said Dorothy, who knew his nerve had failed and just why, and who had been counting the minutes and hours and all the days, weeks, and months till it would.

And who knew, too, who knew nothing of business and wouldn't even learn to write a check for at least another forty or so years that he'd already found his buyer, and that it was Junior Yellin, and that whatever the price was they agreed on would be many thousands of dollars less than what Ted had given for it in the first place.

So Hector Camerando was *her* black market. But one she would hold in abeyance for a while yet, not out of the same cop fear and nerve failure to which Ted, olov hasholem, had been subject (and which she didn't hold against him, honest to God she didn't, not for one minute), but because, exactly like Ted, she was waiting for her price, too. And she had to wait because, quite simply, she didn't know what it was yet.

Had Frank or Maxine wanted for money she'd have withdrawn cash from her S&L and given it to them, whatever they needed. And if they needed more than she had in her account would have closed the account and withdrawn it all, and pressed the money on Camerando, begging him on their behalf to lay it off on the safest, surest, high-odds, long-shot greyhound race or jai alai game he could find, and put it all down for her kids. And if she lost, she lost, he wouldn't hear boo from her. She wasn't, she'd have told him, the most educated person, and wasn't, she'd have admitted, a woman with anything like the sort of knowledge of the world a person her age by rights should be expected to have, yet as God was her witness she'd never bother him again, even though she knew going in there were confidence games—this could be one, she understood that—different scams that occurred, that suckers were born every minute, that you couldn't get something for nothing, that even widows and orphans were vulnerable, especially widows and orphans, often the first to get hurt, but no matter, if worse came to worst, all he could expect from her was gratitude, thanks for having gone to the trouble.

Though thank God they didn't. Frank or Maxine. Want for

money. They had enough. If not rich then certainly comfortable. Even, comparatively speaking, well-to-do. Her son was chairman of the sociology department at the university. Throw in the royalties from the sale of his textbook (more than three hundred university adoptions to date, plus the book was practically required reading and was on almost all the freshman sociology course reserve lists, plus there were copies in almost all the public libraries, plus there were plans for the book to go into a third edition) and you had all the makings of a nice nest egg. Maxine was no slouch either. Her husband had been with the same insurance company for many years and in virtually every one of them was in the running for its highest-earning agent.

So there was plenty to be thankful for, touch wood. The children all had their health. They weren't lame, they had no blood or muscle diseases, they didn't smoke or take drugs, and they were all careful drivers. Donald was smart as a whip, on the dean's list at his school. Judy was pretty. James, who worked for his father, was learning the business. Barry was an automobile mechanic, but to look at his fingernails you wouldn't guess it in a million years. So maybe he wasn't as book smart as his cousins—well, look who'd raised him after poor Marvin died—but he was good with his hands, well, he got that from Ted, and Mrs. Bliss would bet you anything he'd have his own shop one day. Not like most garages, but spic and span, and who's to say, maybe he got that from his grandmother. Well, they were all good kids, she had nothing to complain of in *that* department. They were all of them making their way.

She didn't play favorites. If she had them she'd never admit it, or ever acknowledge, even to herself, which grandchild she'd miss most if all, God forbid, were suddenly taken away. In the love department she was strictly a stickler, steady in her loyalty as the biggest patriot. That was one reason, over the years, she sent everyone the same gift. Never mind age, grades, the value of the dollar, never mind anything, everybody got the same, fair and square, even Steven, no exceptions. What was good for the goose was grease for the gander. Long ago, before Ted passed even, she'd developed a sort of sliding scale based on the particular occasion. Bar and bat mitzvahs, twenty-five dollars; Hanukkah gelt, five dollars; birthdays, ten; grade school, high school, and college graduations, eighteen (for life and luck). For their weddings she gave all her children and grandchildren one hundred dollars, for their anniversaries fifty. Everything equal, no one should think they had an advantage over anyone else.

Well, *almost* everything equal. To a certain extent (this puzzled the kids, but she never explained her reasons) she made individual exceptions. Barry, for example, had never gone to college. Should he be penalized for not graduating, which would put him eighteen dollars behind his cousins forever? At thirty-four, brilliant Donald was still a bachelor. Wasn't that heartbreak enough, did he have to suffer financially, too? So, to make a long story short, the upshot was that when she saw him she sometimes slipped Barry a few dollars on the side until he was even with the rest. And she gave Donald extra money, too, a hundred more than his married brother and cousins, and so on and so forth until everybody was all caught up with everyone else. She kept strict accounts and recorded every transaction in a little black date book. You'd think she was saving receipts for the IRS. To tell the truth, it was a big pain in the neck but, what the hell, it was only money, and what else did she have to do?

Though she had a secret fear that she lived with constantly: Suppose one of them should die before their next mitzvah? How could she make it up to them for all the birthdays, anniversaries, and whatnot they would never live to enjoy? How could she even calculate what she owed them? And it occurred to Dorothy that that's what wills were for, the very idea of inheritance—not to leave your money so that it could be divided up after you died, or pay grief bribes to the survivors. No, not at all. It was to participate, *after you died*, in their celebrations, to live on in their accomplishments and special occasions. Maybe that was what death and the afterlife were all about. Didn't a person make a list of the presents they received, of who sent this and who sent that, just so they could write a thank-you note afterward? People never threw those lists away, they kept them always. Dorothy did. To this day she could tell you, just from referring to her papers, who had given them a particular tablecloth or bedspread or pair of candlesticks, whatever, when they were married. Maybe all immortality came down to was the lists you got put down on when you gave away a present.

But was this a reason to go to Camerando? To put together in

her old old age enough cash to go on some last big spending spree
so that, over and above what she provided for them in her will,
she could make one last grand gesture presenting them, not just
her children, their husbands, their wives, their children, *their* husbands, *their* wives, and so on and so forth, but the entire family,
her sisters and brothers, Ted's, *their* loved ones, all that extended
mishpocheh, with some unlooked for, even uncalled for, auf tzul-
uchan gift. On the occasion of what? Celebrating what? Why, there
wouldn't even be a list they could mark it down on! How, she
wondered, would she even fix on a figure what to send? If she gave
Frank, say, x number of dollars, it wouldn't be hard to fix on the
sum that would be proper to give to Maxine, but after that it got
trickier. After a certain point love and blood didn't come in easily
discernible fractions, and after another it couldn't be understood
not even if you had all the decimal places in the world to work
with!

So her children, who were pretty well fixed and already had
enough money, were out, and the four grandkids who were all of
them making their way, even poor Barry (but she wouldn't play
favorites), were.

This was the problem with holding what Mrs. Bliss didn't even
know was called a "marker," though she well enough understood
that someone like Camerando would expect her to call it in. It
wasn't transferable, and it wasn't negotiable. It was like holding
onto frequent flier miles when you couldn't make up your mind
where to go and weren't sure if you were up to the trip even if
you had a destination.

She obsessed on it, and almost felt like going back to Toibb,
her recreational therapeusisist, to see what she should do. Maybe
she could spend Camerando's money on some new interests.
Though unless someone like Toibb told her what that might be, she
had no new interests. The hard thing, the really rock-bottom tragic
thing, was she had no old interests either. She supposed she was
in her early seventies now, give or take those two or three irrecov-
erable, unretrievable years of Mrs. Bliss's life her mother had so
shamelessly given up to the immigration official. Years, she now
understood, she might have used to better advantage, planting incipient interests, resources she could, in this twilight, or dusk, or
full dark night of her life, have drawn upon now—learned to drive,

perhaps, or read better books so she could use a library card, or gotten more out of the papers, reading the editorials even, the col- umns . . . anything, really, kept a diary, or written her thoughts down in letters.

She didn't get such a kick out of cards anymore, and nothing, not the cruises (though she was scheduled to go on one next month and had already paid her nonrefundable deposit), not food, not the Saturday night entertainments in the game room, not movies, not television, was of much interest anymore.

The truth of it—she should bite her tongue—was that even her family, although it would kill them to hear it, no longer interested her so much. As, at bottom, though it didn't bother her, didn't cause her to turn a hair, or lose a moment's sleep over it, she was sure she no longer was of much interest to them either.

Maybe this was why the whole family—her, Frank, Maxine, even the kids, Barry, James, Donald, Judy—were practically burn- ing up the long distance these days, keeping in touch, wig-wagging their desperate messages of furious reassurance, that all was well, the weather fine—that they loved one another and couldn't wait till the next time they would be together.

She was too old to feel guilty, and supposed herself too near death to count the pennies.

Once or twice she genuinely contemplated suicide. What stayed her hand was the fact that she wasn't much interested in death either.

And another time, because she was practically going batty from boredom, she went to an unfamiliar restaurant and ate a pork chop. She rather liked the flavor but didn't think, as it had taken her seventy-four years (give or take) to eat the first, that she would ever order another.

On still another occasion she forced herself to ride the bus not only into downtown Miami (which she hadn't seen since the night Alcibiades Chitral bought Ted's car), but on through the Cuban and even black neighborhoods. She didn't get off, not even when it came to the end of the line. She paid the driver for her return fare and transferred at the big new mall downtown, where she'd never been and did not explore now, and waited for the bus that would take her back to the Towers.

It was a week after her marathon bus ride (she hadn't peed the whole time she'd been on her expedition, and had had to hold it in all day, not such a big deal because even on long car trips, no matter how Ted might laugh and tease her, she couldn't bring herself to go, or do anything more than make a show of going into the Ladies, not even at the cleanest rest stops or the biggest, most modern, up-to-date Shell stations; what could she do, she couldn't help it, she couldn't force herself to squat over a strange toilet) when Mrs. Ted Bliss found herself by the little telephone table in a corner of her living/dining room area dialing her daughter in Cincinnati. You can imagine her surprise when a woman not Maxine picked up at the other end and said she'd reached the offices of the Greater Miami Recreational Therapeusis Research and Consultants. She hadn't called the number in years. How, she wondered, had she still remembered it?

"Greater Miami Recreational Therapeusis Research and Consultants," the woman said. "How may I help you?"

"Maxine?" Mrs. Bliss said.

"I think you have the wrong number," the woman said.

"Oh, I know," said Mrs. Bliss. "I can't understand it."

"You probably just made a mistake dialing."

"No," said Mrs. Bliss. "I was his patient a few years ago. He didn't have such a big operation back then."

"Who?"

"Dr. Toibb. He didn't have such a big operation. Consultants, secretaries to answer the phones, maybe nurses on call. You're still on Lincoln Road?"

"Yes."

What a piece of work is the mind, thought Mrs. Bliss. How many years had it been? Four, five? This was the trouble living in a climate where there weren't any seasons. You were without landmarks to mark the time—record snowfalls, ice storms, heat waves. Her landmarks were all written down in her little black date book, so she never missed anyone she sent a birthday or anniversary card. (She sent out, she supposed, more than a hundred a year. Nieces and nephews she sent, grandnieces, grandnephews, cousins of all degrees she sent, mishpocheh. And though she made a check by the names of those who didn't send her back, she wasn't smallminded, the next year she sent a card, anyway. In Mrs. Bliss's mind, who couldn't read Hebrew, or, now she was a widow, go often to services, it was a way of keeping up her Judaism, the collective mazel and yontif, all the high holiday greetings of celebratory Jewish life.) But to hold some since-several-years used number in her head without any black book, this was something extraordinary. It wasn't, thought Mrs. Ted Bliss, accidental. It was bashert, maybe even psychiatric. And hadn't she, it couldn't be more than a couple of months ago, been thinking of Toibb?

"So how's Dr. Toibb these days?" asked Mrs. Bliss.

"Didn't you know?" said the secretary. "Toibb's dead."

"Dead? He died, Holmer Toibb?"

"Over a year ago."

"Over a year?"

"He was murdered."

"What? He never! Murdered?"

"Oh, yes."

"He was a physician. They killed a physician?"

"Well, you know, technically he wasn't a physician."

"He was a great healer," Mrs. Bliss said. "A *great* healer."

"The consultants miss him. We all do," the woman said. "I was working here only a few months when it happened. *I* miss him."

"Well, of course," Mrs. Bliss said. "Besides being a good man, healers like him don't come along every day. I feel sorry for his patients. What do they do now?"

"There's others to fill his shoes," the secretary said. "Toibb had foresight. He was no spring chicken, you know. He studied with Greener Hertsheim. He was with him practically from the start of the movement. So he knew. He did. He knew. He had the insight and foresight to bring other practitioners into the practice and give them the benefit of his knowledge. Oh, I'm not saying he expected to be murdered. People always think that's something that happens to the next guy. And more power *to* them, I say! Because what's the use of living if all you do with your life is go around all day with a long face like a scaredy-pants? *That's* no way. A person has to have more of an interest than *thaat*.

"You said you were who?"

"Mrs. Ted Bliss," Mrs. Bliss said.

"And you were Holmer's patient?"

"It's been a few years."

"We'd still have your records. He kept very good records. That was *his* interest."

"My records?" Mrs. Bliss said.

"Well, the notes poor Toibb made on you."

"Did they catch them?" said Mrs. Bliss. "Do they know who did it?"

"They haven't closed the case yet. The detectives still come in from time to time. Do you know what I think? I think you should ask to see one of the consultants."

"Why?"

"Well, you *did* ring this number. And as you say, 'It's been a few years.' And you *were* his patient. And you thought so well of him."

"I'm sorry to hear what happened."

"He was very highly respected."

"I don't understand how he could have been murdered and I never heard about it. Was it in the papers? Was it on the news?"

"Well, that's the thing," this odd but quite friendly woman said, "they're keeping it quiet. It's how they've chosen to operate on this one. They're waiting for someone to slip up. They always slip up."

"Detectives come in? What do they want? What do they do there?"

"Oh, they just nose around. And we cooperate. Well, as much as we can. *You* understand. But not to worry. The therapeusisist/ client relationship is sacred.

"I really think you should make an appointment for a checkup," the woman said ominously.

Mrs. Bliss's first thought when she hung up was to get in touch with Manny. He was the one who'd given her Toibb's name in the first place. The difficulty was she was reluctant to call him. They still saw each other of course. In a community as tight-knit as the Towers they could hardly have avoided running into each other, but the fact was Manny had taken up with other widows by now. With widowers, too. With anyone, really, to whom he could play Dutch uncle, all that wide-eyed, teeming lot of poor, tempest-tossed masses and tired, yearning, wretched refuse.

Really, Dorothy thought, in a kind of way it was as if she'd passed through a sort of second immigrant phase and, sloughing

Manny from the building, taken out final papers. In unconsciously turning to Toibb, for example, deciding to go first class with her troubles, take them professional.

Of course she *missed* Manny. And when she saw him these days, and the helpless, troubled people who looked to him for support, it was quite as if she had dropped into an old neighborhood where she'd once lived. She often longed to tell him how she was doing, and to thank him. He had helped her, he really had, and she could never repay him, but now, in her new, unfocused, listless dispensation, Mrs. Ted Bliss had gone offshore so to speak, moved beyond the three-mile limit of Manny's weak jurisdictionals. Which isn't to say she didn't occasionally feel flashes of a vestigial jealously, short twinges of a peculiar envy, not, she hoped, knew, because others now basked in the attention of the real estate lawyer who, with the death of his wife, had been thrust into an abrupt, sudden eligibility.

Rosie had passed away two years before from a massive coronary explosion.

Mrs. Bliss had gone to the funeral services and, afterward, to offer her condolences to the new widower. Manny's condominium wasn't large enough to accommodate so massive a shivah and they'd had to move it downstairs into the game room. Dorothy, no one, had ever seen anything like it. Not to take anything away from Rosie (though she was a decent, patient woman, everyone knew who the real star of the family was), but the tribute was to Manny. But, Rosie, Manny, those seven days of shivah would come to represent the benchmark of mourning in the Towers, possibly in all Miami Beach. Mrs. Bliss had approached the grieving widower, still a wide, relatively youthful and handsome man—he couldn't have been more than a few years younger than Dorothy—oddly even more virile and distinguished-looking beneath his three- or four-day stubble like a loose gray veil of grief. "Oh, Manny," Dorothy had said, "I'm so sorry. Listen," she'd said, "if there's anything I can do, anything."

"I know, Dorothy. Thank you," he said. And added, "You know what this means? It's taught me a lesson. You're up, you're down. Life's like a wheel of fortune. See, see how the tables have turned?"

Though they hadn't, not really. Manny was still like some

Johnny-on-the-spot with the men and women. If anything, he volunteered even more of his time now Rosie was dead than when she was alive. He'd even been singled out by a rabbi as one of the "just men," one of those holy three dozen on earth who helped keep the good order of life. He was still, that is, on call, but these days Mrs. Ted Bliss had passed out of the range of his influence and was not at all envious of those people who were the beneficiaries of Manny's new second wind, the brighter, even warmer glow of his radiating goodwill, so much as, well, a little sorry for them. They had more sharply defined needs than she, a different order of need—acute, short range, easily dealt with, like heat exhaustion, say. All they needed was to be pulled into the shade, given water, have cool, wet cloths applied to their temples and brows.

Mrs. Ted Bliss, on the other hand, had passed over into a new state of being, existed on a plane different from grief, out of reach of cumulate time's ministering comforts and platitudes. Why, *she, she* had lost not only husband and family and self and appetite (that savored, one-shot pork chop for which she would never again feel a yen) but all urge and interest. The baleboosteh part of herself complete, her house at last in order, and order at last seen for what it finally was: the rule of regularity, habit ground down to the trim, plain, ugly shipshape of the deadened dinky, like all that long, perpetually cared for rectangularity in the Chicago boneyard. Urge and yen and craving subsided, absent from her life. Life absent from her life. So that all she could muster for this season's batch and crop of bereft, forlorn survivors was a pinch of indignation, as if they were suckers of heartbreak, rubes and rookies who hadn't seen nothing yet.

Oy, thought Mrs. Ted Bliss. Oy and oy. Oy, oy, a thousand times oy!

How come then, she thought, that such acceptance and coming to terms was so disquieting, so unsettling when everything the complete baleboosteh could hope for was to have all her decks cleared, squared away, every last hospital corner pulled taut and smooth, as if what life had been all about was preparation for some final white-glove inspection? What, she *didn't* think in terms of a life in the barracks? But, surely, that's what so much of hers had been all about. And now it was as if she'd been presented with a statement, some red-tape thing, complicated, governmental, bureaucratic, vaguely whiplashed through interagency (Part A's uncertain relationship with Part B), like Ted's Medicare bills almost a year after he died—THIS IS NOT A BILL, THIS IS NOT A BILL, THIS IS NOT A BILL—until one day one arrived inexplicably stamped Paid in Full.

So that if they had pressed her she could almost have told them, "Girls, they tell you time heals all things? Time heals nothing. What, you think you're unhappy now? You think because your husband is gone this is the worst, the storm that breaks the camel's back, water in the basement and climbing the stairs, that it's up over the lip of the threshold and coming in under the door in the hall, that it's destroyed the linoleum and already lapping the wall-to-wall, licking high up the legs of the dining room chairs, the mahogany sideboard and credenza, that it's covered the tiles, and slipping down the side of the tub like dirty bathwater, is above the box spring and even with the mattress, is inside the chest of drawers with your things like stockings and underwear left to soak overnight in the bathroom basin.

"Or that the final slap in the face is when the insurance claim comes back marked 'Sorry, not covered, act of God'?

"You think?

"You think so?

"Or from all that pile-on and pile-on of tsuris, the kids' bad grades and the death of friends, your own decline, the failure of beauty, of memory, incontinence, shortness of breath, the inability not just to climb steps but to cross the room without pain?

"And that that's the *worst* that can happen, one by one, or served up like so many courses at a dinner? Or that *that* is?

"You think, you think so? Well, all I can say is wait till *next* year! Because didn't I already tell you you ain't seen nothing yet? No, no, no, girls, there's no such thing as a rock bottom to bottom!"

Though to tell the truth, she wouldn't have told them a word. They couldn't have *dragged* it out of her.

Meanwhile, there was *still* something on Mrs. Ted Bliss's plate. Something left over that, though she knew, or thought she knew, to leave well enough alone, she continued to worry like a loose tooth.

It was what that awful woman had said, the secretary, or nurse, or maybe consultant herself, *whatever* she was who'd answered the phone when she rang Maxine and her head had accidentally dialed the wrong number and put her through to the Greater Miami Recreational Whoosis where Toibb had once had his practice—that he'd been murdered in some high, hush-hush covered-up crime and, more ominously yet, that they still held her records, whatever notes Toibb had written down when she'd spoken to him. She remembered his surprise (remembered it the very second the women mentioned the killing) when he found out she'd known Tommy Auveristas—"Tommy Overeasy" Dr. Toibb had called him—as if he'd discovered both shared some incredibly exotic, important secret that had raised her in his eyes to some new visibility; and recalled now, too, Hector Camerando's sudden arousal to the bait, that at the time she hadn't yet known was bait, when she'd asked him if he knew Auveristas, and how the pay dirt she thought she'd hit had suddenly exploded into his audacious assertions, like a stream of wild oaths, of the power and influence he held in south Florida, and that, moments later, had declined into all those favors and markers he'd thrust into her hands and which, for years, he practically begged her to call in, and which, for years, she just couldn't bring herself to do, seeing it now, suddenly, as out of the blue as Overeasy's name (that's how Mrs. Bliss thought of him now, too) had years before let loose all that skyfull of pay dirt like a gusher of crude, uncapped connection, and which only now she had begun to sort out.

Mrs. Bliss, God bless her, was an old woman now. For a Jew her age she'd been spared a lot. She hadn't lost anyone close in the Holocaust. Indeed, only very, very distant relatives of relatives, people whose names were vaguely known to her but whom she had never met. It was outrageous that anyone should have gone into Hitler's ovens, of course, but that she and her family had been spared was, for Dorothy, one of the few proofs she had that there was a God. On the other hand, fair was fair, He didn't exactly have an exemplary character. Hadn't He cooked poor Marvin's goose for him? Didn't He run His own damn ovens? *Hotter* than Hitler's! Leaving a mother's heart to boil over when He laid His dirty hands on her child. Marvin was lying next to Ted in that old cold, queer Chicago cemetery this very minute. Every time she thought of that it pushed a chill through Dorothy's system even in the Florida shvitz. Why, it was like a ghost story. Marvin had been in the ground even longer than Ted. In a way, thought Mrs. Ted Bliss, that made him not only her husband's senior but her own as well, and had transformed the boy into a sort of ancestor, a death veteran. And that was another proof there was a God. Such magic, such fooling around in the supernatural.

Still, knock wood, she had to admit that for someone who was almost a *very* old lady a lot had been spared her. A lot. Not that she was counting her blessings. What, are you kidding? What blessings? All right, the kids, even with their little handful of troubles, and she had what to eat, shelter, places to go, reasonably good health, kayn aynhoreh, even enough money so she didn't really want for anything, but most people had those things. Except maybe for the good health part, almost everyone in the Towers did.

So why, after she had made that accidental call, did she feel so suddenly fearful and bereft? Why had she had to run to the toilet with the same sort of nervous diarrhea she hadn't experienced since she had worked in the dress shop for Mrs. Dubow when she was a girl? All right, Toibb, a man she actually knew, had been murdered. But so ill at ease? Come on, she'd lost closer every year, and now, at this time of life, every few months practically. In Chicago, the gang was falling by the wayside all over the place, losing their battles to cancer, to heart attacks, to all the dread whatnot of old age. (Even not so old, Irving's boy, Jerry, and Golda's kid, Louis, both dead of AIDS, and though nobody said it out loud, Betty, her distant forty-year-old third- or fourth-remove old maid cousin was thought to be HIV positive.) "I'm telling you," her sister Etta had said when Dorothy had gone north for their sister Rose's funeral last year, "it's getting to be like there was a war." It was at that funeral, so poorly attended—their death-thinned gang—that Mrs. Bliss decided that enough was enough, and that next time she wouldn't be in such a hurry to get on an airplane and fly to Chicago to see someone else she loved shoveled into the ground, particularly if such a sad occasion should take place in winter, or summer either for that matter. In spring, maybe. Indian summer. But she'd been living in Florida too long now. She couldn't take cold weather, or wear herself out in hot, shlepping so many miles, with suitcases, with the formal, constrictive clothing you were expected to wear on such occasions. (People who didn't live there didn't understand. They thought you were putting on airs, pretending to make out you were better than other people, finer, but it was a scientific fact that once your system got accustomed to the Miami climate it wasn't so easy to go back to a harsher one. And anyway, even at her sister Rose's funeral, so poorly attended, not *everyone* was dead. Believe me, plenty stayed away just from being fed up with death. No love was lost between Dorothy and Golda. No matter how hard Ted pooh-poohed the idea, Mrs. Bliss was convinced her brother-in-law's wife cheated at cards. (She'd caught her at it.) Yet, considering she was already in mourning for the fairy, how could she blame Golda for taking a rain check at Rose's funeral? She didn't need her as a reference of course, but Golda's example had been good experience for Dorothy. Besides, to whom was she answerable these days? Her children and grandchildren. If, God forbid, her brothers should die, her surviving sister, but let's not kid anybody here, she would certainly be taking the weather into account. Beyond the tight half dozen of her two children and four grandchildren there were no guarantees. None. She hadn't played favorites, she'd been a loyal family member, but she was depleted and you drew the line somewhere or you died. *Then* what would happen to that tight dozen? So, though she thought she'd never live to see it, she wrote off Ted's side of the family completely, she wrote off most of her own right down to her great-grandchildren. To tell you the truth, she thought that if anything maybe she was a little late in coming around to this thinking. I mean, just look how poorly attended Rose's funeral had been.

Spared a lot or not, if you lived long enough all that drek you thought you'd been spared caught up with you. And then some! Because now look what she'd been hit with out of the blue.

Look here what they were threatening the spotless baleboosteh. The strange woman at Miami Therapeusis with her dark hints about Toibb's murder, and the case is still open, and we have your records and we think you should come in for a checkup.

Threats? At her age? Just when she thought she had cleared all her decks? What did they want from her, anyway? *Her good name?*

SIX

"**I** have an appointment? Dorothy Bliss?"

"Have a seat, Mrs. Bliss, a therapeusisist will be with you in a minute. While you're waiting, if you can fill out these forms, dear. Do you have a pencil?"

"Medicare covers this?"

"It doesn't cost anything to fill out the form."

"There're four pages here."

"Fill out what you can."

"This last page. It looks like a petition."

"We're a grass-roots movement, we're lobbying Congress with the acupuncturers and hypnotists."

Dorothy removed the petition from where it was stapled at the back of the other forms and handed them to the receptionist.

"You're not standing with us, dear?"

"Ich hob dich in drerd," Mrs. Bliss cursed her sweetly.

"Is this your first visit then, dear?"

"Two or three times a few years ago once."

"It shouldn't be long now."

Dorothy sat back down on the leatherette sofa where she'd filled out the forms the woman had handed her. "There's no magazines," she said.

"I keep them back here, dear. Otherwise, people walk off with them."

"They do?"

"You'd be surprised. Or cut out recipes, or rip whole articles from them even. Would you *care* to look at a magazine?" she asked suspiciously.

Mrs. Bliss wondered if this was the same one she'd spoken to on the phone. It didn't sound like her, but she was getting so deaf it was all she could do to distinguish a man's voice from a woman's these days. For the most part she depended on the little whistle a woman's higher pitch set off in her head. It was the queer combination of intimacy and attitude that reminded Dorothy of that other one. She asked her outright.

"That must have been Iris. Iris is with another client now. You'll probably see Milt."

"Milt."

"Milt's one of the best. He bought in as a partner."

No one came in, no one came out. Magazineless, Mrs. Bliss sat in the empty waiting room. The one who wasn't Iris had turned back to do whatever it was she'd been doing before Mrs. Bliss had first given her her name. "I have to do my billing now," she said. The old woman, who could see her at her desk, was surprised to notice that she worked on an old manual typewriter, a portable, not even a heavy upright. She used carbon paper, and typed hunt-and-peck with only her pinky, forefinger, and thumb. Every time she made a mistake she pulled the sheets of typing paper out of the roller, crumpled them, and tossed them into a wastebasket. Then she made a big deal about setting the carbons and fresh paper into perfect alignment and inserting them in the platen.

In the twenty-five or so minutes that Mrs. Bliss waited the phone didn't ring once, and the girl made out only one bill. Then she kicked back and picked up one of the magazines she kept with her in her tiny cubby of an office and idly turned its pages. Either the Greater Miami Recreational Therapeusis Research and Consultants was experiencing a slow period just now, or the fact of Toibb's unsolved murder was scaring clients away. (As it had scared Mrs. Bliss into coming back again.) She wondered if recreational therapeusis still made the all-night call-in shows, or if it, too, had gone the way of all flesh as had the great days of the chiropractor/M.D. wars, the fluoridation/pure drinking-water ones. Though she still slept with her radio turned on all night, she was too deaf to take in very much of what was actually being said.

"I've been here almost forty minutes," Mrs. Bliss said suddenly, going up to the little counter that separated the waiting room from the girl's office. "Where's Milt?"

"He went out for a sandwich," the one who wasn't Iris said.

"I had an appointment."

"It's not down here that you asked to see anyone in particular. We penciled you in for who was available. Iris is busy, Milt's out to Wolfie's for a sandwich. It shouldn't be—See, what did I tell you? That was Milt's buzzer. He signaled he's back in his office."

Dorothy put down to her deafness that she had heard no buzzer. Often, in the Towers, people would literally lean against the buzzer at the entrance to her condo for minutes at a time before she passed by the hall door close enough to hear it. Frank, who'd shown a late-blooming, surprising mechanical aptitude, had recently installed into his mother's telephones lights that flashed whenever the phone rang. He had an illustrated catalog from the Center for Independent Living with maybe three or four hundred separate listings of aids for people who had a use for their special gadgets because of a handicap. He would clip them out of the catalog and send them from Pittsburgh to his mother in Miami Beach with a short note: "For your consideration, Ma: These are for the bath. The bar screws into the tile, you can let yourself down in the tub and hold it to pull yourself up. The friction strips bond to the bottom of the tub with a watertight sealant so you don't slip. I can put them in the next time I come down. Let me know what you think. Love, Frank." "I don't remember if you still have that whistling teakettle. This works for coffee *or* tea. It whistles when the water comes to a boil if you're making tea or by fixing it at the coffee setting when you make coffee. Give me the word and I'll have it sent out. Love, Frank." He called her at least twice a week, but except for these clippings and his brief explanations rarely wrote. He didn't bother with birthday, New Year's, or even Mother's Day cards, so Dorothy was touched by these proofs that he thought of her and filed them away in her bedroom closet on the same shelf she kept her photograph albums. The reason she usually turned down these gadgets was that she had no wish to parade her infirmities before every Tom, Dick, or Harry who might stop by for a cup of coffee or ask to use her toilet. The lights on the phone were something else again. People knew she was deaf, and anyway how often did the phone ring on the rare occasions when someone was in her apartment?

Still, when the not-Iris one indicated that Milt was back in his office, she wondered how many times she had missed visitors by not having some special sort of light that flashed throughout the condo when people were at the door? Nah, she thought, it wasn't worth the convenience if you had to live out your life in a rigged environment.

"I didn't see anyone come in, even."

"Oh, he didn't come in *here*," the girl said. "Milt's office is next door. This is Iris's suite. The consultants use it as a waiting room for *all* the clients. As you go out, it's the first door on your left."

Milt's name wasn't on the door, or a legend to indicate that it was part of the Greater Miami Recreational Therapeusis Research and Consultants organization. Indeed, it didn't even have a number, and for what was supposed to be an office in an office building was about as anonymous as a spare bedroom in an apartment building.

Dorothy's first thought was that Toibb could have been murdered here, or behind any one of the blank-looking doors up and down the long corridor.

There wasn't a buzzer. She wondered if she should knock first or just open the door and go in. She wondered if she should go in at all. And was about to turn, was in fact already partway around and starting to move off when the door opened and she was confronted by a large, broad man standing in the doorway, his head with its dark, thick hair inclined downward as he rifled through some papers on a clipboard that appeared—she recognized her blunt handwriting—to be the forms Mrs. Bliss had filled out in GMRTRC's waiting room.

How did they work that one, Dorothy wondered.

"Come in," the man said and, assuming her compliance, was already headed toward a chair behind a desk Mrs. Bliss instantly recognized as the same one Holmer Toibb had sat behind years before.

How can I know this? she asked herself, and she answered, How did my fingers know his number when I was dialing Maxine that time?

"Dorothy, what'd you do with the petition?" Milt said, still gazing downward and looking very closely, like someone terribly nearsighted, for that last sheet she had pulled from the back of the forms.

"I decided not to sign it."

"Why? It's important."

"I didn't want to get involved," she said, staring straight at him and pointedly addressing him as Junior.

Because as it happened, "Milt" was Junior Yellin, né Milton, Ted's former partner, Herbie Yellin's kid. "Milt" was Junior Yellin, the new nickname crowding out the older one. He was Junior Yellin, the butcher book futzer. *That* Junior Yellin. The Junior Yellin turned realtor and, later, farmer in his own right when he bought back her dead husband's spread (if that's what you called a black-market slaughtering house) for a fraction of what Ted had given him for it in the first place. Junior Yellin, the handsome gutter boulevardier and drunk, gambling man and philandering father of two who'd once felt up Mrs. Ted Bliss herself right there in her husband's shop when she was helping out behind the counter, behind her behind behind Ted's back before Ted's customer.

She blushed to remember it, felt a sort of intense, localized internal heat slide through her face that only grew warmer as she realized that even with *their* shared history he didn't know her from Adam.

She couldn't have said which humiliated her more, that he hadn't recognized her, that she should be consulting someone she knew to be a crook who over the years had cost her family thousands, or that she was in the presence of the only man beside her husband ever to have confronted her sexually in the whole history of her life as a woman.

Was this some new fraud (not that this time around he'd set up as a recreational therapeusisist; she knew of course that *that* was a fraud), but his failure to acknowledge his name by so much as a blink? Was the new fraud the complete annihilation of his own old self? Was he wiping his slate? Would he no longer carry baggage for his former Chicago, Las Vegas, and Michigan farm-cum-abattoir lives? Without quite realizing why (and all this—her surprise at discovering him, her complicated humiliation and shame, her new wonder—taken in in an instant), Mrs. Bliss was overcome by a depression and sadness unlike anything she'd ever known—unlike mourning, unlike bad news, unlike trouble, unlike the recent, piece-meal unraveling of her old confidence and well-being, and the re-mains of the kickless, disinterested life she allowed herself to play out in her kickless, disinterested exile.

It was almost as if, she made a stab at explaining herself to herself, she were not so much furious at as jealous of this new man. He'd been Milton Yellin; he'd been Junior; was now Milt—all his a.k.a.'s subsumed in discrete avatars: butcher, flirt, bum, partner-in-bad-faith, black marketeer, and, now, recreational therapeusisist in a long white coat like an actual doctor's. But no. Now she looked closer. It wasn't a doctor's white lab coat at all. It seemed rougher, heavier. Why the son of a bitch, it was one of his old butcher's jackets!

Mrs. Ted Bliss glared at him, the flush of shame she'd felt ear-lier when she remembered his having groped her gone now and the warmth converted into a sort of angry energy as she collected the features of her face rather like a telescope collects light, and attempted to project them at him as she willed him to recognize her.

Whatever she was sending, Milt wasn't receiving, and for a moment Dorothy wondered whether she had the right man and, for another moment, worried that, even if she did, whether she were so very changed, her good looks so lost to her that she might have appeared now like someone damaged in an accident or burned in a fire.

"It's Dorothy," she said.

"Yes, Dorothy, I know," he said, "what can I do for you?"

"No," she said, "Dorothy *Bliss*. Ted's wife."

The butcher/therapeusisist looked at her closely, almost ex-amined her.

He don't look so changed, but he's old, she thought. His eye-sight ain't good and he's too vain to wear glasses. Whatever shame she'd felt, whatever anger, she relented. Pity broke the fall of her resentments, she buried her hatchets.

"*Teddy* Bliss?" he asked, astonished, and, or at least Dorothy thought so, overcome by something closer to real fondness than genuine nostalgia. "*My* Teddy Bliss? Oh, God, Dorothy, sit, sit. It's been a thousand years."

"More than forty," Mrs. Bliss said, and now it was Junior who was blushing, perhaps remembering the precise terms of their queer old relationship. She thought there was a sort of moisture behind his eyes. What, was he going to break down and blubber? It was several seconds before he spoke. "I was sorry to hear about his death," Junior Yellin said (for it was as Junior, not Milt, that he spoke). "I was shocked, shocked. I was out of town and couldn't get to a phone. Did you get my card?"

No, she didn't get his card. She didn't get it because he'd never sent one. She knew because she had painstakingly written out thank-you notes to everybody who had. She still had every letter and condolence card anyone had ever written to her when Ted died. They were filed away in shoe boxes in the same closet she kept her photograph albums, and Frank's little notes, and all her other personal papers.

"It must have been awful for you. Well I know from my own dad, cancer's no picnic."

"Yes, I heard," said Dorothy. "You have my condolences."

"Yeah, he was a good man, the greatest dad a kid could have. Well, *you* know. You probably recall when I had some trouble with Ted's books that time. My behind could really have been in a sling if Dad hadn't been there for me. He was a great dad, a *great* dad. Between you, and me, and the lamppost, he was a greater dad than I was a kid. You're not contradicting me, I see. The motion carries.

"Hey, will you just listen to me? Going on about *my* troubles, *my* tragic flaws and little circumstances. Looks like I haven't learned anything over the years, looks like I'm not only back at square one but that I never left it. I'll let you in on a little secret, Dot—does anyone else still call you that?—the reason why is square one's where I live. It's practically my home town, square one. Square one zip, visitors plenty. I'm not ashamed to say this on myself even if I am a fellow almost in his seventies.

"Because the secret of life is not to change, Dot. Never. Never ever never. To thine own self be true, do you know what I mean? I'm speaking as a therapist now, so the rest of this is on the meter."

Some therapist, thought Mrs. Ted Bliss. Oh, yes, she thought, I can just see that. I can't wait to tell the children. I got a therapist tells me I should go live on square one. She had to laugh. Despite he was a momzer and gonif there was something almost charming about him. There always had been. That was probably why Ted had been taken in by him so often. Vaguely he reminded her of some of the Latins.

"So, Dorothy," he said, "I haven't had a chance to look at your chart yet, so can you just fill me in on this a little? How may I help you, dear?"

Well, that was a stumper, thought Dorothy Bliss. How could he help her, this guy who all along had helped only himself? What was she supposed to tell him, make restitution? See to it restitution's in my hands by five o'clock, first day of business next week, or else? She had to laugh. She'd been crazy to come. What'd she been thinking of? Well, the murder, but why did she suppose anyone could think she'd have been the least bit implicated in something like that? She was no sophisticated lady, but even Mrs. Bliss understood she didn't fit the profile. She was the longest shot in the world, and gave herself high marks in the innocence department. Murderers, she knew, would have to come to their calling moved by passions she could never even begin to understand. Just look how easily a putz like Junior found higher ground if not in her estimation—he was a liar, he'd lied to her not three minutes before about something so low on his priorities as a seventy-five-cent sympathy card; she did not esteem him—then in her too flimsily swayed judgmentals. Why, she'd found him *charming!*

The question sprawled open before them: How might he help her? Well, he couldn't, but she was too much the deferential man-pleaser, even at her age, to say as much.

"Oh," said Mrs. Bliss, "I'm just getting old, I guess. There's nothing anyone can do about that."

"Let's see your hands, Dot!" Junior Yellin said.

"My hands."

"Yes, please. If you don't mind."

"You read palms?"

"No, no, of course not. I have to look at your nails. It's something we do."

"Toibb never looked at my nails."

"Toibb *trained* me," he said. "I studied with Toibb who studied with Greener Hertsheim. This is like a what, a dynasty. I want to help you, Dot. We go back. Whatever I may have been in the old days, I'm a solid RT man. I'm highly regarded in the field. Didn't I already reveal to you the secret of life?"

At that minute he looked stunningly defensive. He held out his hands, waiting to receive hers.

My hands are one of my best features, Dorothy thought. If he's looking do I bite my nails, I don't. It's a disgusting habit, I never acquired a taste for it. She placed her hands in the old philanderer's. He's a doctor, she thought, it don't mean nothing. Still, when he took them, Dorothy was conscious of every liver spot, each pellet like a small devastating explosion of melanin that traced the ancient fossil record of her skin, age locked into the soft geology of her flesh like rings on trees. She sat exposed and could not have felt more vulnerable if she'd shown him her sagging breasts. Hey, she thought to comfort herself, what's he, a spring chicken? But sat, tentative and alert, ready to pull them away in an instant, like a child whose hands hover above her opponent's in a game of Slap. And self-conscious, too, in some loopy fool's sense, as though each dark freckle felt a faint, dizzyish sting of warmth and pleasure.

He's going to bring them to his lips and kiss them, thought Mrs. Ted Bliss, and was ashamed for the both of them.

He's going to, he is, she thought, and was transported back almost half a century to when he stood behind her as she stood behind the display cases in her husband's meat market, his hands down low, hidden under his butcher's apron, folded they must have been, as though he were warming them, but goosing her really, ramming them up under her behind, pushing and trying to separate the cheeks of her tochis, using only his knuckles in a kind of weird foreplay or, as she would see years later in educational nature programs on public TV, like males of one or another species in a kind of sexual butting. She had not realized till now how much her memory of this moment had persisted.

"Hold still, please," said Junior Yellin, and continued to draw her hands closer to his face.

He's crazy, she thought, and was about to jerk them away just as they came within range of his limited focus and Junior began to examine them. Oh, she thought, it's only his eyes: astigmatism, not love. And that half century she thought she'd lost came back to her again. In spades, compound interest. It was exactly like waking from a perfect, to-scale, very realistic dream in which she was a child again, only to find that she wasn't a child, merely herself, with her aches and pains and duties, an old, old lady as distant and distinct from that careless, romping, laughing child as the conscious state is from the sleeping one.

Not only wasn't he going to kiss her, but the incident in the butcher shop had never, at least for Yellin, even occurred. It was astonishing to her that she should feel actually rebuffed, two-timed, done dirty, played for a fool.

Meanwhile, Junior separated each finger, raised it by a knuckle, brought it close, made soundless this-little-piggy's.

"What are you doing?"

"I'm looking for Beau's lines."

The term sounded vaguely nautical. "What's Beau's lines?" asked Mrs. Bliss.

"They're transverse grooves in the nail plate, and they're caused by various systemic and local traumatic factors."

"I've got Beau's lines?"

"I won't be able to tell until you take off your nail polish. Here," he said, "I keep a bottle of remover right in my desk. Use this."

"What does it mean if I have them?"

"Well," Milt said (for it was as Milt he spoke, he had gone back into the Milt mode), "it's just this sort of ballpark test we do to give us some idea of a patient's general health."

"Patient? I'm a patient? Toibb, may he rest, never called me a patient. I was more like a client than anything else. He wouldn't even let me call him Doctor, and all the times I saw him he never searched me for Beau's lines either."

"He never examined you for Beau's lines?"

"Never."

"Recreational therapeusis has come a long way since Toibb's day, you know."

"He studied with Greener Hertsheim," Mrs. Bliss said. "You studied with Holmer Toibb. It's like a dynasty you said."

"Greener Hertsheim was a giant," Milt said, "a very great technician, but the world don't stand still, Dot."

"You're telling me," said Mrs. Ted Bliss, who in the fifteen or twenty minutes she'd been in the crackpot's office had been whiplashed through time, fifty years gone here, another twenty or so taken away there (those years as a child in the dream), plus all the compounded-in-spades interest that had been dumped on her by Yellin's forgetfulness.

Or what if it hadn't happened? What if it were Mrs. Ted Bliss who out of pure raging distaste for the man—the way, again and again, he'd taken in Mr. Ted Bliss—had manufactured the incident behind the meat case? What would *that* mean? (Could this be what Frank and Maxine—oh, she listened; she hadn't always followed, but she listened; listened? she'd *basked!*—home on vacation from their colleges had meant with their discussions about high things like psychology, fancy-shmancy tricks the mind couldn't help playing on itself. Sure, all right, she understood, but the minds her kids talked about were usually inside the heads of some pretty strange customers. Did that stuff work for the mind of a baleboosteh?) Either way, if it happened and she was sore because Junior had forgotten all about it, or if it hadn't happened and it was only her head looking for revenge, what did that say about her? Either way, she didn't see herself getting out of this one alive. (Though of course she hoped that the filthy things she remembered had actually happened. Sure, let it be on his head, not hers!)

"Okay," Junior said (as far as Dorothy was concerned the bum was Junior and would stay Junior), "we'll forget about the Beau's lines for now. If you could give me a rough idea what's been bothering you."

Oh, boy, Mrs. Ted Bliss thought.

Because she couldn't. Even if she understood her restless heavy-heartedness she couldn't have begun to explain it, wouldn't have wanted to discuss with someone like Junior Yellin the deep, deep misery of the last few years. She couldn't have told Manny about it, or anyone close to her in the Towers. She couldn't have told the gang. She couldn't tell Frank, or Maxine, or even her still-living sisters and brothers. If she still even had any. And for an actual moment really couldn't remember if she had. She'd lost track of who died—so many had died; she'd stopped thinking of "lost" lives—and who still hung on. It was too awful, too awful to live so diminished, it was too awful, such unhappiness too shameful to share. Maybe, she thought, maybe if Marvin still lived, maybe she could have explained it to him. Maybe, sitting by his side as he lay on his deathbed in the hospital, maybe she could have tried to decipher it for him. He'd been unhappier than all of them, after all. Maybe only poor suffering Marvin could have taken it in.

Wasn't it strange, Mrs. Bliss thought, her old age? She wasn't thinking of her beauty. That had been gone years. It wasn't frailty or the breakup of memory. She didn't forget the names of her children or confuse a grandchild with an old pal in Russia, a fellow in the building with her dead husband. Her disabilities had nothing to do with the flow of blood in her head. How could she explain to anyone that her great regrets and disappointments had to do with the mistakes she had made? The sale of the Buick LeSabre, the failure to carry through on her determination to visit Alcibiades Chitral in his prison. How could she explain her fascination with Tommy Auveristas or all that unfinished business with Hector Camerando and the marker she failed to call in and which Camerando himself (on the increasingly rare occasions she saw him hanging about the Towers) had long since failed to mention to her?

He was going to charge her anyway.

Whatever he did, or whatever he failed to do for her, whatever advice he did or did not give her, she would be billed. Forget old times—he had, the son of a bitch—forget the money the momzer had already stolen or charmed out of her husband, his deliberately cooked books and wiseguy's crooked real estate deals, let alone what he'd once tried to do to her in her husband's place of business—oh, he'd done it, he'd done it all right; she hadn't made that up, she wasn't *that* far gone—a bill would be presented, payment on service, and, old times or no old times, it would be a stiff one and, forget they went back, all the stuff that had happened, that he knew her when or she knew him, and without a dime's worth of discount, and that's just when she saw his sign—WE DO NOT VALIDATE PARKING TICKETS!—and decided, All right, that's it, this rotten Moishe Kapoyr is going to give me my money's worth!

"Milt," she said, "forgive me but I can't help remarking, the last time I was here Holmer Toibb told me his patients had to be in perfect health before he'd consent to see them. He said I first had to see a doctor and get an evaluation. You don't go by this rule?"

"Dorothy, Dorothy," Junior said, an edge of disappointment with her in his voice, "didn't I ask to see your Beau's lines? Didn't I offer you nail polish remover from my desk drawer?"

She held out her left hand.

"What?" Junior said.

"Go ahead," said Mrs. Bliss.

As he removed the polish from Mrs. Bliss's ring finger, Dorothy leaned back, shut her eyes, pretending to luxuriate in his ministrations.

"Looks good," Junior said. "No transverse striations. You're fit as a fiddle."

"You can tell this by examining one finger? You don't have to look at the others?"

"I extrapolate."

"Oh," Dorothy said, "you *extra*polate." She held out her right hand. "I'd like a second opinion."

He brushed Cutex across her thumbnail.

This time Mrs. Bliss watched him critically, appraising his technique and hoping he got the impression that she saw something menial in what he was doing, a man his age—almost in his seventies my eye, thought Mrs. Ted Bliss, he should live so long he sees seventy again—who instead of buffing old ladies' fingernails ought to be retired with the other alter kockers.

Though if she embarrassed him he never let on. If anything, he seemed quite happy to tell her she'd passed her Beau's lines test with flying colors, that she didn't sport a single Beau's line. As of today, he said, she was spotless, pure as the driven snow, clean as a whistle Beau's line-wise. Despite the fact that she didn't trust him as far as she could throw him, she was pleased to hear it.

"He asked what were my interests, Holmer Toibb," she said. "He had me make a list. I forgot to bring it, so I recited it for him," she said, and thought, it's strange, you know? She thought, I didn't forget to bring it. I brought it. I was sore at him. Sometimes, for a minute, I'm not always sure who's dead, who's alive, and here's a lie I told years ago I repeat word for word practically.

"What are they?" Junior asked.

"My interests?"

"Yes."

"I don't remember," she admitted dully. "Whatever they were they're gone. I don't have them anymore."

"I'm sorry," Junior said, and Mrs. Bliss suddenly felt a little better about Milt, or Milton, or Junior, or whoever he was. It wasn't his sympathy. He was a crook and crooks didn't feel sympathy. If they could they wouldn't be crooks anymore. So if it wasn't sympathy, what was it? What it was, she thought, was probably only regret. She'd failed to take him seriously. He'd warned her never to change. This was his considered therapeusisist's opinion. It was on the meter. If she'd lost her interests she'd changed. His regret was she'd failed to live according to his secret of life.

"I'd have a chart, wouldn't I?" said Mrs. Ted Bliss. "I know he took notes. The interests I told would be in my records." Actually, she'd forgotten why she'd made the appointment, her original reason for coming, but she was very excited.

And why not? Here she was, doing heart-to-heart with someone who'd known her when. When she lived in Chicago. When she was a beauty. When she still had a husband. When she was the mother of three living children. When. If she'd never trusted him, if he'd taken everyone in a dozen times over if he'd taken them in once, well, even that had to count for something. *When.* This strange man who said he believed in changelessness but who had himself changed, making himself over and over through his shifting avatars, his continuous changings and callings—butcher, realtor, black marketeer, farmer, recreational therapeusisist. (My God! she thought. Like Ted! Who'd been almost all of those things himself. Not a recreational therapeusisist of course, and not a realtor though he had once been a landlord. My God! she thought, my God!) A man with a single unchanging strand run through his being like character—the furious ad hoc course he pursued, opportunistic as a refugee fleeing for his life. She felt an odd tenderness for him then, for just a moment, come and gone like gooseflesh.

She remembered why she'd come and, though she knew the answer, asked him a question as devastating as it was pro forma, asking it disinterestedly as a good detective.

"Milt," Mrs. Ted Bliss asked him, for it was as Mrs. Ted Bliss she spoke, not as Dorothy, not even as Mrs. Bliss, "did you kill Holmer Toibb?"

"What? Did I—What did you say, what did you say to me? What are you, crazy?"

"No, no," Mrs. Ted Bliss said, "you don't understand. I didn't say 'murdered.' You wouldn't murder anybody. I mean, what is it they say on TV? 'Death by misadventure'? 'Manslaughter'? Something in the second or third degree. Self-defense even."

"Boy oh boy," Yellin said, "do *we* have a lot to work through!"

"It's all right," she said. "I was only asking. I'm sure you had nothing to do with it, that you bought into the practice fair and square."

He had set her mind at ease. He really had. Though she couldn't have explained it, she had asked him the question out of duty to and respect for Ted, to clear not her husband's name so much as his character, who only seconds before she had seen trailing amiably along in this fellow's careless footsteps. She was completely satisfied by Junior's answer, reassured as much by what by second nature he immediately realized he stood to gain by her mad question as by his outrage. Indeed, Mrs. Bliss was no longer sure there had even *been* a murder, that that Iris hadn't made the whole thing up on the spur of the moment, told her the bobbe mysehs just to get Dorothy to come in.

Sure, she thought, a trick of the trade. What fools old people were! The crazy things they fell for! Wisdom? You thought *wisdom* came with the territory? It was a myth of the young. Only terror came with the territory. The young were stupid and the old were terrified.

There ought to be a law, she thought, against all the song and dance they foist on you if you live past sixty. The victims they turn you into, the scams they run. It was on all the programs. Bunco squads working around the clock every day of the year didn't make a dent in it. They were easy pickings, old folks. Mrs. Bliss was, easy pickings. Old as she was, she could have been born yesterday.

The Greater Miami Therapeusis. What an operation. It was so shabby, you'd never believe how shabby. She was like a visionary now, the almost deaf and varicose goddess, shabby herself, the former beauty who disgraced bathing suits and, over the years, had paid out a small fortune in hard cash plus tips for swimming lessons to various lifeguards and cabana boys but who had never learned to swim, or maybe never even had the knack for it, ludicrous, suspicious in pools, who always wore clogs to keep herself above the unseen dirts, the terrible sediment of pee and scum and hair and scabs settled at their bottom there, at once repelled and fascinated by the mystery of water, the disparity between its clarity and weight, her very lightness in it impeded by its unseen resistances as, in inner tube and water wings, she moved her arms to the Australian crawl, not even omitting to take a breath every other stroke as she slowly mimed her way across the shallow end of the pool; she, Mrs. Ted Bliss, laughingstock, and good sport, too, consciously playing this holy clown for all the visiting grandkids, gin rummy contestants, and kibitzers gathered there, as much perhaps for the exhilaration of it as the attention, it being a great comfort to her wrapped in a riddle of water to know that anyone might know she knew she was in over her head and depth even at this low end, and would jump in and save her if it ever became necessary; she, Mrs. Ted, suddenly sighted as an oracle or priestess, seeing and knowing and understanding all, everything, her heart breaking because she knew that Toibb had not been murdered, that he'd met his death as almost everyone met their deaths, by natural causes—heart attack, cancer, a bad fall resulting in a broken hip, a slipup on the operating table—*natural* causes; that it had been only a whim, a cheap ruse, desperate Iris's desperate move on just another silly old lady to perk up a moribund business.

What had taken her so long? Why hadn't she caught on during that first, infuriating phone call? How could she not have seen through all the shabbiness right down through its full-of-malarkey, melancholy roots to the fundamental, underlying bedrock shabbiness that supported it? She should have known the minute she saw the manual typewriter, or the hunt-and-peck way the presumptive secretary had used it, or when she learned that the girl kept the magazines (if, in fact, there had ever been more than the one the girl was reading) behind the desk with her. Gypsies, they were gypsies and con men the lot of them, Iris, not-Iris, Junior Yellin. Even dead Toibb was a gypsy. Well, they all were, up to and including old Greener Hertsheim himself probably.

It was plain as the nose. She was a visionary now. Recreational therapeusis was a sham, fodder for old call-in shows. She was a visionary now and she knew. She knew *everything*. (She even knew the character actor—speaking, for example, of good sports and holy clowns, she had become everyone's ecumenical, cutesy-wootsy, Yiddishe mama and bobbe.) Sure, she thought, some visionary.

So why was she enjoying this so much? Why had she agreed to make another appointment with Junior Yellin in a week, sooner if there was a last-minute cancellation and he could squeeze her in earlier?

Why? Because she'd get a kick out of it, that's why. The wild-goose chase she'd take him on. It was worth it. It *was*. Every penny she wouldn't pay him when he submitted his bill. He could stand on his head, or send her letters from lawyers. Just let him try. Lawyers? Two could play at *that* game. She could always dust off good old pro bono Manny from the building. (Of whom it was said, though Dorothy—being herself of a generation of a different age, a generation when gender did not pit itself against gender, when men, throwing up their hands, might very well have exclaimed "*Women!*" but meant nothing more by it than that they were a difficult sex to read, while it would have never occurred to the ladies to make any such pronouncement—"*Men!*" in her day meaning something exactly the opposite, that they were all entirely too easy, the poor, simple, bumbling, babied dears, to understand, there being nothing more harmful in them than their set ways and peculiar male crotchets—couldn't quite bring herself to believe it, that he was seeing someone now, had become, less than a full year after Rosie's epic, historical shivah, an available man.)

He told her to dress casually and to wear comfortable shoes, and that meanwhile he would hunt up her chart in the files and see what that was all about.

It was worth it and, believe it or not, she went away happy.

A coincidence occurred.

Just as she had last time left her therapeusisist's office on Lincoln Road and, waiting for her bus, spotted Hector Camerando, so did she this time, too. This time, however, she didn't wave. The opposite in fact. Seeking to call no attention to herself, she forced her expression to remain fixed in place, her attitude one of suspended engagement, the neutral look of someone, well, waiting for a bus.

It was, she reflected, an odd position to be in, as though, by seeking to evade confrontation, it was Camerando who held her marker rather than she his.

It was apparent to her, however—her inspired visionaries were still upon her, her prescience and magic clarities—that Camerando himself was attempting to steer clear. He crossed the street, she saw, at very near the same pace and angle he'd crossed the street last time, and wore (allowing for subtle evolutions of fashion) the same sort of clothes as last time, too. Then she realized (no, knew, because if those high clarities she'd experienced at Junior Yellin's slanted her self-awareness backward in time, she'd been bombarded, too, with perfect memory maps in sharp, precise relief) that it was the same time of day, as well.

But if this were a contest in mutual, studied avoidance, well, it was no contest. Camerando, a kind of gangster and man of the world, was so much better at it than she was that despite herself it became too embarrassing for Mrs. Bliss to keep up. She was, as it were, the first to blink.

She greeted him almost as he passed her.

So it shouldn't be a total loss she kidded herself that she did it because all these coincidences and circumstantials—the same reason for her being on the corner of Collins and Lincoln Road this time as last, his crossing at the same corner just as she was waiting for the bus, his wearing this year's version of the same snappy clothes he'd worn that year, the fact that it had been of him she'd been thinking the other time they'd met like this and, what she didn't acknowledge till now but knew she'd known from the moment she'd spotted him—that he was coming from the same place as he had come from then—of their twice meeting this way struck her as so unusual that they would be interesting to him, too.

"Gee," said Mrs. Ted Bliss, "how come we always run into each other like this? You got a special friend down here, Señor Hector?"

She thought he was going to strike her. That's how angry he seemed. Indeed, so violent was the shift in his expression, its explosion from some vaguely impatient neutrality of disengagement into feral, sudden alarm, that it was as if he *had* struck her. As she, Mrs. Bliss saw, had struck him. He even raised a finger to his lips as if to see if she'd drawn blood.

"Oh," said Mrs. Bliss, "I didn't mean to startle you."

"What?" he said.

"I'm sorry," she said, "it was like you were a million miles away. I didn't mean to startle you."

"No, no," Camerando said, "not at all. It's good to see you again, Dorothy Bliss."

Mrs. Bliss—those crystal clarities, transparent, fluent as glass—

saw what he was doing. He was collecting, composing himself. She saw what she had done. She had drawn blood.

Then he did something astonishing. He sat down beside her on the bus bench. Even when he'd spoken so rudely to her in his car, when he'd come to her door to give her the money he said she'd won on a bet he'd put down for her at the dog track, when she'd seen him in the corridor at the Towers that time and ducked into a neighbor's apartment to avoid him, even then she had never felt so fiercely pressed and intimidated by a man. Compared to this, his looming, heavy presence, Junior Yellin was a piker, his goosing her behind a freezer case mere kid stuff.

"Oh," said flustered Mrs. Bliss, at a loss for words whose thoughts were so piercing, "you don't have your car today? You're riding the bus?"

Camerando looked around to see if the coast were clear. Leaning in toward her, he lowered his voice. "I have my car," he said so softly that Mrs. Bliss had to strain to hear him. "It's in its customary parking space. Well, you've seen where I park. It's very convenient. A cop watches it for me."

He's paying me back, Mrs. Bliss thought, all her clear certainties on her like a head scarf. It's my marker. He thinks he owes me. I don't know why, it isn't honor, it isn't anything. Maybe it's superstition. Sure, she thought, it's the marker. He wants to be done with me. He's going to pay me off big.

"You got me dead to rights, Mrs.," Hector Camerando said. "I see a woman down here. Her name is Rita de Janeiro. This is only her stage name."

"Please," she said. "Mr. Camerando." It was her stage name, Rita de Janeiro? She didn't want him to tell her her two-feet-on-the-ground name, her floor or earth name. She didn't want him to tell her anything. She didn't care to hear his secrets. What, this was how he was going to pay her off? This was what the street value of her marker came to? She'd have been better off with the cash. And besides, now she knew what she'd stalled him for she finally decided what her payoff *should* have been.

She heard him out, but barely listened to Hector Camerando where he sat beside her on the bench in the little wooden bus stop shelter whose vague simulacrum of a confessional she wouldn't have noticed even though she understood that what she was hearing was a confession and that he offered it to her not so much in the spirit of closing the books as to someone in authority in whom he'd vested an almost magical power of forgiveness and amnesty. No one, not Frank, not Marvin on his deathbed, not Ted on his, had ever spoken to her like this.

"She's a topless dancer. She makes me crazy, she drives me wild. Did you see *The Blue Angel*? Emil Jannings played a good part in that picture. He was an important professor but he fell in love with a nightclub singer, Marlene Dietrich. He'd do anything for Marlene Dietrich, anything. She took him for all he was worth, but all she ever did was make a fool out of him and give him the horns.

"I'll tell you something about myself. I'm not a professor. I don't live with my head in the sky. Well, you know from personal experience what I can do. With the jai alai. With the pooches. Dollars-and-cents-wise, I turn water into wine. I got so much juice and clout I have to watch myself.

"Now I want you to understand something, Mrs. B. Excuse me, but I was never particularly horny. I was never particularly orientated to a behind or a leg or a bust line. Excuse me, but I was never *particularly* orientated even to the big C or any other of the female parts and features—the eyes, the hands, the teeth, a smile, the skin. For me it wasn't even the whole person I was interested in.

"What I'm talking about, and I think *you'll* understand this, is general passion, consuming lust."

"I don't understand it," Mrs. Bliss said.

"I mean, of *course* Rita de Janeiro is her stage name. Oh, I don't mean it had to be Rita de Janeiro. That's just a flag of convenience, that's just what her and her manager agreed on. It could have been anything. It could have been Mrs. Ted Bliss."

Mrs. Ted Bliss winced.

"She'd just had her first period when she started. So of course she had a stage name. The truant officer would have reported her otherwise. And they wouldn't just have shut that place down,"—he pointed toward a small brick building on the other side of Collins Avenue, undistinguished except for the fact that it looked more like a Chicago saloon (down to a high rectangular window built into the side of one wall like a wildly offset postage stamp) than

Miami's usual stucco, faintly iridescent pastel, mother-of-pearl, plaster-of-paris structures—"they'd of burned it.

"Hey," Camerando said, "I'm not kinky. I don't have nothing for little girls. Only this little girl. Only Rita."

"She's what, twelve?"

"Twelve when she broke into the business," Camerando said. "She'll be a senior next year. She's sixteen. Next week she takes the test for her driver's license. I'm going to surprise her with a car if she passes. Hell," he said, "even if she don't pass. I got this cute convertible in mind. Her little ass was just made for it."

He didn't bother to keep his voice down now. He'd set decorum aside, safety, almost as if he'd become Emil Jannings himself, Mrs. Bliss a version of Marlene Dietrich. God knew why, but he'd identified a power in her, too, offering his confession like a sacrifice. She knew she could take advantage of him. She still held his marker. She could take him for all he was worth.

"Can you get me in to see Alcibiades Chitral?" This was the marker she had wanted to call in.

"Hey," Camerando said.

Because now she was on his turf again. And she understood that whatever powers he'd granted her, whatever the specific amounts he permitted her to draw upon from her letter of credit, they were not infinite. They were only social, friendly. They were merely honorary amounts and powers.

"But you *said*," Mrs. Bliss said, her tone quavering, a whiny, petulant register that, even had she heard it clearly, she might not have recognized.

"*What* did I say?"

"About the water and wine," Mrs. Bliss said. "All you could do," she said, her voice trailing off.

"Agh," Camerando said, "I'm all talk."

He wasn't of course. It was just more of the same. Another way to put you on, trip you up—YOU, DOROTHY BLISS, HAVE ALREADY WON . . . And there were all her prizes, written down, in black and white, the number to call. No fine print. No hidden clauses. Just go try claiming them. See what they do to you. Tie you up in the courts years. Make you sorry you were ever born.

But he wasn't. If he was all talk, life was all talk; God, death, blood, love were all talk. The world was all talk.

She, she was helpless. *She* was. Look at him, smell him beside her there on the bench, all his showy shtarker maleness. His expensive, dry-clean-only necktie and matching pocket handkerchief, the shine on his expensive shoes. See how at ease he is, how he sits on the bus bench as if he owns it, though Mrs. Bliss knows it must be years since the last time he waited for a bus. So don't tell *her* he's all talk, or that he couldn't get her into the prison to see Alcibiades Chitral if he wanted, or maybe only if she hadn't made it all sound so urgent and by letting him see how much she wanted it, that that gave him just that much more advantage over her. Though God only knows why he'd want it or how he would ever use it. Except, Mrs. Bliss thought, that's why people accumulated power and advantage, like misers socking it away bit by bit for a rainy day.

"All right," she said, "if you can't, you can't. Here's my bus."

The very next day, when she went down to pick up her mail, Louise Munez greeted Mrs. Bliss, though no one else was in the lobby, with a series of elaborate, conspiratorial winks and hand gestures. The woman, who struck Dorothy as having grown even more increasingly bizarre over the past few months, had mimed a sort of no-hurry, it-can-wait, take-your-time, I'm-not-going-anywhere message. To her surprise Mrs. Bliss was able to pick up every nuance of this strange foreigner's perfectly syntaxed body language—that after she'd retrieved her mail, and if the coast was clear, she should stop by the security desk before going back upstairs.

"What?" Mrs. Bliss asked. "Did you want to see me?"

The Munez woman reproached Mrs. Ted Bliss with a scowl, as if to warn her that the walls had ears. She shook her head sadly.

"What?" Mrs. Bliss said.

"You should have let him," Louise said.

"What? Who? What should I have let him?"

"Your boy Frank," Louise said, "the last time he was down here. You should have let him put up a signal light in your apartment that tell when someone at your door, or even if your intercom is buzzing. Those things are perfected now you know. They're state-of-the-art. If you're waiting will there be improvements down the line or will they come down in price, I can say to you that in my opinion there won't, and they'll never be no cheaper than they are right now either. It's your business, Mrs. Bliss, but who's Security here, me or you?"

She's loony, Dorothy thought, but where does she get her information? Did I say to her about Frank and the gadgets? Does she read my mail? Should I tell her poor mother? Nah, nah, thought Mrs. Ted Bliss, the both of them are unfortunates. Why should I mix in? Does it cost me anything she reads my mail? Do I have secrets? The mad woman, Louise, maybe she guards Building One to protect her mother. What damage is done?

"You wanted to see me?" Mrs. Bliss said.

Louise selected two keys from an immense ring, opened a drawer in her desk with one, a long black metal box like a safety deposit box with the other. With silent, formal fanfare she took an envelope out of the box and handed it to Dorothy.

"A messenger brought it for you in a limo."

"In a limo he brought it?"

YOU, DOROTHY BLISS, she was thinking, HAVE ALREADY WON . . .

"He wanted to take it up but I thought, No, let him give it to me. She won't hear the door, she hasn't got signal lights. I say, 'When she come for the mail I hand it to her.' He didn't want to give it to me. I don't know, maybe he don't want to go away without his tips, I don't know. But he comes in a limo. This is suspicious. 'What's the matter,' I tell him, 'you can't read? It don't say on the sign tradesmen got to leave stuff at the security desk?' "

It was from Alcibiades Chitral.

"My dear Mrs. Bliss," wrote Chitral in the letter Louise had handed her, "technically, of course, your lawyer was right when he advised you that it would be extraordinarily difficult for you to arrange to visit me in prison. In their paranoia, governments often write laws to protect themselves from all sorts of contingencies, real and imagined. In this instance they were seeking, on the basis that a prisoner might be engaged in filing an appeal, to limit congress between a felon and any material witness whose testimony was substantively instrumental in the felon's conviction.

"So Manny was right, though he overstated the case. He's a good lawyer and you're lucky to have him, but when he told you that a visit between us was out of the question he should really have said that, from the system's point of view, it was inadvisable.

"The law is a genius, really. I refer, as you know, to all its elegant ad hoc acrobatic flexibility.

"Well. In the event, I should like to see you, too, Dorothy—may I call you that?—and have made arrangements, unless you advise otherwise, for a driver to pick you up at the Towers @ 9:30 A.M. Tuesday next.

"I hope you enjoy the roses, Señora."

When she went back to the lobby she was so furious it was astonishing to her. It was so long since she'd been angry that she was not entirely certain she had it right. Was it always such a drain on the body? Did it usually dry up your mouth so bad that it was difficult to pronounce your words? Had it always made her nauseous? Indeed, she felt so ill that she was quite amazed, she was able to speak at all. For her years Mrs. Bliss was a relatively healthy, vigorous woman, but she would have sworn she felt blood pressure rising in her veins and heart and blood. She felt it seep into organs she could not even name.

She demanded. *"What did you do with my roses?"*

"What roses is that?"

"That he brought with the note in the limo!"

"The messenger?"

"Yes, the messenger. Who else would I be talking about?"

"Please, Mrs. Bliss, there were no roses. He didn't bring no roses."

She'd terrified her. The girl with the gun and the flashlight, the handcuffs and nightstick and two-way radio. She'd reduced her to tears.

"No roses," Louise Munez said. "I swear you, no roses. You gonna tell my mother there was roses?"

All anger left her. She felt incredibly empty, almost hungry.

"No, no, of course not, Louise," said Mrs. Ted Bliss. "I'm sorry. It was a mistake about the roses."

It was a mistake, but not Louise's. It was something she didn't understand, but somehow she understood there hadn't been roses. Oh, the world was so difficult. Alcibiades Chitral's note had come the day after she'd broached the question of a visit to Hector Camerando. It had to have been Camerando who got word to Chitral that she'd asked for a meeting. And then all that stuff about the law and felons and material witnesses and appeals and difficulties, the difference between out-of-the-question and the inadvisable.

What did she know of the world and its kingpins?

Who ruled here? Did the dog track and jai alai interests hold sway over the drug ones?

A word to Camerando, a note from Chitral. Yes, and the mystery of the missing roses. Louise was a little crazy and a blabbermouth but she was honest as the day is long, responsible, an ethics stickler, too conscientious to quit her post for so much as five minutes to stash stolen roses. No, *that* was out of the question. Speaking of which, she remembered having brought up the whole visit business with Manny after she heard about Alcibiades Chitral's hundred-year sentence, and recalled that the lawyer's response had been those words exactly! How could Chitral know? Was Manny from the building working both sides of the street? Impossible, she thought, what could the real estate lawyer get out of it? Or Chitral either? I mean, she thought, they gave the guy a hundred years. What was that supposed to be, a reduced sentence? Or maybe Manny was even a lousier lawyer than Maxine thought he was. Impossible again, thought Mrs. Bliss. The South American was a hotshot drug lord. Those fellows could afford nothing but the best. It was a mystery. It was *all* a mystery. Like all those cop and detective shows she liked to watch. It was as if—Tommy Overeasy flashed into her head—her 5,512 chickens had come home to roost. Though the mystery of the missing roses was maybe the biggest mystery of them all. Her part in the affair, too. Lashing out at the girl like that—with all she, Louise, had to worry about. It wasn't like Dorothy. Even though Dorothy didn't always know what Dorothy was like these days. The sudden, terrible reappearance of temper like a renewal of feelings she almost couldn't remember ever really having. And suppose when he said that about the roses all he meant were those original roses, the ones he brought the night she sold him Ted's car. She reread the letter. No, he said, "I hope you enjoy the roses." That could only mean today's roses, not roses he'd given her years ago. Unless he thought, and here Dorothy felt herself blush, remembering all the times in the game room when the men had spoken openly of her beauty, and been asked to guess her age as if she were some girl at the fair, she kept them pressed in a book somewhere. Oh, God, thought Mrs. Ted Bliss, don't let him think *that*, anything but not that.

Who ruled here? What did?

Why, the mysteries. It was like the puzzle of the jai alai and drug and dog track ascendancies. It was like those words her children had spoken before throwing out their hands in that game. What was that game? Lom Som Po. Paper covers rock! Rock smashes scissors! Scissors cuts paper! It made her head spin. Such a mishmash of claims on her attention. The hidden secrets of the upper hand.

SEVEN

There was no guarantee he'd show up. Probably he wouldn't. But why take chances? So when Dorothy went to bed that night she set the alarm to go off an hour earlier than it usually did. She set it to go off the same time it would if she had an appointment at the beauty parlor, or the doctor's, or she wanted to beat the heat on a day she went shopping, or if she were going away on a trip. This way she had time for her bath and to lay out her clothes the way she wanted, and to eat her breakfast without having to rush.

She was down in plenty of time. She had time to spare, even. As a matter of fact, if it hadn't been such a beautiful day she would have gone back inside and sat down on a bench in the lobby till he came. (If he was coming.) But it was, so she was content to stay put, to get away from the air-conditioning and stand out in the wondrous weather. (If it even *was* weather, and not some gorgeous potion of perfect idealized memory, the luscious aromatics of a childhood spell say, Mrs. Bliss's, Dorothy's, charmed skin fixed in the softened, smoothed-over stock-stillness of all temperate sufficiency. If it even *was* weather this temperate ate sufficiency as absent of climate as a room in a dream.)

She wasn't the only resident of Building One content to be there, happy just to stand in place, apparently with neither a desire to go back indoors nor the will to continue on the errands that had

146

brought them outside in the first place. Those who'd come down to walk their dogs remained where they were, and so did their animals.

They marveled at the temperature, they complimented the perfect humidity, They congratulated each other on their decision to have chosen south Florida as a place to retire.

"They bottled this stuff they'd make a fortune," one of them said.

"Put me down for a dozen cases. Money's no object."

"It is, but not under the circumstances."

"Weather like this, you couldn't *bribe* me to go inside."

"What's that smell? Oranges?"

"Lemons, limes. Something citric."

"It's like you just stepped out of the best shower you ever took."

"It's paradise."

"I wish my kids were here today. They never catch the really good weather."

"I know. Mine are always complaining, 'Ma, it's too hot,' 'It's too cold,' 'Don't it ever stop raining?' "

Mrs. Bliss joined in the laughter. It was true. They had a day like this once, maybe two times a year, tops.

"And not every year," someone said as though continuing her thought, or as if she'd spoken it aloud.

What's that all about, Mrs. Bliss wondered, startled, returned suddenly to her mission, and nervous because the atmospherics were a distraction and might hold them there until the car came for her. (If it did.) What, did she need this, a bunch of strangers standing around like they were seeing her off? (Because, Mrs. Bliss noted, most of their faces were new to her. She'd laid low the past few years, did not often go to the parties in the game room these days, was less and less comfortable shlepping along with her married friends like a fifth wheel. And with her fellow widows, so unhappy and lonely, it was even worse. She didn't need no grief support groups.) The presence of so many onlookers made Dorothy self-conscious. And if the driver showed up—he was already ten minutes late—in an actual limousine she wasn't entirely sure she might not just disappear into the small crowd, turn around, and go right back into the building. Louise could make up some excuse

for her. Because the thought, just the thought, of these people seeing her helped into a long white stretch limo—she could picture it:
the automobile with its gleaming silver wing-shaped antenna
mounted on the trunk and the one-way glass that made the passengers invisible; its spic-and-span leather interior got up like a
fancy motel room with its absurd built-ins—the speaker phones
and cable TV and wet bar and sun lamp and a desktop you let
down like a tray top on an airplane—would diminish her more
than she already was, turn her pathetic, as if there were no quicker,
more obvious way of pronouncing this some redletter day in the
life, summing her up in the measly bottom lines of her dressed-up,
shined-shoe, queen-for-a-day happiness. What, did she need it? Did
she need it?

And then, suddenly, their chatter ceased. They made a collective sound of awe and wonder. The limo pulled into Building Number One's driveway and stopped beneath the canopy.

The driver got out and walked around the immense length of
the car. He was in black livery, and wore high black boots and a
chauffeur's inky cap.

He came directly up to Dorothy.

"Mrs. Ted Bliss?"

"Yes?"

"I apologize for the delay, Madam. There was construction on
163rd Street, and the traffic was backed up."

"That's all right," Mrs. Bliss said.

"When ain't there?" said the man who wanted to be put down
for a case of the perfect weather. "There always is, 163rd Street is
murder."

"Dorothy," Edna Baim said, one of the few people Mrs. Bliss
recognized, "the car is for you?"

"I'm going on a trip. He's taking me to the airport."

"You're going on a trip?" said the one who thought the air
smelled like oranges. "So where's your luggage?"

Dorothy looked past the driver to the extravagant car. "What
I need I'll buy when I get there," she said, and allowed the chauffeur to hand her into the limousine.

The penitentiary had been built on landfill along the northern, central edge of the Everglades. They had left the Tamiami Trail some-

where between Sweetwater and Monroe Station and plunged north onto a gravel road that cut through vegetation that reminded Mrs. Bliss of a kind of gigantic tropical salad. The trees here, she supposed, bore the sort of fruit whose names she recognized—guava and plantain, currant, avocado, gooseberry and huckleberry and elderberry, damson and papaya—but had never tasted or, vaguely thinking of them as somehow gentile fruits, brought home for her family. It seemed curious to her now that she had never encouraged them away from their old appetites.

She'd never been much of a sightseer when Ted was alive, and now, even on cruises, was content to play cards in her cabin or poke about in the duty-free shops searching out gifts she could bring back for her children and grandchildren. Ashore, in colonial port towns, it was all her companions could do to coax her to ride with them in an open landau drawn through the narrow cobblestone streets by a team of paired horses.

"Oh that," Dorothy would say, "that's for the tourists."

"And what are you, Dorothy, a native?"

"We should hire a guide and let him take us around in a taxi."

"And deal with *two* shvartzers?"

"Shh," Dorothy said.

But she was oddly moved by the journey today, the sight of such ancient, lush significance on either side of the tremendous car that skated over the loose gravel on the slender little road like some sleek, fearless, predatory beast, its flanks mere inches from the edges of what in places seemed more path or trail than road, brushing the rough saw grass that grew along the queer, amorphous, indeterminate earth like clumps, paddies of unfamiliar geography.

Thinking, this is how they took him to prison. These are the last things he saw before they threw him in jail.

Though she knew he hadn't been "thrown" into jail, that he had too much influence, too much imagination and power, that even now, behind walls and locked up in a cell, they let him take calls (it had been the next day she'd heard from Chitral, the day after she'd made her wish known to Camerando), and let him put calls through, to arrange to send drivers with gracious notes and imaginary roses.

"Oh," she told the chauffeur, "that reminds me," she said, inspired, "I never thanked you for bringing me those beautiful roses."

"What beautiful roses would those be, Mrs. Bliss?"

"Why the roses you brought with you last week when you delivered that letter to the Towers."

"I'm sorry," he said, "but the first time I was to the Towers was when I picked you up this morning."

Amazed, thinking, oh, *two* drivers!

Thrilled retroactively who'd never met a man who hadn't impressed her, swept away by men, not in any sexual or romantic sense but rendered dumbstruck by all the ways they seemed to fill up the world (so overwhelmed by them that she had had trouble with the notion of disciplining her male children, this so apparent to the two boys that even when they were still quite small they behaved in front of their worried, vulnerable mother like visitors in a sick room), stunned by their stature and brisk efficiency (their perfect businesslike forms built for a power and efficacy that spread through their bodies like steam pushed through a radiator, *their* unadorned flesh not expended in breasts or useless piles of complicated hair, and even their privates out in the open, functional as hand tools), by their willingness to go forth and wrest bread and victory from their lives in the world, clear down to changing a tire or starting a fire from scratch or handling the money or initiating love, by their gruff and bluff and boldness, and all the rest of their dangerous, hung-out, let-loose ways.

Awed by the driver, too, overcome with wonder and admiration by the sureness with which he negotiated the fragile, narrow gravel road, the toxic-looking swamps—logjammed, she was sure, with alligators—on either side of the winding, puny spit which they did not so much travel as traverse. He must be a convict, Mrs. Bliss thought. Probably a trustee or something. Which just goes to show, thought Mrs. Ted Bliss. Wouldn't you have to be as smart as you were probably brave to know how to walk the fine line between the guards with the guns on the watchtowers and the vil-deh chei-eh killers, kidnappers, and bank robbers in the prison yard? If that wasn't man's work she didn't know what was. And if that wasn't going forth and wresting bread and victory from his life in the world, then she didn't know *what* it was. It's a man's world, thought Mrs. Ted Bliss, and between you, me, and the lamp-post, he's welcome to it.

"Excuse me, sir," said Mrs. Bliss, "you're from the federal penitentiary, too?"

The driver may not have known she was addressing him. They were the first words she'd spoken since she'd asked about the roses.

"Yes, ma'am," he said.

He spoke very softly. She might not have been able to hear him in an open room, but in the big airtight automobile his voice was startlingly clear, even intimate.

"You work there," she said.

"I'm a con. I live there."

"Oh," she said, "you *live* there."

"Yes, ma'am."

"It's none of my business, you'll excuse me for prying, but what did you—"

"Forgery. I forged things."

"Oh," she said, "you *forged* things."

"Passports. Liquor and drivers' licenses; when the elevator was inspected."

"Oh, I don't think I could do that. It must take so much skill. I'd get caught."

"I got caught," said the convict.

Mrs. Bliss didn't answer. Yes, he got caught, but he proved her point. Men were more gifted than women. They could make a fire, rotate the tires, and forge important papers, too.

What men did took nerve and a steady hand. It took brains and courage. Here was this nice, polite, and, as far as Mrs. Bliss could tell, very bright young man who had managed so well in the penitentiary that he had not only worked his way up to trustee but had climbed so high in the system that they trusted him to drive a great powerful limousine all the way out of his prison in the high Everglades, down the gravel road to the Tamiami Trail, across to Miami, and up to the Towers in Miami Beach. He was a man. He was brave; he had nerve. At any time during his journey he could have stepped on the gas and made his escape by outdistancing anybody who might have given him chase. But he was a man, he knew better. He knew it would be other men who would be sent out to find him.

"You know," said Mrs. Bliss when they had gone a few more miles, "you wouldn't believe it to look at me but a long time ago in Chicago I used to carry a gun."

"You did, ma'am?"

"Yes," said Mrs. Ted Bliss. "My husband owned a building on the North Side. It wasn't a good area. I took it with me when we collected the rents."

"I'm damned," the driver said.

"I never took it out of my purse. Not once. These were very rough people. You know why I did it?"

"Why?"

"I thought I could save my husband's life," Dorothy said and, so quietly she didn't think he'd notice, she started to cry.

"Look there," the driver said some minutes later. "That's where all the magic happens. I'm home."

The guards at the gate didn't need to see identification. They didn't even ask her her name. They didn't bother with the driver either, just waved him on through as though he were pulling up to discharge a guest in front of the entrance to a hotel. When he stopped before what Mrs. Bliss took to be some sort of administration building he got out of the limo and came around to Dorothy's side to open her door and help her out. Now she was there she wondered why it had seemed so important to come.

"It's a big roomy car and very comfortable," Dorothy said, "but three hours in a closed automobile is a long time to sit. I wonder could I stretch my legs a few minutes before I go in?"

"Stand around in the yard? It's your call, Mrs. Bliss, but not all these guys are as civil as yours truly. Not everyone here is in for a victimless crime. Ain't all of us forgers, what I'm saying." He winked. "Some of these characters ain't seen a woman in a long time." Quite suddenly Mrs. Ted Bliss was alarmed. She was well into her seventies and what he said seemed one of the cruelest, most patronizing things anyone had ever said to her. So much for men's bravery and nerve. Mrs. Bliss felt quite ill and turned to enter the building. The driver touched her arm as if to stop her. "Hey, no, I'm kidding," he said. "It's like they say in the papers. The place is a country club. You see anybody with his back on a bench lifting weights? You see a single tattoo, or some bull con make eye contact with some cow con? No, Mother, you stay outside and enjoy the fine weather, I'll go tell Señor Chitral you're here."

Before she could object the man had disappeared. Terms, things, conditions, had certainly changed, but Mrs. Bliss could not have said what or how. Of course she felt odd standing by herself out in the prison yard—she was sure that's what it was; dozens of men dressed in what, despite the neat, neutral appearance of their cheap, open white dress shirts, tan slacks, and inexpensive loafers, could only have been uniforms, loitered or strolled about the quad-like yard like students at a university between classes—but not in the least vulnerable, as safe, really, as she would have felt at the Towers. (And it *was* a fine day. It seemed strange to Mrs. Bliss that they could have stepped into a car three hours ago and stepped out again three hours later into the same fine weather. This was a penitentiary at the edge of a swamp. How could it have the same climate as the world?) She hardly believed she was in a prison among desperados and villains. People conducted themselves in perfectly ordinary, orderly, civilized ways. They might *indeed* have been scholars discussing the issues and topics, illuminating for one another the ramifications and fine points. Dorothy wondered if the inmates had "quiet" or "free times" imposed on them like children at summer camp, say, or if this was the way they walked off their lunches. There couldn't have been more than forty-five or fifty of them about, perambulating what were more like kempt grounds than anything as sordid as a prison yard. She wondered if the rest of the population might not voluntarily have gone back to their cells—rooms?—to nap or write letters. It certainly wasn't what she expected, or like anything she'd seen in the movies. Yet it *was* a prison yard. She saw guards with rifles, with guns in holsters, and all the rest of power's lead and leather paraphernalia. They weren't on the tops of walls in little tollbooths on watchtowers, though, but walked about, almost mingling with their prisoners. If anything should happen, thought Mrs. Ted Bliss, the guards would be in one another's way. Everybody would be in everybody else's line of fire. Yet neither guards nor inmates seemed particularly wary. Individuals greeted each other easily, indifferent as old acquaintances, al-most, she thought, the way residents of one Towers high rise might say good morning and ask after someone else's health who lived in a different building. What they didn't show you in the movies was how ordinary it all was, the simple, edgeless decency of people who had been arbitrarily thrown together. Or was this simply the cream of the crop, the best a place like this had to offer?

They greeted Dorothy, too, some of them, inmates as well as guards, and inquired, solicitous as clerks in department stores, if they could help her.

"Oh, no," Dorothy told them, "thank you, I'm just waiting for somebody."

They were charming, charming. Of course, Chitral had been charming, too.

A guard came up to her.

"Excuse me," he said, "I understand you're here to see someone. It could be a while. Bob Gorham's fixing to practice his touch-and-go's in a few minutes. He's got a beautiful day for it. Why don't you come watch? Rodge'll let you know when your party shows up."

"Rodge?" Mrs. Bliss said.

"It's Roger. Rodge is just what they call me," a second guard said.

"Come on," the first guard said, "runway's round the side of this building."

Mrs. Bliss went with him. Most of the convicts were headed in the same direction. It wasn't a long walk and the guard was careful to set his pace to Mrs. Bliss's. In minutes they were within sight of the runway. "We can stop now," the man said. "We'll be able to see just fine from right here. Plus this way, when your party comes, you won't have so far to walk back."

"That wasn't far," Mrs. Bliss said.

"Well, I know it," the guard said, "but . . . I'll be honest with you. You promise not to tell?"

"Tell what? I don't know what you're talking about."

"Bob's a square shooter. Well, for someone of the criminal classes, I mean. But the true facts of the case is that this is the first time he done this without his flight instructor riding shotgun. There's always the possibility that him and fate could run afoul. From here you get a good enough first-rate view, but you're still standing far enough back and to the side of the airstrip that if he loses control or his engine stalls and his plane, God forbid, drops out of the sky you'll be protected."

"This happens?"

"*Could* happen, *could* happen, but it won't. One-in-a-million," he said dismissively.

Mrs. Bliss was reminded of Hector Camerando and his talk of long shots and locks and fixes. What, did most people live beneath such heavy protection? Mrs. Bliss couldn't remember when she hadn't played cards. Poker, bridge, the rummy variations. But for her, for all of them, the stakes had always been the coffee and coffee cake, the sweets and kibitzing and gossip and conversation. She couldn't remember the size of the biggest pot she'd ever taken or even, over the years, whether she'd won, lost, or broken even. Perhaps she was foolish, she thought, not to keep better records.

But then, about fifty yards away, she saw a man in an inmate's vaguely preppy uniform, wearing goggles and a tight, old-fashioned cloth aviator's cap on his head, climb into the cockpit of a small, single-engine plane. A moment later Mrs. Bliss heard him start up the engine.

"But isn't he a prisoner?" Dorothy said.

"Bob Gorham? Five to ten years' worth. He's got but months to serve before he's up for parole, but shoot, I guess he was bored."

"You mean it's only a few months until he gets out and he's taken up flying?"

"Got a beautiful day for it. *Beautiful* day."

"The government pays a professional instructor to teach him to fly?"

"*Heck* no," the guard said. "Taxpayers'd never stand for nothing like that. No, ma'am, there ain't no professional instructors. We had a guy here used to drop dope on the beaches. Flew his own plane. That con taught another con and that con taught the next. And so on and so forth. It's a wonderful program."

"Where do the planes come from?" Mrs. Bliss said, although she knew the answer before she asked the question.

"Government confiscates them," the guard said levelly, and looked the woman straight in the eye.

He knows about the LeSabre, Mrs. Bliss thought, shuddering in the perfect weather.

Then the plane, gathering speed, started to move down the runway. Soon it was in the sky. She watched it turn in a wide arc, bank, and come in for a landing. It touched down and immediately took off again. Mrs. Bliss's stomach tightened. Her throat burned with bile. Far off, the convicts cheered each time Gorham took off and touched down.

"What if he tries to escape?"

"Escape?" the guard said. "Escape? Lordy ma'am, his tank ain't filled with but fifteen minutes' worth of gas."

She was thinking locks, fixes, and long shots. She was thinking fifteen minutes of gas in the tank and that there couldn't be more than seven minutes' worth left. She was thinking about the guard's one-in-a-million and, for a moment, hoped against hope that if it had to happen, she'd still be standing there when it did.

Rodge was not with him when Chitral came up to her.

It had been years since she'd seen him but it might have been only a few months ago. That's how little he'd changed. If anything, he looked not youthful but as if age had refined his best features. His skin, once ruddy, was tan, and his white wavy hair had lost some of its coiffed character and now looked faintly roiled, roughed up. Even his black, bushy eyebrows didn't seem faded or thinned out but culled, less a suggestive Latin caricature. Though still a large man, he seemed sparer, healthier. Dorothy had forgotten how white his teeth were when he smiled. He still had the Cesar Romero good looks but they seemed, against the adjusted colors of his fresh adaptations, somehow more trustworthy.

Of course, Mrs. Bliss thought, I already sold him the car and don't have to bargain with him now.

"Dorothy," he addressed her when he spoke, not "Señora" or "My dear Mrs. Bliss." This seemed appropriate, thought Mrs. Ted Bliss. My testimony helped put him away for a hundred years. That ought to set up at least something of a bond between us.

"I apologize for making you wait," he said, "but as you may well imagine"—his arm took in the prison yard and its buildings, the cadre of armed guards and their wards, even the small plane just now touching down to the accompaniment of applause and a cheerful, unfeigned approval for Bob Gorham's perfect three-point landing—"we don't set our own schedules or march to our own drummer here."

"That's all right," Dorothy said, "I didn't wait long. Sometimes I have to wait more than forty minutes for a bus. Those schedules aren't worth the paper they're printed on."

"At least you have a nice day to be outside," Alcibiades Chitral said.

"Yeah," said Mrs. Bliss, "by us, too."

Chitral nodded solemnly. Dorothy solemnly smiled.

"Well," said Alcibiades.

"Well," said Mrs. Ted Bliss.

Why, he's as embarrassed as I am, she thought, and felt this small nausea of disappointment. He'd sent a car to pick her up and bring her all this way. He'd written her the most fluent letter she'd ever received. He'd spoken of the genius of the law and said things she barely understood. He wanted to see her, he wrote, and suggested that a visit between them was not out of the question but merely inadvisable. He'd mentioned mysterious roses. So Hector Camerando or no Hector Camerando—after all, Dorothy thought, Chitral was the one in jail for a hundred years and had nothing to fear from a free Camerando, unless the dog track and jai alai were even stronger medicines than actual drugs—she'd supposed he had things to tell her. Long ago, through Manny, if he even ever passed it on, she'd made a promise that, if he ever wanted her to, she'd visit him, so why wouldn't she assume there were certain things he wanted to get off his chest? Because as God was her witness she'd been having plenty of second thoughts about why she had wanted to come in the first place.

"Hey," said the guard who'd taken charge of Mrs. Bliss, "look at me horning in on your visit. I'll just get out of your way."

"Thanks for looking after her, Bill."

"No problem, Alcibiades," he said, and fell in with a group of prisoners just then passing by. In their white shirts, tan slacks, and loafers, they reminded Dorothy of college glee clubs she'd seen on the television. A couple of convicts had clapped their arms around Bob Gorham's shoulders. He was still wearing his aviator's cap.

"Hell of a landing there, Bob," Chitral called out.

"Thanks, pardner," Bob Gorham said, "glad you could come."

"You have a couple of letters waiting for you," Alcibiades said. "I left them on your bunk."

The prisoners passed on, leaving Chitral and Mrs. Bliss by themselves. It was a little awkward. Then Chitral asked Mrs. Bliss if she'd eaten.

"Oh, no," she said, "I'm not very hungry."

"Because there's a cafeteria."

"Oh, no," she said. "Thank you."

"Are you sure?" Chitral asked. "They do a swell bread and water."

Mrs. Bliss stared at him. "Look," she said, "they subpoenaed me. I was subpoenaed."

"Of course," Chitral said. "Of course you were, Dorothy."

"So long as you understand that."

"Oh, I do."

"Well," said Dorothy.

"Well," said Chitral.

Mrs. Bliss, conceding still more than what she had already conceded, let him in on something. "I have," she said, lowering her voice even though no one was about, "to go to the washroom."

"You didn't go?"

"No."

"Not since you got here?"

"No."

"Not since you stopped for coffee?"

"We didn't stop for coffee."

"You never pulled into a gas station?"

"No," she said.

"Not since you left the Towers this morning?"

"I already told you," Mrs. Ted Bliss said, "I was subpoenaed by the government."

"Oh," said Alcibiades Chitral, "you think *you* were subpoenaed!"

"Never mind," said Mrs. Bliss. "There's a cafeteria? They must have a rest room. I'll find it myself."

"No, wait," he said, "I'm sorry."

Maybe she shouldn't have, but she stopped dead in her tracks. They moved about the yard dressed like announcers at a golf tournament, they learned to pilot airplanes on maybe two dollars' worth of gas, and the guards seemed more like park rangers than policemen, but this was still a federal penitentiary where they could lock men up for a hundred years. There was no telling what such men might do to you when they knew they had nothing to lose. And if she could find the ladies' on her own that didn't mean she didn't need someone to stand just outside the door like a lookout even if she was an old woman because, after all, everybody knew, didn't they, that rape and perversion had more to do with violence and control than ever they had to do with sex, and if she had to depend on Alcibiades Chitral, a man, she now realized, who evidently still begrudged her the testimony that helped send him into the swamp for another ninety-some-odd years, he was still, or at least had once been, a neighbor, and who else could you turn to in a time of need if not to a neighbor? He would be her Manny from the building in the Everglades, and she stopped dead in her tracks while she waited for him to catch up.

Mrs. Bliss was satisfied that whoever cleaned the place didn't do a bad job, and if the pervasive smell of Pinesol bounced off the tile like the odors in a high school—the room smelled exactly like the lavatory in Maxine's old high school back in Chicago—at least the toilet seats were clean, and there was plenty of toilet paper, even extra rolls if it should happen to run out, and Mrs. Bliss had the place to herself. She locked herself into a stall and quite comfortably peed. She even managed to move her bowels, and felt a certain pride in the civilized ways the government used her tax dollars. When she was done she washed up at one of the sinks and stepped outside.

Chitral was talking to an extremely well-groomed prisoner dressed in clean, just-pressed pants, a fresh white shirt, and loafers that practically sparkled. He introduced Mrs. Bliss.

"You're Mrs. Ted Bliss? Really? I'm pleased to meet you. Al speaks of you often."

The prisoner moved off.

"You're sure you don't want to grab something in the cafeteria? It's right here," Chitral said. "It's a good place to talk."

"Well," said Mrs. Bliss, "if I'm not keeping you."

"No, of course not," he said, "I'm one of the prison mailmen. I've already done my rounds. There's nothing on my plate until lockup, and that's not for another seven hours."

She selected fruit salad in Jell-O, some buttered toast, and a tall glass of iced coffee. Abashed, Chitral admitted that it was the end of the month and that he hadn't much money left in his account and permitted her to pay for both of their snacks.

"I feel just awful about this," he said, "but, to tell you the truth, those roses I sent set me back."

"I never got roses."

"What, you never . . . Are you certain?"

"I'm sent so many flowers I can't keep track?"

"Not all red this time," he explained, "a mixed assortment. Yellow roses, white, purple, blue."

"No. No roses."

Chitral seemed crestfallen, anguished, but when he spoke, it was in the spare, furious, explosive gasps and outrage of someone who could no longer hold his breath. "Cheats! Liars! Crooks!" Though he was not shouting, Mrs. Bliss touched the controls of her hearing aid. "Now listen to me," he said, calming down, "were you home when the messenger delivered my note?"

"I was at home but he left it with the girl."

"The security guard? Louise?"

"You know Louise?"

"I've seen her and I know her mother. She's a very strange girl."

Mrs. Bliss remembered how frightened she'd made her. "I asked her about the roses. She started to cry. Really," Mrs. Bliss said, "she's very honest. She wouldn't steal the roses."

"No," Chitral said, all anger gone out of him, "you're probably right. This place," he said suddenly, "this place with its civility, with all its spic-and-span toilets and you-could-eat-off-the-floor amenities, with all its flying lessons, music rooms, and bridge tournaments, you forget where you are, you really do. You forget where you are and who you're with. Of course you never got my roses. After passing through the hands of all the brokers, go-betweens, skimmers, and middlemen around this place, what'd be left? The stems and thorns? Jesus," he moaned, "seventy-five bucks! Who'd I think I was dealing with? Some greenhouse established 1857? Everyone takes out his percentage of the roses. I'm sick about it. Just sick."

Later, when she had time to think about it, Dorothy had to wonder (though she knew she'd never know) if he'd gone to all this trouble and shlepped her all that way just to get her to buy him lunch and take her for the hundred dollars she'd insisted on pressing on him.

In the cafeteria there, she looked at him in wonder.

"What?"

"Nothing," Mrs. Bliss said, "it's just that, well . . ."

"What?"

"You hear about 'country clubs.' Just today the driver who brought me said this place is a country club."

"What's he know about it?"

"Well, he's a criminal, *too*," she said in his defense. "I mean *he* has a record, *he* was arrested. *He* had a trial, and when the jury found him guilty *someone* sentenced and sent him here.

"Anyway, it isn't at all what I expected. It's just that you hear about these places, and everyone says that we're soft on crime and about coddling the criminals. It's on all the talk shows. I'm pretty old," she said. "Not that I know it all or anything, but I've lived long enough to know at least a thing or two, and what I'm saying is that when you hear all this stuff—soft-on-crime this and country-club that, it's a little like the jingles I used to hear for laundry powder on the radio. After a while you don't believe it anymore and think that someone is just trying to sell you something."

"And?"

"And? And so naturally I'm a little farmisht, mixed up. It's not like in the movies, it's not like on TV. Out where I was waiting for you? Before that nice man, the guard—what was his name, Bill?— came up, I thought I heard a band playing, and when I looked around to see where the music was coming from I saw these people blowing in trumpets and banging on drums, the last of them marching and turning the corner at the other side of the building. I mean, they were prisoners, too, right?"

"They play in the prison marching band."

"A prison marching band! Alevai! Kayn aynhoreh!"

"What?"

"I mean that's wonderful. I mean if you got to be here for a hundred years, then I'm pleased it's a country club and you got a prison marching band. I mean it's exactly like you said to me, 'At least you got a nice day to be outside.' "

"Outside?"

"Well, no, not outside, I don't mean outside. In a place like this, I mean."

"You like it."

"In my wildest dreams I wouldn't have imagined such a spotless toilet," Mrs. Bliss said. "I wouldn't have imagined Jell-O molds, or an airplane, or everybody's nice clothes."

"So you feel a little better about that subpoena."

"Well, yes," she said. "Yes, I do." This was after she had bought his lunch but before she pressed her check for a hundred dollars into his hand when the driver came by to take her home. "It's only a little later than the middle of the afternoon," she said, "and you've already delivered your letters and have the rest of the day off. In a little while you'll probably have even more privileges. You'll work your way up to a trustee like the driver."

"I'm already a trustee," Alcibiades Chitral said. "Everybody's a trustee. They make us trustees when we get here, right after they delouse us and give us our nice uniforms."

"Everybody's a trustee?"

"Every kidnapping, tax cheating, counterfeiting, serial killing mother's son of us. Everyone starts off with his pieces intact. It's like checkers or a game of Monopoly. You lose by attrition. So sure, everybody's a trustee. This place. This place is some place this place. It's the clowns with the longest time who get the wear and the tear. Sure, we're *all* trustees. Only it's not like the Towers, Mrs. Bliss. It's a retirement community in reverse. Oh, yeah," Chitral said bitterly. "I'm through for the day. I start at nine and knock off at two. Only, you know what my job was the year I came? I stuck in the video, started it, and rewound the tape when it was through. Your limo driver is here a couple of months, maybe. Tops, a couple of months, and he's off the grounds more than he's on them. Sometimes the warden sends him to Tallahassee, gives him chits for meals and a motel, a few bucks walking-around money, and has him bring back fresh rolls the next day. All the leisure's up front, my dear Mrs. Bliss, and the cons who made that toilet of yours shine so, pull K.P. and do the lifting, are all old men who work around the clock and have been here thirty years.

"A hundred years. Thanks to you I'm doing a century of time here, lady!"

He wanted me to feel terrible, Mrs. Ted Bliss thought. He wanted me to feel terrible, and that's why he sent for me. He wanted me to feel terrible, the son of a bitch.

And then, for the first time not just that day but since he was sentenced, she understood exactly why she'd wanted to see him. She knew the reason she was there.

But so much had happened, she had so much new information.

She was only a helpless old woman, and this place, for all its collegiality, for all its laundered kemptness and, she suspected, quasimilitary, quarters-bounced-on-the-beds baleboss, was so un-relentingly masculine, that she had to proceed slowly, carefully. But even if it weren't, even if she'd been talking to her mother, to her sisters, even if she were speaking to her own children it would have been difficult for her to blurt out what was on her mind. Even, for that matter, if it had been Ted. There was only one to whom she might have broached the subject sucking at her heart, and he, may Marvin rest, she would never see again.

So she had to sidle up to it, deflecting real concerns with minor ones.

"Tell me," she said, "would you happen to know if by any chance that car you bought from me is on the property?"

"The property?"

"The grounds, the facility, the installation, whatever name this place goes by. Because the guard told me that that airplane some convict taught your friend to fly was confiscated. Maybe that's how they do things. Maybe that VCR you started out on originally be-longed to some other jailbird. Maybe the limousine did. And tele-vision sets and all the trumpets and drums and everything else around here are hand-me-downs, too. Maybe that's how the gov-ernment saves its money. By never throwing anything out. Any-thing! Neither the, what-do-you-call-them, big-ticket items, nor all the drek and chozzerai. By, what-do-you-call-it, recycling every-thing. *Everything!*

"So, well, naturally, I thought of the Buick LeSabre. I mean, well, even you admired its air-conditioning and electric door locks and windows. The FM and AM. You gave me over and above the blue book value. It drove like a top, you said."

Whatever she decided about sidling up to her subject, stepping gingerly, refusing to introduce the real, though till now undiscov-ered reasons that brought her, that motivated her to speak with circumspection, Mrs. Bliss was surprised to discover she had lost her temper. It wasn't the real offensive yet, but the noise she made, the gauntlet she flung down, startled poor Chitral.

"So what do they do with it? How do they use it? Ted used to pick up the White Sox. On all of our drives, on all of them, the thing he loved most was to pick up the Sox games on the radio. Is that what you do? Is it? Because if it *is* what you do I could almost forgive you. Only I'm sure it's not. So what *do* they do? Use it for parts?"

"My dear Mrs. Bliss," Chitral said, "why are you upset? Pardon me, but I'm certain this can't be good for you. Pardon me, but I think you should make an effort to calm yourself. I assure you, Mrs. Bliss, I assure you, Dorothy, your car isn't on the premises. I don't know what happened to it. Probably they auctioned it off. That's what the government usually does with the property it confiscates.

"If you watch the papers, every once in a while they take out an ad back in the section where people post those little disclaimers about how they're no longer responsible for some other party's debts. It's the law, they're required to do that, and if you wanted you could actually go out and bid on it yourself. Just as if it were an ordinary estate sale and not some piece of evidence they once used to deprive a person of his liberty for a hundred years.

"That's one thing the government does with the property it seizes," Chitral said. "The other thing it might have done was have it shredded in the hammermill and sold for scrap."

It didn't matter that Mrs. Bliss was still angry or that she despised this man. It didn't matter that his answer to her question about Ted's car had been laced with intentional mockery and cruelty. If she was nervous of her anger, if she was reluctant to confront him, if she was reticent or shy, shamed, or even a little embarrassed by what she had to do, it was the nervousness, anger, reticence, reluctance, shyness, shame, and embarrassment of someone turning state's evidence, or of one thrown hither and yon by contradictory principles. On the one hand, there was her loyalty to Ted, on the other her long recruitment and service to a talismanic trust in the temperament, nature, and credibility of men as a pure idea. When she spoke it was as if she were betraying her country.

"Did you have so much disrespect for me you had to use me? What was I, your, what-do-you-call-it, pigeon?"

It was almost as though Alcibiades had anticipated her question, almost as though he'd prepared for it, and now aced it like a student who'd been up all night cramming for an exam.

"Disrespect? No, *no* disrespect. On the contrary, out of my sense of your honor. Your softness and sweetness and priorities. My belief in the reliability of your taste."

"My *taste*," Mrs. Bliss, chided for years by her children for the absence of that attribute, the frugality of clipped discount coupons piled up and banded in her kitchen drawers like the mad money of a miser, scolded for the meanness of her saving ways, how there were slipcovers like so much plastic rainwear on all the furniture and how even the tanks and lids of her toilets were swaddled in bulky terry cloth as if to keep them dry, and her reinforced shower curtains (always decorated with marine life blatant as cartoons, sea horses like armored, gothic font riding their perfect verticals, smiling caricatures of fish about to bite down on cheerful hooks) thick and heavy as tarp, said scornfully.

"Yes, señora. Your very dependable taste, your naïveté like a racial trait. Excuse me, lady, I like you. I do more, I admire and cherish you, and wish in my heart the tables were turned, that I had not cast my lot with the adventurers, or been born with this piratical soul like a birth blemish. Oh, I'm a cliché of a fellow, and if I don't feel conspicuously ill-used you may mark that down—I do—to a failure of impatience on my part, to a sort of, well, lazy eye, some high romp of the blood. You, please, Mrs., you mustn't misunderstand me, are like a paraplegic. You, your people have the gift of sitting still, I mean. Had you been here when we came to the New World we'd have made you slaves, stolen your gold and smashed your temples. We'd have wiped out your mathematics and astronomy and forbidden you access to your terrible gods. No offense, ma'am, but there's something loathsome and repellent to persons like me in persons like you. Perhaps your passivity—I bear you no grudge, Widow Bliss, I've no bones to pick with your kind—is at odds with our conquistador spirit, something antithetical between our engagement and the Jew's torpid stupor, his incuriosity and dead-pan, poker-faced genius for suffering, like a cartoon kike's stoicism struck in a shekel. You were *born* sticks-in-the-mud. Why, if it weren't for people like me, like Pharaoh and Hitler, the Cossacks and Crusaders, and whoever those kings were who kicked you out of France and England, the diaspora would never have happened. The diaspora? Shit, señora, your people would never have learned to cross the street!

"So of course you were a pigeon! You were pigeon and dupe, scapegoat and laughingstock—a little menagerie of sacrificial lamb, cat's-paw, and gull. Of *course* you were!

"Oh," he said, "I've offended you. Entirely unintentional, dear. You've mistaken my meaning. Haven't I already said I admire you? Didn't I speak of the Jew's charms—his patience and innocence and naïveté and passivity? Even the imperfect posture of your people's priorities has its charm. The anti-Semites get it wrong with their wild, extravagant claims—all that international-banker crapola and Trilateral Commission hocus-pocus, all those cabala riffs and lame spew about controlling the media. The illuminati this and Protocols of the Elders of Zion that. No, they've tin ears for Jews, Jew baiters do. They go on forever with their Zionist conspiracies and Israeli lobby and Jerusalem-Hollywood nexus. My God, Mrs. Bliss, they can't even drum up a convincing case for your stringing up Jesus!

"Haven't I already said I cherish you? Don't I admire your sweetness and softness, your honor and taste? Yet you ask why I chose you.

"Well, I'll tell you. I chose you because you were available, a surefire target of opportunity. *I did you because there were seat covers in your husband's automobile! I did you because you're descended from a great race of babies!*"

Now she'd heard everything, thought Mrs. Ted Bliss. Twice in her long life she'd sensed herself slurred, once when they'd owned the farm in Michigan and in the deepest part of winter, dressed to the nines, she'd walk to the village on the simplest household errand, then again when the DEA agents had come into the garage in Building Number One and made cracks while they cordoned off Ted's car. But even on those occasions none of the townspeople had ever said a word to her about her religion and, years later, not even the agents (who she felt had been using Manny, talking through him so Mrs. Bliss could overhear what they said) had mentioned Jews. If she'd felt herself personally derided those times perhaps the reason was she'd felt outmanned, outgunned in the presence of so much sheer, overwhelming Americanism. Even as a child in Russia, Dorothy had merely heard of pogroms. She'd never even seen a Cossack. What she knew of anti-Semitism she knew by hearsay, word-of-mouth. It was rather like what she knew of ghosts and haunted houses.

This was something else. It was the last thing she'd expected, and for all that Alcibiades Chitral had couched his attack in different terms, taking care to distinguish himself from the ordinary Jew-hater and seemingly apologize to her as he went along, she knew she was getting it all, being hauled up on all the charges he could think of. She was having, she thought, the book thrown at her. By Alcibiades Chitral's lights it was as if Dorothy Bliss had been found guilty and sent up for a hundred years.

So now she'd heard everything. Everything. Full force. Flat out. It was like having the wind knocked out. It took her breath away. Determined as she was to maintain her calm—it was what Chitral himself had told her to do; even before he'd attacked her, he'd warned her against her anger—she found herself breathlessly hiccuping, then choking.

Chitral moved behind her, clapped her sharply on the back. Astonishingly, it worked. Her hiccups were stopped as effectively as if he'd clasped his hand over her mouth to keep her from screaming. Now, tentatively, as though she were testing the waters, she drew deeper and deeper breaths. She felt a little light-headed and, peculiarly, disheveled. She was conscious of fanning her hands before her face, of making various fluttery gestures of adjustment, silly, girlish, inappropriate Southern belle movements about her septuagenarian body. It was as though she were frisking herself and, try as she might, could not make herself stop. She felt as if she were in Michigan, performing for the townspeople again.

"Do you want some water? I'll get you some water," Chitral said, and left the table.

If I die now, thought Mrs. Ted Bliss, they'll see how upset I am and I'll get him in trouble.

But then, a *little* more sanely, she thought, a hundred years, isn't that trouble? And thought, anti-Semite or no anti-Semite, could she blame him? She had testified against the man. She thought, she *knew* the blue book value. She thought, she had sold Ted's car to pay off a property tax of two hundred dollars. She thought, I made a profit five thousand dollars over and above the blue book value and *still* I threw him in jail!

Was it so terrible what Chitral did? All the business part of their married life the Blisses had lived by markup. She'd made a twenty-five hundred percent markup on the deal! Ted would have been proud. Even what the Spaniard had done with the car hadn't been so geferlech. What, he'd chosen it because who'd ever suspect that a Buick LeSabre equipped not only with seat covers but with all the other features, too, plus a permanent personal parking space out of the rain in a big, mostly Jewish condominium building, could be used as a sort of dope locker? So Ted was a butcher. He stored meat in lockers. Meat, dope, it was all of it groceries finally. A hundred years? Would they have given Ted a hundred years if they had discovered he'd once had dealings in the black market? A hundred years, thought Mrs. Ted Bliss, a hundred years was ridiculous. It was longer than even she'd been alive.

Still, she felt bad Chitral had such a biased picture of Jews. This didn't sit well. But a leopard couldn't change its spots. He couldn't make it up to her for his anti-Semitism, and she couldn't make it up to him for his hundred years.

So she split the difference, and while he was still looking for her glass of water, she took out her checkbook and wrote a check to him for a hundred dollars—making over to him exactly half what it would have cost her in property taxes if she'd never sold the car to him in the first place.

They were quits, thought Mrs. Ted Bliss.

And, in the limo, on the long ride back to the Towers, Mrs. Bliss took comfort in the fact that she was at last even a little better than quits. Now she knew why he had picked her out of all the possible people in south Florida with all the possible used cars they had up for sale; she was finally satisfied that an unthinking promise she'd made all those years back to come on this, what-do-you-call-it, pilgrimage, could be stamped paid-in-full and she'd never have to think about the nasty Jew-hating bastard son of a bitch again!

EIGHT

It was April, and Mrs. Bliss had agreed to spend the Passover holidays with Frank and Frank's family in Frank's new house in Frank's new city of Providence, Rhode Island. Maxine and George would be there with their kids, the beautiful Judith and chip-off-the-block, entrepreneurial James. Frank was said to be helping out with Ellen's fare (her daughter, Janet, was still in India) and with poor Marvin's son, Barry's, the auto mechanic. Frank's own boy, the brilliant Donny, who could have bought and sold all of them, would probably be flying in from Europe.

All this had been arranged months before, in December, and Dorothy had agreed because who knew what could happen between December and April? In December, to a woman Dorothy Bliss's age, April looks like the end of time. She didn't see any point in refusing. But as early as February Mrs. Bliss had begun having second thoughts.

If he still lived in Pittsburgh, *if* there were a nonstop flight from Fort Lauderdale to Providence, *if* he still had all his old friends from the university in Pittsburgh instead of a whole new bunch of people she'd have to meet and whose names, chances were, she'd probably never even catch because, let's face it, people all tended to arrive together on the first night of a seder and who could distinguish their names one from another in all the tummel with all their vildeh chei-eh kids running around, never mind remember them. If this, if that. But the fact was it was already late March and she had to purchase her airline tickets if she wanted to qualify for a cheap fare and escape the "certain restrictions apply" clauses in the carrier's rule book.

She made her reservations on USAir the same day she realized it was already late March and she had better get packing. There was a direct flight to Providence—you had to land in Washington—but no nonstop one, and it turned out it was the only flight going there, so she didn't even have her choice of a departure time. Mrs. Bliss wasn't afraid of flying so much as she was of landing in strange cities and having to sit in the plane while it changed crews or took on fuel or boarded new passengers. (Also, she knew about landings, how they were the trickiest part of the whole deal.) But what troubled her most, she thought, was what to take with her. She'd never been to Rhode Island and it was Frank's first year there so he really wouldn't be able to tell her. She found an atlas of the United States in the building's small bookcase in the game room and looked up Providence. It was north of Chicago, north of Pittsburgh, north of New York, and all that stood between it and the rest of cold, icy New England and Canada was a wide but not very high Massachusetts.

Mrs. Bliss had lived in south Florida since the sixties. In another year it would be the nineties. Over that kind of time span a person's body gets accustomed to the temperature of a particular climate. Take the person out of that climate and set him down in another and she's like a fish out of water. The blood thins out; the heart, conditioned to operate in one kind of circumstance, has to work twice as hard just to keep up in another. There were people from up North, for example, who couldn't take the Florida heat. Their skin burned, they ran a high fever. Except on the hottest days, and even then only when she'd been waiting for a bus in the sun or carrying heavy bags of groceries back from Winn-Dixie, Dorothy didn't even feel it. By the same token she'd noticed that in Chicago or Pittsburgh or Cincinnati on visits, she needed her good wool coat on what everyone else was calling a beautiful, mild spring day.

But who knew from Providence? So for a good two months before she left for that city Mrs. Ted Bliss studied the weather maps and read the long columns of yesterday's, today's, and tomorrow's temperature, the lows and the highs, and prophetically shook her head from side to side whenever she saw the dull gray cross-hatching of fronts and weather.

So, just in case, she packed almost everything, bringing along her heaviest woolen sweaters, scarves, even gloves. Her two big suitcases were too heavy and though she hated to impose on him she called Manny from the building and asked for his help.

"You look like you're moving for good."

"I never know what to take, not to take."

"The summer Rosie died I went back North to see the kids. You don't think I froze?"

"Here," she said, "let me help you."

"That's all right, I'll make two trips."

She should have waited for the van and given the driver a tip a dollar. It was like seeing some once familiar face from television who popped up again after an absence of a few years. She still recognized him, but there was something pinched about his eyes, or his mouth had fallen, or his body had become too small for his frame. Something. As if he were his own older relative. She hated to see him shlep like that.

"You're going to . . . ?"

"Frank's."

For a second the name didn't register and, even after he smiled, she felt a small stab from a not very interesting wound. Dorothy knew Manny knew Frank had not liked him much. He'd resented his mother's dependence on the guy after Ted died. It was nothing personal. There was no funny business to it. No one, not Frank, not Dorothy, certainly not Manny, had any crazy ideas. It was a compliment, really. Frank felt bad she was all alone and a stranger had to do for her.

How, she wondered, when she was on the plane and had finished her snack, and returned the tray table to its original upright position and drifted off to sleep as the airline's inflight shopping catalog with all its mysterious, unfathomable tsatskes, exercise equipment, short-wave radios and miniature television sets, motivational self-help videos, garment bags, and special, impregnable waterproof watches guaranteed to a depth of five thousand feet slipped into her lap, did I get to be so smart?

Though she declined when the hostess asked if she wanted to request a chair to meet her in Providence, she had treated herself to a ride in a wheelchair in the Florida airport even though she'd allowed herself plenty of time to get to the departure gate, and as she dozed it was of this she dreamed. Dreaming of unaccustomed, incredible comfort, dreaming right-of-way like a vehicle in a funeral procession, dreaming alternating unseen skycaps behind her who pushed her in the chair—Junior, Manny, Tommy Auveristas, Marvin, Frank, and Ted—as she sat luxuriously, dispensing wisdom, eating up their attention like a meal.

Despite the pleasure she thought she'd taken in her dream, she woke with a bad taste in her mouth, thinking: The same thing that gives us wisdom gives us plaque.

"How was the trip, Ma?"

"Fine."

"Make any new friends?"

"I don't talk so much to strangers anymore."

"Here," Frank said, "give me the baggage checks. I'll have the skycap bring your bags out to the curb."

To Frank's surprise, his mother surrendered the claim checks without a word.

Mrs. Bliss was surprised, too. She dismissed any idea of the sky-cap's trying to make off with her things.

Something else that surprised her was that in the months since she'd last seen him, Frank had become very religious. He insisted, for example, that she accompany him to synagogue. And not just for the relatively brief Friday evening service but for the long, knockdown, drag-out Saturday morning services, too. Now he and May, his wife, had never been particularly observant. Their son Donny had been bar mitzvahed but the ceremony had taken place in the nondenominational chapel of Frank's Pittsburgh university. A rabbi from Hillel had presided. The boy had been brilliant, flawlessly whipping through his Torah portion, and doing all of them proud, but Mrs. Bliss knew that afterward he didn't bother to strap on his phylacteries, not even during the month or so following the bar mitzvah when the flush of his Judaism might still be presumed to be on him. (His grandmother had been impressed with the grace and speed he employed in getting out his thank-you notes, though, blessed as he was with a sort of perfect pitch for gratitude. Each note was bespoke, custom cut to the precise value of the gift. He did not rhapsodize or make grand promises about how a $10 check from a distant cousin would be deposited into his college fund, but would instead fix upon a specific item—film, say; a tape he wanted; a ticket to a Pirates game.)

Both Mrs. Bliss's sons had been bar mitzvahed, Marvin as well as Frank, but neither could be said to be very religious. When Marvin died it was Ted, not Frank, who rose before dawn every day for a year to get to the shul on time to say Kaddish for their son. When Ted died it was no one. She'd *begged* Frank, but he refused, a matter of principle he said. So Dorothy, who was as innocent of Hebrew as of French, undertook to say the prayers for her dead husband herself. She read the mourner's prayers from a small, thin blue handbook the Chicago funeral parlor passed out. It was about the size of the pocket calculator Manny from the building had given her to help balance her checkbook after Ted lost his life. She read the prayers in a soft, transliterated version of the Hebrew, but came to feel she was merely going through the motions, probably doing more harm than good. If Mrs. Ted Bliss were God, Mrs. Bliss thought, she'd never be fooled by someone simply *impersonating* important prayers. It was useless to try to compensate for her failure by getting up earlier and earlier each morning. God would see through that one with His hands tied behind His back. If there even was a God, if He wasn't just some courtesy people politely agreed to call on to make themselves nobler to each other than they were.

So Mrs. Bliss's first reaction to her son's new piety was mixed not just with suspicion but with a certain sort of anger.

Especially after Frank made them all sit through the long seder supper, unwilling to dispense with even the most minor detail of the ritual meal. He didn't miss a trick. Everything was blessed, every last carrot in the tsimmes, each bitter herb, every deed of every major and minor player, one grisly plague after the other visited by God upon Egypt. It was a Passover service to end all Passover services. Indeed, Mrs. Bliss had a hunch that there wasn't a family in all Providence, Rhode Island, that evening that hadn't finished its coffee and macaroons and gotten up from the table before the Blisses were midway through their brisket and roast potatoes.

May seemed imbued with more baleboosteh spirit and just plain endurance than Dorothy could imagine herself handling during even the old golden glory days in Chicago with the gang. She

wore her out, May, with her hustle and bustle. And for at least a
few minutes Mrs. Bliss actually considered herself the victim of
some clumsy, stupid mockery. As a matter of fact she was almost
close to tears and, though she slammed down her will like someone
bearing down on the brakes with all her weight and just managed
to squeeze them back (she wouldn't give Frank—or May, who
might have put him up to this—the satisfaction of volunteering to
help clear away the dishes), she could almost feel the strain on her
face and only hoped that no one noticed. She sat through the re-
mainder of the meal with an assortment of smiles fixed to her face
like makeup.

When it was finally done she was one of the first to pile into
the living room, and found a place for herself in the most comfortable chair. She took some great-grandchild onto her lap like a
prop and started to rock the kid, who was already half asleep.

I'm going to get away with this, she thought. I'm going to act
like everyone here expects me to act and come away scot-free without giving a single one of them the satisfaction of believing they
ever got to me.

And would have, too, if her pious son hadn't seen through to
the depths of her heart.

"Something wrong, Ma?" Frank said in a low voice at the side
of her chair.

"You're the spiritual leader here," Mrs. Bliss said, "you tell
me."

Her son looked genuinely puzzled, even hurt. He'd been a
good boy. Quick in school, responsible, considerate to the family,
never demanding on his own behalf—they had to remind him that
what he wore was wearing out and that he needed new clothes;
they had to ask him what he wanted for his birthday; throughout
high school they raised his allowance before he ever asked—she'd
never had occasion to punish him, or even to yell at him. Her heart
went out to him. This was the young man who couldn't do enough
for her, who was always on the lookout for special gadgets to make
her life more comfortable and, though he seldom wrote, called even
when the cheap rates weren't in effect. He called as if long distance
grew on trees.

So of course she was sorry she had spoken harshly. Of course she could have bitten off her tongue rather than speak without thinking or cause him pain.

Only she hadn't spoken without thinking. She'd been thinking for a long time, for years as a matter of fact, whether she knew it or not. And though this was hardly the time (the first night of Passover when the Jewish people sat down together to celebrate their deliverance), and certainly not the place for it (her sole surviving son's new home where he'd be making a new life, which, let's face it, he was no spring chicken, so how many new lives could he expect to make for himself from now on, and his mother didn't think he'd be asked to take another job so quick), there were plenty of good reasons to get what had been eating at her and eating at her off her chest.

"What?" he said, following her down the hallway as she sought the spare room where they'd put her up as if it were a neutral corner.

"What?" he repeated. "What?"

"You're so religious," said Mrs. Ted Bliss. "How come you couldn't say Kaddish for your father? How come I had to depend on Manny who volunteered to say it for him?"

"Ma."

Maxine was standing in the doorway, looking in; George, her husband, was.

"I *begged* you," Mrs. Bliss said.

"Oh, Ma," Frank said.

"No. A stranger. A stranger you despised, that you humiliated in my home, my guest—you saw him, Maxine, you were a witness—that you gave him five dollars that time like you were throwing him a tip."

"Five dollars?"

"You don't remember the pocket calculator?"

"Come on, Ma. He makes me nervous. Sticking his nose in everywhere it don't belong. All right, maybe I wronged him, I admit it. How is he, anyway? I haven't seen him in years. I'm sorry if I hurt his feelings. If you want, I'll write him an apology. I'll call him up. We'll make friends."

"How is he? He's old. Like everyone else. And don't write him, don't call him up. He probably forgot. What's done is done. Let sleeping dogs lie."

"What's done is done? If what's done is done, how come you introduce a topic I haven't thought about in years? If what's done is done, how'd you happen to drag this particular Elijah into my house with you in the first place? Come on, Ma, is this really about Manny? Is it really even about my father?"

"Oh, you're such a smart fella, Frank. You're such a fart smeller," said Mrs. Ted Bliss.

"I haven't heard that one since I was a little girl," Maxine said. "Daddy used to say that one all the time."

"My father said it, too. I think it was the only joke he knew," George said.

"That's old," said one of Frank's new Rhode Island colleagues, "that's an old one."

"If you don't mind," said Mrs. Ted Bliss, "family business is being conducted here."

"Sorry," the colleague said, "I came for my son."

He reached out to the child Mrs. Bliss had been rocking in her lap in the living room. The little boy had apparently followed her into the room with Frank.

" 'Fart smeller, fart smeller,' " the kid squealed, "Great-Grandma Dorothy called Great-Uncle Frank a fart smeller."

Why was he calling her his great-grandmother? Who were these strange children, these outlanders, who apparently just latched on to the nearest, most convenient old lady and assumed some universal kinship? How could parents let their kids get away with stuff like that? Didn't they realize how patronizing it was? It made Mrs. Ted Bliss feel like someone's Mammy. (Though she felt for the child, too. How needful people were to belong, to be cared for.)

Her grandson Barry had squeezed into the room with the others. The auto mechanic slapped his tochis and guffawed.

"You mind your manners, Grandmother," Barry said, "or we'll have to wash out your mouth with soap. Strictly kosher for Passover. Ha ha."

"Please," Mrs. Bliss said, and again she was close to tears.

"Mama, what is it?" Maxine said.

"Give her some air, for God's sake," George said, and began to shoo people from the room.

It was a good idea, Mrs. Bliss thought. Why hadn't someone

thought of it earlier? "Yes," Mrs. Bliss said, "give me some air. Stand back there," she giggled, "make room. Oh," she said, "I'm so full. Everything May put out was delicious. The brisket was sweet like sugar, she'll have to give me her recipe. But so much? You could feed an army."

"A question is on the table, Mother, I think," Frank said.

"What question was that?" Mrs. Bliss asked wearily, sorry she'd taken her disappointment public.

"Is this really about Manny? Is this really about Dad?"

"No," she said, her long life draining from her in buckets, "it's really about why you never said prayers for your brother."

Maxine made a noise as if she'd had the wind knocked out of her.

Frank moved toward the door of the first-floor guest room they'd set up for the old woman, shut it, and turned back again to his mother.

"Just what kind of son of a bitch do you think I am?" he demanded.

"I don't think that," Mrs. Bliss said.

"Hypocrite then. I mean, Jesus, Ma, do you really believe I'm that scheming and political? Do you actually think that just because some damn zealot decided to drag my name into an op-ed column in the *New York* damned *Times* that legitimates his crazy charges?"

"Charges? There are charges? What did you do, Frank? Are you in trouble? Do you need a lawyer?"

"I got a lawyer, Ma. Manny from the building's on retainer."

"Manny from the building?"

"He's kidding you, Mother," Maxine said. "Frank, you're scaring her half to death."

"What's going on?" Mrs. Bliss said.

"She doesn't know?" Frank asked Maxine. "I mean her son is famous and she doesn't even know?"

"What's going on?"

"Mother, Frank left Pittsburgh because—"

"Was driven out of Pittsburgh," Frank said.

"—some political correctness jerk did this high-powered deconstructionist job on him. He said Frank deliberately eschewed the Zionist movement and swung over to Orthodox Judaism to privilege the word of the father over the writings of the son."

"You did this?"

"Of course not, Mother."

"Anti-Semitism!" Mrs. Bliss said.

"Well," said her son philosophically, "you know these guys, they get off on demystifying the whole hierarchy."

"They threw you out?"

"Let's just say they made the workplace hell for me."

"The grinch who stole Pesach," Maxine said.

She told them she was tired and said she thought she'd rest a while before going back out to help May with the dishes.

"May has plenty of help, Mother. You just get some sleep."

"Tell her everything tasted wonderful, a meal to remember."

The children came to the side of her bed. Maxine adjusted the pillows beneath her mother's head, kissed her cheek. Frank pressed his lips against her forehead.

"I have temperature?"

"Temperature?"

"That's the last thing I did after I put you to bed."

"I remember," Frank said.

"To check to see if you had temperature."

"Oh, yeah," said Maxine.

"Like clockwork," Mrs. Bliss said. "Sometimes I'd get up in the middle of the night and I couldn't remember. If I did, if I didn't. Then I'd have to go back to your room and do it again. Otherwise I couldn't sleep."

"Oh, Ma, that's so sweet," Maxine said.

"I'd always check to see if you had temperature."

"I'll turn off the light. Try to nap."

"You I'd check. I'd check Frank. Marvin I'd check."

"Oh, Ma," Maxine said.

"In the hospital, even when he was dying from leukemia. Can you imagine? Did you ever? The biggest hotshot doctors, the best men in Chicago. And there wasn't a thing anyone could do for him. The doctors with their therapies, me brushing his forehead with my lips to see did he have temperature."

"Please, Ma," Maxine said.

"Maxine's right, Ma," Frank said. "You've had a long day. Try to get some rest. I can hear them in the living room, I'll tell them to hold it down."

"They're your guests. Don't say nothing."

She couldn't have napped more than fifteen minutes. She'd fallen asleep watching one of her programs on the little bedside TV and when she woke up the show was just ending.

"Grandma? Grandma, I hear the TV. Are you up? May I come in?"

So she didn't know whether it was her grandson's knock, or his voice, or the sound of the television itself that had aroused her from sleep. She was as surprised as ever by the effectiveness of a brief snooze. Yet she rarely lay down before it was actually time to go to bed, and wondered at those times, like this one, how it was a person could doze for only a few minutes but wake completely refreshed whereas she could sleep through the night, or at least a whole block of hours, yet still be as exhausted in the morning as she was when she went to bed. What an interesting proposition, she thought—old people's science, septuagenarian riddles and the deep philosophic mysteries of experience. There should be men working on this stuff in the laboratories and universities. And, as usual, these questions were as immediately forgotten as the time it took her to think them. Which, she thought, was something else they should be working on. And immediately forgot that one, too.

"Grandma?"

"What?" said Mrs. Bliss. "Who's that, who's there? James? Is that you, Donny?"

"It's Barry, Grandma. Can I come in?"

"All right, Barry."

"I'm sorry if I woke you, Grandmother."

"You didn't. Maybe you did, I don't know. It's all right."

"Well, if I did, I'm sorry."

"Make the light, I can't see you."

He stood in the room in the light.

"Let me see your fingernails," his grandmother said.

"Grandma," he said.

"No, don't pull away your hand. You know what, Barry? You got fingernails like a piano player, like a banker. A surgeon who scrubs all the time don't have cleaner nails. What do you do, go to a beauty parlor?"

She'd been giving him the business about his nails all these years, ever since he first became a mechanic in a garage. It was true, his nails were immaculate, his hands were. There wasn't a drop of dirt on them. They were rough, but pink as a girl's. Ted had ribbed him, too. Now, though, she saw his small, sly, proud smile and Mrs. Bliss was a little ashamed of herself, and sorry for her grandson. How he must have worked on them, buffing and polishing and soaking them, it wouldn't surprise, in warm emollients and lotions. Soft, buttery waves of a thin perfume rose off his fingertips like distant, melting light refracted in a road illusion. It was terrible, she realized, the lengths to which he must have gone to rub away all the appearance of failure, and Mrs. Bliss understood as suddenly and completely as she'd awakened to the laws of old people's science how it was with poor Barry, in thrall, pursued by the reputations of his brilliant, successful cousins—Judith, Donald, James. And now it occurred that she didn't remember ever seeing him in anything less formal than a jacket and tie since he was a child. At cards, at family gatherings, on picnics, Barry was the one who always showed up overdressed. She wondered if he even *owned* a sport shirt and had never seen him in a bathing suit. And though none of his clothes seemed particularly good or fashionable, they were as carefully chosen to create an impression (or counterfeit one) as if they had been made to his measure.

Poor Barry, thought Mrs. Ted Bliss. Poor fatherless Barry. Who, for all that he went about dressed to the nines, leading with his perfectly manicured screen actor's fingernails, seemed somehow covered up, masked, as though the carefully groomed hands were only part of a magician's practiced, deliberate distractions, some noisily flourished razzle-dazzle that deceived no one and, indeed, there was something depressingly coarse about him, like a man with an awful five o'clock shadow. There was something loud and awful too about the conservative colors of even his darkest suits, which were always too black, a step removed from patent leather, or too brown, like woodstain on cheap suites of furniture. If Mrs. Bliss, a woman whose habits and heart did not allow herself to pick and choose between the members of her family, had let her guard down long enough to admit of a particular favorite, of her four grandchildren Barry might well have received the lion's share of her love, been chief beneficiary of the small store of her dedicated, egalitarian treasury. Indeed, if she could admit to the world what, even with both hearing aids turned up to their highest volume, barely registered on her consciousness (her still, small voice small still), she might have allowed herself to acknowledge that Barry took pride of place, said, "To hell with it!" and gone ahead and bought him that garage he was saving for.

But then, she thought, she'd have had to buy *all* of them garages.

He pulled an uncomfortable-looking slatted wooden chair (like the chair in the bed-and-breakfast that Frank and May had found for them the time she and Ted visited London during Frank's sabbatical year) up to the side of his grandmother's bed and sat down.

"So how are you, Grandmother?"

Mrs. Bliss started to laugh. Barry looked hurt.

"No, no, Barry. It's just, when you asked, you reminded me."

"What of?"

"Who's afraid of the big bad wolf, big bad wolf?" sang Mrs. Ted Bliss.

"Oh," Barry said, "yeah. Sure."

"No," said Mrs. Bliss, "*I'm* the big bad wolf. What did you bring me?"

"Questions," Barry said meekly.

"The better to see you with. The better to hear you with. The better to eat you with, my dear."

"About my dad," Barry said.

She'd never been one to carry on. She didn't make fusses, wasn't the sort of person who liked to impose. Outside the family, for example, she knew she made a better hostess than a guest. And if she had once been beautiful or vain, then the beauty and vanity were aspects of those same hospitable impulses that went into her lavish wish to please, to be pleasing to others. She wasn't stoic or invulnerable. If you pricked her, she bled, if you tickled her she laughed, de da de da. It was just that same baleboosteh instinct to clean up after herself, the blood; to cover her mouth demurely over the laughter. It was some Jewish thing perhaps, a sense of timing, knowing when to make herself scarce.

No one, she thought, understood the terrible toll Ted's death had inflicted upon her. Maybe the stewardess on the airplane that time, maybe the woman in City Hall to whom she'd tried to explain the problem about the personal property tax on Ted's Buick LeSabre. But the grief she felt when he died, that she still felt, never mind that time heals all wounds, was a thing not even her children were aware of (and to tell you the truth was more than a little miffed about this, not because they were blind to her pain so much as that their blindness gave her a sense that whatever they'd once felt about Ted's death had gone away), though she wouldn't have let them in on this in a million years. It wasn't that she meant to spare them either. They were her kids, she loved them, but maybe they didn't deserve to be spared. It wasn't even a question of why she spared them. It was *what* she spared them. Mrs. Bliss's loss was exactly that—a loss, something subtracted from herself, ripped off like an arm or a leg in an accident. It was the deepest of flesh wounds, and it festered, spilled pus, ran rivers of the bile of all unclosed scar, all unsealed stump. How could she ever ask anyone to look at something like that?

But Barry, with his grief for his father, for himself, was a different story altogether.

"He loved you, Barry. I never saw a prouder father. You were tops in his book. Tops."

Barry watched his grandmother carefully.

"You were," she said. "No father could have been closer to his son. He cherished you." She turned, facing him on her side, her weight uncomfortably propped on her forearm, the edge of her thin fist. "Lean down," she whispered.

Barry moved toward her, stretching tight his still buttoned suit jacket. "Yes?"

"It's a secret," she said. "Don't tell your cousins, it would hurt their feelings. Marvin got more naches from you than Aunt Maxine and Uncle Frank got from all your cousins put together."

"Really? No."

"Sure," said Mrs. Bliss. "It was written all over his face whenever you came into a room. Or maybe you'd just left and I'd come in and I'd say, 'I just missed Barry, didn't I, Marvin?' Sure, I could tell," she said, "it was like a big sign on his face."

"I don't remember," Barry said.

"You were a kid, a baby. What were you when your father, olov hasholem, got sick, eight, nine?"

"He died just before my tenth birthday."

"That's right. And before that he was in and out of hospitals for months at a time for an entire year. The hospital wouldn't allow

visitors your age, and when he was home he was too sick to play
with you. Except on those few days he seemed to be feeling a little
better we tried to keep you away from him. We thought it was best
that a child shouldn't see his daddy in those circumstances. We
were trying to do what was best by both parties. Maybe we were
wrong. We were probably wrong. What did we know? Did we have
so much experience? Were we so knowledgeable about death in
those days?"

She was as moved by what she said as Barry himself, but then,
olov hasholem, she knew that both of them, maybe all three of
them, deserved better, that a debt was owed to what really happened.

So she told him the truth: that in that last awful year of his life
he was too sick for pride, for favorites, big bright smiles, or any
other sign unconnected to his pain and suffering, too sick for the
least little bit of happiness, or, on even those rare, blessed days of
unlooked-for remission presented to him like a gift, for gratitude,
let alone having enough strength left over, or will, or determination, or drive, for anything as rigorous as love, or even common,
God forgive me, fucking courtesy.

It was different then. This was not only before death with dig-
nity, it was before pain management. It was the dark ages when
doctors and nurses didn't always play so fast and loose with the
morphine, and patients had to wait on the appointed, exact minute
of their next injection like customers taking a number at the bakery.
So when Dorothy sat with him in the hospital that year, always
putting in at least five or six hours a day and often pulling ten, or
more even, on the days when Marvin—olov hasholem, olov hasholem, olov hasholem—was out of his head, chained up and screaming at his torturers like a political prisoner, she felt the pain almost
as keenly as he did, fidgeting, uselessly pressing her lips to his head
to feel the fever, kissing his cheeks, wiping his face down with wet,
cool cloths in an effort to console him, even as he thrashed his head
and neck and shoulders about, forcefully (who had no force) trying
to escape, throw her off, shouting at her, actually cursing her, this
good tragic son (whose tragedy was, for Mrs. Bliss, suddenly,
sourly, obscurely underscored by the three- or four-year seniority
his wife had over him in age, so that, if he died, he would seem,
young as he was, even younger, and even more tragic) who'd never

so much as raised his voice to her before; yes, and felt his relief, too, as her son's vicious pains gradually subsided when he received the soothing sacrament of the morphine, but, exhausted as she was, not only not daring, not even willing to sleep during the three and then two and then one good hour of respite that the drug provided lest she miss one minute of what, despite all those hours of her visits to the hospital in the last year of Marvin's life, she still managed to fool herself into believing was the beginning of his cure.

They never got used to it. Not Ellen, not Ted, not Dorothy or Frank or Maxine, spelling, relieving each other on the better days and, on the just-average-ordinary, run-of-the-mill lousy ones only long enough to dash down to the cafeteria for a bite or out to the waiting room to grab a smoke or to the vending machines for a soft drink or cup of coffee, while on the five-star, flat-out rotten ones they never even got that far, but chose instead, like captains of doomed, sinking ships to stay with their vessels, who if they could not go down with them could at least bear witness. So that Marvin became at last not their son or brother or husband at all but some all-purpose child, the rights to whose death they collectively demanded. They *never* got used to it. Why should they? When they never even got used to the diagnosis?

A cracked rib? What was the big deal about a cracked rib? All right, it was uncomfortable. It was painful to draw a deep breath, and you had to walk on eggshells when you climbed the stairs, and be very careful not to make any sudden movements if you wanted to save yourself from a painful stitch, but a cracked rib? How serious could a cracked rib be if all they did for you was tape up your chest? It was like breaking a toe where *maybe* they might go to the trouble of fixing it in a little splint while the bone went about the business of healing itself. It was a nuisance, of course it was, no one denied it, but serious? Come on! It was about as life threatening as a black eye, except that with a black eye you always had the added humiliation of explaining it away, trying to put it in the best light.

All right, *two* cracked ribs, the second following about a week after the first one got better, and Marvin unable to explain how he got it except to tell the doctor he felt this wrenching pain as he was bending over to lift a bag of Ellen's groceries out of the backseat to carry into the house for her. But tests? *Tests?* Okay, the X ray they could understand, but sending the poor man off to the hospital for blood tests Dr. Myers said he didn't have a way to take and have analyzed in his office quickly enough?

It was probably nothing of course, but just to make certain, be on the safe side.

His mother went white when she heard and Ellen's pleas for her not to interfere, and to let Myers take care of it and just stay out of the doctor's hair and not act like some ignorant greenhorn while they waited for the results.

Ignorant greenhorn? I'm his mother!

Of course you are, Ma, and I'm his wife, and I'm as scared as you are, believe me, but I don't want the whole world in on this. It would only terrify Marvin if he found out.

The whole world, the whole world? I'm his mother. What did he say, the doctor?

Let's take it one step at a time.

Let's take it one step at a time? And you didn't ask questions? You didn't press him?

I pressed him, I pressed him. Okay? I asked him what's the worst-case scenario.

What is?

Leukemia. Blood cancer. Are you satisfied?

Leukemia. Oh God, oh God, oh my God.

Myers didn't *say* it was leukemia. What he said was that was the worst-case scenario. We have to wait for the tests, we have to take it one step at a time.

Leukemia. Oh my God oh God oh my God, my son has leu*kem*ia.

"He doesn't have leu*kem*ia," Ellen said. "We have to wait for the tests."

But of course that was just what he would have, Mrs. Bliss knew. Since when does a perfectly healthy young man crack a rib from picking up a bag of groceries out of the backseat of a car? It just doesn't happen. And when the results finally came back—and it wasn't that long; what took time were all the additional tests they added on to those initial ones they sent him off to the hospital for— the reports from hematology, the pathologist's opinions—and it *was* leukemia, Mrs. Bliss, God forgive her, couldn't quite absolve her daughter-in-law from at least a little of the responsibility for her son's illness. Who asks a man who's just recovered from a painfully cracked rib to stoop over and pick up a heavy bag of groceries for her? What was she, a cripple? She wasn't saying that that's what caused him to come down with the disease, but maybe if she'd shown a little more consideration, if she hadn't been in such a hurry, if she'd waited until he was a little stronger, Marvin wouldn't have cracked another rib and his body would have had a better chance to heal, and the leukemia might never have happened.

"That's silly," Ted Bliss said. "How was it Ellen's fault? This was something going on in his blood."

"Leukemia. Oh my God, oh my God, my son has *leukemia*."

They accepted the diagnosis, they just never got used to it. Just as, God forgive her (though she knew better and had known better even at the top of her anger and denial as she pronounced her awful thoughts about Ellen to Ted), to this day she couldn't get past the idea that if his wife had taken better care of him, if all of them had, her son might be alive today.

So it was his death she never got used to.

Mrs. Bliss wasn't ignorant greenhorn enough not to understand the nature of her son's disease. The white cells were amok in his blood, she told him. The chozzers gobbled up the red cells like there was no tomorrow. They had a picnic with him.

"I never gave in to them," said Mrs. Ted Bliss. "It wasn't the easiest thing because, let's face it, your mother was right, I *am* a greenhorn. What did I know about blood counts? About platelets? Did I know what a leukocyte was?"

So she made it her business. Not just to sit there. Not just to feel his fever or wipe his brow. She made it her business to study the numbers, to live and die by the numbers. Just like her son, olov hasholem, and learned to work the proportions between the white cells and red cells as if she were measuring out a recipe. And thought, If she *knew*, if she *understood* . . .

"Because I never believed he would die," Mrs. Bliss said. "This I *never* believed."

And spoke to Myers. And asked if everything that could be done was being done. Because didn't she read in the papers and see on TV that breakthroughs happened all the time, that cures for this and cures for that were just around the corner? She wanted him to tell her where, in the city, they were doing the best work. The city? The country, the world! Myers, God bless him, was a good man but very conservative. Maybe not, Mrs. Bliss thought, up on everything. He told her, 'Dorothy, dear, he's too sick to be moved.'

" 'So if he lays still he'll get better?'

" 'Dorothy, he's not going to get better.'

"You think I accepted that? You think Grandpa or your mother did? We looked it up, we asked around, and what everyone told us was that if, God forbid, you had to be sick the best place to be was the University of Chicago hospital. So that's where we put him, in Billings, where they were doing advanced work in the field, experimental, giving special treatments which the insurance company wasn't willing to pay for, and where Myers himself wasn't even on the staff, where he had to have special permission—wait a minute, it wasn't a pass—where he had to have reciprocity, reciprocity, just for permission to look in on him."

So that's where they moved him, and called in the highest-priced Nobel prize specialists to let them have a go at him.

"But you know? It wasn't they didn't know what they were doing. They tried the latest chemotherapies on him. One drug Marvin was the first patient in the state of Illinois to receive it. And there were definite benefits. His white count never looked better.

"Only . . .

"Only . . ."

"Only what, Grandma?"

"Barry, he was *dying*."

"Oh, Grandma," he said.

"We didn't know what to do." Mrs. Ted Bliss sighed.

"Oh, Grandma."

"That was when we were there practically around the clock. The room was so crowded you almost couldn't breathe. We didn't even spell each other anymore. If we went out now it wasn't for a bite or to get a cup of coffee. It was to give the air a chance to recirculate."

"Oh, Grandma."

She went out to the waiting room this one time. She didn't pick up even a magazine. There was a newspaper. She hadn't seen a paper in days. The headline was in letters as thick as your arm. She looked but couldn't take any of it in. She remembered thinking, Something important has happened, but what it was, or who it had happened to, she still couldn't tell you. The year was a blur. The only current event she could remember was her son.

"There was a man in the waiting room. I'd seen him before, so naturally I thought he was a close friend or relative of one of the other patients on the floor. Though I'd never said a word to him. Listen, I didn't look at a magazine, I couldn't take in a headline. You think I was in the mood to make small talk with a stranger?''

She must have been crying. Sure, she must have been crying, because all of a sudden the man got up from where he was sitting and crossed the waiting room to where Dorothy was.

'' 'How's your son today, Mrs. Bliss,' he says, 'not so good?'

"I'd never spoken to him. How did he know my name? How did he know I was Marvin's mother? He could have been reading my mind. He introduced himself, he gave me his card."

His name was Rabbi Solon Beinfeld, and if she hadn't been holding the card in her hand she'd never have believed he was a rabbi. He looked more like a lawyer, or a businessman, or even one of the doctors. He didn't even look particularly Jewish to her if you want to know. And he could have been reading her mind again because he explained how he was the official chaplain for all the Jewish patients in Billings Hospital. She asked him, well, if he was the chaplain how come when she saw him he was always sitting in the waiting room.

'' 'Patients are often self-conscious. Sometimes I embarrass them. And though I'm here to listen to them, or counsel them, it's always an awkward situation. The waiting room is where I pray for them.'

"And you know, Barry, when he said that that's the first time I really believed he was a rabbi, or even a chaplain. I mean, there we were, in Billings Hospital on the Midway campus of the University of Chicago, with all its high-powered specialists. What was I expecting, that he'd be dressed like a Hasid in a big black hat and have a long beard and side curls with tzitzit peeking out from under his vest? The only thing that surprised me was that he wasn't wearing a long white lab coat."

He wanted to know if she was Orthodox, Conservative, or Reformed.

He was a rabbi, a man. She wanted to please him.

"I bentsh licht," she said, and looked down modestly. He waited for her to go on. "In Russia," she admitted, "girls didn't always get a Jewish education. I don't read the Hebrew."

Suddenly he seemed uneasy, and Mrs. Bliss put two and two

together. It was awkward, he'd said. He was there to listen to patients, to counsel them. What could he tell Marvin, to what would
he listen—his cries and whimpers, his demands for injections?

He was there in the waiting room praying for her son, praying
for Marvin and he was right, she *was* embarrassed. She'd put two
and two together. More than from the evidence of his only inter-
mittently improved blood counts or his brief pain-free periods
when he seemed not only better but actually perky, or from those
rarer and rarer times when the blood seemed returned to his cheeks
(the red returning blood cells from the higher and higher doses of
the heroic new devastating chemotherapies and almost steady
transfusions he was getting now) all the more bright for the flat,
colorless palette of his pale illness, it was her knowledge of the
chaplain rabbi's prayers for her son that depleted her hope, and
made her want to die.

"You know something I don't know, Chaplain?" Mrs. Bliss
asked almost viciously.

"No," he said sadly, "I think you know everything."

He was not only a man, he was a rabbi, and despite her heartbreak, Mrs. Bliss still wished to please him.

"It was all I could do not to let myself cry out in front of him.
I *knew* he was a rabbi. I *knew* it was his business and that this was
the way he made his living, just like Grandpa was a butcher and
you're an automobile mechanic," she told her grandson. "Still, it
was all I could do not to run away from him or stop myself from
howling in the street.

"I didn't completely trust Myers? I wanted a second opinion?
All right, here it was. The chaplain practically praying over your
father's body right out in the hall!

"It was too much to ask. What, I *shouldn't* break down? I wasn't
entitled? Character is a terrible thing," she said. "Who knows what
who knew what back there in Marvin's room? If I screamed now
they'd hear me and come running to see. Maybe your father himself
would hear me and know how it was with him. Because it's true
what they say, 'Where there's life there's hope.' What right did I
have to take that away from anybody just because I'd put two and
two together and understood he was a goner?

"Character is a *terrible* thing. Because all it is is habit.

"So instead of screaming, I started to moan.

" 'Marvin!' I moaned. 'Marvin, Marvin, Marvin! Oy Marvin. Marvin, my poor precious baby!'

" 'Shah!' the rabbi says. 'Shah! Shah!' And actually touches his finger to my lips. I couldn't have been more amazed than if he'd kissed me!

" 'Shah!' he says again, quiet now. 'Shh, shh.'

" 'He's my son,' I say.

" 'Don't call his name.'

" 'Don't call his name? Marvin's my oldest. He's going to die. I shouldn't say Marvin?'

" 'Don't say his *name!*' It's a command. This guy is commanding me not to cry out the name of my dying baby.

" 'Your boy,' he says, 'what is this fellow's Hebrew name?'

" 'Marvin's Hebrew name—' "

" 'Don't *say* his name! Is this chap's Hebrew name Moishe?'

" 'Yes,' I tell him, 'Moishe,' "

Which is when Beinfeld explained it to her.

When a person is supposed to die, he told her, God sends out the Angel of Death to look for the person. Now the Angel of Death is the stupidest of all the angels, and sometimes, not always, he can be fooled. Doctors often fool the angel with certain operations, or at times with special medicines. He's a stupid angel, yes, but not a complete idiot. He's been around the block and he's picked up a thing or two. Only the thing of it is that of all God's angels he's not only the stupidest but the busiest. He hasn't got time to hang around trying to figure out how to undo all that the doctors have done for sick people with their operations and special medicines. Which is why certain patients go—*swoosh*—just like that, and others, like Moishe, linger on for a year or more.

All he had to go on, Beinfeld told her, was a list of names. In certain respects he wasn't all that much different from a postman who has to match up the name of the addressee with the name on the mailbox.

" 'This party of whom we were speaking,' the rabbi says, 'tell me, he has a middle name?'

" 'Yes.'

" 'Whisper it to me.'

" 'Sam. Shmuel.'

" 'Harry,' he says. 'Good. In Hebrew, Herschel.' "

So Beinfeld changed his name. They went into Barry's dad's

room, and Dorothy introduced him and explained to everyone
what was going to happen. It may have been the first time the
chaplain had ever seen who he'd been praying for. He made out a
paper. He even had the hospital type up a different band and put
it around Moishe Herschel Bliss's wrist. They did a new card at the
nurses' station and substituted it for the one on the door outside
his room. Beinfeld turned the clipboard around at the foot of the
bed holding you know who's chart on it. Then the rabbi offered up
prayers around the bed to spare the invalid's life.

Mrs. Bliss hadn't had a Jewish education; by her own admission
she didn't know Hebrew, and though she had no understanding of
what Beinfeld was saying, she caught him repeating Moishe Herschel's "name" throughout the course of his prayer. Well, she could
hardly have missed it, could she, because each time he said it he
seemed to say it more loudly as though the Angel of Death were
not only stupid but maybe a little deaf, too.

He signaled the family out of the sickroom and instructed them
that if they *had* to call Marvin by name they call him Moishe Herschel, or Marvin Harry, *never* Moishe Shmuel or Marvin Sam.

" 'Excuse me, Rabbi,' your grandfather said.

" 'Yes?'

" 'That prayer you prayed.'

" 'Yes?'

" 'Didn't you pray it to God?'

" 'To God, yes. To God.'

" 'And this Angel of Death, ain't he God's angel?'

" 'Of course. God's angel. So?'

" 'So,' " said Ted Bliss, " 'don't the left hand know what the
right hand is doing?' "

Which took the wind out. Out of his grandmother, too.

"Except," Mrs. Bliss said, "I was his mother. Didn't I make a
fuss with Myers? Didn't I go over his head to put Marvin into
Billings? Where they were doing the advanced work, the special,
experimental treatments? We were losing him, Barry, what harm
could it do? So maybe what that chaplain rabbi was trying to do
on a spiritual level was just as much in the experimental stage as
what those doctors were trying to do on the scientific one. We were
losing him, Barry, what harm could it do?"

"Oh, Grandma."

"Only I could never say it," she said softly.

"What?"

"Only I could never say it, say Moishe Herschel. He was my first-born, he was my son. I couldn't call him different."

"You called him Marvin?"

"I didn't call him anything," she said, and wept while her grandson tried to comfort her.

Later that night, when the guests had all gone home, and the house was quite dark and everyone was sleeping, Mrs. Bliss woke from her sleep. She was very thirsty. She put on her house slippers and, making no noise lest she rouse somebody, went to the kitchen. She meant to get a glass of water at the sink and had to turn on the light to see what she was doing. She was astonished. May had made no effort to wash the dishes. Mrs. Bliss would have started them herself but was afraid, one, that she'd make too much noise and wake them up upstairs and, two, that May would take it as a reflection on her housekeeping when she came down the next morning to find everything cleaned and put away. Mrs. Bliss took pride in being a model mother-in-law. She stayed out of people's way, kept her opinions to herself, she didn't interfere.

So she decided to get her drink of water and go back to bed. Except every surface was covered with dirty dishes, she couldn't see a clean glass anywhere. So she went to the cabinet where she thought her daughter-in-law might keep her everyday water glasses. She reached overhead and opened the cabinet.

It was filled with unused Yortzeit candles, glasses filled almost to their brims with a dry white wax and they must, Mrs. Bliss thought, forgiving them all, have been waiting on the anniversaries of everybody's death.

And still later that night, when she'd drunk her fill from the cold water tap in May's kitchen, when she'd quenched her thirst and slaked at least a little of her disappointment at the remarkable though oddly reassuring sight of the well-stocked cupboard of all those candles, and she was once again back in the perfectly comfortable bed in the perfectly comfortable little first-floor guest room Frank and May had set up for her, you'd think, thought Mrs. Ted Bliss, I'd be able to sleep. You'd think, she thought, that after what I told Barry about his father's last days, it would be like a weight off my back. She saw that the poor kid hadn't known bubkes, and speculated that it was probably a sin to keep things from people who needed to know them more than you needed the distraction and comfort you got from not having to explain everything. It was a kind of protection racket they ran on each other, but the only ones they protected were themselves. Even Marvin, olov hasholem, had been kept in the dark about what was what with him and was never brought up to speed on how he was really doing. They conducted themselves that year like they were managing a cover-up. Did this one know what that one knew? How could they keep so-and-so from finding out such-and-such? It wasn't power they sought, advantage, only the control of information, charging themselves with a sort of damage control.

And she still couldn't understand why Frank had become so religious, or what the real story was—throw out the flim-flam—why—a man his age—had ever left Pittsburgh. She was, there in the dark, in the dark, Mrs. Bliss was, about her children's lives. As much as they were in the dark about hers. People were through with each other *before* they were through with each other, and explaining yourself was just too much trouble. How could she tell them, for example, that Junior Yellin was back in her life, or that they'd been talking about going on a cruise together some day, staying on the seafront property of Caribbean resort hotels, or that maybe, to cut down on costs, they'd been thinking about sharing the same cabin, the same room? How could she speak of the Toibb mystery, or of Hector Camerando and what he'd offered to do for her, or ever hope to explain why, after what he'd put her through, or laid on the line what he thought about Jews, she'd given Alcibiades Chitral the hundred dollars, or her visit to the prison, or the question of the roses, or even, for that matter, her conversation with the driver who took her into the Everglades? Or so much as hint at the crush a woman her age could have on Tommy Auveristas, or the fact that Manny was no longer in a position to help her, their trusted, very own envoy and in loco parentis guy in south Florida? They wouldn't have understood anything, anything. They wouldn't have understood, she didn't herself, how even peripheral people— Louise Munez, Rita de Janeiro—had taken up the space in her life that they had once rightfully occupied. Not anything, none of it, nothing, anything at all, as in the dark about her life in south Florida as she was about theirs in any of the half-dozen places they lived their own mysterious lives.

NINE

Dorothy was surprised by the paltry turnout of mourners at Manny from the building's funeral. Compared to the great hosts of people only three or four years earlier who'd not only come to the chapel to pay their respects when Rosie lost her life but come out again the following day for the funeral service and gone on to the cemetery itself, many of them on walkers or in wheelchairs, to witness the burial proper, Manny's obsequies were not merely negligible, they were all but intangible. Rosie's shivah had broken house records. So, of course, did Manny's, but from the wrong end of the telescope. One of the few people who showed up at Manny's apartment—notices had been posted in each of the Towers' game rooms—for Manny's pathetically small farewell party looked around and remarked to the young man who'd opened the door for him, "Jeesh, this seems to be just about the coldest ticket in town, don't it?" It was unfortunate that the person to whom he made the remark was Manny's only attending relative, and when he was informed, by Mrs. Bliss as it happened, to whom he had passed his comment, he could have bitten his tongue in half.

"Hey, forget it," said the guy he thought he'd aggrieved. "I'm only a distant nephew. I barely knew him. I'm his lawyer. Uncle Manny hired me over the phone to buff up his affairs if anything happened to him. I'm just here on the case, no harm done."

Mrs. Bliss wasn't so sure but held her tongue.

The harm, she supposed, was to Manny's spirit. Olov hasho-lem, Manny, she thought, and even, she thought, may have mut-tered aloud. (She was deafer than ever these days, and couldn't always distinguish her thoughts from what she actually said.) At any rate it wasn't the little nephew lawyer pisher to whom the harm had been done. It was an insult that there couldn't have been more than ten people in the place. And even at that, no turnover to speak of because Mrs. Bliss had been there all evening practically and for every two or three people who left barely one arrived to take their place.

It was just too bad there really wasn't anyone to be sore at, for the fact of the matter was that in the just four years since Rosie's death the Towers had practically emptied out. There just weren't that many old-timers or familiar faces left. When someone died their children, who usually had no use for Florida, would either list the condo with an agent or hang around for a month or so to try to sell it themselves. The price of these places had gone through the floor, and the sad truth was that Mrs. Ted Bliss could have had the biggest, highest-priced condo the Towers had to offer (except for the penthouses of course) for many thousands less than what she and Ted had given for their own only medianscale suite of rooms back in the sixties.

"Did you know," Junior Yellin said beside her on Manny's long white leather sofa, "the silly son of a bitch arranged for the caterer himself?"

"He was my friend, I won't listen to gossip about him," said Mrs. Ted Bliss.

"What gossip?" Junior said. "His nephew told me."

"Shh!" Mrs. Bliss, whose increased hardness of hearing en-couraged her in the belief that people tended to raise their voices when they were around her, waved down the volume of Junior's voice.

"I don't know did he, didn't he, but the kid gave me his word as a lawyer your pal not only knew who would and who wouldn't be here today, but pretty much sized up the collective tastes of the crowd. That's why you see more decaf and sweet table than lox and pastrami. They're counting cholesterol, they're stinting on fat."

"It's ridiculous he had his own shivah catered. It's ridiculous, it's nuts."

"Is it, oh yeah? Wasn't he a lawyer, didn't he have a head for contingency and probability?"

"What's that got to do?"

"What's *that* got to do, what's *that* got to do?"

"Shh!"

"Look at this place, will you," Junior said. "Who are these people? They sit off by themselves. They could be patients in the waiting room reading my magazines."

Mrs. Bliss glanced around the room, which, except for Junior, herself, and the nephew, had only two other visitors left. "Since when," she asked, "has your waiting room been this full?"

"Wise guy," Junior said, "it gets me through my days."

"Oh, now," said Mrs. Ted Bliss.

" 'Oh, now? Oh now?' Dorothy, this is the way goyim talk. Maybe you've been in this place too long."

It was true, thought Mrs. Ted Bliss, the Towers had gone downhill. Many of the Cubans and Latin Americans had moved out to Palm, or farther down Collins to South Beach, or bought in the Keys, while a lot of the Jews had died off or moved out altogether. Ted, she reflected, wouldn't recognize the place today, and then corrected herself. Yes, he would. Sure he would. Of course he would. It wasn't all that much different from the fifty-unit Chicago apartment building he owned on the North Side where Dorothy went with him on the first Monday of every month to collect the rents, covering for him with a gun he hadn't even known she had.

So sure he would, he'd have known in a minute, failing only to recognize that this, in the end, was where he'd chosen to bring her, to live side-by-side with those same old Polacks and Slavs her family had fled when she was a kid. Only, in an odd way, she had the upper hand while they, the new goyim, were the interlopers.

Change, she reflected, between crumbs of sweet coffee cake she licked from her fingers, if you just managed to live long enough, even change changed.

Because here was Mr. Milton Junior Yellin beside her—butcher, farmer, realtor, bookkeeper, philanderer, black marketeer, recreational therapeusisist, and general, all-round-who-knows-what-all, a bona fide quick-change champion in his own right, transmogrified again from masher to friend, then friend, absorbed into friendship, something even more valuable—mutual witnesses to each other's lives, necessary kibitzers. So that they could, even at their age, get down, Yellin reserving the right to accuse her speech ("Dorothy, this is the way goyim talk"), Mrs. Bliss at liberty to discuss the fiction of Junior Yellin's "practice." It was heady stuff, heady, and, quite frankly, they may have embarrassed Manny's nephew executor with their open laughter.

Because with the exception of the nephew, Mrs. Bliss, and Milt Yellin, Manny's condo was now quite empty of mourners. It must have seemed that there was no one left in the entire world who genuinely missed him, this once minister-without-portfolio who did so much for so many of them in the Towers complex that he seemed to have become a kind of precinct captain and ward heeler for them. (All this was in the old days, of course. Though, really, Mrs. Bliss thought, the old days weren't all that long ago. Hadn't she pressed her claims on Manny's mysterious volunteer spirit as recently as last year when she'd packed two or three times more than she needed and counted on what even then as well as in hindsight was an already thinning, short-winded huffer and puffer who shouldn't have been called upon to so much as snap her valises shut let alone carry them from her apartment all the way down the hall to the elevator, albeit he made two trips with one suitcase held out in front of his belly with both hands—the way children carry weights too heavy for them—rather than two suitcases, one dangling from each hand and swinging along beside him as if to the marching music of youth and strength? And didn't, for a short-winded old man, two trips with half a load each create a greater threat to the constitution than just some single let's-get-it-over-with effort of the double weight? So it was only fitting, she thought, that she who had added to his burdens the longest should have stayed the longest, making the most of his death even at the expense of wearing out her welcome.)

The sun had already begun to set before Dorothy realized that though they'd been talking together for some hours now they'd never been formally introduced. She broke off in the middle of a reminiscence to do the honors.

"I'm Dorothy Bliss," she said, "and this here is Junior Yellin."

"Call me Milt."

"Oh, I'm sorry," the nephew said, "I'm Nathan Apple."

"Pleased to meet you."

"Pleased to meet you."

"Pleased to meet *you*," said Nathan Apple.

"Excuse me, Nathan, but I have to get this off my chest. You mustn't judge by what you saw today."

"Saw today?"

"Well, *didn't* see today. The turnout. Your uncle was one of the most popular, well-known, best-loved men in Building One. Were you at Rosie's funeral? Your aunt's?"

"My mother's sister's half-sister."

"And I've been thinking, the reason Rosie had so many people and Manny so few in comparison, no disrespect to your aunt, wasn't so much a tribute to Rosie as a show of support for her husband. Also, you've got to remember that many of those who dragged themselves out to her funeral on walkers back then are now in wheelchairs, and that a whole bunch of them who were in wheelchairs are now restricted to their beds. Many of the rest, may they rest, are dead. Others may not really have gotten to know him because he was already too old by the time a lot of them moved in for him to help them out much. Sure," she said, "by that time Manny was the one who needed help. So I'm just saying, you mustn't feel bad."

"I appreciate what you're saying, Aunt Dorothy."

Aunt Dorothy? Mrs. Bliss thought. *Aunt* Dorothy? She was stung by this smart aleck's familiarity. Why, when you reached a certain age, did they rub your face in your harmlessness? That guy at Frank's house in Providence should have smacked his kid for calling her his greatgrandma Dorothy.

"So tell me, Nate," Junior Yellin said, "you got plans for this place?"

"Plans?"

"You know. How you intend to market it."

"We haven't really gotten that far in our thinking, Milt."

"We?"

"Aunt Rosie's and Uncle Manny's legatees."

"You know best, Counselor, but I figure you're down here— what?—only one or two more days? Probably figure to list your uncle's condo with an agent and skedaddle the hell out of here before you even get to know the lay of the land."

"*Junior!*" said Mrs. Ted Bliss.

"Well, he was hired over the *phone*, Dorothy. He's . . . what . . . a distant nephew? Manny and Rosie were from Michigan. *That's* distant. Am I getting warm, Nate?"

"Well," Nathan Apple said.

"Sure I am, I'm getting warm. All I'm saying, son, is that I've handled a few real estate transactions in my day. Aunt Dorothy can tell you. As a matter of fact I had at least a *leetle* something to do with some property she and her husband had a few years back. That was in Michigan, too, now I recall. Tell him, Dot."

"*Junior!*"

"Tell him."

"My husband bought a farm from Mr. Yellin."

"*Through* Mr. Yellin. I know you're already the executor, young Nate, but if it makes you more comfortable why don't you consult with the legatees and see what they want to do with the place? Tell them you have a man who might be willing to handle it for them without, under the circumstances, taking a commission."

"Under what circumstances?" the lawyer said.

"Well, it's sentimental," Junior Yellin said. "I know how helpful Uncle Manny was to Mrs. Bliss. How indebted she was to him. In her book he was practically Uncle Johnny-on-the-spot."

"Come on," said Mrs. Bliss, "cut it out."

"He was, wasn't he?"

"He was very kind to me," Mrs. Bliss admitted.

"I'm afraid I don't see—"

"Tell me your price range. Maybe I'll buy it myself."

"I don't know," Nathan Apple said. "I don't know the lay of the land. You said so yourself."

"Ballpark."

"I don't know," he said. "It's the most expensive of the three basic floor plans. It's got a beautiful panoramic view of Biscayne Bay. And didn't my uncle refurnish the place a few months after Aunt Rosie died?"

Junior nudged Mrs. Bliss and winked. "He don't know he says, he don't know. Is this guy Mr. Perry Fucking Mason or what?"

"I don't know," Nathan said. "A hundred seventy thousand dollars?"

"Jesus," Junior said, "he *don't* know!"

Mrs. Bliss was amazed by Yellin, who seemed in the few minutes he'd been talking to Apple to have climbed down from all the moderated energies he'd displayed for her since coming to Florida and renewing their (in a sense) practically historical relationship, and reverted to his old piratical ways. The seamlessness of the transition was what most surprised her, some now-you-see-it, now-you-don't quality to his character palpable as a magician's trick. Old and diminished as he'd become, conversational, anecdotal, at times almost soliloquial in some gentle, calm, barbershop sense of mild, almost privileged reflection; then, quick as snap, there he was, back in business again. He was no slouch. And neither, Mrs. Bliss saw, to judge by the kid's $170,000 gambit, was young Nate.

She was probably just a foolish old woman, thought Mrs. Ted Bliss, but she had a sense that at least a bit of this male flourish and display were for her benefit. Even the pisher's. It was a proposition incapable of being tested, but she had the impression that if she weren't there to witness them, their moves and positioning, their vying, would never have been near so blunt. It was astonishing to her how people just couldn't help themselves, fantastic they should be so mired in gender. Then she thought, look at the pot calling the kettle black. What, I'm not getting a kick out of this? And surrendered to what, in all the most ancient parts of her old being, she hoped would prove to be spectacular.

And egged it on even.

"A hundred seventy thousand dollars," she said, almost like someone in a prompter's box reminding the players where things stood, pronouncing this as the prompter would, without emphasis, neutrally as she could, almost meaninglessly.

"Ballpark," said Nathan, picking up his cue.

"Yeah, sure," Junior Yellin said, "ballpark. But Yankee Stadium?"

Mrs. Ted Bliss loved it. It was delicious. She ate it up.

"Okay," Nathan said reasonably, "all right. I forgot about your loyalty to Uncle Manny and Aunt Dorothy. I forgot about your willingness to sacrifice your usual commission. What's five percent of a hundred seventy thousand? Eighty-five hundred, am I right? A hundred seventy thousand take away eighty-five hundred is what . . . ? A hundred sixty-one thousand, five hundred."

"Absolutely," Junior said. "Back in Grosse Pointe. Down here they go by the new math altogether."

"The new math."

"Yeah, well, first of all we start from an entirely different commission basis. The agent takes ten percent, not five. Already that brings us down to one hundred fifty-three thousand, and that's without even factoring in the buyer's initial additional expenses."

"*What* initial additional expenses?" Apple said.

"The initial additional expenses of refurnishing this place."

"That's no problem," Nathan said, "we're selling it furnished."

"You decided that? You and Aunt Rosie's and Uncle Manny's legatees?"

"I'm the executor."

"I guess it just wasn't meant to be," Yellin said. "We're at an impasse here, Dorothy." Junior sighed sadly. Nathan Apple, deep in thought, stroked his chin.

"Let's see," he said, "maybe not." And looked up brightly. "Tell you what," he said. "You gave up your agent's commission, I'll give up my executor's commission. But you know," he said, "my hands are tied. We're paid on a sliding scale. In most states, in an estate like Uncle Manny's, the lawyer is entitled to a two and three-quarters percent fee. Anyone have a pocket calculator?"

"I do," said Mrs. Ted Bliss, "your uncle gave me this in a time of trouble." She handed it to him. "It works on solar," she said.

The lawyer punched some numbers into the little machine, then showed them the numbers that ran along the top of the keypad like a faded headline. "I make that $4,207.50," he said. "Subtract that from . . . We'll use your $153,000 as a base price, Milt. There, it's $148,792.50."

"Tell him, Dorothy."

"Tell him what?" said Mrs. Bliss.

"Tell him about the neighborhood."

"I want to stay out of this," said Mrs. Ted Bliss.

She did. She wanted to stay out of it altogether. She wished only to sit there, comfortably ringside, and watch these two champions go at each other. Rivals, she thought girlishly. Rivals for my hand. She almost laughed at the absurdity. She was eighty years old. If she had once been beautiful it would have taken the genius of some paleontological vision to restore her from her fossil clues and data. Bands of archaeologists would have had to reconstitute her from the geological record. It wasn't vanity, she wasn't vain. It had to do with that old gender mire. It was that they couldn't help themselves. They couldn't.

"Go on, Dot. Tell him."

"You tell him, Milt."

"Tell me what?"

"It's sociology," said the jack of all trades.

"Sociology."

"And style. Sociology and style. Sociology and style and evolution, both progressive and retrograde."

The jack of all trades was into his recreational therapeusistical mode now with more than a touch, thought Mrs. Ted Bliss, of his handy-dandy bookkeeping and old black-marketeering skills than of his realtor ones.

"Because what you've got to remember," Junior Yellin said, "is that this place, south Florida generally, is a one-industry town—the weather industry. Now you've got to refine that to read the *winter* weather industry. Not like Vermont, of course, or Vail, Colorado, but in some it's-June-in-January sense. Why, it was practically invented by people with bad circulation. Well, it's called the Sunshine State, ain't it? They stick it on the goddamn license plates!

"All right, so what we essentially got here isn't so much a place to be as a place to *come* to. You're a kid, or in your thirties or forties or fifties, the blood is running, your daddy's rich and your ma is good lookin', and you've barely even *heard* of it. Maybe Disneyworld, maybe Cape Canaveral. Maybe stone crabs, maybe Key lime pie. Because your nose is to the grindstone, your shoulder to the wheel. Because, jeez, you're too busy even to notice the temperature, and if you did, so what? Because weather is a thing you strive for. You sock it away for a rainy day. I mean for when the blood turns to sludge, to thirty-weight oil. I mean for when the damp shtups mold and arthritis into your bones.

"So that's when it happens. People live longer and longer, you know. The mean average dead man today is twenty or thirty years older than when Hector was a pup. So there's this like sunshine boom now like once upon a time there was a gold rush. And then they put in the toll roads and interstates, and discovered stucco and air-conditioning, and invented beaches and tall buildings to put them up on. Tall, taller, tallest. And every year a new amenity. Once it was enough to have these huge game rooms where they'd bring in a songstress with an accordian and an old tummler from the Catskills on a Saturday night. Or have some circuit-riding rabbi who came around on Shabbes with a Torah, a bema, and a portable ark. Or they put TV monitors in the lobby you think you're in a newsroom. Restaurants they had, Chinese take-out, cineplex, Banana Republic.

"That's what they already got. You know what's on the drawing boards? Condos like resort hotels—horseback, snorkeling, golf. One place a little north of here has its own trails. Next year they're opening a building with its own community yacht!

"Paradise is a growth industry, the good life is. That leaves only the poor who'll have to make do with global warming. The rest are flocking to Florida in droves, Southeastward ho!

"The only drawback, Nathan, is that the neighborhood's changing. Dorothy will tell you. It's going down steep as a thrill ride. Every year it becomes harder and harder to put a minyan together. I'm an old-timer, I don't look so much to the future. What does it mean to me? I got enough to last me. And a little for a modest burial and maybe a few bucks left over for my own legatees and if the future is the wave of the future, so be it, I say. Others may have the energy for it. I don't.

"You know what the Towers have become, Nathan? An itty-bitty American metaphor. What, I'm making you blush? Relax, it's no big deal. All I mean is it's waves of immigration. All I mean is it's peoples after peoples making a clearing in the world and then, soon as they see smoke from the other guy's fire, they do a deal, they make an arrangement. The Jews are a very ancient race. If they didn't always make the clearing they at least staked a claim and moved in. Sure, and then came the Spaniards. Just like the old days. Conquistadors with their macho dope rings and plunder. Aunt Dorothy could tell you stories would curl the hairs in your ears. You lived side-by-side, didn't you, Aunt Dorothy? Who moved out on who is a nice question, but the bottom line is those waves of immigrants. Investment ops. Jews and South Americans falling all over each other. Until with a whoosh and a bim bam boom all of a sudden it's the march of time and the South Americans are selling out or renting to some of the lesser Latinos. And even Jews beginning to sublet to WASPs down from up in the north country or a few worn-out old farmers in out of Iowa and the rest of the Midwest. Even, if you want to know, to a couple of handfuls of deserving poor who might actually qualify for food stamps if only those proud, worn-out old farmers and subsistence-level golden agers climbed down from their high horse long enough to register with the authorities.

"So that's the story, Counselor. That's why I won't waste your time by pretending to consider your $170,000 or $161,500 or even your $148,792.50 price for Uncle's condominium. Now, if you'd come to me in the flush old days when the Towers were regarded as one of your hot, cutting-edge, state-of-the-art, pushed envelope, growth-industry properties, it might have been a different story altogether. I mean I still wouldn't have given you your $148,792.50 asking price of course, but I don't think I would have felt myself so personally insulted.

"Here's what I *will* do. If you get it repainted and bring the cosmetics up to code we'll split the difference—loan me the calculator, Dorothy—and I'll make you an offer of . . . $74,396.25."

"That's very funny," Nathan Apple said.

He's stalling for time, Dorothy thought. He sees his work's cut out for him and he's stalling for time. He's figuring what can he do with a guy like this. Personally, she almost had goose bumps. She hadn't felt so important since the evening, years ago, when she'd gone to Tommy Auveristas's open house and he'd sat next to her on one of the living room's three sofas. She couldn't imagine what the nephew would say, but he'd have to go some just to earn a draw. It was wicked, really, thought Mrs. Ted Bliss. *Men*. Really, she thought, the lengths to which they went to flash their plumage in front of other males. It was flattering to the ladies, but sometimes she wondered if it was intended for their benefit, if they'd ever bother to get themselves up in their colors if there were only females around to catch their act. Otherwise, well, otherwise they might just pick out the one who'd caught their eye, knock her to the ground, and take her. Perhaps the reason for courtship at all was the same reason soldiers lined up in ranks for parades. Maybe all that display was the only way they knew to civilize themselves.

Well, look at Dorothy Bliss, will you, thought Dorothy Bliss. Was this Alcibiades Chitral's pigeon, damned for her stupor and incuriosity?

Certainly she'd been entertained by Junior Yellin's aggressive arguments. Certainly she'd anticipated that Nathan would counterattack. But she'd stopped just in time. (Because if there was no fool like an old fool, what sort of old fool would an eighty-year-old woman make?) Flattered, but short of taking it personally, a privileged witness to their swagger and strut. While quite abruptly reminded of Ted's ways with his customers: charming them into one cut rather than another, selling them three pounds rather than two, and with no more plumage on him than the dried blood across his apron and, when Junior was not in the shop, the only witness to his sweet talk Dorothy herself for whom he passed in parade.

The nephew was staring straight into Junior Yellin's eyes.

"Done," he said sweetly. "If you can talk Aunt Dorothy into selling me hers for fifty-five thousand."

"What about it, Dot?" Junior said. "You willing to trade up? There's bedrooms and toilets galore. I could move in with you. We'll split the nineteen-some-odd grand right down the middle. That would put us in Manny's apartment—just a second—for $9,698.12. I won't pressure you, I leave it entirely in your hands. I mean, I see the guy's game. He buys the place, turns around and sells it on the open market. He could clean up, but what the hell, the laborer is worth his hire, and the two of us got a luxury apartment we could get lost in. Come on, kid, what do you say?"

"I say," said Mrs. Ted Bliss, "I'm a married woman. I say Ted, olov hasholem, would turn over in his grave."

Now she was eighty-two, the mysterious, discrepant matter of her age seemed to have resolved itself. Without proof, without seeming even to have been aware of how or why, she at last knew how old she was. Not in round, approximate figures but exact sums. It was as if all the peculiar spring-forward, fall-back, daylight savings and central standards and fluky international time lines and zones of her personal history had been fixed, repaired, tuned to some Greenwich Mean of the ticking world. She had a birthday now, and though she had not yet officially observed it (and had no plans to), it was as if all the square feet and exact specs of the properties and registered deeds of her existence had at last been revealed to her.

This was, of course, essentially useless, but like other essentially useless things, an old person who earns a bachelor's degree in her last years, say, she received a genuine sense of accomplishment and pleasure from it. She finally knew, or if she didn't actually know then at least had finally fixed upon the age she should be.

She did nothing about it. She didn't rectify her social security records or notify Medicare. Nevertheless, she could now fit numbers to her life and this was somehow as liberating as the emerging knowledge of who she was and of what she had been.

She was eighty-two. She was a very old woman. Junior Yellin, whose very name suggested that she was his senior, was a very old man. Mrs. Bliss knew that if she had taken Yellin up on his offer to move into Manny Tressler's apartment, Ted would not have turned over in his grave. He wouldn't have so much as stirred. Ted had been fond of Manny and, despite all the awful stuff Junior had pulled on him, had always been rather more well-disposed toward him than otherwise. Ted had been dead almost fifteen years. The world had changed, attitudes had. Scandal had been all but wiped out in her lifetime, even, had he lived a little longer, in Ted's. Since the sixties there had been a general, accelerating erosion of the shameful. It wasn't that goodness was on the rise but that a general sense of evil—Think, Mrs. Ted Bliss thought, of the terror Mrs. Dubow, the first wife in Illinois forced to pay the husband alimony, evoked; that was a shocker that brought the house down—was being absorbed into the atmosphere. She saw it on the morning programs, she heard it on the call-ins, she read about it not only in the tabloids at the checkout in the supermarket but in the legitimate papers, too.

Who knew what went on behind closed doors, of course, but in her and Ted's day married people had been generally loyal to each other. Except for Junior Yellin and his bimbos, Mrs. Bliss didn't think she could name a man who ran around on his wife. Today it was a different story. In just her own family, hadn't both Jerry, Irving's boy, and Louis, Golda's, died of AIDS? (And Louis had been married!) And hadn't she recently heard that Betsy, a distant cousin she'd known only to say hello to who'd tested HIV positive, had come down with full-blown AIDS? (And why had her

grandson Barry never married? What was what in that department?) And what was going on with the shaineh maidel, Judith,
Maxine and George's exquisite daughter, a girl in her mid-thirties
if she was a day, who had probably been with at least a dozen men
(and lived with three of them), so beautiful she could have afforded
to remain a virgin forever but who instead—her grandmother
should bite her tongue—chose to think with her panties the way
some men had their brains in their pants? Or, while we're on the
subject of disgrace, was Frank and May's Donny, the brainy one, a
target of a grand jury investigation or not? He hadn't flown in from
Europe that time when Mrs. Bliss had gone to Providence for the
seder. The fact was that Dorothy hadn't heard from him in years,
neither through a letter or a phone call (who used to call her with
regularity), and whenever she had a chance to ask Frank about him,
her son was uneasy, or put her off with a vague answer, or changed
the subject. (Were they tapping her phones? Was that why Donny
didn't get in touch anymore? It wasn't so far-fetched. She had a
sort of record with federal people. Her Camerando connection. As
far as she knew the government still held Ted's Buick LeSabre under impoundment.)

For that matter how hotsy-totsy could Frank's and Maxine's
marriages be? You couldn't tell *her* there wasn't any funny stuff
going on back in Providence—probably the result of Frank's picking up his Pittsburgh roots and setting them down in Rhode Island.
She and Ted had done the same, and when they were even older
than Frank and May, but let's don't kid ourselves, thought Mrs.
Ted Bliss, Frank and May were a horse of a different color.

Dorothy and Maxine were close as ever, so Mrs. Bliss didn't
have to speculate why her daughter was having such a tough time
of it these days with George. The insurance business was practically
in ruins, at least at George's end of things. Whole life was out, a
thing of the past, along with the agent who sold such policies, a
relic. These days all the money was in term. It was entrepreneurial
James who spotted the trend before his dad and left him to go with
another company.

Life had lost the oom-pah-pah of fabulous things. Everyone
lived shmutsig today, everyone had a rough time of it. The Mr. and
Mrs. Ted Blisses were as dead as the dodo, olov hasholem. Which
isn't to say that some of their angels didn't have dirty wings. Sam

not only cheated at cards but on occasion might clumsily palm a loose quarter or fifty-cent piece if one were tossed to the ragged outer edge of the pot. And Philip wouldn't give you a true whole-sale price if your life depended on it, and Jake—who did he think *he* was fooling?—changed his name and signed up his sons for a Christian boarding school, while Joyce was a shnorrer first-class who gave cheapo wedding presents, bar mitzvah gifts that were practically an insult, and somehow never managed to have the right change in her purse when it came to sharing a cab or splitting a check.

But all that was piker sin, a kind of four-flusher pride, committed not so much in the name of fun as the spirit of edge.

Ted, taking the long view, had lived in a permanent state of forgiveness. He was too benign to have died of malignant tumors. (Mrs. Bliss recalled the last year of his life, how generous he was, how proud he'd been of her, how tirelessly he'd joined in on the grand joke of her beauty at those spirited underauctions where the bidders tried to guess her age.) So it was almost impossible to argue he would have been shocked by Junior Yellin's suggestion that he move into Manny Tressler's with her. (Whoa. Wait a minute. Was that the real point of the game? Was part of the pleasure Ted took in her sixty-some-odd-year-old beauty some old trap-more-flies-with-honey thing? Was it a routine he went through to make his wife more attractive to the bachelors he knew would survive him? Had it been more some midway trick in a carnival than an auction? Was Dorothy supposed to be the grand prize on the booth's upper shelf?) *Shocked?* If she knew her Ted, he would have been thrilled! He could not bear to die and leave her a widow. He wanted to make sure she was settled, cared for, supported, unlonely. Thanks but no thanks, thought Mrs. Ted Bliss. Surely even Ted could not have wanted Junior Yellin for a legatee. Her condo plus $9,698.12? Not at *those* prices!

It was another thing altogether that they should turn out to be friends. *Ted* had made friends with him. Or if not friends exactly, then at least come to terms with the man. Sitting back amused, enjoying for all he was worth just watching the man operate, even if it was at his own expense. Not to pick up tips, tricks of the trade, not in any way trying to apprentice himself to the gonif, but like some scholar or philosopher, to see how far Yellin would go, to study the ways he had up his sleeve to get there. What did they call it, a sting operation? A sting operation, but with nobody jumping out of the wallpaper at the end of the show to point a gun or slap on the handcuffs.

So who knows, thought Mrs. Ted Bliss. Maybe Ted wouldn't mind even if she took Junior up on his offer. Maybe Mrs. Ted Bliss was part of a sting operation, too. Maybe Ted was dead today because he was ahead of his time (just as Dorothy had been behind hers) all the years he had been alive. Maybe he was the first one ever to have lost the sense of scandal, the one man to have taken in that first whiff and understood that evil was only another unpleasant smell, like mold, say, in a summer house.

But that's where they parted company. If it suited Ted's plans for Dorothy to participate in her husband's experiment, it did not in the least suit Dorothy's. Not only was *she* too old, Junior Yellin was. She'd been by herself too long now. She was settled, she could take care of herself, and her misery, whatever else it may have been, was not loneliness. Manny from the building had been more support than Yellin.

Would Junior shlep for her, drive her around on her errands? Would he have taught her to make out a check, or advised her in legal matters? In the drive and shlep, practical information, and stand-by-your-side departments he wasn't worth the paper he was written on, and although—it was probably a sin just to think about this part—were both of them thirty or forty years younger they might have made something or other with the bedroom thing, Mrs. Bliss still wouldn't have touched him with a ten-foot pole. For one thing the man was a born chaser. He would have broken her heart.

Mrs. Bliss gasped at the thought. Quite literally it took her breath away. The idea, just the *idea*, that Mrs. Ted Bliss could have been a candidate for a busted heart was enough to make her laugh. Or cry. For all her odd old vanity, the pride she'd taken in her beauty, in all the fastidious, just-so arrangements of her old life (the two and three daily baths, her painstaking toilet, her wardrobe, even the old baleboosteh care she lavished on the plastic seat covers over her furniture, the sky blue water in her commode, the shined surfaces of her breakfront and wood tabletops), she'd never been much interested in sexual relations. (Ted had rarely seen her nude and, with the exception of his illness, Mrs. Bliss, when she had helped him in the bathroom or washed him in their bed, had just as rarely—had in fact gone out of her way to avoid looking—seen her husband's naked body.)

So it was pretty ridiculous to think of herself with a romantically broken heart. Marvin's death had broken her heart, the deaths and divorces of certain close relatives, the failure of the Michigan farm, and other times her husband had sustained business reversals or been forced to sell at a loss. Her grandson Barry broke her heart. Losing Ted, it goes without saying. But a sufferer because of romance? Never. Never!

But that was one thing. Friendship was another. Surprisingly, astonishingly, really, she and Milton Yellin had become good friends. Pals, if you want to know; buddies, partners in crime. It was almost as if, like kids, they were cut from the same cloth. That's the way they were with each other. They *played* together. This quite new to Dorothy's not exactly vast experience (something she actually had to learn and the only thing in the world Junior Yellin could teach her), new to the experience because, for all that she was eighty-two, she'd never had a friend. And why would she have had? She'd never had a childhood either. What she remembered of being a kid was what she remembered of being an adult: her family. Brothers and sisters and cousins of various degree, but no friends. No, what Junior called, "asshole buddies."

"There's," he'd say if people were watching as he stopped to pick her up outside Building Number One on days he was off, "my asshole buddy, Mrs. Ted Bliss. How you doin', Dodo?"

"How many times do I have to tell you," Dorothy, blushing, would scold him, "you're embarrassing me. You're embarrassing *them*."

"Yeah, well, the day I can't get a rise out of people is the day I might as well drop dead and die."

In his old age he drove big four-wheel-drive vehicles, Jeep Cherokees, Land Rovers, other such machines that he would borrow for the day from various people he knew with whom he was cooking up schemes. "Arrgh," he'd say with a certain self-loathing, "I'm too old for this stuff, I ain't got the balls anymore. I give them away. They can have them with my compliments. All my best-laid plans of mice and men. They can have them for free. Surefire shit. They take a flier on the least of my ideas, they'd double, *triple* their investment! 'Gee, Milt,' they say, 'if it's half as good as it sounds why don't *you* get in on the ground floor? Why don't *you* put up some dough?' 'Me?' I say, 'I'm content to trade you my ideas for a box at the Dolphins game, or take your car out for a spin with my asshole buddy, Dorothy.' I get a rise out of them, it gives them a laugh. So they humor me. Twirps in their fifties and sixties, what do they know from getting old, cutting their losses, tossing their towels in?''

"Oh, you haven't tossed in your towel," Mrs. Bliss reassured.

"Damn straight I ain't," he told her, cheering, "there's still a few miles left in this model. So what do you want to do today, kiddo? Go fishing out on a charter? Catch the helicopter and do the beaches or downtown Miami? They got a new one in Fort Lauderdale. Takes us up the coast to Palm. I slip the guy ten bucks, he buzzes the Kennedy compound or flies low over the country club and spooks the polo ponies."

"Oh, Junior," Mrs. Bliss said laughing, "where do you get your ideas?"

"Oh, my ideas," Junior Yellin said, "my ideas are a dime a dozen. What *I'm* looking for are a few good years."

He really is a death-oriented man, thought Mrs. Ted Bliss. It was odd, death was something you worried about in middle age, or while your family was together. It was something she gave little thought to these days. Manny had drawn up her will shortly after Ted had died and, to tell you the truth, her death was the last thing on her mind—except those few times when she wished for it. So she was bothered to hear Junior talk this way.

She had an idea. She told Junior she had to go to the bathroom and asked if he would stop at the next gas station. When they stopped Mrs. Bliss went up to an attendant, turned, and walked back to the car. "You need a key," she explained, but when she went into the office she took a small notebook from her purse, found a number she'd written down, then searched the purse for a quarter and called Hector Camerando from the pay phone.

She returned to the big off-road vehicle.

"I have an idea," she said.

"Yeah? What?"

"Why don't we go to the jai alai?"

"Oh," Yellin frowned, "the jai alai's a crapshoot. It's fixed as wrestling. You don't know that? Everyone knows that."

"So what if it is?" said Mrs. Ted Bliss. "What if it is if a person happens to know a person in a position to know which players are going to do what to which other players?"

Something in Mrs. Ted Bliss's grin caused Junior to examine her closely, almost to appraise her.

"Dorothy?" he said.

"Junior?"

"I know you what, five decades?"

"Something or other."

"Sweetheart," he said, "apples don't fall far from their trees. Ted, may he rest, was a sweet, stand-up guy. You heard of painless dentists? Well, your husband was a kind of bloodless butcher. He took practically all the cholesterol off a steak he trimmed the fat so close. That's how honest he worked the scales. I'll tell you the truth, I was a pig in comparison. I'd weigh in my thumbs, my wrists. Sometimes I'd sit with my tochis up on the scale to help make us break even. If I made him a patsy, if I wronged him, it was just to get even—almost like honor.

"Well, you know how I screwed him over—the books, the farm. From my point of view it was a . . . vindication. But what troubles me now is how you, who I had this idea lived in his moral shadow, all of a sudden pops out from the shadow to tell me she may know a person who knows a person who can chisel the jai alai.

"Do you know what you're saying bites deeper than mafia? It huffs and puffs harder than the trade winds the drugs blow in on. It's one of the grimmest shows the INS runs. We're not just talking Basque separatists, we're talking international terrorists.

"Dorothy, dear, tell me, how did you come to know such a person?"

"Well," said Mrs. Bliss, "I'm—"

"No, don't tell me," Yellin broke in.

"I'm holding his marker."

Junior Yellin scrutinized the old lady.

"Back at the gas station. You called him?"

"We could go to the greyhounds," she said.

"The greyhounds, too?"

"I'm holding his marker."

The jack of all scams weighed the odds.

"How much?" he asked finally. "What are we talking here?"

"The sky's the limit," said Mrs. Ted Bliss.

Yellin shut his eyes, his face lost in concentration. It was as though he were trying to guess in which hand an opponent was holding a coin. He opened his eyes. "The jai alai," he said hoarsely.

They drove in silence to the white rectangular building, long and low as a huge discount store or a factory in an industrial park.

"So what did he say?" Junior asked when they were inside.

"Didn't I tell you?"

"I was making a speech," Junior said shyly. "I never gave you a chance."

"Oh," Mrs. Bliss said, "his line was busy."

It was only minutes before the first match was scheduled to begin. They were standing near the five-dollar and ten-dollar windows. Yellin looked stricken. "The line was busy? It was busy, the line."

"I tried two or three times."

"Try it now," Junior pleaded, "if he hasn't got anything for us in the first match, then maybe a later one." His eyes shone with an immense idea. Mrs. Bliss thought he looked fifteen years younger. She turned to go. "Oh, and Dorothy?"

"What?"

He signaled her closer, then, when she stopped, he stepped forward and closed the gap between the two of them even more. Mrs. Ted Bliss, who'd never see eighty again, watched him warily.

"Nothing," he said. "Only when you talk to him, it might not be a good idea to tell him someone else is in on this, too."

She was old; for a moment she'd had a crazy thought that Junior had been on the verge of trying something. She was relieved when he hadn't. The shine in his eyes, the sudden, transient, ischemic pallor on his face like a sort of youth—she thought she'd felt the last weak rays of lust radiating out of him. She had, thankfully, misrepresented its source. It wasn't the love of an old lady that had excited him but the action. The excited, polyglot voices of the crowds milling around the betting windows—his sense of connection and edge like deep drafts of ozone.

Mrs. Ted Bliss laughed. "What," she said, "you think I was born yesterday? Why would I tell him I have a partner in crime?

As it is we'll be pushing up the daisies soon enough. Let's just let nature take its course. Oh," said Mrs. Bliss, "I'm sorry. I know this man, he wouldn't lift a finger." She was trying to comfort him. The pallor had returned to his face. All he wanted, he'd said, was a few good years. His bloodlessness was a sort of reverse blush. She understood. He was embarrassed by death. "Really," she said, "if I call, I don't even have to mention where I am. Maybe you've changed your mind."

"Well," Junior said, "if you're holding his marker."

It was odd about the high rollers, thought Mrs. Ted Bliss. Their lives, built around some tender armature of chance, were always deeply grounded in hedged realities. Briefly, Mrs. Bliss pitied the man, came within a hair of writing him off. If she got through to Camerando she might not only tell him up front where she was but tell him Junior Yellin's name, too.

As it happened, however, she still couldn't reach him. A phone company recording came on to tell her the number she was calling had been disconnected.

She went back to Yellin to tell him the news.

"No luck," she explained, "the number's been disconnected. I don't understand. When I called a half hour ago I got a busy signal."

"Hey," he said, "no problem. It's not a big deal. They're here today and gone tomorrow these guys. Come on," a restored, relieved Junior Yellin told her, "who needs the son of a bitch? If we hurry, we still got time to lay a bet down on the match. Any of the names of these bums mean anything to you?"

After that they were closer than ever. Junior was actually relieved to be back on terra firma. Perhaps the idea of edge, of extravagant advantage, made him nervous. It wasn't the first time she thought the old bully was a piker, daring enough in his own small ponds but quick to lose heart where he knew he was beyond his depths. It was an insult to Ted, finally, whose measure he'd taken and relegated, whom he'd comfortably fit into manageable scale. On her behalf she was furious, on her husband's, amused, come to terms with Ted's forgiveness and understanding and philosophic scrutiny. On her husband's behalf they were closer than ever, Mrs. Ted Bliss taking up their friendship like someone pledged to carry on the unfinished work of someone who'd died. Even that first day at the jai alai she allowed herself to be drawn into his piker schemes.

Freed from the obligation of taking a risk, they agreed upon a system whereby they pooled their money and, by wagering on opposing teams, in effect, covered each other's bets. Even Mrs. Bliss understood that this was more like accounting or balancing her checkbook than like gambling. Except for the fact that neither of them stood to win or lose much money, Mrs. Bliss was content to go along with Junior's reasoning that, what the hell, at the end of the day they'd gotten several hours of quite good value for their entertainment dollars—the price of admission, the cost of their programs, the tabs for their hot dogs, their coffees and Cokes.

And, for Mrs. Ted Bliss, it *was* entertaining. She meant the jai alai, the power and flexibility and stamina of the athletes, their lightning hand-eye coordination, the way they scooped up the small, heavy, hard-rubber pelota into the unyielding woven reeds of the curving cesta attached like a long, predatory claw to their arms and drove the ball flying back against the main granite wall. For all their athleticism and diving, driving speed, within the relatively close quarters of the wire mesh ceiling and vaguely chicken wire fencing of the viewing wall, they seemed to Mrs. Ted Bliss, protected only by their odd, single-winged arm, like nothing so much as wounded, desperate, captive birds fighting for their lives inside a terrible caged battlefield.

She was close enough to smell their heat and sweat. It was awful. It was wonderful. She was at an age, she reflected, past (if she'd ever been capable of them) such odors. Even her fevers when they came would be back-burner, a dry, desiccate desert heat—the almost pastel fragrance of old bone, ancient skin. Her stools, too, had lost force and sting. Only the ammonias of her pee seemed cumulative, consolidate. But she couldn't remember when she had last perspired. On the hottest, steamiest days of the Florida summers she had felt the heat really as a kind of comforter across the lap of the sore, listless, stymied blood of her advanced age, and she could only marvel at the smells spilling from the cage of athletes even in the middling distance of her and Junior's seats.

"Why did you cheer," Yellin asked her, "for Berho and Hiribarren? Those characters were on the other side. Our guys were Darruspe and Urritzaga."

She would have tried to tell him how she was drawn to what she could only have explained as their rugged vividness, but she would have sounded crazy even to herself.

So they played together. And it really was, Mrs. Ted Bliss supposed, quite like playing. She used as models her memories of Marvin's and Frank's and Maxine's Saturday afternoon excursions with their Chicago buddies to the Rosenwald Museum of Science and Industry, or the Field Museum of Natural History, the Shedd Aquarium, the Adler Planetarium, double features at the Southtown or Hyde Park, or important single features at big, first-run theaters like the State and Lake, the McVickers, the stage shows at the Chicago and Oriental; their forays into Jackson Park to the golf course and tennis courts, or out to see the Golden Lady, or the Japanese Gardens, to the archery range on the beach at Lake Michigan where they rented bows, arrows, leather bands for their arms, or their trips to the downtown stores on the I.C., or all the way to Wilmette to view the splendors of the Bahai Temple, shining, white as the Taj Mahal. And as asexual at her age with Junior Yellin as she assumed the children would have been when they had been tourists taking in the sights of *their* times.

So they played together, revisiting the jai alai, accompanying each other to the greyhounds, the track. Sightseers they were, the only difference between herself, Yellin, and her kids and their playmates was that Mrs. Bliss and Junior had more money to spend, but friendship at their level of disengagement as essentially touristic and hands-off as the kids had been when they aimlessly wandered from hole to hole on the Jackson Park golf course, or chased balls for the tennis players when they had been hit over the chainlink fences.

Playmates.

On rainy days playing the gin rummy variations (Hollywood, double points if the call card's a spade, or being unable to knock until you had gin; the extra points, bonuses, and boxes in these refinements like a kind of runaway inflation) as her children might have stayed home and played Monopoly. Or shmoozing in restaurants over coffee after they'd eaten the Early Bird special. Playmates, but almost like courtship without any of courtship's attendant anxieties. As comfortable with each other on these occasions as gossipy girls. (Junior Yellin unmasked, unmanned, sent home again to some almost virginal, pre-big shot condition, like a lion or tiger whose jaws and teeth are still undeveloped. Dorothy in her own way almost the same—their gossip making her nostalgic for something she'd never actually experienced, a life that, outside of family, had not yet happened.)

Queerly dependent on each other as a sort of stranger, castaways, say, or folks thrown together on a difficult trip. With nothing but time on their hands now, and nothing to do with that time—it's still rotten out, say, the weather still threatening—but fall if not into the story of their lives then at least into some confessional sideshow aspect of the story of their lives, not the high points so much as the oddities, like freakish, unbeautiful geological formations in nature.

Mrs. Bliss, for example, offered a few of the reddest herrings from the last third of her life.

She told Yellin about the sale of Ted's Buick LeSabre and of all the trouble that had gotten her into, and was quite astonished to learn that Junior had seen the car, had ridden in it, and, when his own was in the shop, had actually driven it once.

"What? No. Impossible."

"What impossible? Why impossible? A seventy-eight, right?"

"Yes, but I could have told you that."

"You never mentioned it. It was green, I think."

"Not a dark green."

"No, not a dark green. Ted wouldn't drive around in a pool table. A light shade, I think. Like the background color on a dollar bill."

"That's right," Mrs. Bliss said. "But this was 1978, we were already living in Florida."

"Didn't he go back to Myers for a second opinion?"

"You know I forgot?" Mrs. Ted Bliss said, astonished. "So much happened that year." Confused now, surprised she could have forgotten something like that but amazed, too, that Ted—the whole trip had taken less than a week—would have gone out of his way to look this man up, this son of a bitch who'd taken such advantage of him over the years and then, to add insult to injury, asked to borrow his car, a man who'd driven God knows how many miles all the way to Chicago to get a second opinion on his *cancer*—it was . . . it was *outrageous!* Why, her husband mustn't have been so much amused by the man as absolutely *fond* of him!

She could do nothing more now but surrender to her dead husband's wishes.

So she offered him Alcibiades Chitral, too, and Tommy Auveristas, and finally gave up Hector Camerando himself, the bizarre terms of Camerando's arrangement with her.

"Four hundred dollars? A setup like that and all you took him for was four hundred dollars? Whatever happened to the grand views of Biscayne Bay, the penthouse in West Palm? You let that crazy spic off the hook for a lousy four hundred dollars?"

"It was embarrassing to me."

"Embarrassing," Junior said. "You got some sense of the proprieties. Didn't it occur to you you might be hurting his *feelings* by running away from his generosity? *Jesus! Dorothy!*"

"It's over anyway. His number's been disconnected."

"That don't mean he's dead. Where there's life there's hope, where there's a will there's a way. I bet that Alcibiades Chitral guy could put you in touch. One da dit dot dash on the jungle telegraph would do it."

"An anti-Semite? I wouldn't stoop."

"Tommy Auveristas, then. I can't get over it. You know Tommy Overeasy."

"Well, *know,*" said Mrs. Bliss dismissively.

"You were in the man's home."

"It was open house."

"He put a napkin over your lap. You sat on a sofa with him and ate his food."

"Oh, his *food,*" said Mrs. Ted Bliss. "Drek, chozzerai. I barely moved it around on the plate."

"You were the belle of the ball. You went mano a mano with him, you went tête-â-tête."

"You know," she said, "I've been thinking about that. This was right after my testimony. I think he may have been sizing me up. I think he must have been trying to see how much I really knew about Alcibiades Chitral. About Alcibiades Chitral and himself."

"How much did you?"

"Nothing," Dorothy Bliss said, surprised. "Nothing at all. My God," she said, "I don't even know Hector Camerando's phone number. I can't remember the last time I saw Tommy Auveristas," she whispered, suddenly frightened by how much she had lost. "Can you imagine that?"

Junior Yellin shrugged. "Spilled milk," he said.

Suddenly she felt a duty to be interested. She leaned toward her companion cross from her on the faux leather banquette in the fish restaurant. "Holmer Toibb must have told you plenty."

"Holmer Toibb?"

"The man who trained you, whose practice you bought into."

Yellin didn't even look shamefaced. Or stare sheepishly into the dregs of his coffee cup.

"Friends?" he said.

"Of course friends," Dorothy said.

"Well, the fact of the matter is I didn't know Toibb. I never even saw him."

"You told me he trained you."

"Trained me. I'm an old dog. You can't teach an old dog new tricks."

"And Greener Hertsheim?"

"A legend."

"A legend?" Mrs. Bliss said.

"Like Robin Hood. Like George Washington and the cherry tree." Mrs. Bliss scowled. "Friends?" Yellin asked like a professional wrestler extending his hand for forgiveness.

"But Junior, you *billed* me!"

"You never paid."

"You threatened to turn it over to a collection agency!"

"Did I follow through?"

"It would have cost you *money* to follow through."

"What are you so cockcited? You knew I was a fake. What troubles you, I was an untrained fake?"

"Junior, you're dealing with people's lives."

"Oh," Yellin said, "people's lives."

She took his point and smiled.

"Sure," Mrs. Bliss said, "friends."

TEN

loser than ever now.

Who did absolutely nothing for each other: Yellin pulling Mrs. Ted Bliss into what were for her uncharted but thoroughly buoyant waters; Mrs. Bliss reciprocating with an openness so total she might well have been dealing in the naked heart-to-heart of a child with an imaginary friend. And, as in such friendships, they often arranged strange adventures—journeys and tasks neither would have undertaken on their own. Of course, Mrs. Bliss reasoned, she at least had been preparing, training for, and, in a sense, behaving in such "public" ways since coming to the Towers almost thirty years earlier. For what had those demonstrations and makeovers been that she and the other tenants had gathered on the decks of the rooftop swimming pools to witness and participate in? What had the tango lessons been? The lectures and language classes? The Yiddish film festivals and landscape painting courses? Las Vegas and Monte Carlo nights? The good neighbor policy and international evenings? What had all those participatory crash courses in winning bridge, golf, tennis, and chess and even deep-sea fishing instructional programs amounted to, finally? Well, not to very much because for all the initial enthusiasm—Mrs. Bliss did not exempt herself—these courses of study may have elicited, few who signed up for them (and paid their good money) persevered long enough to earn their merit badges.

And it was just this, Mrs. Bliss saw (and explained to Junior Yellin), that as much as age was at least part, and maybe most, of the cause that had contributed to the breakdown and deterioration of what could only be called "the spirit of the Towers."

"Well, sure," Mrs. Ted Bliss said, "what then? You don't see that even the dumbest of us didn't understand we were barking up the wrong tree? A person don't take up chess, deep-sea fishing, and the tango just because there's a sign-up sheet in the game room. You got to have a better motivation than that. You got to have a calling. You ask me, the recreational therapeusisists have it bass ackwards. Fresh interests in life? Who has the time? All right, okay, we got the time. We do. What's missing is the energy. Piecemeal, this has to have its effect. Piecemeal, this has got to lead to the conclusion that no matter how hard you work you're never going to be any according to Hoyle or Bobby Fischer or Gussie Moran. Piecemeal, you lose the will to put in the time practicing or do your homework or just show up for the weekly meetings. There ain't enough left in the class to make up a pair for what would have been the gala at what would have been the end of the term.

"So this is one of the ways the neighborhood changes and gets to put a damper on the spirit of the Towers."

The old therapeusisist blushed.

"Guilty as charged," he said.

"Oh, no," said Mrs. Ted Bliss, "with you it's only business. You're no more to blame than the art teachers and French cooking specialists we used to bring in. It wasn't their fault we dropped out like flies."

"Because," Junior Yellin said shyly, "it just so happens I've taken up an interest of my own. I read an article about it in the Sunday paper. It was very interesting. Right, you might say, down my alley."

"What?" Dorothy asked.

"I read up on it first."

"What?" she said. "What?"

"In fact, I thought it might be something we might do together. We'd get some fresh air out of it if nothing else and, if we ever got lucky, maybe something even more substantial."

"What already? What?"

Then he told her about the metal detector. His trip to the library to see could he find them evaluated in back issues of *Consumer Reports, Consumer Guide*.

"You'd be surprised, they can be very complicated. Did you know that they work by means of radio waves? I mean, when you come to think the whole planet's like some enormous orchestra that plays this ongoing set that never takes a break. It just keeps on blasting out the music of its treasures—all its locked-up silvers and golds and other precious metals. All its buried iron-padlocked chests and trunks, caskets and hidden, bundled safes. Earth's hush-hush, top-secret knippls and pushkes."

His voice was hoarse, his eyes wide and oddly lively, as if his pupils had been dilated. He was as excited as she'd ever seen him. No, he had *never* been so excited.

"You've seen them. Haven't you seen them, Dorothy? Old guys in the park in the grass combing the lawn as if they were sweeping it with a broom or going over it with a vacuum cleaner?"

"Sure," she said, "I always wondered what they found. Bottle tops, beer cans, old tins of Band-Aids?"

"Oh, no, Dorothy," Junior Yellin said. "There's caches of valuable stuff everywhere, the world littered with stash like carpet laid down by pirates. Rare coins and crashed ransoms, stolen goods like a scavenger hunt dreamed up by gangsters."

"It was a hobby, a fad," said Mrs. Ted Bliss. "You don't see it no more so much."

"What, are you kidding me? Maybe up north, maybe the fields are played out in Minnesota and Wisconsin, but down here, down here it's still practically a natural resource. Only cordless phones outsell the metal detector in the greater Miami Radio Shacks."

"This is true?"

"Cross my heart."

"I don't see it so much no more," said Mrs. Ted Bliss.

"You don't see it so much no more because you don't get out so much no more."

"I get out."

"Where? To a Jewish-style restaurant for the Early Bird special? To the movie in the strip mall for the rush-hour show? Where, where do you go, Dorothy? When was the last time you been to the beach?"

"I got a pool on the roof, what do I need the beach?"

MRS. TED BLISS ~ 223

"Entirely different story."

"What, I should lay in my bathing suit on a blanket in the sand with a portable radio? A woman my age?"

"I'm not arguing, I'm just saying. Anyway, don't change the subject, I want you to come in on this with me."

"Come in on this what?"

"Metal detectors. What else have we been talking about?"

"Oh, Junior," said Mrs. Ted Bliss, "I think you got a bug up your ass with these metal detectors. If you want one so bad why don't you just go out and buy it?"

Here Junior Yellin looked down at his shoes. Suddenly, and to his great disadvantage, he seemed years younger, almost childish, the expression on his face at once sheepish and serene and, for Dorothy, triggering vague memories of if not of similar occasions then at least of times when she had seen this peculiar amalgam of defeated triumph and victorious shame, the scared pyrotechnics of someone narrowly escaping a threat to his life, say, like someone getting away with murder in a near fatal collision of his own making. It was, Mrs. Bliss realized, the look of one whose prayers have been undeservedly answered.

"Well," he said, looking up, "you know me, Dot. I always feel I have to have a partner."

It was true, and she suddenly remembered the look. It had been there when old man Yellin bailed him out after Junior had worked over Ted's books, and there it was again when his father had settled his gambling debts, all the times he had sprung to his son's defense, made good on his losses, the thriving, striking codependency of his thievery, principle standing firm in the defense of what was only finally family. Yes, it was true. He *had* needed partners. Ted. The Greater Miami Recreational Therapeusis Consultants gang. Even, for a time, Hector Camerando, whose name he did not know and refused to hear. And now Mrs. Ted Bliss.

"Are they very dear?" she asked.

"No, no, not at all. There's different models of course. There's low end and high end, but they're all pretty reasonable. They go for between thirty-nine to a hundred ninety-nine dollars. There's a good one put out by Radio Shack for about eighty-nine dollars."

"What's the difference?"

"Sensitivity," he said. "You're paying for power. The cheaper ones usually just pick up iron, the pricier jobs have a finer discrimination. But even the eighty-nine-buck jobs work in up to two inches of water."

"You seem to know a lot about it."

"Fools rush in, Dot."

"If we do this," said Mrs. Bliss, "what would we be looking for?"

"Like you said, the sky's the limit, kid." He looked at her solemnly, levelly, and uttered the remark as soberly as if he were offering inside information.

What he couldn't know, of course, was that Mrs. Bliss had no use for inside information, or for his project, or even (it could have been the differential in their ages) for the limitless opportunities of young Junior's sky. If she did this thing she would do it, quite simply, because, as he said, he needed a partner. He'd been a baby even when he was a young man. Now that he was an old one he was an even bigger baby.

Not for old time's sake, not because he was one of the last direct living connections to her dead, beloved husband. Not out of sentimentality, and not out of any need for companionship, but simply because he was too used to his character and, partnerless (though much of his banter with Nathan Apple was pure snow job, he'd been caught at least a little short by her refusal to allow him to move in with her), he would flounder and wither and die.

She made a further show of interest by throwing faint demurrers in his path.

"Oh, no, Dorothy, quite serious people are engaged in this activity. Policemen in police departments hunting spent bullets and shells, actual murder weapons—guns, knives, and hatchets."

"I hope we don't find anything like that."

"And lose out on the reward money?"

"Just the same," said Mrs. Ted Bliss.

"Treasure hunters," Junior mused. "Archaeologists. Prospectors."

At Yellin's insistence they bought two devices. So they could halve the size of their sites. So they could double their efficiency. Nor was he content to buy one of the cheaper models. He argued more bang for the buck and quite agreeably forked over two hundred dollars for Radio Shack's deluxe detector. Mrs. Bliss, who felt she'd done her part by agreeing to go in with him in the first place, was not to be bullied into buying something beyond her price range. This was Junior's hobby-horse, not hers, and if he chose to ride it in some Cadillac of metal detector, Mrs. Bliss was content to go with a perfectly serviceable Buick LeSabre. She bought the one for eighty-nine dollars, batteries not included.

Despite what he'd said she had no idea how the things worked, so naturally she was a little surprised when he came by for her that first day in one of the various off-road vehicles to which he seemed to have such unlimited access. He handed her a trowel, a small shovel, a sort of short-handled hoe.

"What's this?" Mrs. Bliss asked.

"Don't worry about it," Yellin said, "we'll settle up later."

"No," she said, "what is this? We're digging a garden?"

"A treasure garden, what else?" Yellin smiled. "What, you thought this was a magnet? That all you have to do is run it over the ground and it picks stuff up like a Hoover?"

As a matter of fact that pretty much was what she thought and, feeling how foolish she must seem to him, blushed.

Junior grinned and tried to explain how the metal detector was actually a kind of transmitter that sent out waves. These were amplified, converted into signals that were then reflected back to the instrument. Listening to him, hearing him out, patiently trying to absorb the information he attempted to hand down from the superior heights of his male, mechanical inclination and intuitions, Mrs. Ted Bliss gave up years, returned in seconds to the trusting, contingent condition of her brief girl- and maidenhoods, her extensive marriage, much of her almost as extensive widowhood. Yellin might have been some faintly ill-willed Manny teaching her the art of balancing checkbooks, the two DEA agents violating her husband's car, Holmer Toibb giving her homework assignments, a Hector Camerando laying down the who's whos and what's whats, or Alcibiades Chitral describing for her the limits of her humanity. He might have been Rabbi Beinfeld alerting her to bold, arcane death escapes, tricks of the trade. He might, God bit her tongue, have been a sort of Frank, or for that matter, any man who'd ever rushed in to instruct her—even her beloved Ted.

Junior Yellin was like any other man. She was old, and couldn't hurt his feelings.

As Yellin explained she remembered the year in Michigan, the last time she'd been a farmer. Well, farmer's wife, actually, with her chores (which she didn't mind) and discomfort (which she did), and proposed that she first go upstairs to change into more suitable clothes.

"But you look fine," Junior objected, anxious to start.

"I thought it was magnets," Mrs. Bliss said. "I thought it would be more like fishing than digging and pulling." Before he could object further Mrs. Bliss turned and walked back into Building One. Upstairs, she improvised a costume she thought more suitable for the work that lay in front of her. She exchanged her wedgies for a pair of Isotoner slippers and took off her polyester pants suit and put on a long, loose-fitting sun dress with a white blouse. She found some light cotton gardening gloves (from her days as a landlord's wife), and finished off her outfit with a big, white, wide-brimmed straw hat beneath which she fitted a large silk scarf that she drew down the sides of her face and tied under her chin.

"Excuse me, Dorothy dear," Junior Yellin said when she returned to the strange vehicle, "but you look like a fucking bee-keeper."

Because even though she'd lived in Florida for all these years she was terrified of the sun.

As frightened of it as one living above a fault line, or on the side of a dormant volcano, or in the direct path of tornado activity, the Florida sun an object of dread and superstition to her, some poisonous sky augury like an ominous arrangement of planets. Moving to Florida had been her husband's idea and, when they first started their forays into Miami Beach back in the fifties, often with other couples and always over the Christmas and New Year's holidays, the winter warmth after the bitter Chicago cold had been an agreeable novelty. During the days they shopped or played cards under immense beach umbrellas and ordered sandwiches and bottles of pop from the towel boys. At night they shuffled from hotel to hotel catching the shows, Sophie Tucker a headliner, Jack Carter, Myron Cohen, Buddy Hackett. They were hardly aware of the sun and, after the first time or two when one or another of the group suffered bad sunburns, they gradually learned to budget the time they spent outdoors, which hours of the day were the safest to go.

Living there all year round was something else altogether. You made a different accommodation, an accommodation, Dorothy understood, which was no accommodation at all but more like surrender, as one's life in an inner city, say, would be like surrender, a life that couldn't be budgeted, lived around the times the hooligans were not in the streets, but had to be plunged into daily and at all hours, inescapable as air. Unless you turned yourself into a kind of invalid.

As I have, I have, thought Mrs. Ted Bliss, astonished at herself, to realize what she was doing even as she permitted herself to be helped into Junior Yellin's borrowed dune buggy. This was one of those machines that tended to tip over. She had seen a story about them on "60 Minutes," how their odd centers of gravity made them dangerous to ride in. With their twin roll bars the machine looked vaguely like a stripped Conestoga. Dorothy at eighty-two and Junior in his late seventies had, between them, to be at least one hundred sixty years old. To anyone who saw them riding in such a young person's toy they would seem ridiculous.

Yet it was neither her queer appearance (dressed "like a fucking beekeeper"), their ridiculousness, nor the clear and present danger the dune buggy represented that terrified Mrs. Bliss; it was its topless nakedness, its awful exposure to the sun.

She didn't fear cancer, and after all these years felt herself immune to the danger of a bad burn. It was just that she knew (as a lifetime ago her parents had been anxious at the proximity of Cossacks) that so close to the sun, taking its direct hits as one might take "incoming" in a fierce battle in war, she was in the presence of the enemy. That she was willing to go on with their ludicrous expedition was an indication of just how far she had come, strayed, from her life.

She'd thought there'd be someplace they could go to try out their equipment, imagining something like a driving range or the big empty parking lots and lightly traveled roads where Ted had taken the children when he taught them to drive. Yellin had different ideas and as soon as he could pointed the big clumsy dune buggy toward a long stretch of occupied beach where bathers lay about on blankets taking the sun. (She did not worry about them or project any of her own private fears onto their situations. Indeed, had this actually occurred to her, it would have amounted to an invasion of their privacy, crazy, like someone frightened of elevators warning people away from them in department stores.) It may have been the open car in combination with the vast sandy beach, all that fearful light burning up the sky. Whatever it was, Mrs. Bliss was very nervous, almost carsick.

"Slow down, slow down," she pleaded.

"I'm not even going twenty miles an hour."

"There's children," she said, "there's people on blankets."

"Relax. You don't think I see them?"

"You're knocking my kishkas."

"We're almost there."

"Where?"

"I'm looking for a spot. Don't you think I know what I'm doing?"

If he were looking for a spot, Mrs. Bliss didn't know how he'd ever find it. God knows where they were. All she could see on her right was open ocean, on her left a bright but bland skyline of beachfront high rises and motels. They bumped along in a sickening no-man's-land of sand and sun and sky. She didn't know whether they were still in Miami Beach, or even in Dade County. They might have been in Fort Lauderdale or any, to Dorothy, of the nameless suburbs that had risen beside the coast like a kind of urbanized landfill.

She wished he would stop the car and then, quite suddenly, he did.

"We're there?"

"Didn't I tell you?"

He was bullshitting her, but he'd stopped driving and she forgave him. She climbed down out of the dune buggy and immediately felt less exposed to the sun, her stomach still queasy because they were still squarely on the beach in what was not quite yet the middle of the day.

"I know what you're thinking," Yellin said. "You're thinking how is this spot different from any other spot on the beach."

"I *am* thinking that," said Mrs. Ted Bliss.

"It's got the proper ratio of sunbathers to swimmers. It doesn't seem to be all played out, worked over by other metal detectives. I like the demographics."

"The demographics," Mrs. Bliss said.

"Hell yes. Superb demographics. Terrific demographics. Wonderful distribution of yuppies, the recently retired, and old folks. White people, coloreds."

"Please," she said.

"You think I'm depending on just that two-hundred-dollar gadget I sprang for? Don't underestimate me, Dorothy. In this business you got to have a dowser's heart. Let's set up."

Dorothy read to him from the manual as Junior poured out parts from the box holding her metal detector onto a sheet and began to assemble it. He was wonderfully efficient and often went on to the next step while Mrs. Bliss, trying to absorb what she had just read, fell behind. If she lived *another* eighty-two years, she thought dispiritedly, she'd never get the hang of mechanics. Always she'd believed this was some man/woman thing, but Mrs. Bliss was aware that fresh returns were still coming in from the feminists and the fact was she was more than a little annoyed with herself.

Junior fit the batteries into Mrs. Bliss's metal detector and pronounced it ready to go. First, though, he would have to put his own together. At more than twice the price of Mrs. Bliss's, Yellin's metal detector seemed at least three times more complicated, and now when she read the directions to him he frequently stopped her and asked her to repeat what she'd read. At other times he grabbed the manual out of her hands, checking to study it himself or maybe to see if she'd read it correctly. Mrs. Bliss, already upset by the brightness of the sun, began to transfer some of the anger she'd been feeling about herself onto Junior. The metal detectors should have been assembled before they'd left. Even if he didn't do it at home he'd have had plenty of time while she was in her condo changing her clothes. At least to get started. Whose idea was this? It wasn't hers. He should have taken the responsibility. What did she think she was doing, anyway? Yellin was Ted's buddy, not hers.

"All right," he said at last, "that's it. Let's rock and roll."

Mrs. Bliss, sick to her stomach, thought he sounded like a fool.

She was, kayn aynhoreh, a healthy woman. Indeed, the last time she remembered feeling nearly so ill had been the hot day she'd left Holmer Toibb's office and was spotted by Hector Camerando as she waited for her bus and he'd offered her the ride.

She'd been breathless, disoriented. That had been about treasure, too. Her conviction that they would round a corner and come upon Ted's Buick LeSabre, reborn, gleaming at the curb as the day he must have first seen it in the showroom. When she saw it was Camerando's Fleetwood Cadillac she couldn't catch her breath and started to cry. She felt faint and Camerando had drowned her in air-conditioning. He advised, she recalled, not to let things slide, to see a doctor.

Well, she was with one now, wasn't she? And knew he would fail her. As all doctors ultimately failed all patients. As Toibb before him, as Greener Hertsheim before Toibb, all the way back to the experimental research scientific ones at Billings, and Rabbi Beinfeld, and good old Dr. Myers before all of them. Nobody, she thought, could help anyone really. It was nobody's fault. Help just wasn't in the cards. The cards? The deck!

What she did now, she saw, was for herself. Not for auld lang syne, or Ted, or companionship in her old age, and not, finally, because Junior Yellin might wither and die if she rebuffed his attentions and kiddy enthusiasms, but out of her *own* needs, her *own* kiddy enthusiasms that until a few moments ago she still believed—in spite of the presence of the shadeless, roofless ruthlessness of the overbearing sun and the distant twitch of a returning interest in interest (fresh interests lay at the heart of recreational therapeusis; she'd known that going in), in spite, too, of her dissipate concentration over the incomprehensible chop suey of the owner's manual, and her patient rereadings of the most pertinent sections—applied and that she felt, up to that raw moment when Yellin slapped her hands away and pulled, ripped, the owner's manual from them. As if he were denouncing her, as if he were saying, *"This is the owner's manual, I am its owner!"*

So the shoe was on the other foot. What, he was doing her a favor? Leading her into direct sunlight, dragging her beneath its spooky field as if under some cruel astrological influence. She no longer cared that he was too used to his character, or that he'd always had partners, projecting her anger where it properly belonged—Rage to Bliss to Yellin like a double-play on her husband's radio.

The more she thought about it the madder she got. The nerve

of that guy! Snatching the book away like I'm not even here, like I'm invisible. To hell with him. To *hell* with him!

And gathering up her metal detector, her trowel and shovel and hoe, and taking her fine paleontologist's brush made off down the beach on her own, passing by groups of discrete populations— couples from the hotels stretched out on bath towels; women older than Dorothy on beach chairs of bright woven plastic, indifferent as stylites, their skin dark as scabs; men, the ancient retired, chilly in suits and ties; girls in thong bathing suits, their teenage admirers trailing behind them like packs of wild dogs; kids, overexcited, wild in the surf, their parents frantically waving their arms like coaches in Little League; waiters, kitchen help, and housekeepers on smoke breaks; small clans of picnickers handing off contraband sand-wiches, contraband beer; lovers kneading lotions and sunblock into one another's flesh like a sort of sexual first aid. Mrs. Ted Bliss, like some fussy fisherman, as inconspicuously as she could moving past these people toward a yellow patch of empty beach, for all her stealth reminded that she must appear at least as idiosyncratic (though not nearly so fashionable) as the girls in the thong bikini bathing suits, at least as idiosyncratic (though, again, not nearly so fashionable) as the superannuated gentlemen in their tight shoes, suits, and ties—a little old "fucking beekeeper" lady and her elec-tric broom.

Somewhere in a narrow clearing between low and high tides she set up shop, took a last look at the directions to see how one turned on the machine, flicked its toggle switch, and opened the store.

"What are you doing?" a little girl of eight or nine asked about ten minutes after she started.

"Looking for buried treasure, sweetheart," said Mrs. Ted Bliss.

"Did you find any?"

"So far," said Mrs. Ted Bliss, "they're not biting."

"Oh," said the kid, "may I try?"

"Be my guest," Mrs. Bliss said.

"Really? No fooling?"

Mrs. Bliss handed the metal detector to the little girl.

"What do I do?"

"Make little half circles."

"Like this?"

"Looks good to me."

"This is fun," the child said in a few minutes without really meaning it.

"Take your time, darling."

Mrs. Bliss watched the little girl, self-consciously comparing her to her own children when they were her age, to her grandchildren, their children, her sisters and brothers at that age, ultimately to what she could remember of herself when she had been nine. Drawing a blank here, recalling as through the vague narcotic muffle and babble of an interrupted dream only the interest she'd had in detail, the remarkable sum of unrelated parts, a sort of silly wonder and flawed attention. She was sorry she didn't have an orange in her purse, or candy, or gum to give the kid, anything, really, to keep up her flagging interest. Suddenly, inspired, she reached into her change purse, found a quarter, put it back, and took a dollar out of her billfold.

"Here," said Mrs. Bliss.

The look on the little girl's face changed from the curiosity and enthusiasm she'd shown when she'd initiated their conversation to that of suspicion, almost alarm.

"It's your treasure," Mrs. Bliss started to explain, but before she was sure the words were out of her mouth or, if they were, whether the child had heard or understood them, the kid dropped the metal detector's long handle down on the sand and ran off.

"What was *that* all about?" said Junior Yellin, coming up to her.

"Oh," Dorothy said, "oh."

"What's up? What's wrong?"

"I scared her. I tried to give her a dollar." Mrs. Bliss was almost in tears.

"You scared her? You tried to give her a dollar? To hell with her. She can go to hell."

"She thinks I'm a witch out of some fairy story," Mrs. Bliss said.

"Let her go screw herself she thinks you're a witch. She's a son of a bitch. So what did you find?" She was thinking about the little girl. She didn't understand what he meant. "Hey," Junior said, "she threw it on the ground. What does she think, it's a toy? It's an advanced piece of machinery, it isn't a toy."

"It's a toy," Mrs. Ted Bliss said.

Yellin looked around to see if anyone were watching. "Look," he said, "look inside." He was wearing a sort of creel. He raised its lid. Inside, dark at the bottom, Mrs. Bliss saw that he carried a kind of loose, unset metal jewelry.

"You found these?"

"Shh. Yes. And more, but people were getting curious so I kicked sand over the area and came to look for you. I took coordinates. I could find the spot again anytime I wanted to."

She'd forgotten the little girl. "What do you think it is?" she asked.

"A battle, what else?"

"A battle?"

"A battle, a shoot-out, a fistfight with guns."

"On the beach?"

"On the beach? The beach? Dorothy, *dar*ling, this is the hallowed ground of drug lords. Just look at these shell casings, will you; look at all these bullets. I don't know my ass from a hole in the ground, millimeter and NRA-wise, but I'm telling you, kid, this stuff has all the markings of Uzis, AK-forty-sevens, rubber landing craft on moonless nights. Cocaine-wise, it must have been the Bay of bloody Pigs. I was a butcher, I know."

"It's ammunition?" Mrs. Bliss asked nervously.

"It ain't arrowheads."

"But what do you do with it?"

"What, are you kidding me? We could open a smuggler's museum. We don't have enough yet. Anyone can see it's just the tip of the iceberg, but we can always come back. I mean, I know where the mother lode is. Hell, Dorothy, there must be a couple hundred dozen mother lodes up and down all these beaches. And let's say I bring some of my Land Rover chums in on this. And you've got an in with the DEA guys. Working together with our friends downtown and if we put in a little research on the mainframe, we should be able to establish the like provenance of these drug wars, the circa and circumstances. I mean, face it, what's a tourist do with his time after he's checked out South Beach and been to Little Havana? He wants the big picture on the culture his next stop has to be the Dope Runner's Museum. What do you say? I'm offering you the ground floor. What do you say, what do you think?"

What she said was nothing. What she thought was that he was crazy. Yet a part of her couldn't help but admire him. Even to stand in awe of his nutty energy. Who, she wondered, was the true baleboosteh? Not Dorothy, who could not remember when she had given up clipping coupons out of her newspapers and junk mail, or ceased to bother with all the heavy hospital corners of slipcovers, blue water in the toilet bowl. Not Dorothy, who often as not these days let a pot of coffee stand overnight and warmed it up the next day. Not Dorothy, who no longer always bothered to bring back to her condominium the doggy bags and uneaten rolls from restaurants but who, when she did, let the rolls stand out on the kitchen table and warmed them in the toaster oven the next morning to eat with her breakfast, just as she put the contents of the doggy bag not into her freezer but in the refrigerator so she could make her next meal out of the merely day-old leftovers.

So if there were a new baleboss in town, unlikely as it seemed, it had to be old Junior who baked the bread. How different was the way he plotted his campaigns from the way Dorothy had once planned meals for her family? Peculiarly, not that she gave him any credit for it, this made him seem all the more male in her eyes. Driven, she meant, unable or unwilling to let anything go, his hold on life greedy with strength. (She knew, for example, that even after discounting the two or three-year seniority she held over him he was bound to outlive her, to outlive everyone with whom she had struggled for edge over the course of his life.)

"But what did *you* come up with? Never mind," he said, glancing at her tools, "those ain't even got dust on them. I could eat off your trowel." He picked up her metal detector. "Is it turned on? Are you sure you even know how to work this?"

"I flip the toggle switch. I make little half circles."

"Well," Yellin said, "maybe you hit a dry hole here. But that's hard to buy into. I mean this place is a billion years old, you had to come across *some*thing. Beer tabs, bottle caps. The key from a sardine can. A tin of old condoms, for Christ's sake."

He spoke as if she'd let him down. Surprisingly, she was not at all surprised.

"No," said Mrs. Ted Bliss coolly, "no beer tabs, no bottle caps. None of that other stuff either." She wanted to tell him she had found gold—what do you call them?—doubloons, silver spoons, forks, shining jewels set in precious metal rings. That she held her tongue was a tribute to the great age she knew he would live to be, a lonely old man surviving his children and grandchildren, surviving everyone he had ever known or taken advantage of. She did not wish to add her sarcasm to the weight of his possible regrets.

"It could be defective, I suppose," Yellin said. "Let me take it out for a spin."

Dorothy Bliss shrugged and Junior, reactivating the machine he had just switched off so as not to drain its batteries, began going over what seemed to Mrs. Bliss exactly the same ground she and the little girl had previously covered.

"We already did over th—"

"Quiet," he said, "I think I've got something. Hand me that shovel." He scratched furiously at the packed sand as if he'd hit pay dirt. "See" he said, "see?"

"Have you found something? Is something there?"

"My God," Yellin said, "it's sending out signals like a sinking ship. Give me a hand, will you? Use the hoe, get the trowel. Yes, right, good girl, bring the brush."

Mrs. Ted Bliss, excited, in the sand, on her knees, beside him, leaned into her effort. Breathlessly, she pulled sand from the hole he was digging as if she were bailing the beach. But for the pressure she felt along her arms and in her chest (and her fury), it might have been more than a half century earlier on the shore of Lake Michigan with her children and nephews and nieces, Mrs. Bliss dispensing pail-and-shovel lessons, overseeing pretend burials. The thought brought her up short. She dropped her hoe. (Marvin was dead, some of his cousins; not buried to the neck in Lake Michigan sand but in that cold Chicago boneyard, even their nostrils clogged with dirt, covered by death shmuts.)

"No," Yellin said, "don't let up. Why are you stopping?"

Mrs. Bliss shrugged. "What's the use?" she said.

"What's that, philosophy? The use is we're onto something here. Christ, Dorothy, this is hot work."

Yellin stopped just long enough to wipe his face and neck with a handkerchief, then quickly resumed. "Listen to that. Your metal detector's beeping away to beat the band. The sound wasn't nearly as loud at my dig."

What was he talking about? What beeping? What sound?

"What beeping?" she said. "What sound?"

He stopped digging.

"What beeping? What sound? You don't hear it?"

"No," said Mrs. Ted Bliss.

"Jeez, Dorothy, don't you have your hearing aid in?"

"Sure I do," she said.

"You see?" Yellin said. "You see what happens you don't go for the upscale model? Where are your bells and whistles? On my device there's even a light that flashes when you're over something. The bigger the find, the brighter the light. That's the sort of thing you need."

She thought of the light Frank had installed on the phone in her bedroom. She thought of all the people she'd missed who said there'd been no answer when they pressed on her buzzer. Not so many. Maybe not so many who said that they had.

"It's a good thing I came over," Junior said. "We would have missed this, whatever it is." He took up his position again over the hole he had dug in the sand. "Wait," he said, "I think I just heard the shovel clink against something solid. Give me a second here."

Dorothy watched as Junior Yellin moved the shovel aside and reached his arm deep into the hole, almost as far as his shoulder. "My hand is on it," he said, making no sound but moving his lips. Before he pulled it out he looked over at Dorothy, staring at her, she thought, almost murderously. "This is a fifty-fifty arrangement, you understand. I mean by actual legal rights it probably ought to be sixty-forty, but I'm bringing you into it because you're my friend, you staked the claim, and it was your machine even though you missed it and I ended up having to do all the work."

She watched him carefully.

"What do you say, Dorothy? Shake?"

She couldn't believe this son of a bitch, but thinking again how long he'd survive her and wishing him only the saddest, dreariest memories, she put her hand out slowly and slipped it into his. Junior smiled. "Done? All right then, done. A deal's a deal!" he said triumphantly. "So let's see what we got here."

He jerked his hand away as if he'd been stung. "Jesus! Son of a bitch! I think I cut myself." His knuckles and fingers were covered with wet, compacted sand, almost the texture and color of mud. "Can you see, am I bleeding?"

"I don't see any blood."

"Some of this buried shit can be jagged, sharp. That's why they say to wear gloves. You could get a very ancient strain of tetanus. No," Yellin said, "I don't see any blood either. I was lucky. That stuff can be a bitch to cure. More painful than rabies shots, they say."

Mrs. Bliss nodded.

"Think I could use your scarf to wrap around my hand?"

"You give me fifty-five."

"Ri-i-ght," Yellin said. "There's life in the old girl yet, hey Dorothy?" He winked. "Okay," he said, and reached down into the hole again. "He stuck in his thumb, and pulled out a—Jesus, Mary, and Joe," he said. "What do you suppose this is?"

Hand over hand he drew more of it up.

The metal had lost definition. It was corroded, discolored, had been transmuted, undergone some heavily inverted oxidation by age and weight and water. Vaguely, pieces resembled figure eights, others, enormous, indistinguishable lumps of wadded gray chewing gum. Mrs. Bliss, who'd never seen anything like it, recognized it at once.

"They're shackles," she said. "For slaves. Shipped over from the islands."

"Jesus, you think?"

"Shackles. Handcuffs. Neck rings and leg irons."

"For shvartzers?"

Mrs. Bliss looked at this Junior Yellin. "For the doorman. For the girl who comes to clean once a week. For the man who brings the car around."

"Escaped? You think maybe escaped? I mean we're a little too south of plantation country. They couldn't have been tobacco and cotton niggers, do you suppose?"

"There's storms," said Mrs. Ted Bliss. "Ships founder and sink. Rocks scrape their sides and they go down."

"Absolutely," Junior Yellin said. "I agree with you, but how do you think—"

"Bodies bloat. They decay. Death puffs them up and lets out their air like leaky balloons. Elements—seawater, the air—chip away at their skin like tapeworms. They melt. Fat lets go. Bones do. And gasses." *The sun!* she thought. "Then what's left to hold them?'' Mrs. Bliss pointed to the sordid cache at their feet. ''This iron? They slip these useless nooses like Houdinis.''

''Yeah,'' Junior said, ''I guess *so*. We write that up on the little cards. We do the whole megillah. Dramatic, hard-hitting. They come away with something to think about. Yeah,'' he said, ''yeah.

''I think this introduces a whole new dimension,'' Yellin said. '' 'Smuggler's Museum' won't work anymore. Or 'Dope Runner's Museum' either. We've got to change it to something more universal. 'South Florida Museum of Havoc and History'? It needs work. Nothing's written in stone. But in the ballpark. Think about it. You have a gift for this particular aspect.''

Mrs. Bliss shook her head.

''What?''

''I haven't got the bells and whistles for this work,'' she said.

''Oh, come on,'' Junior said, ''sure you do. You do. You're the brains of the outfit.''

Mrs. Bliss found it difficult to look at him. The same poisons that radiated from the sun seemed to pour from his eyes.

''I get it,'' Junior said, ''you think maybe this is some soft soap I'm handing you. You're knocking it back to what I said about partners. You probably put that down in case I need someone to help take the load off if I screw up. Well, nothing could be further from the truth. Nothing.''

''Will you tell me something?'' Mrs. Bliss said.

''Will I *tell* you something? Will I *tell* you something? Of course, sweetie. What have *I* got to hide? We're old friends. We know each other our whole lives practically. Ask me something, I'll tell you something.''

She pointed up the beach to where he'd left the dune buggy.

''Where,'' she said, ''do you get those things? Who gives them to you? All those Frank Buck motorcars you ride around in?''

He seemed flustered, humiliated. Then he was angry.

''All those . . . What, you think it's all up with me?'' he shot back. ''That it's all over but the shouting? You think that ATV shit is too sporty for a guy like me? Listen, you. I'm a character, I'm colorful. All my life I'm a heartbreaker. My wife, the ladies, my daddy, the kids. My partners. Ask Ted, olov hasholem, you don't believe me. They held their breath to see where I'd jump next, to see where I'd land. I'm in the air *now!*''

"Where, Junior?"

"*You see?*" he exulted.

"No. Where? I mean who gives them to you? What strange lies do you have to tell them?"

Junior Yellin glared at Mrs. Ted Bliss. He held her eyes. Unmoved, she stared back at him. It was an old game she remembered from childhood. She used to play it with her brothers, her sisters. Even in America they played it. Even with her younger cousins Dorothy was always the first to look away, her concentration broken by some comic shame. This time, though, it was Yellin who looked away. He stifled a giggle. "Jesus, Dorothy," he said.

"No, Milton, I mean it. How do you get those machines? What do you have to pay for them to give them to you?"

"Theah delez plays," Yellin mumbled.

"What?" she said. "What?"

"They're dealer's plates."

"I don't understand."

"Yeah, well," he said, "that's because you think there ought to be some sort of statute of limitations on trying to stay alive," he said malevolently.

"No," said Mrs. Bliss, "no."

"Bullshit," Yellin growled. "I tell them I'm opening a business to take seniors on tours off the beaten track, rides in the sand, into the woods. Land cruises. That I put them in all-terrain vehicles on forks in the road. It's a terrific idea. They all think so. And it is. Just what we came across today, for example. We'd do a land-office business. We'd clean up. I tell them I just have to take it out for a spin. Safety factors. Official vehicular approval ratings."

"They fall for this?"

"I'm a heartbreaker, they eat it up. Half of them want to come in on the deal with me."

He *was* a heartbreaker, he really was, and he made her as breathless as he must have made Ted and all the other dupes and suckers who'd ever had dealings (the dealers) with him. It occurred to her as he ran through his wild defenses that she was not properly dressed for him, that she should have worn the garments of Saharan nomads; that she had made a mistake not to sport gleaming robes, complicated headgear; or to have rubbed heavy sunblock into every pore like a minstrel. That he gave off a sort of cancer, had power to kindle headaches, to dehydrate the heart.

She needed to get back to her apartment.

"So soon?" he said mildly. She was astonished. He'd forgiven and forgotten.

"No, really. I have to."

"Dorothy. Sweetheart. No one's here. I'll turn around, I'll shut my eyes. Take off your bloomers and walk in the sea to your waist. Raise your dress, tinkle in the ocean."

It wasn't his business. She was furious, but despite herself she told him she didn't have to go. She didn't. It was the old business of her bladder shutting down on her when she wasn't near a familiar toilet. Ted had teased her about it in the old days. Even Alcibiades Chitral had questioned her when she'd visited him in the penitentiary. People thought she was too modest, a prude, ashamed, for all her vanity, the pride she'd once taken in her looks, in her body. It was probably true. Though it rolled off other people like water off a duck's back, she may have been one of the last alive who hadn't come to accept scandal. Who, though she watched with the same avidity as anyone else the morning TV shows, the mass public confessionals on which everyone—incesters, whores, cross-dressers, the sex changed, the housewives who stripped, fat admirers, klansmen, wife swappers, self-proclaimed thieves, rapists, child abusers, the murderers, the specialist serial killers—admitted to anything, still wanted to cover her eyes, her ears, who couldn't have fantasized a fantasy if her life depended on it (even that Ted was still alive, even that Marvin was), and who wouldn't for the world have gone on any of these shows to admit that she had ever had anything so intimate as a body, or that even if she had, it could have found itself on national TV owning up to anything as personal (and it was this, not their standards and practices, that scandalized her) as a function or a need.

It was remarkable to Mrs. Ted Bliss that the whole world did not seize up when it was out of range of a toilet.

And she didn't care to hear any mishegoss about repression, thank you very much. No. If she wanted no part of Junior Yellin right then it was because he embarrassed her. His remark about peeing in the ocean was the least of it. It wasn't *any* one thing. His plans for a museum, what he'd said to the dealers, all the silly, heartbreaking highwire of which he was not only capable but proud, even the fatuity about the superiority of his metal detector, the baloney about the "spot" he was looking for, his crap about the demographics—all his crap. It was amazing, a revelation. She had perhaps at last met a man (taking nothing away from the natural gifts and bona fides of his manhood) whom she couldn't entirely trust.

But she was his last connection to earth, the life he'd known before he'd become such a caricature of himself. How could she tell him goodbye and good luck, how could she write him off?

Because, sadly, the truth was that if she was his last connection to earth, he was pretty much hers, as well. Maxine, thank God, lived; Frank, whatever his new, changed circumstances, did. George, Judith, and James; Ellen and Barry; Janet and Donny and all of them, thank God. But there was no getting away from it. She was at an age where distance and separation had been transformed into something more important than memory. Or, if not memory (she was too old to tell herself lies), then at least involvement, hands-on concern, the simple day-to-day of all her maternals and sororals and familials down past the most distant cousin to the last of her mathematically attenuate mishpocheh.

She loved them. In some platonic piece of her heart they loomed larger than nations, than civilization itself. It wasn't a case of out-of-sight out-of-mind. It was much more complicated. As complicated as distance. She was old. She had her health but she was old, and it would have been as difficult for her, as much of a mental and physical impossibility and strain, to bear down on them, on their collective griefs and individual concerns, with the brute force of her concentration as it would have been for her to catch a rubber pelota in the clawlike cesta at the jai alai to send it flying back at the wall, or run after the rabbit at the dog track.

She still spoke to them regularly on the long distance, but the truth was she spent more time idly chatting with Louise Munez at her high-security kiosk and newsstand than with all her children and grandchildren and relatives combined.

No, thought Mrs. Ted Bliss, though she wouldn't go in with him on his schemes, she couldn't abandon Yellin. No more than she could have stopped putting through calls to her children, or taking them either. But, face it, she was pulling in her horns almost

as deliberately as she was just now taking up her tools and sub-
standard, unbelled, whistleless metal detector and starting off in
the direction of the ridiculous dune buggy for the long ride home
under the unrelenting sun.

ELEVEN

Mrs. Ted Bliss's daughter-in-law Ellen had used her two-week vacation from the shoe store to come down to visit from Chicago.

Typical, Mrs. Bliss thought, the woman didn't even wait to be invited, just picked up the phone one night to announce when she'd be arriving. She wanted, she said, to treat Dorothy to lunch. Were there any particularly good health-food restaurants her mother-in-law had not been to?

"I haven't been to any," Dorothy said. "When I eat out, I eat out. I don't go for a treatment."

"Oh, Ma," Ellen said lightly, "what am I going to do with you? Never mind, I'll ask Wilcox. He'll know a place."

Wilcox was Dr. Wilcox, Ellen's holistic chiropractor. His practice was in Houston, Texas, and three times a year Ellen flew there to be adjusted and to find out what was new in the New Age.

Because the truth was Mrs. Bliss had a blind spot when it came to the question of her problematic daughter-in-law. Though she knew better, she still held something of a grudge against her son's widow. After all—she knew she was being ridiculous—Marvin had died on the woman's watch. This was before all the mishegoss of the herbal teas and honey; the wheatless, flourless breads and leaf jams; the baked soybean stand-ins for meat and the vegetable compote dessert substitutes. It was before all the noxious, mysterious

243

beverages she had learned to mix in her blender, before all her long, awful witness of her husband's horribly drawn-out death. In fairness, though, it was only tit for tat. Because on Ellen's side, too, wasn't there the same unspoken accusation? If Marvin had died on his wife's watch, hadn't he also died on his mother's? Of course, neither of them ever mentioned to the other their vague mutual suspicions. Though they screamed at each other plenty and, behind one another's backs, passed remarks, Ellen finding fault with her mother-in-law's stolid Russian reluctance to consider other options, or color outside the lines of her character, and Mrs. Bliss resenting her daughter-in-law's resentment, her unyielding attempts to look for miracles, stubborn as a cultist or orthodox. Did she think Wilcox some magician who could push back the borders of death, protect her with elixirs and potions? (And wasn't Janet still in India? India, noch! Why not Oz?) That having surrendered poor Marvin to death at the hands of the doctors (who had failed her only after Marvin died), she could so arrange things with her diets and ointments and fancy Houston, Texas, backrubs and spells that no one would ever have to die again.

It wasn't the first time Ellen had visited Dorothy on a moment's notice, and, though the women didn't get along well, didn't for that matter even like each other much, for Marvin's sake neither wished to call it quits. Mrs. Bliss even had a grudging admiration for her son's wife. It was, in an odd way, a little like the esteem in which she held men. After her husband died, Ellen had become astonishingly independent. With no Manny in her life to give her widow tips she'd gone on not only to raise two very sweet children but to become a genuinely first-class businesswoman. Salesperson of the Year eleven of the fourteen or fifteen years she'd been with Chandler's Shoes on Randolph Street (the flagship of the big Chicago chain), she had won giant, bigscreen television sets, state-of-the-art computers, all-expense-paid trips to London and Cancun, grand prizes of every description. One particularly good year they had presented her with five thousand dollars' worth of company stock.

But then she remembered Providence, the seder at Frank's. Her son had paid for Ellen's airplane tickets, for Barry's. Why had she let him? Mrs. Bliss wasn't one to wonder what this one or that one did or did not have in the bank, but she knew damn well that her daughter-in-law could afford to buy her own airline tickets, Barry's, too. Why did she make herself out to be such a chozzer?

Though, of course, thought Mrs. Ted Bliss, that wasn't putting the case accurately. Anyway, Mrs. Bliss didn't really believe Ellen's greed had anything to do with money. It was greed of a baser sort. It was oy vay iz mir greed, poor-me greed, the greed of insistent vulnerability and grudge, the pressed, put-upon passion of complaint—a greed that lived by its own jealous counsel and kept its own sharp accounts, bookkeeping loss like an underwriter. It was almost, had Mrs. Bliss understood the complicated laws of the lines of succession, a sort of royalty by remove. Thus Ellen (according to Ellen according to Mrs. Ted Bliss) would always qualify as Marvin's chief mourner, outranking Maxine who had merely been his little sister and had a good, living, faithful husband, and a beautiful daughter (Judith), and entrepreneurial James; and Frank, the baby of the outfit, but the one who published books and had celebrity and whose son, Donny, was the richest and smartest of the bunch. If she had competition about who had taken the heaviest hit it had to be, thought Mrs. Ted Bliss, Mrs. Ted Bliss herself. And Dorothy she'd have written off because though Dorothy had lost her son and her husband, too, at least had had the husband long enough to see most of her children married and to have grandchildren. Also, Ellen's son, Barry, though a kind and gentle man, was a lightweight, and Janet, her daughter, a lost, almost middle-aged spinster, was in India, searching for her life in a place she'd never been where she could ever conceivably have lost it. These were the reasons she took airfare from Frank, and fought like cats and dogs with Dorothy.

Which she proceeded to do the very day she arrived in Florida.

Dorothy was scrounging around in the cupboards.

"Ma, why are you standing on that chair?"

"I'm looking to see what I can make for supper."

"Do you want to fall? Is that what you want? To fall and possibly break a hip?"

"Did I fall yesterday? Did I fall once all the years you weren't around to catch me? I didn't fall yesterday, and I didn't fall thirty-five years before yesterday. You know what I do when a lightbulb burns out in the ceiling fixture and the maintenance momzers lay down on the job? I get up on a chair and change it myself!"

"Ma, you're playing with fire. Get down, I'll find what you're looking for. You know," she said, "if you'd tip the man a few dollars you wouldn't have to put yourself at risk."

"Sport," said Mrs. Ted Bliss, "big sport." She let herself cautiously down from the chair. "There's nothing here, not even a can of soup. We'll go shopping tomorrow. I'll see what's in the freezer."

"Not for me," her daughter-in-law said.

"There's lamb chops, there's chicken. There's leftover pot roast. There's some delicious soup I froze."

"You know that stuff's poison, don't you?"

"What's poison? I don't make poison."

"Of course not," Ellen said. "You're a wonderful cook. It's just something Dr. Wilcox told me the last time I was in Houston. Freezer burn breaks down the nutrient molecules in meat and makes dangerous microbes. Fresh meat's bad enough but leftovers will kill you."

"You have a freezer. You freeze food."

"I threw it out when I heard. I threw out over a hundred dollars' worth of meat. Just like that I got rid of it."

Mrs. Bliss glared at her crazy daughter-in-law. "Your father-in-law was a butcher. You fed your family years on free meat."

"Yes," she said coolly, "I know."

"You've got something to say, say it."

"I've got nothing to say," Ellen said diffidently.

She needed this? She didn't need this. She'd lived alone too long ever to have to bicker with people again. (And wasn't that one of the chief purposes of retirement, even of leaving the places you'd lived most of your life, the people you'd lived with?) So the signs and prospects for the vacation didn't look so hot. Indeed, one of the first things Ellen had said after she kissed Mrs. Bliss and was inside the door was that she'd left her return ticket open-ended.

"What, I'm on trial, Ellen?"

"Ma," she'd said pointedly, "I think we both are."

This was a Tuesday. Mrs. Bliss knew she'd have to stay over a Saturday night to qualify for the discount. This meant the shortest she'd be staying was, what, five nights. What would she do with her? Just the problem of feeding her seemed insurmountable. There was nothing in the house. Ellen wouldn't eat anything from the freezer, and she'd already alerted Mrs. Bliss to her thing about the health restaurants. Drek! Reeds and straw!

"Milchiks?" Dorothy suggested.

"Dairy, Ma?" Ellen said. "Are you trying to kill yourself?"

"With what? A whitefish? An egg? A slice of cheese and fruit?"

That first night Ellen prepared a salad for the two of them. Mrs. Bliss was out of kale, haricot beans, eggplant, and pumpkin, so she improvised with tomato, lettuce, some cucumber, and onion. She found a box of dry, uncooked oatmeal and sprinkled a liberal handful over both their plates.

Mrs. Bliss tried, but could barely get down a single mouthful. She was wiping bits of oatmeal from the corners of her lips with a paper napkin while Ellen studied her narrowly.

"Ma?"

"What?"

"I'm not trying to upset you," she said.

Instantly, Mrs. Ted Bliss was overcome by a sense of shame and guilt. She crumpled the napkin and laid it in her lap.

"It's all right," Dorothy said. "I should have remembered about your special dietary needs and laid in what you like. But you know, sweetheart, it's harder than keeping kosher shopping for somebody so frum about what she eats. Tomorrow," she promised, "tomorrow we'll go shopping. First thing in the morning, before it gets hot."

"Fine, Ma, whatever," her daughter-in-law said, "but you know," she said, "I really don't mean to upset you, I don't. Everyone's entitled to live their life as they please. That goes without saying, but what I'm suggesting is for your own good. May I ask you something personal, Ma?"

Something personal? She wanted to ask her something personal? An eighty-two-year-old widow? This would be good, this would be very, very good. Mrs. Bliss's guilt disappeared as if it had never existed.

"Sure," she said, "as personal as you please. Think up your most personal question and ask away. Go ahead, shoot."

"Have you ever had a high colonic rice enema?"

"A what?"

"Coffee beans, then. Wilcox thinks highly of coffee bean enemas, too."

"Ahh, *Wilcox*."

"I could give you one. Wilcox showed me, I know what I'm doing."

Wonderful, thought Mrs. Ted Bliss. Now she knew what they could do together while her daughter-in-law was there waiting out her stay-over-Saturday discount. They could give each other enemas. First Ellen could give her a coffee bean enema, then they'd trade off and Dorothy could give her daughter-in-law a lovely rice enema. Coffee beans, rice. It was six of one, half a dozen of the other. Tomorrow, tomorrow they would lay in provisions.

"No enemas," Mrs. Bliss said.

"Ma, I see how you eat. I don't think you know how they can clean out your system."

"No enemas. Enemas are out, no enemas."

"All right, all right," Ellen said, "don't get so excited. It's been a long day. I had to eat that airplane food. Would you object very much if *I* took one? I brought my own enema bag of course. There's a box of wild rice in my suitcase."

It was at least half a minute before Mrs. Bliss could answer. "Use the guest bathroom," she pronounced austerely. "There's two cans of deodorant spray in the linen cabinet. One is Mint, the other is Floral Bouquet. Please use the mint before you give yourself the enema and the floral bouquet afterward. Yeah, it's been a long day for me, too. When I finish the dishes I think I'll go to bed."

"Ma, sit still. I'll do the dishes."

"No, Ellen," said Mrs. Ted Bliss, "I really wish you wouldn't."

So she was crazy, thought Mrs. Ted Bliss in bed that night. What difference did it make, did it make, really? She had been a good wife to her son. Yes, and an excellent mother when you considered that she'd raised her children practically by herself. Her looniness was only a kind of grief, finally, and Mrs. Bliss, whose guilt had passed, once again started to feel her shame. She began to cry so softly that with her hearing aid out she was aware she wept only when the tears wet her cheeks.

They shopped so efficiently the next morning it took just over half the time it usually did for Mrs. Bliss to do her marketing. Dorothy pushed the cart while Ellen went down the aisles selecting various unfamiliarly shaped cans of strange foodstuffs—raw, unprocessed organics, pulps of queer fruits, minced game, oddball packets of herbs, Oriental chowders. They would have been through in even less time if Ellen hadn't stopped to read all the labels, occasionally pausing before familiar, popular brands, and reading those labels, too, clucking her tongue in contempt at the high sodium and fat levels listed on them. In the produce section she fairly squealed in approval and surprise whenever she came across the exotic vegetables and fruits of distant third-world countries.

"At least it won't take us long at the checkout," said Mrs. Ted Bliss.

"Why's that, Ma?"

"They don't make coupons for this stuff."

On the way back Ellen was insistent about paying for both their bus fares. It was her treat, she said, and wouldn't take no for an answer.

"You know, Ma," Ellen said when they were putting away what Mrs. Bliss couldn't quite bring herself to think of as groceries, "there's really no point in you going out in this heat."

"No? What should I do, ask the neighbors to do my shopping?"

"You could call up and have it delivered. I'm sure in a community where over half the people are retired the stores offer all kinds of services."

"Sure," said Mrs. Ted Bliss, "and you know what they'd charge? An arm and a leg."

"What are you saving it for, Ma? Your golden years?"

This was some Ellen, this Ellen. Daughter-in-law or no daughter-in-law, and mother of her grandchildren (one of whom, Janet, off in India watching the tigers churn themselves into butter, she hadn't seen in years) or no mother of her grandchildren, she was a perfect bully of a woman. She had an answer and a remark for everything. No wonder she'd done so well for herself in retail shoes. Which brought up a small point Mrs. Bliss had wanted to ask about for years but the woman made her so angry, she always forgot. Now, while the iron was hot, she decided to strike.

"Your chiropractor?"

"What about him?"

"Isn't he a special sort of chiropractor?"

"Holistic," Ellen said.

"Yes, holistic," said Mrs. Ted Bliss, "that's right."

"What about him?" Ellen said still more defensively.

"I forget, ain't that where the mind and the body are the same thing?"

"He treats the whole person. What about it?"

"Nothing. I was just wondering why you always wear earth shoes."

"They're not earth shoes, Ma. They're customized. You can't get them without a prescription."

"They're flat like earth shoes."

"They're not earth shoes."

"I see," said Mrs. Ted Bliss. "How come I never see you in high heels? Not at the biggest affairs."

"High heels are very bad for you. They ruin your posture; they can throw out your back."

"Aha!" said Mrs. Ted Bliss.

"What are you talking about?"

"You *sell* high heels! You make practically your whole living selling high heels! And all those prizes and trips? You can't tell me those are from carpet slippers. I see what they get for high heels. The markup's all in high heels. Ask yourself, Ellen, how many people's backs have you thrown out in your time?"

"Caveat emptor," Ellen said primly.

It was an absurd conversation and Mrs. Bliss knew it. Nor did she feel particularly proud of having bested her daughter-in-law. It was no way to treat a guest, let alone a close relative. Plus Ellen was one of the gang. It was no way to treat one of the gang, and Mrs. Bliss's triumph fell hollow in her heart. Yet hadn't she been asking for it since the moment she came into her house? And what about the tsimmes with the groceries? Or paying her mother-in-law's bus fare like she was the last of the big-time spenders? Or that what-are-you-saving-it-for crack? When she must have known one of the things she was saving it for was Ellen's children—the scarce Janet and garageless Barry.

Still, none of that was an excuse. The woman got on her nerves? Big deal. Grin and bear it.

Mrs. Bliss tried to make it up to her but Ellen hung back coolly, parrying Mrs. Bliss's attempts to make up with all the quiet, dignified propriety and hurt she could muster. The only way Mrs. Bliss could think to make it up to her was through the dreadful, suspect teas and jams Ellen had brought down from Chicago. She asked Ellen to prepare it and, oh yes, it might be a good idea to heat up one of those nice rice pies Ellen had picked up at the market this morning.

She had to know what Mrs. Bliss was up to, but Ellen was a good sport, so what the hell, forgive and forget. She prepared the tea for her mother-in-law, steeped the herbs briefly, a lick and a promise, really, cut her a small piece of pie.

And then, over their queer high tea, both women dropped their guards, participants in an undeclared spiritual truce and, very gently, started to become friends.

"I barged in on you, didn't I?" Ellen said.

"Barged in? What? No. Don't be silly."

"Intruded on your privacy."

"Oh, my privacy," said Mrs. Ted Bliss.

"Some people enjoy being alone."

"Who? Why?"

"They catch up on their reading, they can go to the movies in the afternoon without feeling guilty, or watch TV till it comes out of their ears. You love playing cards. In a place like this I bet you play all the card games there are, in a place like this. You must like that aspect at least."

"Oh, cards," Mrs. Bliss said.

"Oh, privacy? Oh, cards?"

"I'm eighty-two years old."

"You act younger."

Mrs. Bliss shrugged.

"The most important thing," Ellen said ruminantly, seriously, deeply, originally, a message from the sibyl, "is to have your health."

Meaning Marvin was dead, Janet incommunicado, Barry failing, Ellen on some mystical quest in Houston, Texas, that would not only resolve her pinched nerves, headaches, and swollen ankles but perhaps restore them, too, all of them, to what they were and whom they were and where they were decades earlier, reincarnating them not so much into different or even higher beings as back into their own old, individual, mean, quotidian averages. Meaning I beg your pardon Ma, but how dare you be bored at your age while you still have health, privacy, books, movies, TV coming out of your ears, and access to all the card games there are?

But meaning, Mrs. Bliss supposed, chief above even all those other things, while you still have most of *your* family intact, if not on call then at least available at a moment's notice—Frank and May, Maxine and George, her grandchildren Judith and James, Donny, even herself and Janet, herself and Barry. And meaning, too, never mind her spirited new Hispanic and Latino friends but the ones in jail, and the ones who'd skipped, and all that crime and excitement unfolding before her very eyes. (People talked, insinuated, implied.) Manny from the building a dear friend, a great loss; Tommy Auveristas, the one that got away; the Kingpin Camerando; Long-timer Chitral; the unresolved mystery of the Buick LeSabre. And Ellen was right. How *dare* she be bored?

But maybe something of disapproval, too, in that long list of overlooked opportunities, perhaps actually accusatory. Not, "You could have gone into retail sales, Ma," although they both knew she'd have been too old even if she'd applied on the day she'd been widowed, but something, anything, something, even if it were only to volunteer to distribute newspapers and magazines from a cart she pushed three days a week along the corridors and into the rooms of patients in hospitals.

"Down here," Ellen said, "don't you at least miss the gang?"

"I miss the *old* gang."

"The *old* gang."

"The gang that got away. The gang that died."

"Oh, Ma," Ellen said.

"It ain't all bad," Mrs. Bliss said. "I got outside interests."

"That's good, Ma. That's swell."

Mrs. Bliss grinned.

"What?"

She smiled broadly, almost laughed.

"Ma?" Ellen said. "Ma?"

"Don't be ridiculous, Ellen!"

"Tell me," Ellen said, "I won't breathe a word."

Mrs. Bliss shook her head.

"Come on, Ma, tell me."

"All right," she said, "but if this ever gets out . . ."

"I swear. What?"

"I'm pregnant."

"You're never!"

"Yeah, I'm pregnant, but I'm thinking of getting an abortion. You think maybe Wilcox . . ."

"Why would you say something like that to me?"

"Come on, it's a joke."

"I could have had a heart attack!"

"I'm sorry, but when I said I had outside interests something tickled my funny bone."

"I could have had a heart attack."

"A few weeks ago I went on a treasure hunt."

"Sure, a treasure hunt. All right, Ma."

"No, I did. I have one of those metal detectors."

"Yo ho ho, and a bottle of rum," Ellen said.

"No really," Mrs. Bliss said.

"Sure, Ma."

"Do you remember Junior Yellin?"

"Junior Yellin, Junior Yellin. Dad's Junior Yellin?"

"Junior's his nickname, his real name is Milt."

"A gonif?"

"Well," said Mrs. Bliss.

"No, I remember. Very presentable. A good-looking guy but a gonif. You saw Junior Yellin? He's still alive?"

"He's in his seventies," Mrs. Bliss said.

"Gee," Ellen said, "it's been years since I even heard his name mentioned. He had an eye for the ladies. He was Dad's partner in the butcher shop."

"Yeah, well, now he's a treasure hunter. He wants to open up a museum. I was supposed to be his partner."

"You're kidding! Junior Yellin. He's still alive?"

"I'm still alive."

"No, well, I mean, but Junior *Yellin*. He burned the candle at both ends." Ellen lowered her voice. Dorothy, who had trouble hearing her, was surprised that a woman like Ellen, who wore earth shoes and took enema instructions from some quack in Texas, who wolfed down the kale and the pumpkin and powdered her salads with raw oatmeal, and could throw a hundred dollars' worth of meat out of her freezer just like that, a woman who sold so many shoes she earned awards that took her all over the world, who went through life at the top of her voice, would ever bother to lower her voice, and was overtaken with a sudden, strange but not entirely off-the-wall idea: that in his salad days Yellin had probably made an entirely serious pass at her young daughter-in-law, as he had once made one at her.

"Would you like to see him?" Mrs. Bliss asked.

"See him? See Junior Yellin?"

"I'll invite him for supper. We'll talk about old times."

"He wouldn't remember me."

"You'll remind him."

Ellen nodded vaguely in the direction of the kitchen table, toward the uneaten scraps of Mrs. Ted Bliss's rice pie, the deepish dregs of her unfinished tea.

"I'll boil a chicken," Mrs. Bliss said. "I'll make some soup. You make the salad, put in some of your organic vegetables."

"I wouldn't *mind* seeing him again," Ellen said.

He didn't. He didn't remember her. No more than he had recognized Dorothy the day she had come to his office on Lincoln Road. Even when Mrs. Bliss identified her as Marvin's wife.

Well, a lot of water had passed under the bridge he excused. The old gray mare ain't what he used to be.

"Isn't the mare generally a she?" Ellen called down from her high horse. "I'd have thought a butcher would know the difference."

"Hey," Junior said, "touché there. But you know," he said, "I'm not a butcher anymore. I haven't been behind a meat counter in years."

"No," Ellen said as Mrs. Bliss poured the wine Junior brought, "Ma says you've decided to become a museum director."

"It's still America, sweetheart," Yellin said and, sensing it might be a long evening, filled his glass to the brim.

He was not a mean drunk. Indeed, thought Mrs. Ted Bliss, he was no longer even much of a wiseass, and reflected that if you both only managed to live long enough your worst enemy could become one of your best friends. The thought made for a kind of nostalgia that inhabited the room like atmosphere, enveloping Mrs. Ted Bliss and, so it seemed to her, Yellin, and perhaps even Ellen herself, though Ellen, Dorothy imagined, had to be coaxed along, rather like someone of two minds in an audience, say, who has been asked to come up on the stage to assist the performer in his act. They finished Junior's wine and Dorothy, on a roll of good feeling, offered to open a bottle of what had to be at least forty-year-old Scotch whiskey—twelve years in the bottle, twenty-eight or so in a drawer of the big walnut breakfront in the dining room, a gift from one of Ted's customers when they left Chicago to take up a new life in Florida.

The women weren't drinkers and Junior usually drank only to pass out, and so had no clear idea of what it was like to be drunk. They supposed it meant something like "tipsy," by which they meant lighthearted, frivolous, cute, a condition summed up by the notion of women in films of the thirties and forties, say, forced by far-fetched circumstance into wearing men's pajamas, several sizes too large for them. This was their collective mood now—an exaggerated comity between them too big for its necessity. They laughed easily, Junior himself joining in as they evoked his old piratical avatars and manifestations like a sort of wild glory.

"Do you know," Mrs. Ted Bliss giddily confessed, "there was a time I thought you'd set your cap for me?"

"Me? Really?"

"Oh, I suppose you don't remember the time you snuck up behind me and tried to feel me up while I was waiting on a customer."

He didn't of course, but smiled sly as an old roué, a heroic rogue in a different movie, and politely wondered aloud how far he'd managed to get.

"I thought of telling Ted on you. On you to Ted."

"I bet you never did," Junior Yellin said.

"You were already in enough trouble."

"I thought," Ellen said, "of telling Marvin."

"Marvin?" said Mrs. Ted Bliss.

She'd struck a nerve, and a little of Yellin's guilty handsomeness drained from his face.

"Only he was already in Billings," Ellen said, the second person there whose mood had cracked.

"Hey," Junior Yellin said, the last, his mood breaking up, run aground on a sandbar of suddenly uncovered memory, "dinner about ready? I guess I'll go powder my nose."

"I think," Mrs. Bliss whispered when he left the room, "he remembers you."

"Oh, Ma," Ellen said, suddenly weeping. "Nothing happened. I swear to you. I swear on Marvin's life!"

"On Marvin's *life?* On his *life?*"

What Mrs. Ted Bliss didn't know was that in the toilet, Junior Yellin raised the toilet seat and peed wide of his mark, drilling some of his urine around the elasticized hem of her terry-cloth toilet-seat cover. Feeling immensely disconsolate about this awkward turn of events, he wet one of Dorothy's hand towels under a faucet in the bathroom sink and tried to wipe away (rubbing it furiously, as one might attempt to clear a stain from a freshly starched shirt back from the laundry on which one has just dripped gravy) the evidence of his marked territory.

"By damn," he muttered, "I am one goofy galoot of a guy."

The sound of the phrase cheered him a bit, but he was thankful he was a little high. Under the influence, he thought. Get a grip, he thought, you're seventy-eight. Sooner or later one or the other of them would have to come in to do her business. We *all* got business. What will it look like if she realizes her dress is DWI due to my carelessness? How many points would *that* cost him?

Because the way Junior figured, life was a little like one of those games—checkers, Monopoly—where everyone started with the same assets and lost when they went bankrupt.

My life, thought Yellin, my life is like that. More Monopoly than checkers, though. I was always the top hat or the roadster, the wheelbarrow or battleship or dog, never the iron or thimble or shoe. Sure, he thought, big man. Big man's man. In your *dreams!* he thought bitterly.

Because he knew there'd always been more smoke than fire to him, to his history. He caused trouble and brought grief down around people's heads—already he could spot a little flame of yellow piss burning through the water spots he'd made doing his repairs. Oh Christ, he moaned, and wondered if Dorothy's wasn't the real reason—that, as Dorothy said, he was in enough trouble already—more women hadn't told on him. My God, how he hated owning an unearned reputation! Still, if it weren't unearned he'd have no reputation at all.

Because, sight unseen, he knew there was little of substance to the contemptuous awe folks held him in. Those out there now, vulnerable to charm but nothing more to it than that, silly as girls at a sleepover, simply had no skill at recognizing a flirt when they saw one. He could hardly believe, for example, that he'd ever tried to feel up that old one, Mrs. Ted Bliss. And as for Ellen, the elderly one, why would he ever have put a move on a woman with a husband in the hospital? It would have been too brave, it wasn't like him.

The whoosie was still damp but he couldn't stay in there forever. He unlocked the bathroom door and went out.

"Sorry," he blustered to the ladies already seated at the dining room table, "had to see a man about a dog. Ah," he said, taking his seat and winking at both of them, "girl, boy, girl. Just the way I like it!"

"On Marvin's *life?*" the outraged Mrs. Bliss was still saying, and Junior Yellin had the impression that time had stood still while he had been in the bathroom, that there was something faintly magical in his ability to charm people, but only faintly magical. Otherwise he would have made a greater dent in the world. He'd be high and dry and sitting pretty instead of just dragooned and press-ganged into a skimpy little company of old ladies. Otherwise, he might have followed his heart and had the nerve to propose to that gorgeous Rita de Janeiro kid and married her.

If he'd a better command of the life cycle of liquor he'd have known that he was coming down from the ledges of optimism and gaiety to the flatlands of despair and self-pity. In the event, the quarrel he'd generated between the two women registered like a chatter of drone.

"Ma, nothing *happened.*"

"On his life? His *life?*"

"If something happened, why would I say so? Just to aggravate him? He made a pass, all right? Big deal, he made a pass. He tickled my palm with his finger. Once he blew in my ear when I leaned toward him to listen to a secret he wanted to tell."

"While Marvin lies dying in a hospital bed."

I tickled her palm? That was my pass? I blew in her ear? That was? Oh, I am so pathetic. I am pathetic. Not a grand galoot of a guy at all. Just a sorry old asshole. I must cancel Miss de Janeiro's flowers. I must remember to tie a string around my finger so as not to forget to cancel her flowers.

What he did or didn't do. As if he weren't even in the room at all. They'd invited him to supper, not the other way around. The boiled chicken could be boiling over. He hadn't come there just to be humiliated. He had better set them straight.

"Excuse me," Yellin said, "but if either of you is thinking of using the little girl's room, may I suggest you use the other one? I'm afraid I missed and made number one all over the toilet-seat cover. I tried to blot it out with hand towels but I didn't do such a good job. It's still pretty damp. Did I really tickle your palm and blow in your ear? Sorry. Maybe I was trying to cheer you up. Dotty, dear, did I really feel you up?"

"Yes."

"Well," he said, "you were both beautiful women. I'm sorry, but I guess I'm not much of a boozer. I'm sorry. I think I've lost my appetite. Just as well, I have to run an errand. Have to see my florist on a matter of some urgency.

"Oh," he said as he reached the door, "they say if you rub it with seltzer the stain disappears like magic."

He disappeared like magic.

That night, after she picked up the empty glasses and cleared the table and washed the dishes—Ellen had offered to help but Mrs. Ted Bliss was still enough of a baleboosteh to do some things by herself and refused her—and Ellen had gone to bed, Mrs. Bliss noticed something out of place on top of the telephone table. It was the directory, which had not been replaced in the little shelf where it should have been. Loose on top of the telephone directory Ellen had failed to put back properly were her airline tickets, spread-eagled to her open-ended return coupon. Without meaning to pry, Mrs. Bliss noticed the price of her ticket. Thinking she'd made a mistake, she checked it again. What had so surprised her was that her daughter-in-law received the same senior citizen's discount as she did herself!

She must have known, she'd sent birthday greetings to the woman for years. Even, though Marvin was dead, cards on their anniversaries. It was easy, if not to lose track exactly then to fix people in time and suspend them there, your near and dear. Growing old was no picnic and though you made allowances for it in yourself, it hardly seemed possible that others, your children and grandchildren, for example, were susceptible to the same erosions. Yet she must have known, she must have. Hadn't Ellen herself brought up the subject, and more than once, of what she intended to do and where she intended to move when she retired? And each time, *each* time, Dorothy had felt uncomfortable hearing such talk, as if, oh yes, as if there were something maybe just a bit disreputable and vulgar about the idea of someone relatively secure and successful in her position throwing it over for the sake of some soft dream. Wasn't this, in some wild way, connected to her feelings about Frank leaving Pittsburgh and moving to Rhode Island? All right, he said he had his reasons, and maybe, as he'd said, the feelings, his and the university's, were mutual, but somewhere there'd been an infraction, disorder on both sides. It was the way she'd felt when Ted had told her he had bought the farm in Michigan. Who knows, it may have been the way she'd felt all those years back when her family uprooted itself and came all the way from Russia to America.

"You've lived in Chicago all your life," she'd told her daughter-in-law when Ellen had first introduced the subject. "All your friends are there, your family. You're no spring chicken anymore, Ellen. Where would you go, what would you do, chase Janet in India? Believe me, darling, if I had it all to do over again and poor Ted was still alive, you think I'd be here today?"

Enough things had changed, she wanted her daughter-in-law to stay put, although even as she made her point she recognized the fallacy in her argument. There was nothing to stop her from picking up and moving back to Chicago. All right, the price of condos in the Towers had plunged. She'd never get back what they gave for it, but so what? Even if she took a loss, even if she sold the place under fire-sale conditions, threw in the carpet, the drapes, her furniture and appliances, all the crap she'd accumulated, the manuals, the letters and cards, pictures and scrapbooks, all the carefully rubber-banded documentation and ledgers of her life, how bad could it be? Wouldn't it, as a matter of fact, be just the thing for her old baleboosteh ways, to clear the decks, make everything neat, one last final spring cleaning of things, the deleavenization of her past? What would she lose? Nothing, zip, gornisht. She could rent a furnished room or even a small studio apartment and live off the proceeds of her red-tag sale. She was eighty-two years old, had her health, but how much longer could she expect to get away with it? Hale and hearty as she was, kayn aynhoreh, how much longer could Mrs. Bliss have left, four, five years? So her estate would drop to maybe seventy-three cents on the dollar when she passed. What difference would it make to her inheritors? They were provided for. Her good husbandry couldn't *really* make a difference in their lives, so what was the big deal? What was to stop her from moving back to Chicago? Nothing. Nothing but her failing energies, nothing but her sense of how disruptive and untrue one must be to oneself even to want to make a new life.

"I was thinking," Ellen had said, "about maybe moving to Texas."

"To Wilcox?"

"You talk about him as if he was a crackpot. Or as if I was. Think what you think. The man has made a tremendous difference in my life. Marvin might be alive today if . . ."

"Ellen!"

"Don't say it, Ma. I know what I know. *Doctors!*" she said.

All right, she was crazy. Driven nuts by her widowhood. Mrs. Bliss had accepted it before, had let her off the hook because she knew deep down, beneath the long bones of her bullying, Ellen had a good heart. But it was one thing to take that stuff off a grieving woman, another entirely to take it from a fellow senior citizen. Oy, she thought mournfully, brought up short, suddenly breathless. If the wife of her firstborn qualified for the senior citizen discount, how much longer could it be before her surviving children would be old people themselves? And what did that mean to her?

Looking back, clear-headed, she was aware that she was a woman who had not much enjoyed her long life. She had done her duty by it, earned the love and respect of her husband, her children, her family, her friends.

The truth, however, was that she had little to regret. Her mistakes, she felt, were only the general failures—lapses of taste; an inability, perhaps the simple stupidity of a failure to risk. Holding her flaws up in a kinder, much more generous light, it might only have been a lazy disinclination to take pains, like anyone else, not to fiddle with the givens of her character, never daring to color outside the lines, her life nothing if not a struggle to stay within them.

She'd done nothing wrong, she meant, only what was expected. And didn't reproach herself for her loyalties, had no argument, for example, with her repudiation of Junior Yellin's ancient crude advances, or thought for a moment she might have wasted her beauty. She was not in the least distressed that she'd ever been anything less than a good, unselfish, loving wife and mother. She would have despaired and been ashamed if she thought that she had, if she'd ever even consented to the soft porn of submitting to anything so mild and innocuous as becoming the recipient of a makeover on national TV. (She had appeared in court once to testify against Alcibiades Chitral, but it had taken a subpoena to get her there.)

No, she had suffered (it was too strong a word even if what she was attempting to come to terms with was the faintly misbegotten shape of her vague disapproval of her life) from a sort of generalized deafness. What did it mean not to hear the accent in which she spoke? Why had she been so stung when Chitral told her in the prison that her people (born sticks-in-the-mud, he'd called them) had a gift for sitting still? Why had she learned to write checks only after her husband had died? Or been so reluctant to exchange her lady's maid status, helping Mrs. Dubow's customers dress in the close quarters of those airless old dressing rooms for what would have been a salesclerk's higher salary up in the front of the store? Why had she kowtowed to men?

Mrs. Bliss was so tired she could barely move. She remembered that when her children were kids, up past their bedtimes and wild, up past their bedtimes, their mood swings fluctuate as white water, gay, crazed, one minute hilarious, the next irritable and quarrelsome as murderers, she'd warned them against overexcitement, threatened they'd become hostage to their overtiredness, would be unable to fall asleep under the weary weight of their crankiness. It wasn't true, she thought now. Nothing could have been more false. As soon as their heads hit the pillow, as soon as hers did . . . Yet all of a sudden Mrs. Ted Bliss, who had wiped up the last of the mess Yellin had made in the bathroom (she'd put it off till last), felt her blood boil up in a kind of rage, the old mercurial irritability of her kids' quarrelsomeness, and she knew she would never calm herself enough to sleep that night and found herself already resenting the hangover she would feel all that next day. The immediate cause had been Junior Yellin's strong, stenchy pee. It still filled her nostrils. She thought she could taste it.

The man was a pig. How do you come into a person's home and pee on a seat cover? How do you go into your hostess's toilet and pee all over, everywhere at once? It was more like an act of vandalism than an old man's inability to direct his stream. And then what does the pig son of a bitch do? He actually tries to clean up his mess with her guest towels! Her *guest* towels. They were useless to her now. The nerve, the *nerve!* How could she ever set them out again? First thing in the morning she would retrieve them from the hamper and throw them away. She wouldn't have waited, she'd have done it right then but knew it was worth her life to enter that bathroom again tonight. She could taste it, taste it.

He was her last connection to earth? Then to hell with her last connection to earth! And to hell with Ellen, too. Oh sure, she'd asked if she could help. Nice as pie in the nice-as-pie department. But gone off quick as you can say Jack Robinson the second her mother-in-law had told her out of a deference she'd have used to any guest, "Go, go, darling, I can do it myself."

And then Mrs. Bliss remembered the phone book the woman had not had the decency to put back where she'd found it. And what were those plane tickets all about? They were supposed to be a threat? She wasn't having a good time, Ellen? Dorothy was forcing the wrong food down her throat? What did she think this was here, a restaurant?

Ellen missed her dead husband more than Dorothy missed her dead son? Because that's exactly what the woman thought, that's what was at the bottom of all her goofy Employee-of-the-Month drive and nutty advice about how other people should live their lives, why she was at once so smug and defensive about Wilcox, at the bottom of why she was not only willing to give up all those free bonus trips to Cancun and London and wherever to retire and move away from Chicago just so she could be closer to her holistic holy man, the Messiah Texas Chiropractor, but even looked forward to it. And if you ask me, thought Mrs. Ted Bliss, it was, at bottom, why Ellen was so tolerant and free and easy about allowing her daughter—my granddaughter—Janet, to go shpatziering all over India looking either for her soul or some swell new herbal tea.

Mrs. Bliss was not an impatient woman. Live and let live. Normally, she bent over backward. But something about Ellen . . . And that open-ended airline ticket planted smack in the middle of the Yellow Pages under the TWA ad like a bookmark. What, she wanted to be begged? Gai gezunterhait!

And now she was really making her sore, because she felt bad about not liking her daughter-in-law better, and wished she did. If for no other reason than that then maybe she could get some sleep and feel fresher, more rested, be better prepared, when the knockdown, drag-out show-down came between them the next morning.

Only that wasn't the way of it at all.

After she'd dragged herself out of bed, after she'd had her bath, after she'd powdered herself, put on fresh makeup and her favorite cologne (the same kind she'd been using since the days of her great beauty), and dressed in a clean new pants suit and come into the kitchen that morning, Dorothy was met with the smell of fresh coffee. Great, thought Mrs. Ted Bliss, she's making herself an enema.

"Oh, morning there, Ma," her daughter-in-law greeted her cheerfully. "Good, you're up. You were sleeping so soundly I didn't want to wake you. Beautiful day. I've taken the liberty of putting up a fresh pot of coffee for our breakfast. What would you like with it, you think? There's no oranges but I found a can of Crystal Light in the cupboard. How do you want your egg? Boiled? Scrambled? Do you want one slice of toast or two?"

It occurred to Mrs. Bliss actually to rub her eyes, to pinch herself.

"Say, Ma," Ellen went on, "do you still have that metal detector you were telling me about? If you don't plan to use it anymore, do you think I could buy it off you?

"You never told me Milt's a recreational therapeusisist."

"Oh, sure," said Mrs. Ted Bliss, "one of the biggest men in south Florida."

"Really? One of the biggest?"

"I'm here to tell you."

"He never told me *that*," Ellen said. "When he called this morning . . ."

"Junior? Junior Yellin called?"

"You were sleeping," Ellen said. "He told me not to wake you."

"What did he want?"

"Well," she said, "I think he called to apologize. He's a reformed drunk, you know, and got a little high and wasn't able to handle it. Anyway, he's terribly embarrassed about what he did in the bathroom. He asked me to tell you."

Dorothy nodded. There was a slightly dismissive expression on her face, as if it didn't matter, as polite as if she were personally taking the apology. Ellen looked relieved, grateful, as though she were Yellin's envoy or held his personal power of attorney. Mrs. Bliss watched as her daughter-in-law lay out two place settings. She made no move or offer to help, and was vaguely dismayed to realize that, except for restaurants and airplanes and those infrequent occasions when she was an invited dinner guest, this was one of the first times in years (even at Frank's seder in Providence she had carried food to the table and helped pass it around) that she was being served. She had to make a conscious effort to keep herself from crying.

Meanwhile, Ellen, chirpy and crisp as a housewife in a television commercial, filled both their glasses with Crystal Light (the can could have been two or three years old by now; she kept it in case some child should show up), and spooned the meat from two perfectly boiled eggs into small dessert bowls. She buttered three slices of toast, gave one to Dorothy, kept two for herself, and sat down.

"So," Ellen said, "do you or don't you, will you or won't you?"

"Do I don't I, will I won't I what?"

"Still have the metal detector? Will you sell it to me?"

"You want to buy my metal detector? Junior Yellin talked you into this?"

"He's actually a very interesting man. Not at all like what I remembered."

"Yeah," Mrs. Bliss said, "very interesting." Don't sell yourself short, she thought, you're pretty interesting yourself.

"He has this theory about AIDS," Ellen said.

"Oh?"

"He believes it can be cured if the patient has a hobby that takes his mind off his troubles."

Mrs. Bliss stared at the woman.

"Of course it has to be caught early enough, while it's still in the early HIV-positive stage. Once it's full blown it won't always work."

"The man's close to eighty," said Mrs. Ted Bliss, and thought she saw her daughter-in-law's face flush as Ellen dipped a corner of her buttered toast into the bowl and allowed it to troll amid the loose yellow islands of her soft-boiled eggs.

"Oh, Ma," Ellen said.

Mrs. Bliss knew what she knew. She remembered that airline ticket and was glad she hadn't permitted herself to complete her thought. That he was old enough to be her father. Well, almost old enough.

"I'm no spring chicken myself, you know," Ellen said, and provided Mrs. Bliss with an insight into how she had been able to sell all of those shoes. Why, on markdown! On markdown and reduction and discount. Perhaps she had found tiny, almost invisible flaws in the merchandise. Maybe she inflicted them herself and then pointed them out to her customers.

Mrs. Bliss shrugged. She lived and let live. She bent over backward. Because weren't people amazing? If only they suffered enough, had been put through enough, didn't they surprise you every time out? Didn't they just? They could knock you over with a feather. With their resilience, with their infinite capacity to adapt, camouflage, evolving at one end of things by suppressing at another. Now, for example, watching her suck down all that cholesterol, Ellen's delight in the incriminating joy she took in all the strange forbidden flavors of her leashed hunger.

"No," Dorothy said, "it isn't."

"What isn't?"

"The magic wand. It isn't for sale. It isn't for sale but take it with my blessings."

"Oh, Ma," Ellen said, beaming like a young girl.

The thing of it is, she wondered, if push comes to shove, does that louse get to call me Ma, too?

TWELVE

It was the only ship-to-shore telegram she'd ever seen.

They were married, Ellen said in the wire, by the captain of the cruise ship himself.

The irony was that Mrs. Bliss got the telegram a few hours before she heard the first reports about Hurricane Andrew that the National Hurricane Center in Coral Gables had spotted 615 miles east miles of Miami growing winds of over 100 miles per hour and picking up speed as it moved toward the Bahamas. The old woman even made a small salacious joke about it.

Oh boy, she thought, Junior and Ellen on the Love Boat. Just married and both so unused to going to bed with anyone they probably started up that wind and those waves by themselves.

It put her in a good mood to think of the two of them together. Which put her in an even better mood.

Because it was a measure, she thought, of cut losses, her emotions in a sort of escrow, the heart in chapter eleven, receivership. Because she would have thought, she thought, she'd have taken it harder. Her widowed daughter-in-law, her dead son's only wife. The real keeper of the flame when you came right down. The one so nuts about poor dead Marvin her grief made *her* nuts. Whose every New Age pilgrimage to the crackpot chiropractor in Houston had been like a feather in steadfast mourning's cheerless cap. So her marriage to Junior was really a kind of defection, leaving Mrs.

Bliss (according to Ellen's own figures) high and dry to bear the lion's share of their leftover bereftness.

Yet she did not feel betrayed. If anything, otherwise. Their absurd new matrimony making her smile, convinced that the joke was on one of them, though she didn't know which.

If not entirely surprised by Ellen's decision to marry Junior Yellin (indeed, the surprise was on the other foot so to speak; she could not have anticipated Junior's proposal), she was at least a little startled by her own reaction to it, or rather by how gracefully, even cheerfully, she first acknowledged, then accepted, then actively embraced the idea. Only briefly, and out of one corner of her mind, did she have this flaring, fleeting synapse when it occurred to her to wonder whether Marvin might be turning over in his grave if he'd heard the news or read the telegram or maybe overheard the actual proposal Yellin had made to Ellen or Ellen to Yellin. This was merely the most vagrant of thoughts, yet in the short transience (that was even less than time) it took to entertain and resolve it, Mrs. Ted Bliss was brushed by what was at once both a conclusion and a conviction: that Marvin had *not* heard the news, had *not* been looking over her shoulder to read the telegram nor tapped into whatever solemn exchange had taken place between Junior and Ellen back there on the Love Boat's high and rising seas.

Marvin was not turning over in his grave, she realized, because, well, because Marvin was dead. These simple, indisputable facts struck like epiphanies: Dead people do not turn over in their graves; the dead have no opinions. Well then, thought Mrs. Ted Bliss, if it's OK with Marvin it's jake by me, and settled, stunningly, gracefully, even peacefully and, at last, conclusively and decisively into the idea that her son was dead. Settling up. I had the pie; you had the sundae; she had the iced tea. Well, thought Dorothy, that's that, then. The kid's dead.

It was this, she knew, that reconciled her to the news in Ellen's telegram. It was this, however odd it might seem, that had produced such calm, allowed such cheer.

She had an idea! And what so delighted her about her idea was the fact that she knew she was rising to an occasion. She was into her eighties now. People in their eighties will have been called upon to rise to occasions countless numbers of times—all those births and deaths and ceremonies; all those pitched battles of obligation that made up a life, constructed it like a laborious masonry of rough expectations. The rare thing, the sweet and marvelous thing, was to rise to an occasion gratuitously, out of some sheer sense of its rightness, its dead solid joy, all its, well, nondeductible, not-for-profit giftness.

She would throw a party for the happy couple when they returned from their honeymoon cruise. Her condo wasn't big enough so she'd host it in the game room of Building One. She'd have to find a date when it was available, of course, but that shouldn't be difficult. Since there were fewer occupancies in the Towers there was less demand on the facilities these days. Indeed, as the idea for the reception formed in Mrs. Bliss's mind it became increasingly clear to her that the affair (the concept of the party already beginning to snowball, transmuting itself from simple party to reception to affair; if she didn't rein herself in at least a little, before she knew it she'd have a full-blown gala on her hands) would have to be catered. This was beyond some one-woman deal. From the first she hadn't even wanted it to be and, even if she did, she knew she wasn't up to the task of preparing the game room, let alone all that food, by herself. The more Mrs. Bliss thought about it the less enthusiasm she had. Who would she invite? If she invited her family, whoever was left, the remnants of the old gang in Chicago, her kids in Cincinnati and Providence, all her globe-trotting, scattered grandchildren and great-grandchildren, it would send the wrong signals. This wasn't intended to be some last hurrah thing. All she'd meant was to introduce the happy couple to each other's neighbors and some of her Florida friends. Maybe she would even send a special invitation to Wilcox in Houston if for no other reason than to witness the cure he'd wrought.

All right, so the snowball was starting to melt, break up under the heat of her cooled-down second thoughts. But that was all right, too. Now she didn't have to worry about arranging for game rooms and caterers and all the foofaraw a gala would involve. Not that she was losing her enthusiasm for the idea of doing something for them, just for the overkill of her first hasty impressions. One thing, though. She had better stop planning for the thing (whatever it turned out to be) and do something before all that was left of the snowball was a great puddle.

Commit yourself, thought Mrs. Ted Bliss, and decided she

would fire off a telegram of her own, offering her congratulations to the bride and groom and announcing her intentions about the party.

Which was easier said than done.

About an hour after she phoned in her message, Western Union called to apologize. They were sorry, the operator told her, but at this point they weren't accepting nonessential civilian communication between the United States and the cruise ships in that area of the Atlantic. Both telegraphic and all two-way air traffic had been put on hold while the weather emergency was still in effect. If she wished, she could cancel her message or, if she preferred, they'd file it with the rest of their backlog and send it first-priority once the ship was out of harm's way.

"Harm's way?"

"Once they're sure which direction this fella's gonna jump," said the male operator at the other end of the line.

Even more out of hunch than superstition, Mrs. Bliss told Western Union to cancel altogether. She'd call back when the coast was clear.

But maybe it *was* superstition. It made her nervous (it always had) to fix on a specific date too long before its time. Even when she'd organized Maxine's wedding she had postponed making the arrangements for as long as she could. Don't get her wrong, she was crazy about George, she was rooting for their marriage, and it had nothing to do with losing the deposit or anything like that. It was only that Mrs. Bliss felt there was something just a little too cocksure about making long-range plans. Man proposes, God disposes. Something like that.

And now, too, something spooky about that out-of-harm's-way business. She was familiar with the phrase. It was something they always dragged out in wartime, impending crisis. She didn't like the sound of it, and though Western Union had been very polite and explained to her about keeping the traffic lanes open between Ellen's boat and the land, once the United States was dragged into it, everything started to seem much too important and official sounding. The United States?

Mrs. Bliss turned on the television to see if they'd interrupt a program for a special news bulletin. Sure enough, she didn't have long to wait. They cut away to an expert standing by at the National Hurricane Center and then leapfrogged to another expert at the U.S. Meteorological Survey in Atlanta, Georgia. Both men seemed very excited. Andrew's winds were gusting from between 100 and 130 miles per hour and had been unofficially clocked as high as 185 miles per hour. If it didn't veer to the east it was expected to hit the Bahamas with heroic force sometime in the middle of the night. It would be, both the Atlanta and Coral Gables guys agreed, the mother of all hurricanes. Already, all ships in the area had been instructed to change course in the hope of either outrunning or evading the storm that was moving along at about 25 knots. She didn't know what a knot was exactly, but the experts couldn't get over it. Between them they had over fifty-seven years in the weather business and neither could remember a storm packing such high wind velocities to travel at such a speed toward whatever would turn out to be its ultimate destination. Because usually the more furiously a hurricane's winds revolved about its eye the more moisture it picked up from the sea and the heavier it became. The heavier it was the slower it traveled toward impact. This one, though, this one was a horse of a different color, and may the good Lord have mercy on whatever got in its way!

Mrs. Bliss, hooked, watched all the channels for the latest developments. Again and again she saw the same experts talking to each of the anchors on the major networks. Idly, she wondered if these experts were paid extra for going on the different shows. Officially, she supposed, they were civil servants. Probably, if it happened, they were paid under the table.

Even the local meteorologists were having a field day. They put their Skywatch and Doppler Weather Alert and Skywarn and Instant Color Weather Radar systems into play, all their latest, fancy, up-to-the-minute machinery. Their jackets were off, their collars and ties undone, their sleeves rolled up. Only the civil servants, Mrs. Bliss noticed, shvitzed in their buttoned, inexpensive, dress code suits, but everyone, from the TV meteorologists to the experts at the National Hurricane Center and U.S. Meteorological Survey served up a kind of short course on hurricanes. Vaguely, Mrs. Bliss was reminded of the lectures delivered by the community college professors who used to come to the Towers game rooms to talk about their disciplines.

It was very impressive, lulling, too, in a peculiar way, rather like the gardening, cooking, and home improvement shows she sometimes watched—programs for young homemakers: furniture stripping, interior decoration, foreign cooking. Before she knew it she was as involved in the science of these powerful storm systems as ever she'd been in an actual entertainment show, absorbed in all the interesting bits and pieces—the gossip of tempest. She learned, for example, that hurricanes could be two hundred to three hundred miles in diameter, that they were nurtured by low pressure fronts and rose in the east and moved west (just like the *sun, just like the sun!* worried Mrs. Ted Bliss) on the trade winds, that an eye of a hurricane was about twenty miles in diameter and traveled counterclockwise from between ten and fifteen miles per hour as the winds blew it along above the sea, sucking up the warm, evaporating ocean. She learned that storm clouds, called *walls,* surrounded the eye, that it was these that caused the most damage, kicking up dangerous waves, called *storm surges,* that forced the sea to rise several feet above normal. Especially destructive at high tide, they brought on terrific, murderous floods.

Every hour or so astonishing pictures of Hurricane Andrew were beamed down to Miami Beach from satellites orbiting the earth. Mrs. Bliss watched, hypnotized, as the photographs collected themselves from a blur of vague dots and electronic squiggles and slowly resolved into clear, enhanced portraits of brutal, rushing power.

Gradually, as hard news started to trickle in (they were talking about a shift in the storm now, how it might miss the Bahamas altogether and then, gaining force, move toward the East Coast, and were even beginning to speak of the storm of the century) the meteorological anecdotes trailed off and they were speculating about momentum, land-fall, and drew thick black lines in Magic Marker, superimposing them on maps as if they were composing best-case/worse-case scenarios, or complicated plays in athletic contests. The wind speeds were stunning, frightful. No one had any idea how many ships might already have been impacted, turned on their sides, spinning like bottles.

Mrs. Bliss thought of the honeymooners, her heart in her mouth.

The storm was moving at thirty-one knots now, an incredible speed. Someone gave the equivalent of a knot to a land mile, and

Mrs. Bliss got out Manny's calculator and tried to work out what thirty-one knots was in real space. She got something like sixty-eight miles per hour and knew she'd made a mistake. No catastrophe could come on that fast. The end of the world couldn't come on that fast.

Her heart was in her mouth, her fingers were crossed. Her heart was in her mouth and her fingers were crossed for the honeymooners, for anyone out there on that ocean.

It was very exciting, more exciting than the greyhounds. She bit her tongue and tried to take the thought back. But it was. It *was* more exciting than the greyhounds. Junior and Ellen racing wind, zigging and zagging through all the choppy minefields of an enemy air, Nature's mortal fender benders, all its angered give-no-quarters. Was will in this, wondered Mrs. Ted Bliss, indifferent, merciless will like the thing of a thug, a sort of vandalism? Though, finally, she didn't really believe it, any of it, as she didn't really believe in God. Only force was in this, a slasher and a burner, making widows and orphans, murdering sons.

More exciting than the greyhounds. Force merely the mechanical rabbit, a towed, insentient tease. Why waste your time? Nah, nah, thought Mrs. Ted Bliss, who, years past, had been on a ship or two herself, who'd wondered during each day's required safety drill, What, I'm getting off this big ship and going into one of those flimsy, tiny lifeboats? What, in *that* vast sea?

So it never even crossed her mind to pray for them. She was for them, for Ellen and Junior; she was behind them one hundred percent, but she wouldn't pray for them.

They were lost, the two of them, somewhere behind the lines of Western Union where neither she nor anyone else could get to them. For what it was worth they had her blessing, though she knew as soon as she gave it what it was worth. You laid your life down for people but you had to be close enough so it would do them some good.

And now (it was August 23; she'd started watching on the twenty-second and fallen asleep in front of the television) they had changed their tune, the weathermen.

The storm had grazed the Bahamas anyway, leaving four dead, and was on its way to Florida, maybe the Keys, maybe farther up the coast. They had changed their tune and were singing a different song. The hurricane was coming, the hurricane was coming to America. Vicious Andrew was serving and the ball could be in Mrs. Ted Bliss's court any time now. It was 287 miles from Florida and the boys were into a different mode. They were giving instructions where to stand if the hurricane hit. (It was *exactly* like those safety drills on the cruises.) And Mrs. Bliss could never keep it straight in her head what you did in a tornado, an earthquake, a hurricane.

And giving words to the wise about provisions, supplies, laying them in. She didn't *have* a flashlight, she didn't *have* batteries, matches, candles, cases of mineral water. She didn't *have* a portable radio. She didn't *have* a first-aid kit, she didn't *have* a generator. What she had were Ellen's cans of minced game, her oddball teas and organic chowders—all Ellen's reeds and straw. What she had was wild rice for the enemas. What she had was a freezer full of doggy bags of her own leftover, uneaten meals.

She was glued to the television reports. And the thing kept on coming and kept on coming. She stayed glued to the television, the only times she left it were when she went to the bathroom. (She didn't *have* a full tub of bathwater for washing the dishes.) Or into the kitchen to eat. (Eating, as she told herself, while she still could, while the stove still worked and her can opener was still driven by electricity.) There was a small radio on one of her countertops, and she listened to it as she waited for her eggs to boil, her coffee to heat up, her bread to toast. The hurricane was on every station but the edge was off. She missed the experts, couldn't take the news as seriously when it came in from disc jockeys, or supplied grist for call-in talk shows. This was why she brought her food back into the living room/dining room area and sat down to eat it in front of the TV set.

And now they were showing a video of the damage in the Bahamas. Awful, terrible. Roofs blown off houses, boats overturned. Hurricane Andrew had caught them with their pants down.

The hurricane would hit the coast of Florida sometime during the early hours of August 24. Maybe it would, maybe it wouldn't. As advanced as weather forecasting was, they told each other, it was still in its infancy, an inexact science, almost an art form. They had the equipment, their scientific, state-of-the-art tools—their radar and weather balloons and eye-in-the-sky satellites, even their own daring, dashing flying squadrons of "Hurricane Hunters" in modified airborne AWACS with all their glowing jewelry of measurement, finely tuned as astronomers' lenses and instruments. Yet even the experts acknowledged the final, awful unpredictability of their art, how their knowledge was humbled before all the intricate moving parts of climate. They trotted out the one about the butterfly beating its wings in Africa. They trotted out the moon and the tides. They trotted out God and force. It might or it mightn't. They hedged their bets and settled for their "best guesstimates."

All that could be done, they admitted, was hope for the best and prepare for the worst.

This wasn't the first time Mrs. Bliss had waited for a hurricane to happen. There'd been warnings and alerts every few years since the Blisses had first come to Florida. There'd been one in the late fifties, when she and Ted were there as tourists. The management of the ocean-front hotel where they were staying announced during the dinner show—the comedian, Myron Cohen, was entertaining—that a great storm was expected and that everyone should proceed to the children's huge playroom in the basement of the hotel to wait it out. There was no need to panic, they should make their way downstairs in an orderly fashion. The checks for their dinners had already been taken care of by the hotel. Myron Cohen would be along to join them and kibitz. Everyone applauded. It was one of the things Dorothy and Ted liked best about Miami Beach, the sense of some deep-pocket hospitality it gave off—fresh flowers in the room and a basket of fruit on the table when you checked in, a personal handwritten note from the manager, then, not fifteen minutes later, a follow-up phone call, were they satisfied with the room, did they like their view, would they permit the management to send up a complimentary drink and a small assortment of hors d'oeuvres. Even, months later, another personal note. Did Ted and Dorothy intend to return next year, would they like their old room—he gave the number of the room—again? The hurricane had passed them by that time. Cohen had never been funnier. The camaraderie while they waited for something terrible to happen to them was something to see. And other times, too. And always they had gotten away with murder. The only time anything significant happened was when a hurricane, diminished by bumping into Cuba and scraping along some of the Keys, had grazed on up the coast until it was at last downgraded to a tropical depression. The storm was still powerful enough to produce gale-force winds and over four inches of rain on Mrs. Bliss's balcony, three iron balusters of which had been knocked loose as teeth that had eventually to be pulled and replaced. Their patio furniture, which never completely dried out or lost its strong musky mildew, they gave to Goodwill.

So though they'd had their share of storm warnings and alerts, nothing had ever *really* happened. With the fierceness of its weather—its four- and five-foot drifts, its killer ice storms—Chicago presented more risk in a single winter than Florida did in all the years they'd lived there.

This one could pass her by, too. It would or it wouldn't. It might or it mightn't. It could or it couldn't. It will or it won't.

And though it was the middle of the afternoon of August 23, the hurricane was still up in the air, so to speak. The experts were still all over the tube with their special reports, advisories, and up-to-the-minute's, but something had happened, a subtle change in the programming, as though the Greater Miami area had been somehow politicized, or put under martial law or vague state-of-siege conditions. City, county, and state officials had begun to appear on her screen—governmental agencies, FEMA, even the Coast Guard.

What these various spokesmen said often contradicted what others before them had said. Thus, on the one hand, Mrs. Bliss was advised that just sitting tight (particularly if one was within a few blocks of the ocean) was like the piggies in their houses of sticks and straw in the story practically inviting the wolf to huff and puff and blow their doors down, and, on the other, not to try to make a run for it, that the danger of traffic tie-ups on the main streets and northbound thruways could create major gridlock, that folks stalled in their cars would be like fish shot in barrels for the pitiless winds but, that if one were absolutely *determined* on escape, one had better carpool. (Mrs. Bliss thought wistfully of the Buick Le-Sabre, recalling the smooth, troublefree rides and trips she and Ted had made in it, endowing it with magical powers like a beast's in a legend. In her daydream Ted turned the LeSabre's steering wheel to the left and it soared above gridlock, setting down on straight empty highways in Georgia, Tennessee, eleven miles from Chicago. He tugged it to the right and they were on access roads, coasting alongside big clean motel chains, their vacancy signs flaring like great cheery lights of welcome.)

They did a job on each other, these municipal, state, and federal spokesmen, a great debate, their raised voices in babble and argument, some great bureaucratic covering of all the bases, particularly, Dorothy guessed, their behinds. They left her, finally, with her options open. She knew from experience, though she didn't know how she knew it, that no final order, no ultimatum, would be given (offered, granted), that everyone was on his own in this one. (Even in extremis, the woman subsumed in the male principle—the spokesmen, the spokesmen.) Though maybe she did know, she thought, how she knew. These guys, they were like Ted's doctors, these guys. (Laying out choices for her, the pros and the cons, shtupping them with pros and cons, making them dizzy with alternative, forcing them to choose—chemo or radiation or surgery.) One of the spokesmen, adding insult to injury, pointing out what a gorgeous day it was, not a cloud in the sky, a regular our-blue-heaven out there.

Which was true. Mrs. Ted Bliss, up to here with the voices on the television, opened her glass doors and walked out onto her small balcony. The day was spectacular, the weather even nicer than the time she went in the limousine to visit Alcibiades Chitral. How could a storm be brewing in weather like this? Which wasn't like weather at all, really, but as comfortable as the neutral, flawlessly adjusted climate on the ground floor of a department store.

She stretched. She took in immense drafts of perfect air, almost gagging on its richness after the close, soiled atmosphere of the condo, which she hadn't left since Friday, the day before she received Ellen's wire, the day before she took up her vigil in front of the television. She was momentarily dizzy, sent reeling on the sweet truth of the world, and steadied herself on the railing of the balcony, her palms spread over the area where the old balusters had been loosened by the storm. Mrs. Bliss had outgrown most of what few superstitions she may once have indulged, but when she realized where her hands had come down to halt her swoon her breath snagged, caught on an omen.

She recovered and had started to go back indoors when she became gradually aware of noises, a hubbub. These seemed to rise all about her, sent from the street to where she stood on her balcony on the seventh floor and, at first, it seemed through all the sharp shrills and trebles of her amplified deafness that the noises—she recognized certain voices—might be calling to her—impatient, urgent sirens. But when she looked down she saw great activity in the streets and driveways of the buildings adjoining hers, in the driveway directly below her own.

She was not so high she could not attach names to the figures making these noises, this frantic bustle, nor so low—at that unlikely moment she was suddenly touched by her dead husband's middling intentions, the normative measure he'd taken of their lives, meaning neither to distance themselves so greatly above the world that they were carefully buffered from it, nor so close to the earth that they could sink into it, but here, just here, precisely in the heart of the building's hierarchy, its Goldilocksian mean—to distinguish what they were saying, their furious gestures. Though she well enough understood what they meant. These were the noises of flight, of refugees, the sound her family might have made when it quit Russia and started its journey. Beneath her, men and women stood by their automobiles hollering orders and questions at their wives and husbands who'd not yet quit their condos, barking last-minute details at each other like the flight checks of pilots before they took off. It reminded Dorothy of the times she and Ted were preparing to check out of motels, Ted at the door and Dorothy making one last surveillance of the room, checking drawers, closets, to see if anything had been left behind. She didn't care how comfortable or unpleasant (she thought of the farm in Michigan) a stay had been, there was always something anxious and a little rushed about every leavetaking, all departure a sort of scorched earth policy.

And now, here and there on the other Towers buildings, she could make out thick, fortifying strips of tape crisscrossing various windows, or wide plywood planks covering a balcony's glass doors, transforming the Towers into a kind of crossword puzzle, or even giant, ambiguous, ludicrous games of tic-tac-toe.

They're getting out while the getting's good, thought Mrs. Ted Bliss a little guiltily. They're making a run for it. They're doing something, she thought forlornly. They'd heard the same pros and cons she'd heard. She'd seen the same programs. More probably.

She hadn't bothered to change her clothes and realized she

must have been wearing them since the day of the telegram. The famous, fastidious Mrs. Ted Bliss had let herself go. The baleboosteh was doleful, almost in tears, and let in a tub for herself. She washed carefully, dried herself on her thickest towels, applied powder, light makeup, perfume, and changed into fresh clothes. She thought, I'm nobody's fool, this isn't some ritual, it ain't my bas mitzvah, I'm not committing harakiri. It is what it is, she thought. I stayed by the TV too long and now it's too late. I'd call but I'd never get a plane out now. They must be booked solid. If, she thought, shrewdly, they're even flying in this weather. (She was an expert, a forecaster herself now. She meant the weather on its way, the hurricane, or even, knock wood, tropical depression. She was just too slow off the dime, and now it was too late. I'll just have to wait it out, thought this little piggy.)

She sat down by the tiny telephone table, found the sheet of useful numbers the condominium complex handed out to all owners, and called Tower Stores, realizing even as she picked up the phone that it was a Sunday, that less than half the staff was on duty on Sundays, that even the lifeguards had Sundays off. On Sundays, in mitten derinnen, it was strictly swimming at your own risk. Gentiles, she figured, showed you no mercy. Therefore, she was actually a little surprised when she got a busy signal. She had to call back three times before the line was free and somebody answered.

"Tower Stores."

"Tower Stores, this is Mrs. Ted Bliss in Building One."

"Hey, Mrs. Bliss. Hola, sholem, how are you?"

"Francis?"

"Si."

"It's Sunday, I thought you'd be off."

"They called people in because of the hurricane."

"You're in Tower Stores now, not maintenance?"

"No, I still work maintenance. It's the hurricane, all hands on deck."

"You think it's going to hit us?"

"Like a potch in tochis."

Francis Moprado was an engineer in the Towers complex. Dark as an Aztec, he was a short, almost tiny man of fierce appearance whose amiability had earned him a kind of mascot status among some of the residents. He liked to spike his conversation with Yiddish words and phrases he'd overheard, and often showed up at many of the community seders (where he'd pretend to steal the afikomen) and even at some of the old Friday night services in the game room. At these times he always wore a yarmulke, not the interchangeable plain black almost patent leather-looking beanies most of the men took out of brown cardboard boxes before they entered the converted sanctuary and put back again when they left but his own knit beige beaded skullcap. Everyone knew he was working the room for Hanukkah gelt and tips but went along with Moprado's bald-faced fawning deferences anyway, reimbursing him generously for favors received, topping him off with gas money for the wear and tear on his car, the rubber he used up when he ran them out to the Fort Lauderdale airport or went out on errands. A taxi would have been cheaper, they agreed, but enjoyed having the patronizing little son of a bitch for a pet. Mrs. Ted Bliss found him a great curiosity, not so much for his blatant ass kissing as his complicated Indian and Hispanic blood. She thought his bland compliance and odd Latino Step'n Fetchit ways an anomaly. Unlike the other Cubans, Central, and South Americans she'd had contact with during her years in Florida, he seemed utterly without machismo, yet she was more fearful of him, of his dangerous smiling mildness, than ever she'd been of all the hidalgos' aristocratic distance, courtesies, tricks, and airs. Somehow she knew his sharp ugly features hid no sweet and gentle heart. She guessed how much he hated them, yet when she heard his voice she felt reassured, almost lucky. She'd found her man.

"When I went out on my balcony," said Mrs. Bliss, "I saw big pieces of wood covering a lot of the glass doors and windows. Can I get those?"

"Oy vay," moaned the Jew hater, "if you'd called ten minutes sooner."

"I've been calling for twenty minutes. The line was busy."

"Yeah, there's been a run on the four-by-eights."

"You're all out?"

"Well," Moprado said, "there's still a couple in back but I wouldn't feel right selling them to you. Warped. Damaged goods."

"Oh."

"Probably I could pound out most of the flaws. It's just the building would have to charge you the same as if you were getting first quality."

"How much?" she said.

He quoted an outrageous price, three times, maybe four, the rate she'd have had to pay if a hurricane weren't on the way.

"That's steep," she said. She could almost see the long face he put on for her at the other end of the phone, his helpless shrug, but when he spoke his voice was bright with consideration and possibility.

"Tell me, you got someone to slap them up for you?"

"No."

"Tell you what," he said, "I could drop by and give you a hand." He'd been pretending to look at his watch now. "I can't tie this phone up much longer. I hate to rush you but there's probably half a dozen people trying to get through. You ought to decide. The staff's getting shpilkes down here, it's got its own tsuris. Their own families to deal with, last-minute stuff. Any minute the Towers will be emptying out like rats jumping a sinking ship."

Mrs. Bliss didn't understand why, but she had a sort of vision, a kind of freestanding knowledge like her shot-in-the-dark certainty of Francis Moprado's hypocritical pantomime of sadness, helplessness, recovery, and urgency. She didn't so much see as feel, visceral to her as sour stomach, raw as sore throat or tender glands, that whatever was going to happen had already happened. It was aftermath, the solemn embering end of the world. Everywhere, filling the landscape of Mrs. Bliss's vision were people, in pairs or groups of three, four, but never more than five or six, clumps and clusters of the lost, encrusted in dirt and filth or in some ragged cleanliness like a scour of rough handling, the work of wind and water, say, a fellowship of bunches, of tufts and clumps of survival drifting in place as if they were trying to stamp blood and feeling back into their feet. Great drifts of the milling, great swarms of the solitary.

Moving in and out through the crowd were gangs of profiteers doing a kind of triage among the numbed and needy casualties, sizing them up, pushing their wares, pitching them, selling them four-by-eights, flashlights, batteries, candles, first-aid kits, generators, matches, portable radios, tubfuls of bathwater at a monstrous going rate, whatever the traffic would bear. Gulling the remnant, ripping them off. Disaster profiteers, they gathered about the disparate rabble selling them canned goods like it was going out of style, like, thought Mrs. Ted Bliss, like, my God, Ted profiteering on meat and food stamps during the war!

"I don't want to handlen with you, Mrs.," Moprado said, "but if you want them up I need at least an hour."

"Want what up?" Mrs. Bliss said.

"The boards," he said. "The sooner I get started the quicker you'll be safe. We've got a pretty narrow window of opportunity here. Time and tide. This damn storm's got bells on. . . . Mrs. Bliss? Mrs. Bliss?"

"I'm sorry," she told him. "I've changed my mind."

"You've changed your mind? You know what the hurricane could do to your place in two shakes of a lamb's tail? You got any idea?"

"Maybe," she said. "I think so."

"I'm not promising there wouldn't be damage. There's no guarantees. But if you put up plywood you'll definitely be cutting your losses. Plus it looks better for the insurance. That you made an effort. . . . Mrs. Bliss?"

"No," she said, "I'd like to see it. I don't want to be shut up in a dark box when it happens. I've been watching the radar on TV for two days. At least I ought to see it."

By ten that evening it had begun to rain. Nothing spectacular. Without her hearing aids in she wouldn't have heard it at all. She might even have gone out on her balcony to see the rain fall into Biscayne Bay had it been coming down a little harder, but now, in the dark, there'd be nothing to see. Sometimes, during a shower, protected from the weather by the overhang, she'd venture outside to watch the rain dimple the water in the bay or lap against the sides of yachts riding at anchor there. At night, after the sun had gone down. It was interesting to her how snug the people aboard those boats must feel, the wet safety of all those bobbing, cradled craft a queer luxury of displacement. She, for example, didn't feel nearly as secure in her rooted, stock-still condominium, but borrowed her comfort from theirs, tapping into their coze and filled with a light wonder that they didn't miss it, her faint stealth adding to her contentment. It was like staring into fire licking at a hearth, and she could have remained like that for hours if the consciousness of her ancient body had not intruded.

Now, of course, it was a different story. Nothing could have forced her out into those elements. She'd already decided not to make a run for it, but her motives had nothing to do with folklore, nothing to do with those legendary old-coot heroics one hears about after a natural disaster. She wasn't standing her ground. She had drawn no line in the sand. She was not in it to defy authority or deny the looters. Indeed, she'd packed a small suitcase, put clean underwear into it, a couple of changes of clothes, soap, a roll of toilet paper, and had been careful to tuck her good jewelry, her bank passbook, and a fresh sheaf of blank checks into its side pocket. She was ready. Had the city issued orders to evacuate the premises she would almost certainly have complied, waiting only for the bus they'd send to take her to the nearest, cleanest shelter.

So she didn't understand the motive that had convinced her not to make a run for it. She had no motive. Simply, it was too much trouble.

Now, inside her seventh-floor condominium, she waited for the winds to start howling, the rains to lash her windows, but all that happened was that the light rain had tapered off, faded to a drizzle. It was almost midnight and Mrs. Ted Bliss was overcome by a peculiar letdown, a fizzle of expectation like the diminished rain, and she turned back to her television set for an explanation.

What they had experienced during the last couple of hours, the local weatherman said, had been merely the weather they would have gotten anyway, the normal working out of pressures and fronts wheeling in from Georgia and the Gulf, and had nothing to do with Hurricane Andrew at all. He was a little embarrassed, he said, but he'd been so preoccupied by the hurricane he'd neglected to give the viewers a less exciting forecast. He apologized, and hoped he hadn't inconvenienced anyone.

If there was lightning, he warned—the storm was expected to strike somewhere in the Miami area between about two and three in the morning—it was advisable to disconnect all major appliances and to avoid using the telephone until the lightning had passed over since it could actually strike either through the ear- or mouth-piece. Mrs. Bliss shuddered, removed her hearing aids, and placed them on the telephone table. She disconnected the television.

Now she was frightened, alarmed, even a little angry at herself for her refusal to pay Francis Moprado his pound of flesh. It seemed inconceivable that she'd be able to sleep. How could she get into a nightgown with a hurricane coming? She'd just have to sit tight with the television on and maybe doze in her armchair. This would make how many nights now she hadn't been to bed, three, four? Excuse me, she thought, but acts of God took their own sweet time to play themselves out, and Dorothy felt more than a little irritable, as if she were in a game of cards with someone who either didn't know what he was doing or was deliberately stalling. She didn't appreciate it in an opponent and she didn't approve of it in God, and was thinking—it was already after two P.M. and she saw no signs of Andrew—come on if you're coming, let's see what you got. She wasn't daring providence, she was just a little cranky and punchy from the fitful quality of her sleep and the sourness of her body.

She roused herself from her wing chair and shambled into the bedroom. Sitting on the side of the bed and, while the rain had stopped and the lightning not yet started, she tried phoning her children for at least the eighth or ninth time that day. And got the same three tones followed by the same recorded message, female, solicitous, and firm. "We're sorry," the voice said, "but due to heavy traffic on all long-distance lines, your call cannot go through just now. Please hang up and try again later." It was the same woman who advised her that the number she had just dialed was not in service, or not a working number, or that she had failed to dial "1" for long distance. She spoke always in the same prim voice, and Mrs. Ted Bliss would have recognized it anywhere. It was the voice of power and denial.

Of course her children would be trying to call her, too. Practically everyone in Miami would have people to report to—their kids, brothers, sisters, concerned uncles and cousins and friends, and all of those people would have people whose safety they would want to check up on.

She tried to think of others she might call, outlanders in communities so remote it was almost statistically impossible that the lines connecting Miami to these outposts would be tied up. She racked her brains to come up first with a locality where she knew anyone well enough to ask them to get in touch with Frank or Maxine and pass on a message for them not to worry, that their mother was safe. She thought of a couple of such places—the small village in Michigan near their old farm, and the town in Wyoming where the airfield might be from which the plane that had borne their ancestral uncle's ashes could have taken off. She could come up with the geography but not with any names, and felt a sense of relief, that it was out of her hands, that she'd done all she could.

Buoyed by this odd sense of achievement she permitted herself a reward and lay down on top of the bedspread, breaking one of her own strictest rules. Even in Chicago when her grandchildren were young and, later, in Florida, when Ted was still alive and they came down with their parents to visit, Mrs. Bliss read the riot act to anyone she found on her bed once it had been made. She wouldn't permit herself to do it and didn't tolerate it in others. Something in the act, its wild disarray, violated her baleboosteh soul, and Mrs. Bliss lost her temper whenever anyone tried testing her on this point. She still remembered the time Maxine had caught Judith and James playing on their grandmother's bed and had warned them to get off at once, that this was their grandma's pet peeve. "Peeve?" she'd shouted. "My pet peeve? It isn't a *peeve*. I hate it! I hate it!" Isn't it strange, Mrs. Bliss thought now, where people drew the line? And, forgiving herself, lay down on top of the brocade bedspread without even bothering to take off her shoes. She swooned into the deepest, most comfortable sleep of her life, snoring evenly, dreamlessly.

When the hurricane woke her it wasn't its noise, its huge winds, loud and great and uninterrupted as a cataract not so much plunged as actually pushed over a steep precipice, loud, louder than a skyful of sorties laying down a carpet of saturation bombing. It wasn't its violent thunder locked up in the wind like the sound of unmuffled drums. It wasn't its mad, wild, tortured, sourceless groans, rasps, screeches, and bestial gutturals—all nature's shrill, scorched harmonics. Though she heard it, heard all of it even without her hearing aids, as anything would have heard it—the windowpanes, the furniture and appliances, its queer, vibrating falsetto so rapid and filled with enough bump and bounce and friction to raise the temperature in the apartment by a couple of degrees.

Nor even the stinging drafts striking her through the imperfect plumb of her windows and coming in over the threshold of her off-true doors like a high tide.

None of these had roused her.

What had were tremendous bursts of light filling up her room and wiping away shadow and night like the fiercest sun in the fiercest noon. She'd been right to fear the sun, going out beneath its blinding, oscillating toxic fault lines like meat in a microwave. Here, in her blinding, strobic bedroom, lightning seemed to brighten every square inch of darkness, filling up, tightening it, pulling the room's disparate angles together like a cat's cradle, exposing everything—her closets, the fluorescent glare off her tile and porcelain in the master bathroom, even patches of dust that had somehow escaped her vacuum cleaner, the damp rags with which she polished the furniture—even the raging winds, and every drop of rain strafing the exterior walls and driven like nails against the window glass.

She felt rested though she couldn't have slept for more than an hour or so. It was exciting to her, waking up in time for the hurricane, though she couldn't know yet, of course, if it actually *was* the hurricane and not just some scout sent out in advance of the party, a tendril of exploratory, devastating weather.

She went back to the television in the living room and, leaning down, plugged it back in. Even after two minutes there was still no picture. What the, wondered Mrs. Ted Bliss, what the, what the. It's picked a hell of a time to go on the fritz, she thought, who had been watching it for at least three days now taking hurricane instruction, but couldn't blame anyone but herself because maybe it said somewhere in the manual. She knew where it was, but trying to read it now would be like locking the barn door after the horse had escaped. She knew better, anyway. Hadn't she scolded everyone who held the refrigerator door open too long, predicting not only that the cold air would escape but that it was a strain on the motor? And warned against running the air-conditioning for more than an hour, or, in the old days, winding watches too tight? So, at least in principle, she knew better. It was terrible that her thoughtlessness had shut her off from the news reports and, remembering the radio in her kitchen, went there to see what she had missed since going to sleep.

But that had broken down, too. She glanced at the electric clock over the kitchen table. It had stopped running. Shocked, in a panic, she realized that the power was out, that what she'd been seeing she'd been seeing only by the light of the thunderbolts, flickering but almost constant, steady as a snowfall.

She wondered if she were the only one who hadn't left the Towers. She was no martyr, not the type to stay behind to guard her property, not one of those who'd choose to go down with the mountain when Mount St. Helens blew its top, or defy catastrophe—floods, volcanoes, acts of God. Such people bought into a myth of their own rectitude and, she thought, felt better about themselves, throwing up first and secondary and tertiary rings of defense around their being as if they were causes, their own holy terms of survival. She didn't give a plugged nickel for that sort of magical thinking. Indeed, thought Mrs. Ted Bliss, didn't it go against her own bloodlines? Technically, she, her family, her husband's, were refugees, and though they hadn't been driven from Russia by an act of God, they had by politics and an old hostility. So it was rather more a breakdown in history and in her character that she should have remained behind in the driving wind and hard rain while just that afternoon she'd seen so much hustle and bustle, the streets and driveways packed with her neighbors taking their leave with something so like gaiety it could have been a party. How much trouble would it have been for her to flag one of them down? Her suitcase was packed. She could have been out of there at a moment's notice if it hadn't been for the time she'd tracked the storm on the television, as tightly wrapped in her fate as someone caught up in a close game of cards. She could give away nothing, nothing, and had to stay the course to see how her hand would play out.

And she had. And had wound up losing all.

She went to the telephone table. And lifting the phone from its cradle found a list of the people who lived in the Towers complex, but the phones were still down of course, and Mrs. Bliss had never felt so forlorn. It was one thing to have lost touch with her daughter in Cincinnati, her son in Providence, but another entirely to be out of contact with all of her neighbors. She wanted some evidence she wasn't alone in the building. All right, the lines were down. This was troubling enough, but suppose service were restored? So many of the owners had unlisted numbers. Mrs. Bliss shuddered. She hadn't realized how many wanted to remain anonymous and thought, irrationally, that these would be the most dangerous. Sure,

or what were they hiding? I mean, she meant, what were they pro-
tecting that made them willing to fork over whatever premium
they'd have had to fork over to Southern Bell for the privilege of
not being listed in the Miami telephone directory? At the very min-
imum they had to be deadbeats covering their behinds from cred-
itors and, since the demographics had shifted, from all those to
whom they owed services. Either way, thought Mrs. Bliss, they
couldn't be on the strict up-and-up.

I'm getting crazy, she thought, suddenly finding enemies, making them up. She'd never expected not only not just to run with
the paranoids but actually pace them. And remembered the call
she'd made to the Towers Stores and Francis Moprado. She wondered if he were still in the building and, jarred by the thought he
might be, slowly managed to piece its number together by the
flashes of electricity in the room and punched Towers Stores up
once again, remembering only after it was too late that using the
phone during an electrical storm was the worst thing you could
do. She thrust it away from her and hoped it had landed where it
belonged. It hadn't and Dorothy, exactly as if a poisonous snake
were loose on the carpet and striking at her heels, made a wild
zigzag move toward the entrance (perfectly describing the wild arcs
and angles of the lightning) to her apartment and pulled open the
door.

Think, she thought quickly, don't lock yourself out and, first
pressing the automatic latch on the door, stepped outside her condo
and shut the door behind her.

"It's too dark," she said in the hallway. "I can't see my hand
in front of my face."

Because the power was still out of course. Because almost no
lightning tumbled over the stunted clearances of the doorways. Because unlike the other buildings in the Towers the architects had
made no provision for windows at either end of the long, dark
corridor. No sudden bolts illuminated the different ends of the
buildings, its distant poles.

With no shapes or dimensions to guide her she felt fear, and
quite lost. Mindlessly, as though its sound were the only orientation
available to her, she called her name aloud, like someone taking
attendance in a schoolroom. Then, feeling her vulnerability, she deliberately began to lurch from side to side all along the walls up

and down the length of Tower Number One and, here and there, to knock indiscriminately at the walls and doors.

It was a lesson to her, how soon the old become lost once they've slipped their tether. She was trying to get back home. That's why she rapped at the doors, why, when she got no response, she fumbled in the dark at their hardware. Though how would she hear one if she got it? She'd pulled the appliances from her ears. "Foolish," she scolded herself, "you wouldn't recognize panic? Some scared 'Who's there?'" Even someone's desperate, alarmed, and rushed elusions, the noise, she meant, of someone else's danger. (She knew these places, their disparate configurations like the back of her own hand, that she, in their place, wouldn't even have tried to hide. She lived, she understood, in a sort of corner. Space here was a fiction.) Only then, when she heard no panic or futile scurrying, when she'd raised some dim light of hope, did she try a door to see if it were hers. Again and again she tried but it never was. Then one was, and thinking some looting rapist killer lurked behind it, she turned the doorknob.

No one jumped out at her but this didn't calm her. He could be lying low, he could be playing possum. Such was Mrs. Bliss's fear and confusion that though lightning still flashed (diminished in frequency and intensity) and lighted up the place like flares behind clouds it was at least a minute or two before she was sure she was home.

Thinking: It looks familiar. That's my wing chair, there's my television.

It was the most amazing thing. There was nothing to do. She was bored in mitten derinnen. That's life for you, thought Mrs. Ted Bliss, a surprise in every box. Deprived of television by the power failure, she wondered what to do with herself. Though she understood she hadn't been a proper baleboosteh in years, not since Ted was alive, as a matter of fact. She'd always been fastidious about her housekeeping, she liked to think she still was, but here she was in the middle of one of the most disruptive events that could happen to a woman like herself and what was she doing about it? Nothing. Not a damn thing. She knew the storm wasn't done with her yet and that anything she did now would have to be done over when it was, yet she hadn't even taken the measures taken by those who'd chosen not to go down with their condominiums. Where were the boards on her windows? Had she disconnected *all* her major appliances? Where were the provisions the experts had practically begged her to lay in? What equipment did she have on hand? There was nothing, nothing. Now the toilets wouldn't flush and she had only her pots to piss in.

So she had nothing to do. She was already bored with her emergency and who knew how much longer it would go on?

She forced herself to think about what had happened to Ellen and Junior Yellin, whose cheery wire had indirectly led to Dorothy's first awareness of the hurricane. She wished them well, alevai, but even as she did so felt a spirit of disclaimer come over her, something like the printing on the back of the ticket a parking garage might have handed Ted in the old days. Management not responsible for damage to automobile or for loss of any contents left therein.

She went up to her big wing chair and turned it toward the wide glass doors that led out to her balcony. She sat down. Here and there through the night pieces of lightning still lit up the sky but she could see that the storm, though not yet over, had moved into a new, perhaps even more treacherous, phase.

Mrs. Bliss, staring as far as she could into the western edges of the hurricane, tried to recall what the earnest young weather mavins had attempted to teach her about hurricanes, but except for the big stuff—wind speeds, the eye, periods of low pressure, storm surges, risen seas, terrific floods—it was all blur, a confetti of information. So maybe, she thought, if she just stared at it hard enough long enough, examining its progress and moods, she might be able to tell for herself where she stood, when she could declare the all clear (always mindful, of course, that it was provisional, merely the eye passing through, a grace period like the thirty days the insurance gives you before canceling your policy), and go out into the street again. To stretch her legs, get some fresh air, collect herself, regroup for the next onslaught.

Brushing up, studying, learning, cramming, burning the midnight oil, articling herself to it until she had the hurricane by heart. Making the adjustment from television to her great glass sliding doors as though the activity were only a shift in camera angles.

Mrs. Ted Bliss observing the winds bash the palm trees. Imagining the noise it made, so much it might have been the sound of a thousand fire trucks, as many police cars. Ambulances. An entire motor pool of disaster and death.

Something riding on all this close coverage and up-to-the-minute.

Her respite, that chance to catch her breath, get her second wind. When she realized: *If* the power's back on, *if* the electric is up. Because how the hell else would she be able not just to make it down those seven floors but to climb back up them again, all those flights of stairs? Or even four of them? Or even three? It was maybe her third or fourth hour into the hurricane, and it was the first time she cried. She felt as if all breath had left her body. Breathless, alone, as though the vacant Towers were only another sort of necropolis. She could have been back in the Chicago boneyard where all her dead relatives were buried.

If Holmer Toibb were alive today, thought Mrs. Ted Bliss, I'd breeze through his assignment with flying colors. My self, she'd have explained to him, my self is my interest. Because everything else falls away. Family, friends. Even love falls away. It chips and breaks up like ice. It falls off like a scab.

Oh, I'm not indifferent, she would have told the old therapesisist, if anything, vice versa. She was highly partisan. Were it in her power she'd have done anything to save them. It wouldn't even have to have been them. She would have saved anybody, everybody. She meant it, she wasn't bragging on herself. Still, she had to admit it, she'd have used their salvation to forward her own. So what was the use? Who knows? Maybe she wouldn't have done such a bang-up job on the assignment. Maybe all her good intentions added up to was a gentleman's "C." If it weren't so late in the day maybe she'd have put her money where her mouth was. Maybe everybody would.

In her dreams the hurricane was even more animated than it was in actuality. She got better reception in her dreams. For one thing it was already light out. She couldn't judge what time it was but supposed early morning since she saw no sun. Of course that might have been an illusion created by the gloom—some mean average by-product of the practically biblical rain. So God knows when those first few palm trees flew past her seventh-story balcony. It could have been as early as seven or as late as half-past six in the afternoon. Whatever the time, this was the worst Mrs. Bliss had seen yet. The trees flew past so rapidly and on so horizontal a course they could have been wooden torpedoes. She'd have risen from the wing chair, walked to the drapes to shut them to protect herself from the constant necessity of blinking or throwing up her hands like a boxer trying to protect his head if it hadn't been for her fear that at any moment the wind could shift, *pfftt, bam*, just like that, and drive one of those palms directly through the sliding glass doors. There was nothing more Mrs. Bliss could do. Tracking the hurricane was fatuous now, quantifying it was. She dreamed she had fallen asleep in her chair, she dreamed that the eye of the hurricane had already passed over.

With this, she dreamed of how very depressed she was, for if its eye had passed over, then not only was the worst yet to come (and hadn't it—those palm trees whizzing past—already started?) but she had missed out on what was said to be the most exhilarating aspect of a hurricane—the intense feeling of well-being and soft, luxurious fatigue that accompanied an extended period of low pressure. The experts were all agreed on this part, hammering away at their theme, their own disclaimer. You must steel yourself against the soft seduction of the eye's low pressure, its perfect dust- and pollen-raked sweet room temperature ionized air, as though the same powerful winds that had blown it over and around her had pushed away all shmuts before them like a new beginning of the world. Stay indoors, stay indoors, they warned, drilling its dangers at her like a public service announcement. You couldn't have paid her, who'd missed so much, to miss this.

And now she had, and woke from her unplanned sleep with a fatigue as sour as a hangover.

Confused, disoriented, she saw that it was still dark but took no comfort from the fact that she had not missed the eye's wondrous performance.

A beam of fuzzily focused yellowish light, round and wide as if it were coming out the end of a megaphone, played over Mrs. Bliss's living/dining-room area, frightening her, stiffening her back against the wing chair and forcing her to clutch at its arms like a fugitive flattening himself against a wall.

"Mrs. Bliss? Mrs. Bliss."

She thought she could hear someone call her name, but without her hearing aids she couldn't be sure.

"Mrs. Bliss?"

Furtively, she put her hand into a breast pocket of her pants suit and quietly as she could fumbled for a hearing aid. She didn't think she'd made any noise but the appliance wasn't in yet so she couldn't be sure.

"Mrs. Bliss, are you there?"

"Who's that, who's there?"

She hoped it wasn't Francis Moprado come to murder her for not allowing him to board up her sliding doors.

"It's me."

"What do you want, how'd you get in?"

"Passkey." The security guard walked in front of Mrs. Bliss's chair. "I come to check you out."

"Oh, Louise," said Mrs. Ted Bliss. "I thought you were somebody else."

"No," she said, "it's me. Elaine Munez's daughter." She turned the batonlike flashlight on herself for identification.

"I fell asleep," Mrs. Bliss said. Inexplicably, she felt a need to account for herself, her wanton presence in her condominium in an abandoned building during a hurricane. Idly, she wondered if this were a citable offense, if she could be written up, decided that trying to explain would make too long a story. She wouldn't fight it.

"Did you see my mother?"

"What?"

"Did you see my mother? I been trying to call since the first reports on my scanner. She don't answer, Mrs. Bliss."

"Darling," said Mrs. Bliss, "the phones aren't working."

"*Before* they ain't working."

"People have been leaving the building, Louise. I saw from my balcony. It could have been yesterday. The day before yesterday."

"She didn't sign out," said the security guard. "You got to leave your name with the security guard you go away overnight. I check the books. No Elaine Munez."

"Well, everyone was in such a hurry."

"She know the rule."

"There must have been long lines. Everybody was honking their horns. Does Mother still drive?"

"No."

"There," Mrs. Bliss said, "you see? Her driver was giving her the bum's rush. She probably didn't have time for the formalities."

"Not the formalities," Louise said. She was close to hysteria. "She know how I worry."

"You'll see, Mother's all right. Probably she tried to get a message to you. Everyone was in such a hurry."

Was she crying? It was too dark to see but it seemed to Mrs. Bliss that the strange girl was crying.

"I come to guard her," Louise explained. "To protect her from bandits and stranglers."

"Oh, Louise," said Mrs. Ted Bliss.

"It isn't secure," Louise said, shaking her head desolately. "I'll tell you something," she whispered hoarsely. Remarkably, Dorothy could hear every word. She didn't even have to lean forward, as if there were something in the complicated register of her alarm so insistent it wiped out all silence. "The building ain't vacant!"

"You checked the sign-out ledger. Did many stay?"

"How hard it would be to sign out and stay behind? It make a good alibi," she said professionally.

Mrs. Bliss looked toward the mad, improbable woman. Was it possible she knew what she was talking about? And recalled her paranoia in the hall when she'd called out her name like a talisman and stealthily tried all the doorknobs. But somehow her fear had been short-circuited. Sure, she thought, fear falls away, too.

"She could be anywhere," Louise Munez said desperately. "She could be anywhere on any floor in any building." Then, like a child, she said, "I want my mother, I want my mother," and Mrs. Ted Bliss, who wanted her husband and her dead son Marvin, but now not so much, and her other children, too, and the gang, and all the others whom she loved who'd ever lived, but not now not so much, even Junior Yellin, even Ellen, was astonished to realize that the strange girl—she'd met her when she first came to the Towers— was no longer a girl but a woman in her fifties who even at that age was still forever frozen into whatever loony, skewed relationship with her mother had caused their breach and disappointed the mother forever. (Because of all the things that fall away—and everything did, everything, the whole kit and caboodle, even her condo, even the Buick LeSabre, the color of which she no longer remembered—thought Mrs. Bliss, maybe it's only madness you can hang onto.) And felt something warm, even feverish, take her hand.

It was Louise Munez's hands, covering her own. "Oh," she said, "I have frighten you."

"No," said Mrs. Bliss.

"I will wait with you," she declared. "I will see you safe through the hurricane."

Mrs. Bliss removed her hand gently from Louise's and held her arms open. In the darkness she lifted her left hand to Louise's head and began to stroke the dry hair.

Because everything else falls away. Family, friends, love fall away. Even madness stilled at last. Until all that's left is obligation.